I0760732

THE TWILIGHT OF CHAOS

THE POWER OF GOLD TRILOGY

The Power of Gold

The Call of the Shadow

J. J. LEACH

THE TWILIGHT OF CHAOS

• BOOK THREE •

Leach Books
Flat Rock

Published by Leach Books, Flat Rock.

Printed in the United States of America

Map created with Inkarnate

First edition: 2021

ISBN: 978-1-7360144-6-2 (hardcover)

ISBN: 978-1-7360144-7-9 (paperback)

ISBN: 978-1-730144-8-6 (eBook)

Library of Congress Control Number: 2021903513

The Library of Congress Cataloging-in-Publication Data is available upon request.

Young Adult Fiction/Fantasy/General

To JNo.

For your courage, hope, and laughter.

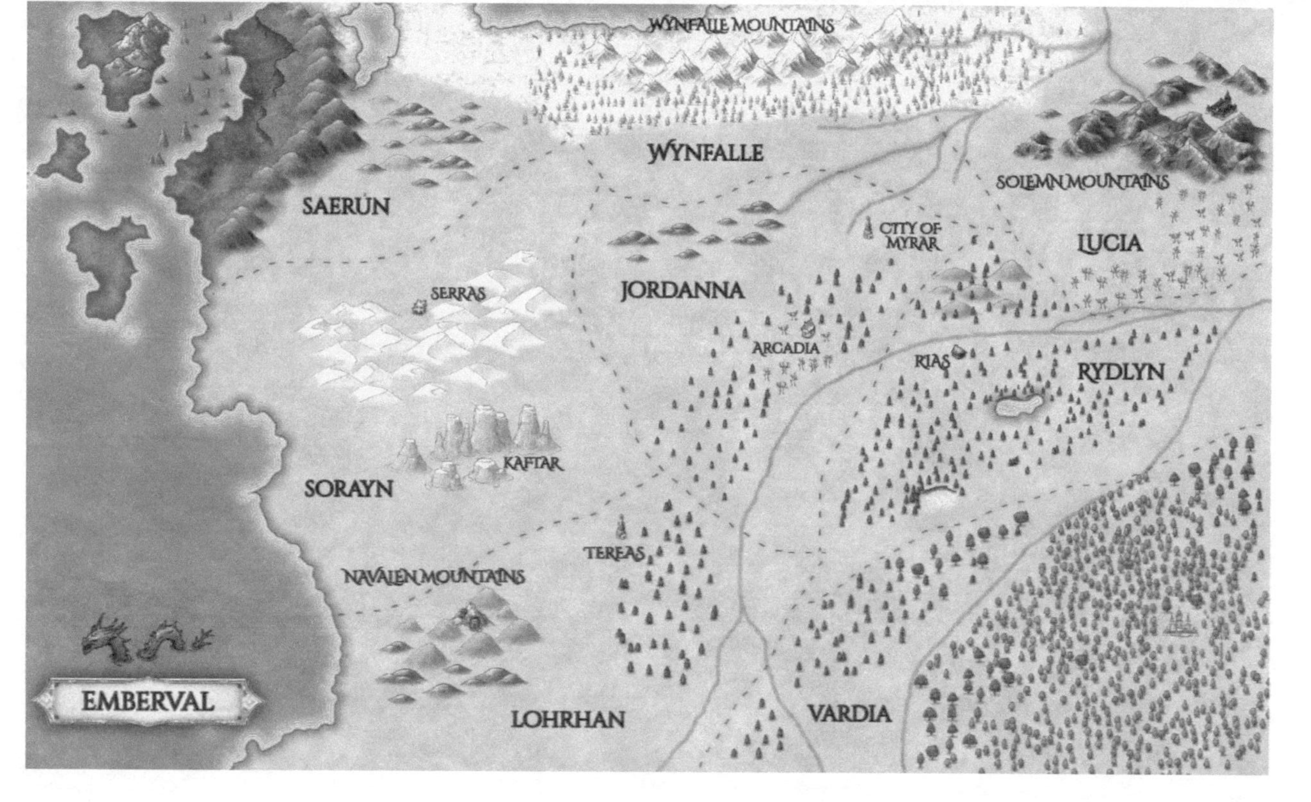
WYNFALLE MOUNTAINS
WYNFALLE
SOLEMN MOUNTAINS
SAERUN
CITY OF MYRAR
LUCIA
SERRAS
JORDANNA
ARCADIA
RIAS
RYDLYN
KAFTAR
SORAYN
TEREAS
NAVALEN MOUNTAINS
EMBERVAL
LOHRHAN
VARDIA

ONE

Spiraling and twisting, the black cloud hovered in the air. I closed my eyes, making contact with the nebulous being with my thoughts, and commanded it to move back into my hand. I felt it linger above my palm. A few tendrils separated from the swirling ball and touched me. My breath trembled from the contact. The cold finger of energy caressed my skin. A smile played on my lips as I opened my eyes and leaned into the mist.

"I understand. I feel the same way," I whispered lovingly.

"Who are you talking to?"

The mist suddenly disappeared, causing an uncomfortable twitch in my stomach. Sighing, I put my hands on my hips and turned toward the intruder.

"How many times do I have to ask you to announce yourself before barging into my tent?"

Anu threw a mischievous smile my way before casually strolling over to me and then sprawled on the sleeping cot.

"Whatever. It's not like you were doing anything questionable, right?" she muttered.

When I didn't respond right away, Anu sat up and looked at me suspiciously.

"So, who were you talking to, Anwen?" Her smile gradually turned into a sneer. "Are you finally losing it? Do Healers go crazy?"

"Ha, ha," I answered insolently. "No. I—I was just talking to myself. Saying the spells out loud makes them easier for me to remember."

I turned away from her and walked to my small desk. Casually, I pulled a notebook over the open black book.

"Anyway, why are you here?" I turned around to face her. "Aren't you supposed to be guarding the camp tonight?"

"I was just out walking." Anu briefly diverted her eyes to the floor before turning back to me. "What will you do if the High Council votes against officially declaring war? Even stopping us from seeking the monks of Saerún?"

"That absolutely can't happen. According to Freyja, the only way to stop Loki is to go to Saerún. They have to let us go. All-out war is inevitable."

I busied my hands with the papers scattered across my desk. Anu understood the frustration of this entire trip and the process of seeking the High Council's approval. I tried to convince both Ansgar and Eydis—the king and queen of Vardia and my grandparents—that it was crucial to keep the journey secret. The fewer people who knew about Freyja's plan, the better our chances for success. But they believed in transparency—never hiding behind secrecy and deception. Especially when they were about to officially declare war on the Kingdom of Lucia.

"And what if they say no to Vardia?" Anu pressed. "Is there, let's say, an alternative plan?"

I understood what she meant. The alternative plan would be to defy the council's decision and proceed alone, instigating war between Vardia and the other kingdoms. Even risking my banishment. I knew it would kill them to have to choose between their own laws and their blood.

Anu wouldn't let the topic go. "Are you going to tell them about our sessions together? About the object mentioned on the obelisk?"

My insides churned with nerves. How could I tell her that I had no idea what I was going to say at this point?

She, of course, was referring to the strange stela I found on our journey back from Wynfalle—a discovery that I could read the ancient language etched into the stone monolith. Seer Herja, Anu, and Vardia's Ambassador Ragnhild were the only ones who witnessed my strange behavior and wanted to keep it that way. Herja had her reasons for not disclosing the information, but keeping the secret from the council and even from my grandmother only added to the distress of this whole journey.

Beyond that deception, the private sessions with Anu—who, according to Freyja, had the answers to destroy Loki somewhere deep inside her—revealed a potential ancient weapon of destruction. Unfortunately, any other information about the mysterious weapon was lost and not found within Anu's memories.

So, my dilemma was how much to reveal to the council—the ancient language I couldn't remember learning but could speak perfectly, or the mysterious weapon that could save our world. I couldn't elaborate or explain to them at this point, either. That's why it was so important to talk to the monks without the council's interference.

"Let's not think about that right now, okay? Eydis is very convincing. Besides, the gods are the ones who sent us to the monks. How can they deny us for wanting to save their kingdoms, save their people from a terrible death?"

I couldn't talk about this with Anu anymore. My head was about to explode.

"I thought you were supposed to be on guard tonight? Why aren't you out there now?" I asked again, changing the subject from her unwanted questioning.

Anu sat up slowly, her eyes cast down to the floor, avoiding the question. Combining her saddened silence with her appearance in her human form, I shook my head with a heavy sigh.

"You were with Halvard."

Anu's back straightened in defiance as she shifted back to her Lirrean form—her true identity. I sat next to her on the cot.

"It is fine, Anwen, I didn't leave my post unprotected," she snapped. "Ivar and Frey took over for me."

Anu sat on the edge of the cot, her coppery-gold skin glowing in the candlelight. I compared her to a penny with a warm patina. Her body darkened with shadows when she was angry—or defensive, which seemed to be most of the time.

"I am not accusing you, Anu," I exhaled wearily, wanting to avoid arguing with her about it again. "It was just a statement. Nothing more."

Anu sighed and rested her head on Anwen's shoulder. "I know, I mean, he can be so stubborn sometimes. He just can't see that we shouldn't be together. No matter how we feel about each other."

The emotion behind Anu's words took me by surprise.

"Love sucks," she whispered, then suddenly lifted her head. "I'm sorry, Anwen. I didn't mean anything against you or Elric."

I looked away, despising the pitiful tone in that single word.

Elric.

I sprang up from the cot and hurried to the desk. I glanced at the black book and touched one of the exposed corners. That simple contact gave me strength when I heard his name. The Shadow brought comfort from my heartache.

Anu stayed silent for a few minutes, aware she had hit a nerve, but she refused to back down.

"What will you say when you see him tomorrow?" she asked softly. "How long has it been? Ten months, almost a year, since you heard anything from Elric?"

My heart shattered at the sound of his name once more. Even though Anu and I have begrudgingly built a friendship over the past few months, sometimes I wondered if she enjoyed my pain.

She knew I didn't want to talk about seeing him again—that he was all I thought about for those long ten months.

When Elric and Queen Sigrún left Vardia in search of a new

home for their people, the Mountain Elves of Wynfalle, he contacted me several times during the first month. However, those quick contacts soon became rare until one day the communication stopped. I went crazy with worry, even pressuring my grandfather to send a rescue team to find him. That was when I discovered the truth: Elric had stopped contacting me personally and had instead begun to reach out to the king. He wasn't injured or worse, dead; he simply didn't want to talk to me.

An angry retort pricked the tip of my tongue, but before I could respond, a blood-curdling scream pierced through the air.

Anu jumped up. "What in the name of the gods?"

Both Anu and I dashed to the tent's opening and pushed the canvas aside. Complete chaos erupted before our eyes. The masked Lokrum discovered our camp.

I pointed to the tent next to mine and yelled at Anu, "Find Jack. Protect him!"

No sooner had I spoken than a powerful force lifted me off my feet, slamming my body into a tree. With my breath knocked out, I struggled to stand, knowing that if I didn't do so immediately, death would come quickly.

The faint but distinct sound of a released arrow made me lunge sideways. The arrow narrowly missed my head, hitting the tree behind me. I turned just as a soldier grabbed my arm and slammed his fist into my temple. Instead of falling to the ground, my body collided with the attacker, causing him to lose his balance and fall into me.

The intense urge to release my energy overtook me. I

climbed onto his chest, placed my hands over his mask, and let the energy take control. The Lokrum soldier struggled and resisted, but I held firm. His body finally ceased convulsing. Grabbing his mask, I yanked it off and saw a disfigured man with lifeless eyes.

Before the realization of taking a life consumed me, another terrified scream sounded in the dark, moonless night. I raced towards the next tent when another Lokrum soldier confronted me.

Without thinking, my hand swung through the air, knocking the soldier away from me and into a tree. A brutal crunch broke the silence of the night as the soldier collapsed to the ground.

I ran around the tent and skidded to a halt just as Eydis pulled her dagger out of a dead soldier. She looked up at me, perfectly calm.

"Are you all right?" I asked anyway.

Eydis dismissed my question with a quick flick of her dagger. Rubies the size of nickels sparkled within the silver filigree—a wedding gift to my grandmother from my grandfather. The dagger never left her side.

She sheathed the dagger with care. "Of course, love. Where is Jack?"

"Anu is protecting him," I proclaimed.

"Anwen, help!" Jack screamed from across the field.

"Jack!" I yelled. I saw the Lokrum soldier grabbing Jack by his shirt, with a knife raised high above him, ready to slice across his throat.

I ran toward them, raising my hand to unleash my power,

but the soldier didn't flinch—maybe a slight hesitation in his downward swing toward Jack's throat, but not enough to stop him. The soldier turned to me with a sneer.

"You cannot hurt me, elf. I have protection," he hissed with contempt.

His body shifted enough so I could see the amulet attached to his armor.

Everything around me went dark. Soft whispers echoed in my mind, craving release. I could feel my body shifting, drawn to the call of the Shadow. My body felt as light as a feather, and nothing could stop the sudden surge of deadly energy erupting from my hands.

A short, but intense, scream pierced the night. The smell of burnt flesh invaded the air. Blackness crowded my vision, followed by welcomed silence.

***

"Anwen . . . Anwen, wake up," a soft voice whispered in my ear. A gentle hand touched my face.

My eyes fluttered lazily, hoping my nightmare was just that—a terrible dream. I jerked forward, but a strong pair of hands kept me pressed down on the ground. I looked up into my grandmother's worried face.

"Hold on, hold on, my love, let it pass," she whispered again. "The magic has not released you yet."

My eyes widened in disbelief. The power inside me still churned. The voices demanded more release—not just the Shadow but something else. I closed my eyes again, hoping to stabilize the energy. Instead, the Okri joined the fight for attention. Fear churned inside me, uncertain of how to quiet the voices—they never possessed my body. Not like this.

Silently, I called out to Freyja, my protector and the giver of my powers, but instead of hearing her response, I felt the pressure of Laga's spell and the mark of Odin.

I opened my eyes, only to see Eydis pulling back slightly. Her eyes flicked down to my neck. A soft golden glow reflected on her face.

"Anwen, control yourself," she said more firmly. "You need to restrain your powers."

Fear cloaked Eydis' words. I commanded the Shadow and the Okri to calm their fears. My commands gave me strength. I controlled my powers. Not them.

Suddenly, I sensed another presence. A loud, commanding voice echoed through my body.

They backed off, leaving my body more relaxed and in control.

"I am fine," I said, sitting up and brushing her hands away. "Really, grandmother, I'm fine."

Eydis looked at me skeptically. I could only imagine the questions racing through her mind. I shrugged it off, knowing I would have to tell her my secret sooner or later. Messing with dark magic wasn't something you talk about with your family every day. She wouldn't approve—actually, none of my friends would support my latest effort to learn the Shadow on my own. Even Herja, who is the only one capable of teaching the Shadow, would have a major fit. But it's not her fault; she has other critical duties. She doesn't have time to teach me properly, but that doesn't change the fact that I needed to learn the Shadow quickly—it's my responsibility to save the world.

And of course, there was Elric. He left me, so I took matters into my own hands.

Eydis grabbed my hand and pulled me up from the ground. All eyes were on me, staring. Thyra held Jack in her arms, holding him back from running to me, while Halvard stood with Anu by his side. Everyone appeared awestruck. Even Ambassadors Ragnhild and Sigúrd seemed impressed.

But not Eydis—she looked prepared to interrogate me. I knew I had a lot of explaining to do.

Halvard reached down to the remains of the Lokrum soldier and picked up a piece of stone hanging from a chain.

"Anwen, you did it!" he muttered. "The protection amulet . . . you destroyed it!"

"Whoa," Jack exclaimed as he hurried to Halvard's side and looked down at the remnants.

I crossed over to where they were standing, making sure not to step on the bits of flesh scattered on the ground. I looked down at my bloodstained tunic and trousers, then wiped my face. Blood stained my sleeve.

Halvard handed me the broken stone and then looked down at what was left of the armored torso. The gold chain was shattered.

"You found a way to break Loki's spell. Well done!" Halvard said, smiling and clapping me lightly on the back.

Yeah, well done, I thought, as a small piece of skin slipped from the stone and dropped to the ground. My insides cringed at the consequences of my magic.

TWO

"But, Anwen, I am ready. Really, I am," Jack whined. "Please teach me some of your magic."

I shook my head and said crossly, "No, Jack, it's not going to happen. Anu has been showing you the Lirrean way, and that's how it should be. You know how I feel about it, so don't bring it up again."

I looked over at him and sighed. His defeated expression pierced my heart. "I love you, Jack. Please understand that what I did last night was new . . . I am not sure if I can do it again, and even if I could, there's no way I am teaching you something like that."

I shivered at the thought of killing someone like that again. I couldn't sleep knowing parts of the soldier littered the ground. So, before bed, Thyra and Ivar gathered the flesh and buried them along with the rest of the Lokrum bodies. No one survived, which was probably for the best. They were scouts, only six soldiers, but still, killing didn't sit well with me. But, as Halvard said earlier, we couldn't afford any of the Lokrum escaping to report back to their leader and reveal the location of our camp.

"Jack, Anwen is correct," Anu interrupted my thoughts, pulling her horse next to mine. "As an almost extinct race, you have an obligation to learn the Lirrean traditional magic. We are the last of our kind, so that fact alone should be enough."

Jack stopped his horse, a chestnut stallion named Volla, and faced Anu. Jack's eyes shifted from blue to black. The gold flecks in his Lirrean eyes flashed with anger. His skin shimmered with a deep gold hue. "NO, I am not just Lirrean, I am half human. And I didn't choose to be experimented on and turned into a monster."

He turned Volla around and galloped toward Eydis, who touched his arm to steady the now skittish horse.

I pulled on Glaesir's reins, turning him around to follow Jack, but Anu stopped me.

"Leave him. His anger is not directed at you or even at me," she said. The horses began walking again. "He has been asking me a lot of questions lately about Corvus and Loki. His anger is directed at them and the circumstances of his origin. Questions that you or I can't answer yet."

"I can't imagine what he is going through. This is all new to him. And his body is changing as well. Did you see his eyes? His skin, too? His anger makes him change."

Anu snickered. "Ah, yes, it does . . . almost like you, don't you think?"

"I don't know what you are talking about."

"Yes, you do, Anwen. When you get angry or when someone you love is being hurt, your magic takes over. Isn't that what happened last night? The Shadow magic was very clear."

I looked from side to side, making sure no one was nearby to hear Anu. I turned to her angrily.

"No, that is not what happened. I was in control at all times," I whispered. "And don't make statements like that around people because they will only worry about me, and we can't afford that distraction."

Anu snickered again. "By all means, but do know this, Anwen, the Shadow is hard to control. Herja would not be happy that you are learning her magic without her guidance."

"Well, drastic times call for drastic measures. Besides, I am not learning the Shadow without her."

I urged Glaesir into a gallop, needing time away from the questioning. Anu may have guessed something was going on with me, but she didn't mention the book. I knew she wouldn't stop until she found out what I was up to. She was too curious. I wanted to make sure no one else noticed and started to question.

***

Thyra held up her hand to stop the caravan, tilting her head slightly to the side.

"I believe we are almost to the rendezvous point," she turned to Eydis. "Your Majesty, let us scout ahead just to survey the area."

Eydis nodded and turned to me.

"Anwen, why don't you take Jack with you?" she leaned closer and whispered. "Make him feel like he is part of the company. He needs to feel useful."

I nodded in agreement and turned Glaesir around toward Jack. "Jack, we need your help in scouting this area before the queen enters. Follow us."

Jack instantly perked up and gently slapped the reins across Volla's neck. I turned back around to follow him and Thyra. I smiled at Eydis as we passed, giving her a slight nod of appreciation for understanding Jack's feelings. Sometimes, all it took was a small gesture of trust and usefulness to make someone feel needed, especially an eleven-year-old.

As we pulled ahead of the group, Thyra turned her head side to side. A frown appeared.

"What is it, Thyra?" I asked.

She shook her head. "I do not know, Anwen. Something just feels different . . . out of place here."

I scanned the area again, trying to find anything unusual. Something prickled my nose, causing my brow to furrow. I extended my hand to the side. The tips of my fingers caused a slight ripple in the air.

"Magic," I whispered. "Very powerful too."

The energy felt strange. It brushed against my outstretched hand—soft and silky waves curled around my arm. I almost laughed out loud at my choice of words, not the usual way to describe a possibly deadly protective spell.

"Where did the magic come from?" Jack asked as he strained his neck to look into the dark treetops. "Is it Kenrick?

Or Corvus?"

I shook my head and turned back to Thyra, but before I could say anything, a sharp voice interrupted.

"No, newcomer, it is not your enemy," the voice said from above us. "But your allies."

Swift and confident, a figure leapt out of the tree and landed in front of Glaesir, who reared back onto his hind legs. A dark, slender hand reached out and grasped the mane firmly, while the other hand splayed on Glaesir's neck, instantly calming him.

Jack and I raised our bows, arrows already nocked, but Thyra held her hand up to signal us to stop.

I looked into a pair of sharp gray eyes. His brown skin shimmered with a thin film of sweat. Strands of dark hair poked out from under a brightly-colored keffiyeh. A breeze moved through the trees, causing his red robe to billow around him. The stranger seemed at ease falling from the treetops, even though his home was in the desert.

He nodded in greeting. "Forgive my sudden intrusion, Healer Anwen. We have been waiting for your arrival since news of the attack. Queen Gamila sent several of her best warriors to monitor this area and wait for you."

He extended his hand, inviting me to dismount. "I am Shu, First Protector for Queen Gamila of the Kingdom of Sorayn."

His hand was cool to the touch despite the oppressive heat surrounding us. His other hand snaked around my waist, pulling me down from Glaesir.

The sight of Shu demanded attention, from his tall stature to his elaborate clothes. Apparently, I was staring a little too long when Thyra cleared her throat.

"Take care, Anwen, when gazing into this one's eyes. Shu has a way of capturing the hearts of many young elves and maybe even a human or two," Thyra laughed. She hopped down from her horse and walked to Shu. "Are you still up to your old tricks, my friend?"

Shu laughed with Thyra, taking her extended arm in greeting and bowing his head.

I was confused by their exchange. Thyra turned to me. "Our kin from the desert have special abilities that soothe their adversaries. Holding eye contact can wreak havoc on one's decision-making abilities."

Shu shrugged and smiled. "Ah, we only use our skills when needed, my friend. It is a gift to make those around us more . . . comfortable."

Thyra laughed. "More comfortable? Is that what you think you are doing to our Healer?"

"But it is hard to control my gift, Thyra, in the presence of someone so breathtaking."

Shu continued staring at me for a few more seconds, but then turned to Thyra and flashed her a charming smile.

"Thyra, you know I only have eyes for you. No one can match your beauty and skill as a warrior," Shu said with a smile full of white teeth, then turned back to me. "But, alas, stories of the Healer's bravery certainly did not tell of her true loveliness."

I smiled awkwardly. Really? Stories about my supposed bravery? And beauty? Thyra was right. I should be careful not only of Shu's overzealous charm but also of his outlandish claims.

Shu realized he might have been too bold, so he bowed his head in apology. "Forgive my forwardness, Healer Anwen. It is an honor to finally meet the All-Fathers Defender."

I wasn't sure if I heard him correctly. "The All-Father's what?"

Shu turned his attention to Jack, who was still sitting quietly on Volla with his bow clasped tightly in his hands. Jack's eyes glowed as his skin flickered briefly between his human and Lirrean forms.

"And you did not tell us about this one, Thyra . . . a Lirrean," Shu's expression showed no anger or hatred, only reverence. The same awe that Herja expressed when Jack's true heritage was discovered.

Jack bristled despite the Desert Elf's calm tone and looked away. Shu noticed Jack's discomfort.

Shu smiled. "This one has great potential—strong and brave—a young one hoping to prove himself to those around him."

Jack's attention perked up at Shu's proclamation, but he still looked uneasy.

I moved toward Volla and patted her neck. "Yes, Jack *is* strong . . . strong-willed and stubborn, traits he's always had. Right, Jack?"

Jack caught my wink, and a slight smile appeared. "Well, I learned from the best."

Thyra laughed, knowing his statement was definitely meant for me.

"So, that is where he gets it?" she exclaimed. "Well, that makes sense. Elric has his hands full with you, Anwen."

She immediately stopped, her head lowering, but not before I saw the panic in her features.

Have I been so distraught about Elric that my friends are now afraid to even mention his name?

Confused by our exchange, Shu started to speak, but Eydis appeared beside Jack. Shu immediately kneeled.

"Queen Eydis, it is an honor. I am here to escort you to the clearing where you will set up your camp. Queen Gamila requests your presence immediately. There is much to discuss before tomorrow's council meeting."

"Very well, I look forward to seeing my old friend," she nodded to Shu. "Have the others arrived yet?"

"King Grannir and his warriors have not arrived, nor Queen Sigrún and her company."

"I hope nothing has befallen Wynfalle again," Thyra stated.

Shu smiled. "The word is that they took an extra night to celebrate."

My ears perked up at the news.

"Why were they celebrating?"

Shu shrugged. "It is not yet known, although many of my comrades have an idea of the happy occasion. I have said too much. Come, let us not tarry here any longer."

Several Desert Elves stepped forward, escorting our group to the campsite. I chose to walk beside Shu instead of riding Glaesir, which gave me a chance to learn about the protective spell surrounding the camp. However, even though Shu was eager to talk about the Desert Elves' magic, I only caught half of the conversation. My mind kept drifting back to the Wynfalle announcement.

A celebration? Did the good news involve Elric? Maybe he was accepted as the Mountain Elves' official Volun? Or, perhaps, they found a new home in the mountains and are celebrating the return of their people to their homeland?

So many questions, but none seemed quite right in my mind. A sliver of anxiety prickled my heart.

THREE

On our journey to the High Council encampment, Grandmother shared frightening stories of Queen Gamila and her formidable warriors. Men and women who could stop the enemy with a single glance, giving them the advantage of a swift death with their deadly, curved swords. Remembering how Shu's gaze mesmerized me, surrounding me with peace and calm, only made me pause now—I wondered what it would be like to be on the other end of that spectrum. How would it feel to know you were about to die and not be able to defend yourself?

A shiver ran down my spine. I hoped he would never turn that specific gaze at me.

My grandmother also spoke of the more positive and artistic side of the Desert Elves—and this was the aspect that faced me now as we entered Queen Gamila's tent. My eyes widened at the size and grandeur of her shelter. From the outside, it looked fairly large, maybe enough to hold several families, but inside was easily the most astonishing sight.

Color exploded around me. Oranges, reds, browns, blues, purples, and yellows inundated every inch of the tent. Intricate geometric designs decorated everything around the tent—from the rugs under our feet to the pillows on the long benches set around it. Beautifully carved screens lined the walls while tiny glass lanterns floated above our heads. Their tiny flames flickered back and forth within their colorful glass cages, casting hundreds of shadows along the canvas.

I admired the calm and cozy atmosphere while standing near the back of our group. Eydis suggested that I stay hidden from the queen until she was ready for me to step forward. I agreed completely, knowing that remaining in the background allowed me to observe the crowd and listen for any signs of plots. From beneath my cloak hood, I kept watch.

The crispness of the evening quickly descended, so the warmth of the tent was welcomed. Winter was rapidly approaching, which meant that the journey to the Sea of Saerún would be hindered by snow. Now, as I looked around the tent and observed the people from the other kingdoms, my task to convince them that I could save their world from three unbalanced beings—a man with a god complex, an elf with unstoppable magic, and a god with a vendetta—was daunting. I shivered with doubt.

As we moved deeper into the tent, our desert kin parted ways. Queen Eydis stopped in front of a petite woman with skin as dark as night. Her chair was elaborately decorated with dark purple and red textiles. She was an elder, so frail-looking, but she stood with strength and confidence. Unusual, yet powerful, energy radiated from her. My steps faltered in her presence.

A smile erupted when Eydis approached.

Eydis bowed as Queen Gamila placed her hand on top of Eydis's head.

"My friend, it has been too long for our eyes to meet again," Gamila whispered softly.

Eydis looked up, unshed tears glimmered in her eyes. She placed her right hand on the shoulder of the elder elf.

"Aye, it has been too long, Queen Gamila," Eydis repeated. She placed her hand on Gamila's. "You are looking well, my friend."

Queen Gamila chuckled. "You are one of the most thoughtful and gentle of elves, Eydis, but you are a lousy liar."

Gamila coughed lightly as she settled back into the cushions with a gentle thud. "I am old, my friend, too old to be considering a war to end all wars."

Eydis smiled knowingly. She understood, like me, that Queen Gamila's cough and her abrupt declaration were for show.

Gamila motioned toward a group of chairs next to her. "Please, rest your tired bodies. I know the journey has been long and draining for my woodland kin."

Eydis sat beside Gamila and took her hand. "It has been a journey of unexpected troubles, to say the least, but the need to gather the council outweighs those hardships."

"Aye, it weighs on all of our minds. The council wants to proceed carefully with this decision—a motion that makes us all cautious. We must not rush into committing our warriors and people to another war. Right now, our success in keeping the tyrant and his monstrous army out of Sorayn is enough."

I bristled at her statement and her isolationist stance. If we didn't act immediately, her kingdom would ultimately fall. Her people would be enslaved or killed. She must see that there could only be one solution—death to Kenrick and Corvus. Send Loki back to the gods' realm once and for all.

Pulling her hands from Gamila, Eydis sat back in her chair. A respectful frown formed. "Yes, I understand the hesitation in declaring war, but the time has passed for us to sit idly by and do nothing. Death and destruction for all will be the only outcome if we do not act now. We cannot let our neighbors fall by the wayside and do nothing. Even the small skirmishes and the destruction endured by others should be acknowledged and addressed. A unified front with all the kingdoms of Emberval must be now."

Gamila's hand swiped the air as she smiled. "Alas, let us not talk of this. Tomorrow will come soon enough for our arguments when the council convenes. Please, I only wanted to greet my friend, but I have kept you too long . . ."

Relieved that the queen didn't request an introduction, I started for the tent opening, only to be pushed back by one of Gamila's guards

"Your Majesty, Queen Sigrún and her company have arrived. She requested to greet you before they set up their camp."

"Of course," Gamila replied and turned to Eydis. "Please

stay, my dear, for I imagine the queen would like to speak to you as well. You are sheltering her people until she finds another home."

Eydis nodded in agreement. "Of course, I am eager to hear how their journey fared."

The canvas opening swooshed back suddenly, making my heart skip a beat. I nervously wiped my hands down my cloak. Jack sidled up to me and grabbed my arm.

"Are you okay?" he whispered.

I nodded sharply; my eyes fixed on the entrance. My breath caught in my throat. Black spots started to form due to a lack of oxygen. I took a quick breath to keep from passing out when he appeared.

Elric stepped through the entrance, holding the flap open as Queen Sigrún walked inside. She paused so her eyes could adjust to the dimness. Her hands lifted to lower the hood.

A few more Mountain Elves entered and made their slow, dramatic walk to the throne. I automatically rolled my eyes and clenched my fists at the silly display. My focus shifted back to Elric. He followed behind Sigrún. His face was emotionless, and his eyes never left her back—not even to acknowledge his Vardian family.

I silently scoffed. Why didn't he notice his friends?

I moved, standing slightly off to the side of our group. Jack followed, taking my hand and gripping it tightly. I felt his energy increase. He also noticed Elric's lack of friendliness.

"Queen Eydis . . . Queen Gamila . . ." Sigrún bowed her head. "I am humbled and honored to be included in the council.

If my father were still alive, he would be pleased with the invitation."

"My dear, it is with great sadness that I hear of your father's death. However, we are overjoyed that your people have chosen you to take his place. We are humbled and honored that you have decided to journey to our council today."

Sigrún bowed her head at Gamila's words. She turned to Eydis, placing a hand upon Elric's arm and bringing him to stand next to her. "Queen Eydis, it has been too long, but I bring wonderful news. We have found a new home."

Queen Eydis stood and tilted her head with a smile. "That is wonderful news. Your people will be very happy to know that your journey was successful."

Eydis turned her attention to Elric and smiled. "And, Elric. You look well. I am sure seeing your homeland again is the reason, but we missed you in Vardia and look forward to your return."

Elric returned her smile. "Thank you, Queen Eydis. You are kind, as always."

I noticed Sigrún's hand tightened on his arm, but he didn't react to her vice-like grip. Why was she acting so protective? My grandmother's compliment was harmless. It had been many months since she last saw Elric in person. Still, Sigrún did not seem pleased. In fact, her expression tensed while her smile looked strained.

Alarms rang in my mind. I thought about the many Vardian remarks concerning their mountain kin. Mountain Elves couldn't be trusted. They had a habit of following the darkness, seeking power for themselves. Maybe Sigrún was following her ancestors' footsteps—Kenrick did offer them the way to regain that glory again.

The Okri stirred. I suddenly felt light-headed. Laga's words burned inside me, my energy twisting to be released. Instantly, I felt a hand on my arm. Anu's eyes cut through me from beneath her hood.

"Control yourself, Healer," she murmured softly.

I took a deep breath and closed my eyes, trying to calm the Okri and my energy. Thyra stepped back from her place by the queen and sidled up to my side.

"Are you unwell, Anwen?" she asked quietly.

Looking up at her, I saw concern in her eyes. I nodded, but I couldn't speak. Too many emotions overwhelmed me—the ache of the Okri, the burning of the goddess's words, and the tearing of my heart.

"Was your journey uneventful, Queen Sigrún?" Queen Gamila asked. "Did you encounter trouble like our Vardian brethren?"

Elric's body grew stiff. He approached Queen Eydis. "What happened, Queen Eydis? Are you unharmed?"

"Yes, of course, but we are all fortunate to be alive after the Lokrum attacked us," she shook her head. "If it wasn't for the sentinels and, of course, Anwen, we would not have made it to the council."

My insides cringed at the mention of my name. I didn't want anyone to know what I did to the Lokrum soldier. Too many questions were sure to follow, and I wasn't ready to tell anyone about my changing magic yet.

The mention of my name instantly made Elric turn his head toward our group. His eyes surveyed the crowd. I moved behind Ivar, silently cursing my grandmother's slip.

"Anwen?" Eydis strained her neck to find me.

Both Anu and Thyra gently pushed me aside, but I stayed put. I refused to lower my hood.

"So, this is your granddaughter?" Queen Gamila asked. "Come to me, child, and let me see the renowned Healer. I have heard the story of your budding powers."

Each step toward Gamila was agonizing. Compassionate whispers mixed with anxious ones. Sigrún's cold, piercing eyes tracked me.

"Please, Healer, show yourself," Gamila requested softly. "I am an old elf. My eyes are not used to the shadows inside your cloak's sanctuary."

My hands hesitated for a moment before lowering the hood.

"Queen Gamila, I am at your service," I said softly. "I am honored to meet the great queen who fought alongside my mentors, Healer Hrafn and Seer Herja."

Gamila smiled, her eyes shifting to the side of my face, and then down to my neck, hoping to glimpse Odin's three triangles and Laga's spell. "No, my dear, I am honored to meet the one who was chosen by the All-Father Odin and the goddess Freyja."

I could feel Elric's eyes roaming over me. His mind probe tried to break through my block. A small smirk escaped, making him try even harder. I sensed his desperate push against my thoughts. I have become stronger during the months he was away. My impenetrable mind-block remained intact. No one could figure out how to break the barrier, not even Herja.

Halvard stepped forward and bowed to the queen. “Your Majesty, if it weren’t for Healer Anwen’s magic, our situation would have been dire, and our losses would have been great.”

I cringed again at the mention of my magic—Gamila and the others grew interested in the details now. I could feel their heightened energy and anticipation. My breath quickened; my lungs tightened.

“Please, do tell us the intriguing story,” Queen Sigrún goaded Halvard sarcastically, but her eyes never left my face.

Everyone waited for Halvard to continue, but he instantly knew he had made a mistake.

My eyes begged him not to reveal the horrific details.

I stole a glance at Elric. He furrowed his brow with concern—my wounds hadn't healed completely, so they were still visible.

Halvard hesitated, uncertain how to proceed. Everyone waited quietly, holding their breath.

“I can only tell you that we were very lucky that Healer Anwen found a way to foil Corvus's magic. She destroyed the amulet that protected the Lokrum.”

A silent sigh of relief escaped my lips, thankful that he didn’t reveal any specifics. I also knew, unfortunately, that they would have to be disclosed soon.

When it became clear that no more information would be shared, Queen Gamila rose and ended the session with a disappointed sigh.

“Well, it seems that the saga will have to wait for another time, my friends. Now, let us rest—tomorrow will be a day of difficult discussions and grave decisions.”

My eyes briefly closed as a moment of relief washed over me. I quickly left the tent, turning away from my grandmother's worried frown and Elric's piercing stare.

I had work to do.

All the amulets needed to be destroyed, and I knew that wouldn’t happen until I discovered how I destroyed them in the first place.

FOUR

The golden sphere of energy hovered an inch above my right palm. Thin, jagged bolts struck the skin every second, sending tingling sensations up my arm. The breeze filtered through the trees and billowed my tunic away from my body. I swiveled my arm and tossed the ball to my left hand. With a fluid motion, my right leg lifted, and the ball hovered on the tip of my boot. Turning smoothly to the side, my arm stretched out to catch the ball again.

My slow but controlled movements persisted. I concentrated on the single ball of energy. With my eyes closed and breathing deeply and calmly, the stress of the day's events started to fade away. Thoughts of the Lokrum, the amulets, the council, and even Elric disappeared into the hidden corners of my mind.

A soft whisper hummed with my movements, and the Okri's purr-like chanting echoed through my bones. A calming symphony that helped my body relax. My energy ball shifted from gold to black, then to blue—the chaos of my magic merging into one.

I was so immersed in my meditation that I didn't notice Elric's approach at first, but then I felt him—his energy was wild, dynamic, and different. Almost too intense and definitely overpowering. His time in the Wynfalle Mountains changed him.

He probed my mind again, but I held onto my block, easily pushing his to the side with little effort. What was he trying to prove with all the probing? That he could easily push my will aside?

No, he couldn't do it now because I am stronger. I hid a smile.

I continued my movements; my meditation was almost finished. When I finished, I stood at attention, head down, arms at my sides then extended forward. My energy ball, now a bright amber gold, shrank to a single point before vanishing.

After finishing my exercise, I brought my arms to the front, pressing them together, and silently prayed to all the powers within me—Freyja, Odin, Laga, the Shadow, and the Okri. I bowed my head and expressed my thanks for their mediation.

When I opened my eyes, I saw Elric's surprised expression.

We stood there, facing each other for several minutes, neither of us speaking. Our emotions swelled inside us. His light blue eyes begged me to speak first, but I didn't know what to say. He abandoned me, and the hurt washed over me, leaving me speechless.

He leaned casually against a tree with his arms crossed. His eyes examined every inch of my face and then slowly drifted down my body. Feeling like he was judging me, I crossed my arms defiantly.

"You've been busy, I see," he drawled. "Herja has been teaching you advanced mediation."

I continued staring at him, hoping I wouldn't break down and wrap my arms around him. My silence must have made him uncomfortable. He pushed away from the tree and looked down at the ground. His feet shuffled uncomfortably back and forth.

"You were hard to find," he said, sweeping his arm around him. "Several miles away from the camp, in the middle of the forest, isn't a very smart move right now, Anwen. Lokrum scouts are nearby, and you would be an easy target while you're lost in your mind meditation."

A sarcastic laugh escaped me. "Really? Lokrum here? Who would have thought they'd bother us . . . oh, that's right, because they have! Yes, Elric, I do know the Lokrum are around here, unfortunately."

I leaned down, grabbed my bag angrily, and started to walk around him, stomping in my fury.

"I just needed to get away from the camp. My head was about to explode with the Okri and all the pent-up energy running wild . . . you should know this . . . you used to care."

Elric stepped in front of me. "Anwen, please. I wanted to talk to you."

I looked up at his face, my anger boiling over. "Oh, now you want to talk? I feel so privileged now that you have something to say to me."

I started to walk away from him again, but something broke inside me. I spun around and pointed my finger at him, pushing it in anger.

"How could you just forget about me? I waited for you to contact me for weeks, and then, when I found out you had been contacting Ansgar instead of me the whole time . . . I never felt so betrayed. I needed you, Elric, and you just left without even considering the consequences. I still needed guidance from you, and with my new power from Laga . . ."

I suddenly felt drained, as if everything I wanted to say to him after all these months just wasn't worth it anymore.

Pain and regret crossed his face. "Herja should be your teacher; she could give you better and more thorough training—more than I ever could hope to provide. And from what I've seen, she's succeeded in ways I can't even imagine. I feel the power in you, Anwen. You're different."

He didn't finish his statement, only looked at me with a kind of reverence, but then it shifted into something deeper and more personal.

"I never meant to hurt you, Anwen. You have to believe me. I didn't intend to stay away for so long, but my people needed me," he said softly.

"Yes, of course, your queen must be very happy now that you've stayed by her side," I hissed. I wanted to hear him say that he was coming back to Vardia, not remaining with his people. Not going back with her. But he shuffled his feet again, avoiding eye contact.

"Well, so be it," I said as I turned away from him and walked off.

"How did you do it?" he asked. "The amulet. How did you destroy it?"

I stopped but didn't turn around. Should I tell him that it might be one of several powers within me—the Shadow, Laga, Freyja, or even Odin—that I didn't understand what happened when the Lokrum attacked our camp.

The magic, well, it just took over me.

How would he respond? Would he be angry that I wasn't in control? Or would he be worried because he still loved me and wanted to help figure out what was going on inside me?

But he lost that right to the truth when he left me. Left Vardia. Of course, he didn't care anymore. His people accepted him now. Their Volun was back. He didn't need me anymore.

So, without turning around, I kept my back straight in self-assurance.

I simply stated the obvious.

"Magic."

And I walked away, ignoring how his anger and hurt grew with my answer.

***

The noise from the large group was almost overwhelming. Everyone had something to say, and surprisingly, most of it was unexpected. Emotions were intense as dissenters against declaring war on Lucia tried to outshout those eager to attack the kingdom at dawn. Unfortunately, the voices opposing Kenrick were barely noticed. Queen Gamila's earlier statement about protecting their own kingdoms echoed through the council.

I pulled my cloak hood further down over my head, tightening my lips. I couldn't believe how anyone could sit and argue to do nothing—a common delusion that Kenrick couldn't have teamed up with a god. Why would the gods turn against them? Kenrick's army couldn't be that powerful. He would eventually run out of ammunition and soldiers to draft. They believed we should wait and let him fail. War should not be an option.

I felt a hand cover mine under the table. I glanced sideways at Jack. His features reflected mine. Anger flickered in his eyes. He knew more than anyone how far both Kenrick and Corvus would go to ensure the success of their evil plan. Jack was part of that plan—we just didn't know what role he played or how they planned to use him.

King Grannir rubbed his large hands together, causing spine-tingling scraping sounds.

"How can ye sit there and tell this council that Kenrick is not a threat?" He pointed his large gray stub of a finger at the queen of the Sand Giants. "But maybe that's it, right? Your people were allies with the Lucians in the Great Purge, maybe ye already made a deal with Kenrick."

Queen Tule immediately stood up. Her large, beige body leaned over the table. The armor scraped against the edge.

"How dare you stoop that low, Grannir. That is ancient history, and my people have suffered enough for their past mistakes. Kenrick and his Mage are causing chaos, but that does not justify the death of my people in a war I believe is unnecessary."

"Not necessary?" King Alvis from the Navalen Mountains in Lohrhan yelled. "Wynfalle was destroyed. The indestructible mountain was devastated by Kenrick and his men. Navalen is in the same peril. My kingdom could be next, and I vote to strike hard against Lucia and even Jordanna. King Lorrin didn't even bother to grace us with his presence or send a representative from his kingdom, so that should say something about Jordanna and their stance against Lucia. War is imminent, and we must act now." His hand slammed on the table. "Before all our kingdoms are destroyed."

"But we forget one thing, King Alvis," Queen Tule smirked. "The gods are on Kenrick's side. How can we possibly win?"

She turned to face me and scoffed. "A mere girl-elf will save us all? From the all-powerful Loki? If the stories are true, why would the gods destroy us? What have we done to them to make them hate us?" Her grin grew even wider. "I know that my kingdom, my people, have prayed and sacrificed to our gods . . . they are not angry with us. Maybe you have not been so steadfast with your devotion?"

Eydis bristled next to me. Slowly, she stood up, her hands clenched at her sides.

"Are you calling our Healer a liar? That our goddess Freyja did not declare that she must journey to the Sea of Saerún?" Eydis enunciated every word slowly and deliberately. "Are you saying, Queen Tule, that *my* people are not suffering now because our Okri have been taken from us? That *my* kingdom, *my* people, are unfaithful to our gods? That *my* husband, along with some of *my* kin, is dying because of Kenrick's deception?"

My eyes stayed forward, flinching slightly at her words. Movement from the group of Mountain Elves caught my attention. I could sense Elric's energy spike in alarm.

Queen Tule shuffled her feet nervously, her eyes cast downward. My grandmother could be formidable when necessary. Many of our allies knew that she was a great warrior, not just an indifferent royal sitting on a throne.

"Of course not, Queen Eydis. I meant no disrespect to your Healer, especially given what your kingdom has endured. I wasn't aware King Ansgar was ill."

Eydis sat down, her head falling into her hands. She was so exhausted. Over the past few months, our people have been battling a mysterious illness. Hundreds, including my grandfather, were bedridden. I couldn't think of anything like it other than symptoms of a flu-like virus that people in my old world would have succumbed to.

"Of course, you did not know, Tule, because we are not one to openly show our weaknesses," Eydis murmured into her hands, but gradually her eyes met Queen Gamila's. "That is why Seer Herja did not travel with us. She is helping my people survive. That is why this council and the decision we make are so important—vital to the survival of my kingdom. Kenrick and Loki are to blame for what Vardia is experiencing now. Our enemies did not attack with soldiers and weapons. No, they were more subtle. They took our ancestors—our life force. My granddaughter, our Healer, can help us. All of us. Goddess

Freyja has given us hope; our All-Father has blessed us. Anwen must travel to the sea. The monks hold the key to destroying Loki, and through that, destroying Kenrick and Corvus. We need to mobilize. We must journey to the Sea of Saerún. We have to confront our enemies. We must declare war. We must succeed—for the survival of our kingdoms and our world. We must trust the gods. We must trust our Healer."

King Grannir glared at Queen Gamila. "I say we should take the vote now. Let us not delay any longer than necessary to stop the destruction of Kenrick and Loki. Those who have spoken, and arrived on time to this important meeting, and have not cowered in silence, should vote." His eyes angrily shifted to the group of centaurs standing impassively at the entrance of the tent.

The centaurs stiffened at the king's accusation. Their energy grew sharper. I leaned forward to the edge of my seat, expecting a fight. But, to my surprise, laughter erupted as a centaur strolled forward to stand before King Grannir. I recognized the large beast as he passed by us.

"It seems the rock king has mistakenly viewed my silence for indifference," the black stallion seethed. "Silence does not mean that we lack a voice. Simply, we have an unfortunate insight into this dire situation. My father's kingdom, our people, are leaving their homes. We are in a hopeless situation. Our warriors are few in numbers now, and the decision of war is not as easy as it may seem to Rydlyn or Vardia."

"Please, Prince Ciar, what has happened to Lohrhan, your kingdom?" Queen Eydis asked. "We have not heard news about your troubles."

The hair on his long, sleek body shone as he made his way to the center of the council. Several of his fellow centaurs followed behind him. A bright white mare with coppery armor stamped her feet while a dark chestnut with a quiver slung across his back sneered at everyone around him.

"Aye, Your Majesty, my father couldn't attend because my kingdom is being burned acre by acre, driving families out of their homes, and my warriors . . ." Ciar paused and looked around, facing each member. His eyes finally settled on me. "My warriors are being roped and herded like wild beasts and forced to carry the armaments of the Lokrum."

Ciar moved forward. His eyes searched my face. "I remember this one, and from the look in your eyes, you also recognize me."

Ciar turned and pointed to Elric. "And the elf . . . we met many moons ago, and it is I who warned you to keep this one safe." He pointed to me again. "I cannot stand by and watch my kingdom destroyed, but I cannot wage war with soldiers I do not have. I know what must be done, but I cannot send this young one to her death. Not now. That is why, with great sorrow, I reject the declaration of war."

Elric began to stand up, but Sigrún halted him. He hesitated, then sat back down, lowering his head in irritation.

King Alvis scoffed. "If you do not declare war, then all is lost for your people, Ciar. I cannot believe your father would allow such cowardice."

Suddenly, Ciar was in front of the dwarf king, his front legs tearing up the ground in anger. "The answer that I have given you *is* from my father, the king. It is not cowardice that I am showing to the council, it is what is best for my people."

Eydis bowed her head, frustration clear as she spoke the next words.

"Are there more dissenters against the declaration of war?" Her voice wavered. "Let me be the first to say that I do not take this lightly, that my kingdom is in desperate need of help, that I may have to send my Healer, no, my granddaughter, to certain death."

Eydis found me in the crowd. "Our goddess told us what needs to be done to save our world, and I believe in Anwen. All I ask is for a distraction, an army that will give Anwen a chance to talk to the monks, to find something, anything, to defeat Loki. That is all I ask."

Queen Gamila stood, shaking her head sadly. She reached out for Shu's arm to steady herself.

"I understand, my friend, but it is a commitment that many of us also will not take lightly, for sacrificing our kin for the word of your Healer is not enough," she glanced at the group of Mountain Elves. "Queen Sigrún and I have discussed our fears and are not convinced this is the right solution. What you ask is too much."

Eydis was just as surprised as I was by the decision. She immediately turned to Sigrún. "Queen Sigrún, is this true?"

Elric leaned toward Sigrún and whispered urgently in her ear. She waved her hand at him, showing indifference to his secret argument.

Sigrún stood and frowned. With a quick nod to Queen Gamila, she turned to my grandmother.

"Yes, Queen Eydis, it's true. However, I wish our hostess had chosen her words more carefully. But the fact remains, I will not send my kingdom to war, not now, when I am dispatching my warriors to Vardia to gather and care for my people. We must travel to our new home as soon as possible."

Eydis appeared shocked and saddened. This was not how I expected the council to respond to our pleas.

Silence was no longer an option.

I pushed my hood back from my face, anger now guiding my words.

"You, Sigrún, of all people, should know that Kenrick will stop at nothing to destroy all the kingdoms," I fumed. My eyes darted to Elric, who immediately stood at my words. "He killed your father, destroyed your home, and now you cower like a bunch of dogs. Herja would be disappointed in you."

The words hit their target. Sigrún's eyes widened in shock, her hatred clear in her gaze. "Herja belongs to me, not you. She is part of my kingdom, not yours, and she will leave with my people. I am her queen."

Her hate-filled words stunned the council. Everyone believed the rivalry between Wynfalle and Vardia would be put aside. Vardia took them in, providing food and shelter. But apparently, that camaraderie was short-lived.

Elric gently placed his hand on Sigrún's arm, as if trying to soothe her. His gesture and the lack of words dismissing her claims didn't go unnoticed by many Vardians, especially me. He was choosing Wynfalle over us.

He sensed my confusion and anger and attempted to probe my mind again. I furrowed my brow at his audacity.

"Council, let us pause to regain our composure," Elric said. "All of our emotions are heightened. That is what Kenrick and Loki want us to do. Turn the kingdoms against each other. Divide us. I must say that Queen Sigrún has every right to question a war that will commit the rest of her warriors, possibly to their deaths. Wynfalle cannot afford any more losses."

Elric paused. "But I cannot deny the truth in Queen Eydis' words. Healer Anwen is our best chance to stop Kenrick and Loki. There has to be a compromise."

Elric's words caught me off guard. Though I valued his loyalty, I still felt my anger bubble up inside.

Heavy silence enveloped the group as they reflected on Elric's words.

Queen Gamila bowed her head. "Volun Elric has spoken wisely, but we will need more than just a break. Let us resume tomorrow and take a final vote on our actions."

I hurried to Eydis's side, eager to leave the tent quickly. Jack was right behind me with Anu. We headed for the entrance.

King Alvis suddenly stood and raised his arms, stopping us in our tracks.

"I would like to welcome all of the kingdoms to my camp for a celebration," he yelled out. "Tomorrow's decision hangs heavily over our heads, but news of an impending marriage has been announced!"

Everyone eagerly waited as the dwarf king approached Elric

and Sigrún.

"Let us raise our glasses tonight to the Queen of Wynfalle and her Volun . . . a longstanding union between the two families."

Nothing could have prepared me for the announcement. I felt the pressure of hands on my back and the distant voices of Eydis and Thyra calling out my name. Everything around me seemed to unfold in slow motion.

Elric searched the crowd for me. His energy surged to an unbearable level. A sharp mind probe tried to invade my thoughts. I used all my strength to keep him out.

Anu grabbed my arm. I looked up into her face; her lips moved, but I couldn't hear any sound. Her agitated state caused her body to ripple from human to Lirrean. It was almost comical to see her body shift back and forth. A small smile formed on my lips at the strangeness, but suddenly an unusual yet familiar feeling overwhelmed me, making my smile falter.

A sudden tingling sensation emerged from the center of my chest and spread down my body, followed by a sharp pain in my arm. My body felt as if it was about to explode. An unfamiliar energy invaded my body.

I quickly looked at Anu in a panic.

A muffled cry escaped before darkness overwhelmed me.

FIVE

The pain in my arm throbbed unbearably. The piercing stab beneath my skin grew worse with every heartbeat. My eyes snapped open to faint candlelight. My head felt heavy and sluggish as I turned it to the side. Anu slumped in a chair beside my desk, her chin tucked into her cloak, sleeping.

I started to lift my right arm, but it was heavily wrapped in bandages. Jack's head rested beside it, his hand gently curled on top, holding my arm down.

My eyes flickered rapidly, trying to understand my current state.

What happened to me?

Everything was blurry and unclear. My throat was parched and scratchy. Coughs shook my body, sending a jolt of pain down my arm.

Bits and pieces filtered through my thoughts—I remembered the council meeting, the argument against declaring war on Lucia, the doubts about my role in stopping Loki. And something else happened, but I couldn't recall what it was. I slowly raised my left arm to pinch the bridge of my nose. The pain started after the announcement.

Tears welled up in response to the unbearable news—Elric's engagement to Sigrún.

And with the horrible news, I felt it.

Another death of a god.

A tear rolled down my cheek. I shifted my arm out from under Jack's hand and turned it over, staring at the linens that concealed the spell etched into my skin.

Which god was it that perished? And where were Freyja and Odin? Why didn't they show themselves to the council or even to me? Why didn't they tell the council the truth and the intentions of my mission?

My thoughts shifted to Sigrún and her decision not to declare war on Lucia.

How could she make that decision, even after everything that had happened to her people and to her father? How could she go against Vardia, the kingdom that helped her people? How could Elric choose Wynfalle over Vardia? Everyone from Vardia, including Eydis, was surprised by her vote. Now, where does that leave my kingdom?

If no one stood up to Kenrick and Loki, could Vardia fight alone?

Elric's betrayal cut deeply. Hearing about his engagement felt like a dagger stabbing right into my chest. How could he walk away from our relationship? I believed he loved me. He claimed he ended things with Sigrún.

I was foolish to believe in him and trust him.

I dragged my hand across my eyes, wiping away the tears. I needed to stop crying. Now isn't the time to wallow in self-pity. Vardia needed help, and if the other kingdoms wouldn't join us, then I had to take action. The alternative plan was in motion.

I carefully lifted my body onto my elbows, testing to see if the pain would come back, but instead, dizziness washed over me. Jack twitched slightly and tucked his now free hand under his chin, but he didn't wake up. Sighing with relief, I looked over at Anu. My breath caught in my throat when her bright eyes met mine.

"I was wondering when you were finally going to wake up," she muttered as she stretched her arms overhead and yawned.

She leaned in and smiled mischievously. "And what do you think you're doing?"

She stood up and sauntered over to the side of my bed. Her eyes shifted to Jack, who continued to sleep.

"Jack refused to leave your side," she whispered. She pulled another chair up beside the bed. She looked at me silently for a few seconds before continuing. "Everyone has been worried about you."

I wiped the tears from my cheeks, hoping Anu didn't see my brief moment of self-pity. "How long have I been out?"

Anu looked at me for a few more seconds before speaking. "Three days."

My heart stuttered. "What? Three days?"

Jack stirred but still didn't open his eyes.

I couldn't believe it.

Three days. Impossible.

I swung my legs over the side, but a wave of nausea hit me. Anu steadied me and then placed my legs back onto the bed.

"You need to take it easy. You had a tough time for a while," she murmured. "Fever, shakes, mumbling in that strange ancient language. Eydis even went so far as yelling at the top of her lungs, demanding that Freyja, and even your mother, help you."

She shrugged her shoulders and grimaced. "It was a spectacle. No one knew what was happening to you. It was different than the last time, you know, when Loki killed Laga."

I tried to recall the last three days, but my memories slipped away. I lifted my arm and scratched at the bandages until my freshly tattooed arm was visible—skin slightly red and swollen, with the black runes glistening, extending from the back of my hand to just below the elbow. The letters looked odd, almost as if a child had scribbled them. I turned my arm over, hoping to find some connection to the god who gave their life. The words wrapped around my skin, leaving hardly any space between each character.

I gently laid my arm back on the bed and closed my eyes. My lips trembled, and another tear rolled down my cheek.

Anu kept staring at me in silence. I understood what she was thinking, just as I was sure she knew what my next question would be. I was acting selfishly. Someone had died because of me, but there was only one person I could think of at that moment.

"If it makes you feel any better, he refused to leave your

side, too," she whispered, but her tone grew more condescending as she continued to talk. "He knew something was wrong with you in the council tent, even before anyone else saw you fall to the ground. He caught you and brought you here. So gallant, I must say. Even when Sigrún ordered him to leave you, he refused."

I shifted my gaze to her, hoping what she said was true.

She scoffed. "I don't understand you. He treated you horribly, but any mention of him being somewhat nice to you, you get all mushy and teary-eyed. The hope on your face disgusts me."

Anu jumped up from the chair and began pacing back and forth. Her movements were erratic. She never said another word to me.

I turned away from her as new tears began to fall. If she saw them, she would probably lose it. She stopped pacing when she heard my quiet sniffles.

Sighing, she walked back over to my bed and stood quietly over me. I thought she had left when I didn't hear anything else for a few minutes, but when I turned back around, she was sitting in the chair again.

"Well, I just had to get that off my chest, okay?" She looked down at her hands folded in her lap. "Anyway, I thought you would also like to know what happened while you were sleeping."

I wiped my face again and nodded, eager for her to continue.

Anu gave me a strained smile. "Well, on top of the

excruciating debate before you went all swoony, the council met the next day, and lo and behold, surprise, surprise, they voted against the declaration."

I threw the cover off me. "They what?"

She leaned forward. "Looks like we are on our own, Healer."

I hurled my legs over the side of the bed, ignoring the wave of dizziness that swept through me. I stood up but instantly fell back onto the bed. Jack leaped up from his chair, his eyes shifting from blue to black. His hand swept to his side, and he withdrew his dagger.

"What? What is going on?" he managed breathlessly. He noticed I was awake. He sheathed his knife and wrapped his arm around my waist. "Anwen? Are you okay? What are you doing? You should rest. You were out for days. I didn't know if you would wake up."

Jack's voice cracked as I pulled him into a hug.

"I know, Jack. I am so sorry I put you through that, but I am better now."

I stepped back and smiled. "Really, I'm better."

My voice also cracked as he pulled me into his arms again.

"I remembered Herja's stories, when Loki killed Laga. How you acted, but this was different, wasn't it?"

I wanted to ease the worry and fear in his eyes and tell him everything would be fine. But I couldn't lie to him, not when our lives and those we love, and even the lives of everyone in this world, depended on us.

"Yes, Jack. It was different," I said, glancing briefly at Anu, knowing the next words I spoke could banish all of us from our kingdom. "I expect a visit from Freyja to tell us whose life was taken, but know this . . ." I grabbed him by the shoulders. "It is up to us now . . . you, me, and Anu. We are on our own. We need to stop Loki."

Jack looked between Anu and me. His face twisted with sudden panic before he lifted his chin with resolve.

"What's our plan?'

I grabbed his hand and Anu's.

I knew the next words would condemn us to certain death. A journey only we could start and finish. Maybe Freyja already knew this—that the council would never declare war on Lucia, and even less so on Loki. They were afraid that if one of their gods turned against them, then what would stop all the gods from lashing out? What would prevent the gods from condemning all the kingdoms to death and destruction?

I saw how the council looked at me—restrained reverence for what the gods bestowed upon me. But beneath that surface of awe was fear. Pure terror of what my powers could truly unleash. I sensed their conflicted emotions. But could I blame them for being scared of me? I might be just one step away from becoming a deranged, god-like elf. They knew nothing about me, only the stories passed between their kingdoms. With only two days to convince the council to trust me, to journey to their sacred lands, and to speak with their revered monks—to save them from a trickster god and an evil Mage and Master—what was I really expecting? It was a crazy plan, even to my ears. The whole thing sounded ill-fated and desperate. No wonder they voted against declaring war.

But as I glanced from Jack to Anu, I knew we couldn't give up. We had to continue with our plan, this practically doomed mission.

"We must leave tonight," I said with resolve. "Just us. We are going to the Sea of Saerún."

SIX

Lately, my sepia-toned dreams have resembled silent movies—no sound, but with strange, fast-paced scenes showing close-ups of my overdramatic expressions. Short clips revealed mysterious yet chaotic magic with a few frames of my smiling face—but it wasn't amusement or happiness. Madness, not joy, consumed me.

Imagine having the same dream every night, to the point where you started to think you were going crazy, that your dreams were part of reality. Whatever happened to those 'feel-good, running through the meadows holding the hand of the love of my life' kind of dreams?

Exactly. That situation never occurred either.

My eyes opened again, hoping to escape the aftermath of my nightmare, only to find myself back in the same place repeatedly.

I finally gave up on trying to get any more sleep and swung

my legs over the side of the bed. I rubbed the sleep from my eyes, hoping to also wipe away some of the sadness.

I shook my head, trying to shake off the remnants of my dream and the lingering thoughts of defeat.

How were we going to pull this entire thing off? Were we really ignoring the council's decision to go after a god and his followers?

My head fell into my hands, and I started to laugh. The yet-to-be-determined plan that will surely banish us from Vardia, if not condemn us to our deaths, even if we did survive the quest?

But what if we succeeded in defeating Loki and restoring peace? Everyone would be proud of us, pleased that we had the courage to take matters into our own hands. Was it truly my destiny to save the world?

I fell back onto the cot and smirked sarcastically. Well, maybe death was my fate. Maybe my death was the key to saving everyone.

I lifted my right arm, staring at the mysterious spell carved into the skin. My arm hovered above me, twisting this way and that. The pain subsided, but like Laga's spell on my neck, it tingled like a small bug slowly crawling on the skin.

My arm thumped onto the bed. I still didn't know which god or goddess had died. Maybe it wasn't Loki. Maybe something else caused the nameless god to die. That would explain why Freyja or even Odin hadn't shown themselves to me.

Suddenly, the candles flickered unpredictably, sending small sparks flying. I sat up quickly and looked around the tent cautiously. The square firebox in the middle of my tent hissed. Flames burst from between the grate, sending sparks everywhere. The temperature inside the tent started to climb.

I jumped from my cot and grabbed the dagger from the desk, spinning around to the center of the tent just in time to see a hand reach out from inside the box and unlatch the door.

A small creature emerged from the flames. I shielded my eyes from the intense light but kept the dagger steady in front of me. I lowered into an attack stance. The flames pulsed even brighter. The figure hesitated as it moved through the opening. It eyed the dagger before lifting curious eyes up to me.

Smirking, the creature stepped out of the firebox. The flames dimmed to a normal level.

My hand, which shielded my eyes from the light, lowered automatically. A bright blue light emitted from my palm.

"Who are you?" I managed to say. "Why are you here?"

The creature casually leaned against the firebox, crossing its arms and eyeing me with skepticism. It was a strange sight—standing no taller than two feet with orange-crimson skin. Its hairless head had deep ridges running from his forehead to the top of his slightly pointy head. And apparently, it didn't believe in clothes.

"She said you would probably ask all sorts of ridiculous questions," he said lazily. "You are the one who called for me, girlie."

"I don't think so," I said, standing a little taller. "I have no idea who you are."

The creature moved away from the heater and walked

toward me.

I raised the dagger higher while my other hand fired a warning burst of energy at his feet.

He stopped and placed his hands on his hips.

"Really? Don't try that magic on me, elfy," he growled. "You *did* call me. Otherwise, why have your altar to invoke me?"

He pointed to the small nightstand next to my cot. Several candles flickered on top of it. My necklace curled around the base of one of the candles, and a bundle of basil sat to the side, apparently a gift from one of the centaurs when I was unconscious.

My confusion ignited the creature's anger, making his skin glow bright red and pulse like a stirred fire.

He turned around and began pacing in front of me, muttering to himself.

"I cannot believe her audacity. I thought she said this elf-girl was clever?" he said softly. He continued to ignore me, walking in circles around me. "She is oblivious to what is happening around her."

"Excuse me?" I interrupted. "Who are you, and why do you keep saying she? What are you talking about?"

My anger intensified as he kept mumbling obscenities.

"And just so you know, I am clever. So there! And powerful!"

I extinguished my magic and placed my hands on my hips, mimicking the little intruder.

"So, leave my tent, or I will turn you into an ice cube!" I mocked with a tilt of my head and a raised eyebrow.

The creature stopped pacing and turned toward me. A smile slowly spread across his face, even though it still pulsated. I was surprised at how a smile could change someone's appearance. Grimacing and yelling, this creature looked like a demon, but when a smile crinkled his face, an almost normal human quality appeared.

"Good, good," he said. "That is what I like to hear. Power is not only in your magic, my lady, but also in your command of words, and of course, attitude is most appreciated. She was at least correct in that regard."

"Who are you talking about? Who is this *she*?" I asked again.

The creature bowed deeply, his hands extending outward. "Please let me introduce myself. I am Kal, your most exalted fire fairy, dear Healer, and the one I speak of is none other than our goddess, Freyja."

"Freyja?" I exclaimed. I immediately knelt in front of Kal. "I have so many questions for her! Where is she? How did Loki find the other god? The one he killed?"

I rolled up my tunic sleeve and revealed the spell.

"I need to talk to her now," I leaned in closer. "Please. No one believes I can defeat Loki."

Kal stepped back and grimaced. It seemed he didn't like how close I was.

"Whoa there, little elfy. You called me, remember?" He pointed to the nightstand again. "Besides, Freyja is too busy to bother with you right now."

"Too busy for me?" Anger flared as I stood up and paced the room. "She's the one who suggested this council. She's the one who told me I had to defeat Loki. What could possibly keep her so busy right now?"

Kal was about to respond when a bright green light flashed in the middle of the tent.

We covered our eyes and stepped back in surprise. The light grew brighter until a round portal the size of a door appeared.

A hand wielding a sword appeared through the portal first, followed by a battle-worn shield. I immediately pushed my hands forward. The changing colors of my energy flashed and sparked to life. My tent seemed to be the center of activity tonight.

I glanced at Kal and saw that he was bowing. What in the world was he doing?

Suddenly, I felt her energy and her presence.

I lowered my arms as Freyja emerged from the portal. The bright green light faded, leaving the tent nearly in darkness, but with enough firelight to see her condition.

She faltered in her steps. I rushed to her side and grabbed her waist. Kal kept his distance until I helped her onto my cot. Her appearance shocked me. Bloodied and exhausted, she turned her face up toward me. She set her sword and shield down. My eyes followed her movements. Blood dripped from the blade of the sword.

"Thank you, Anwen," Freyja muttered wearily. She straightened the armor covering her chest and tossed her wrist guards on the floor. "May I have a drink of water?"

Kal instantly jumped to attention and suddenly conjured a chalice out of thin air. "Please, dear goddess, drink my special elixir. It shall calm you and bring you solace after the battle you have fought."

"Battle?" I asked nervously. "What is Kal talking about?"

I knelt beside Freyja as she took a long drink. My voice trembled. "Am I too late? Did Loki win?"

Freyja gently placed her hand on my cheek.

"No, my dear, not yet. The consequences of Loki's violence have taken hold in the other realms," she pulled her hand away and looked at Kal. "My dearest fairy friend has come to you on my behalf, knowing that what you have decided—to go against your council and even more so, your family—shall have repercussions that may never be fully forgiven. This decision has been foretold in the stars."

I looked away from her and stood up. Anger now replaced my fear. "So, you knew the council would vote against war, that they would not believe me?"

I threw my arms out in disbelief. "Why did we come? Why waste the time asking for their blessing when you knew they would say no?"

Turning away, I muttered to myself, "This is ridiculous. I believed in you. I thought you trusted me."

I twirled around and shoved my arm out for her to see. "Now, because of your decision to waste time, this is what happened. Another god has been killed. Loki has found a way to gather the spells. No god is safe now. I feel so helpless and useless. And when you didn't show up for three days, after the death . . ."

Freyja approached me. Her eyes locked onto mine, never looking at the spell pulsing on my arm.

Motionless and silent, we stared at each other. "Forgive me for not coming sooner, Anwen. I would have come to you if not for the impending battle."

Guilt flooded me. My world wasn't the only one at risk because of Loki. I opened my mouth to apologize, but she shook her head, understanding my intentions.

"No, my dear Anwen, there is no need to apologize. I understand the dilemma you are in. Everyone you love is in danger. Turning away from them is the only way to protect them."

She took my arm in her hands, gently rubbing her fingers over the red skin. "His name was Hermod, the swift, and he was Odin's son."

My eyes drifted to Kal, who was sniffling. Drops of glowing ember trailed from his eyes.

"I am so sorry. Odin must blame me. I would have stopped him if I could have." I said, trying to find the right words. My head dropped into my hands, feeling guilty for another death.

Freyja held me close and softly brushed my hair away from my face.

"The great All-Father does not blame you, Anwen. My brothers and sisters knew that giving you our spells was dangerous, but we had no choice at the time. Live to fight another day—that is what drove us to your mother and finally to you."

She took my head in her hands and gently caressed my cheek. "The plans that you have made with Anu and Jack, you must leave before dawn. You cannot wait. For if you do, all will be lost."

"Why? What do you mean?" I pulled back. "What is going to happen?"

Freyja stepped back from me and grabbed her sword and shield. Another portal of light appeared behind her.

"Wait, you can't go now," I exclaimed. "I need your guidance. I thought Elric would help, but he has turned away from us. I don't know how to get to Saerún!"

"Loki has concealed his thoughts and movements—all the gods have lost contact with him. It's now your turn. Head west, follow the stars, listen to the ancients, and trust your heart. Believe in your decisions, Anwen, never second-guess yourself. Your destiny is calling—trust those who believe in you."

She began to step into the portal, but stopped. She tilted her head as if listening for something. Twisting back around, Freyja fixed her gaze on Kal. Her eyes became stern.

"It has begun. You know what you must do."

And as she disappeared into the light, an explosion shook the earth.

I started running toward the tent opening when Kal leapt at me, grabbed my wrist, and pulled me toward him. Surprised by his strength, I had no choice but to fall at his feet. He dragged me toward the firebox.

"What are you doing?" I screamed, clawing at his fingers. "LET. ME. GO!"

Kal kept pulling me closer to the fire, ignoring the specks of blood seeping from the scratches caused by my nails. He leaned over the nightstand and grabbed my necklace. Turning around, he wore a demonic grin that could have rivaled any monster from my old world.

"Close your eyes, Healer, we're going for a ride," Kal whispered through his bared teeth.

He jumped into the air, pulling me with him. My breath caught in my throat. Everything around me blurred and slowed down. My feet hovered above the floor for a moment, and then suddenly, in a flash, Kal hurled my body into the fire. A blood-curdling scream escaped from my lips.

SEVEN

The smell of burnt cotton filled my nostrils. My head shot up, but I immediately regretted the move as a sharp pain shot through my skull and down my back. Moaning, I lowered my head back onto the ground.

What happened? Where was I?

Slowly, I lifted my head, checking for injuries, and when the intense pain didn't return, I pushed myself off the ground, clawing at the hot sand for leverage. The glaring sun's rays beat down unforgivingly on the land. The heated air flickered and wavered.

Shielding my eyes from the bright light, I gasped at the barren land around me.

"Whoa," I muttered, turning around slowly in a circle.

Ignoring the splitting pain working its way down my body, I took a few hesitant steps forward. The shock left me speechless.

Gone were the tall trees and the lush green hills of Rydlyn. Now, enormous, spherical mounds of rock loomed around me. Deep brown with red veins streaking down the sides, the unsettling formations appeared as if they were bleeding. Each rock varied in size; the smallest was no taller than me, while the largest reached as high as a five-story building.

"Hello?" I yelled. My voice crackled. "Kal? Freyja?"

I looked up at the sky again, noticing the sun was almost directly overhead. How long had I been unconscious? And where was everyone? Why did Kal bring me here?

My thirst became nearly unbearable. I shuffled my feet toward the small shadow cast by one of the mounds. I ran my hand over my body, checking for any injuries. My clothes were torn and blackened from the fire. My fingers traced around my neck and discovered a few spots where I must have been burned by the flames. I continued my inspection, brushing over Laga's spell. A sharp tingling sensation pulsed beneath my fingers, but it didn't last. I kept exploring down my throat and stopped immediately.

My necklace was missing.

I jumped up in a panic. The last time I saw it was on my nightstand—and then Kal grabbed it and pushed me into the fire.

My eyes scanned the ground. Dread flooded through me at the thought of losing my mother's necklace. It had to be here. Why would Kal keep it?

I dropped to my hands and knees, running my fingers through the sand. I stopped as soon as the light brown sand was streaked with red blood. I leaned back in despair. The reality of my loss sank deeper inside.

I shouldn't have removed it. It was my only real link to my mother, and now it's gone. Lost forever.

I held back my tears.

No. I didn't lose it. Kal stole it.

And Freyja told him to do what he needed to do. She knew he was going to throw me into the fire. Or whatever it was. Was it another portal? But to where?

Jaw clenched with determination, I scrambled to my feet once more and scanned my surroundings.

"Hello?" I yelled again. "Anyone out there?"

My echoing voice called out several times, but silence quickly followed. I had to find my way back to the camp.

I walked around the mound, looking up at the sky and along the horizon, hoping to find any other lifeform—yearning to see the familiar figures of my Vardian family. What happened to them? Who attacked the camp?

Did they survive?

That one question lingered and pushed me into action.

I started walking west. Freyja knew my mission. I knew what I had to do to save my people. Maybe that was her plan. But did she know about the coming attack? Did she send Kal just for that—to save me?

I stopped. "Freyja? Are you out there? Please, show yourself. Why did you do this to me? Where did you send me?"

As the sun reached its peak, a distant howl echoed. I shivered. The sound evoked memories of the Kludde, the fierce creatures from Kenrick's army.

My gait quickened as the yelping continued. I had to find shelter before darkness fell, and before whatever caused those noises found me.

***

A light breeze whipped around the mounds. I turned my face into it, enjoying the relief from the heat. The remaining part of my tunic floated about an inch from my body, cooling my sweat-soaked, exposed midriff. With the relentless sun beating down on me and the slim chance of running into anyone in this deserted land, I let go of my modesty. The tattered remnants of my tunic wrapped around my head, covering my exposed neck, which was the only way I thought could protect me from heat exhaustion.

For the hundredth time, I knelt on the ground and sifted through the sand, hoping to find a cache of rocks. If I had a few rocks in my hand, I could try to turn them into water. But, again, my hands came up empty. I thrust my hands out in front of me and tried to conjure my magic, but all I could produce was a few golden wisps of energy. How would I have known that sand wasn't conducive to magic?

Frustrated, I yelled into the bright, cloudless sky. "Freyja? Kal? Is anyone out there?"

I fell back and pulled my knees up to my chest, hugging them in desperation. I had never felt so alone and exposed. Not even my magic was working for me. Tired, hot, and overwhelmed by concern for my family, I was on the verge of tears.

Hopelessness settled deeper inside me.

A faint cry called out.

I quickly scrambled to my feet. My head tilted in anticipation, hoping the noise would repeat. A few seconds later, my name echoed around me.

"Hello?" I screamed. "I'm here."

Turning around in circles, I tried to locate where the sound was coming from, but the echoing in the valley of the mounds made it hard to tell.

A movement from the east caught my attention. I started to run toward the object, but then stopped. Maybe it was a trap? I shouldn't just run into the unknown, even if they were the ones calling my name.

My feet froze with my indecision. I needed to be more cautious, especially if my powers were not working. My eyes scanned the ground for something to defend myself with, but nothing caught my attention. I glanced back up and saw that the person was much closer, arms waving as he walked toward me.

No, that wasn't right. He was sprinting and screaming in terror.

"Anwen! Run!"

I squinted against the sun's glare, and my name, along with the person yelling, became clearer.

"Jack?" I yelled in surprise as I started to run toward him.

"No, the other way. RUN," he shouted, waving his hand. "Run away."

A cloud of dust billowed behind him. He fell several times,

struggling to get back up each time.

What was happening? Why was Jack having so much trouble? Why was he running?

He kept struggling, scratching at the sand to find his balance. He finally got to his feet and began to run back toward me.

The ground trembled beneath me, causing me to sway. I struggled to maintain my balance. Small clouds of dust rose from the ground, forming a perfect circle about thirty feet around me.

My senses flared, warning me to get out of the circle. As I started to run, sand heaved beneath me, throwing me to the ground. With the earth vibrating, Jack screaming, and the sand swirling, I summoned all my remaining energy and threw my hands out, hoping to hit whatever was trying to kill me.

A burst of energy shot from my hands and struck its target. A loud shriek erupted beneath the sand.

I jumped up and tried to run toward Jack, but the ground lurched again, this time with much more force, launching me into the air and onto one of the small rock mounds. I hit with a loud thud, enough to knock the wind out of me, and rolled back onto the sand. Jack darted around one of the larger mounds, eyes wide with fear, but suddenly stopped. A large creature erupted from the ground.

The brown beast shot up into the sky, swirling its mottled body as it gained speed. Its skin scraped against the sand, forcing itself up from deep within the earth. The sand circle widened with the creature's bulk. I turned right, trying to crawl to safety.

From the corner of my eye, I saw Jack do the same as he

made his way around one of the mounds. He held up his hand, stopping me from moving.

The worm-like creature continued swirling, enlarging its hole and making it less stable. Suddenly, it stopped moving upward into the sky. Unfortunately, I didn't notice that it was slowly descending back to the ground, leaving a circle of quicksand that immediately pulled my body toward its depths.

Screaming, I clawed at the sand, trying to escape certain death. There was no way I was going to become this creature's meal.

Jack ran away from the hole, enough to then cut across and head toward me.

"Stop, Jack," I yelled. "It's too risky. You need to get out of here! Climb the mound."

But he didn't listen as he skidded to a stop several feet ahead of me.

"Grab my hand," he grunted, extending his arm. His fingers barely brushed against mine. "I can't reach you."

A second shriek shattered the earth. Several dust pockets exploded just behind Jack's outstretched feet. A second hole formed, but this time nothing erupted from the ground, only a circle of sand rippling outward from the center until it touched Jack's toe. A black, slithering tentacle emerged and wrapped around his ankle, pulling him toward the center of the sand puddle.

"Jack, behind you!"

Jack's body jerked back a few inches. He screamed in surprise.

My clawing became more frantic. I struggled to reach the tips of his fingers, causing my own body to sink deeper into the quicksand. Feeling helpless, I prayed for the Shadow to help save Jack, anything to keep him out of the jaws of the sand creature.

Instantly, I felt a stirring inside me. The tingling of uncomfortable energy grew rapidly, causing pain from the tension for release. I stopped carving into the sand and reached out to Jack. A small, twisting black mist burst from my palm and wrapped around Jack's wrists, halting both of us from descending further into the deadly depths of the hole.

My arms ached from the strain of holding up Jack's weight. I struggled to keep the magic from vanishing.

"Jack, I can't hold on much longer," I gasped, angry tears mixing with sweat as I tried to hold on to him.

Desperation washed over Jack's face. His skin flickered with color as his eyes blackened. The lower half of his legs sank into the sand. He groaned in pain but clenched his grip on the magic tighter and fought to pull himself out of the hole.

I did the same as my feet tried to find anything, any leverage, within the coarse sand.

"Freyja, don't you dare do this to me," I muttered. "I cannot lose him again."

My right hand felt as if it were tearing away from my arm. The magical mist disappeared.

"No!"

Jack's body was almost submerged.

"Hold on!" I yelled in fear.

Suddenly, as if Freyja answered my call, a rope fell from the sky and hit the sand beside me. The sight of a hand pulling Jack out of the sand surprised both of us.

Just as quickly as Jack's body floated up the mound, the rescuer's hand appeared in my face.

Expecting to see Freyja, I looked up with relief.

Imagine my surprise when the outstretched hand reaching for me was not attached to the beautiful goddess, but to my ex-boyfriend.

EIGHT

The sand worms cried out in anger when their meal vanished into the sky. Their long, eerie screech echoed through the desert as they slithered away, feeling defeated, with wild, disappointed thrashing beneath the ground.

Climbing to the top of the rock, I kept a firm grip on Elric's hand. The mound shuddered from the tremors. After a few minutes, I noticed our hands were still clasped together. He drew me closer. My hand automatically rose and rested on his chest. His heartbeat matched the rhythm of mine.

"Anwen, are you hurt?"

Another voice came from behind me.

Instantly, I shoved away from Elric, hard and fast. He stumbled at the force of my push. I looked up into his face, expecting to see anger at my harshness, but only saw hurt. I quickly turned to the person asking the question and was surprised again.

"Anu? How did you get here?" I turned to see all the faces staring at me in disbelief—Ciar, Shu, Thyra, and a female Desert Elf named Menhit.

"How did you get here?" I exclaimed. My eyes landed on Jack, who was clutching his leg.

I rushed to his side. His eyes were still black and gold. A moan escaped him. His skin pulsed slightly as he shifted from his Lirrean form to human.

"Let me see your leg, Jack."

He shook his head, grimacing at that slight movement. I checked the rest of his body for other injuries and found only minor wounds on his temple and chin.

"Jack, please," I soothed, reaching down and peeling his hands away from his leg. "Let me help."

I gasped at the deep gash along his calf. The bone glistened through the cake of blood and sand.

Thyra quickly moved to Jack's side, a soft cry escaping because of the severity of his injury. "Jack, my dear, hold still, let Anwen help you."

She looked at me, fear gripping her. Jack's face turned pale from blood loss. He was slipping into unconsciousness.

Panicking, I looked up at everyone, catching their expressions of expectation. My eyes settled on Elric, and I shook my head. "I don't know if I can heal him. My magic doesn't seem to be working very well here. It comes and goes for some reason."

I glanced down at Jack again, then back up at Elric and said softly, "I might need your help."

He knelt beside me without hesitation, my cold reception to his rescue forgotten.

"I am also having trouble using my magic, but maybe together, we can manage to heal him." He raised his hands.

I placed my hands over Jack's chest. As I murmured the spell, I gradually moved my hands to his head and then down to his leg. Elric began to mutter his spell and mimicked my movements until both of our hands were positioned over Jack's wound.

A trickle of sweat ran down the side of my face. The magic flickered with the different colors of my energy, as if it couldn't decide which one to use. A dull pain spread through my hand and up my arm, making me wince. I felt a hand tighten on my shoulder. Anu knelt beside me, her eyes closed. Words softly formed and escaped her lips. I looked at Elric, and he appeared to have the same problem. His energy pulsed erratically from his hands.

I closed my eyes again and recited the spell more fiercely. The pain grew more intense. The sound of my voice increased. I tried to focus, but it became harder to handle the pain. Anu's hand tightened and pressed down on me with such force that I felt like I was being driven into the stone.

The pain was nearly unbearable until suddenly I felt a strange release inside me—like my body was pitched over the first peak of a roller coaster. If I didn't know I was kneeling on rock, I might have believed my body was floating—light and free. All pain vanished.

I opened my eyes when the sensation faded and saw Elric's

expression. It was obvious he had experienced the same phenomenon.

I felt the pressure of Anu's hand still on my shoulder, but I also noticed Shu's hand on my other shoulder, and I was even more surprised when Menhit grasped both Elric's and Anu's shoulders, forming a circle around Jack.

I looked up at Shu and asked, "How did you do that?"

Shu backed away from me, removing his hand from my shoulder. His skin was slick with sweat, and his face looked strained.

"It is of no concern," he shrugged indifferently. He moved to stand beside Menhit, whose features showed the same tension. "We do what we must to help our friends. And to survive."

Menhit's hand dropped to her side. She nodded and bowed her head to Jack, who still kept his eyes closed. I noticed that his complexion was gradually returning to normal. The skin around his cut was blistered and puckered, but the wound was closed.

"Young Jack will need rest," she turned toward the horizon. "We must find shelter before the storm is upon us."

Elric stood up, shielding his eyes from the sun. "What storm? All I see is clear, blue sky."

"Do you know where we are, Shu?" I asked.

He nodded curtly. A small crease appeared along his brow. "We are in our homeland, Sorayn."

Shu started to turn away from our group, but I stepped forward and grabbed his arm.

"Why are you so worried if this is your homeland? I can

sense your anxiety rising. What is wrong? What are you not telling us?"

He didn't speak at first and glanced at Menhit, whose face mirrored his own expression. She appeared terrified.

"Shu speaks the truth. We are in Sorayn, but it is an area where we are not allowed to travel." Menhit glanced around nervously, watching the sky and horizon in fear. "We need to find shelter before night falls."

Anu snorted in annoyance and placed both her hands on her hips in anger. "So, why would that irritating and insolent monster drop us here? I thought he was saving us, not dropping us in a dangerous and forbidden place!"

I couldn't help but agree with her. "Anu is right. Why would Kal leave us here?"

"Kal?" Shu turned to me. "You know him? The fire demon?"

I shrugged calmly, now somewhat annoyed by everyone's accusatory stares.

"Yes, his name is Kal, and he is not a demon, but rather a fire fairy," I threw back.

"How do you know him, Anwen?" Shu stepped closer. The heat of his gray eyes burned into me.

I looked down at my feet uncomfortably, shifting them back and forth. What should I tell them? That Freyja was the one who told Kal to drop us here? For some unknown reason that she didn't tell me about? Again? Her failure to share any information to help defeat Loki and Kenrick was tiresome and annoying. How can I be this great Healer and the key to saving everyone when the goddess herself cannot be straightforward with me?

Elric moved closer. "Anwen, you need to tell us everything you know. Including anything you know about this Kal!"

I moved away from the group, especially Elric. His proximity and intense emotions were just too overwhelming at the moment.

"Fine!" I shouted. "Fine! Freyja came to me again and told me that Loki was destroying other realms and the gods were fighting! She told me that Odin's son was the latest victim in Loki's plans, and that, of course, it wasn't my fault, but then she said to leave with Anu and Jack as we planned. All hell broke loose, and Freyja told Kal what he must do, and that is when he grabbed me and threw me in the fire!"

I tried to hold back the angry tears, but they still fell. I took a deep breath and kept going. "Don't look at me like that!"

I first pointed at Elric, then jerkily moved around the circle, pointing my finger at each person.

"Don't look at me like I am some wounded animal! Freyja has a tendency to appear in the strangest of places when I need guidance, but did you know that she tells me nothing that helps me? I am alone most of the time, hoping to find some way to defeat Loki and Kenrick," I took a quick breath and wiped my tears with the back of my hand. "Anu is supposed to have some ancient knowledge to help me, but all that has been revealed so far is a nameless weapon that, of course, still offers no helpful information. Elric left me struggling with new powers and no guidance. I couldn't even convince the council to help! No matter what Freyja said, it's my fault that another god died at

Loki's hands. And now look at me. Look at us! I can't even use my powers to save our group from giant worms, let alone save the whole world!"

A hand gently touched my arm. I turned around to see Thyra. Her worried eyes made me pause. A sad smile gradually appeared.

I had forgotten that she was part of the group thrown through the portal. Her hand squeezed my arm. She pulled me into her embrace.

"Anwen, we are not judging you—never about the past or the present. What you have gone through, and are going through, we could never understand. I look at you and see a brave Healer, fighting against the odds, feeling overwhelmed by the pressure placed on her shoulders." She pulled back and placed her hand on my cheek. "We must never question the deeds of the gods, for they know what they do. Our goddess Freyja is guiding you on the right path, even if you might not realize it. Trust in her, trust in your powers. All the pieces will fall into place when the time is right. Have faith, little one, because we believe in you."

She looked at me a little longer. Her hand stayed on my cheek before moving down my neck. I felt the warmth of Laga's words through Thyra's gentle touch. She lowered her hand to rest on my arm, sending the same tingling sensation on Hermod's spell.

Thyra lowered her hand, and the glowing faded.

"See, Anwen? You are never alone," she whispered. "The gods are always with you."

I nodded, sniffling the tears away. A long, slow exhale escaped, providing me with much-needed comfort from her words.

"I am so sorry. I am not sure what's wrong with me," I muttered. My eyes swept over everyone in the group. "Please forgive my outburst. It will not happen again, nor will I fail you."

I bowed my head in shame. The entire incident weighed heavily on me—selfish behavior would never be acceptable again. The silence felt unbearable. I refused to face the group—afraid to confront the shame in their eyes.

The embarrassment continued as my empty stomach rumbled loudly enough for everyone to hear; the sounds were so loud that flesh-eating worms would surely think a dinner bell was calling them back to us.

Menhit chuckled.

"Well, I don't know about you, but I totally agree with Anwen's call to find something to eat! I am starving."

Her broad smile aimed to give me a much-needed break from my self-critical thoughts.

She signaled toward the narrow rope bridge crossing the rock formations.

"It seems the gods entrusted us with helping the Healer in her quest, so let's find shelter for the night and then go hunting for our dinner."

I nodded gratefully and smiled, silently thanking her for the distraction from my poor performance and the awkward timing of my embarrassing hunger growls.

Jack looked up at me, now back in his human form again.

"Good, I'm starving. I could eat a horse."

Elric bent down and picked him up in his arms. He glanced at me and winked.

"Well, that is a good sign that he is back to his old self," he laughed, but nodded his head toward Ciar, who was the first to cross the rickety bridge. "But let's not say that too loudly for the centaur to hear, yes?"

Thyra rolled her eyes at Elric's joke and smiled back at me, hoping to see the same reaction.

"What is it you say . . . always a comedian?" She grabbed my arm and tucked it into the crook of her elbow. "Come on, Menhit is right, we need to find shelter and food, and then we will come up with a plan, all right?"

I gave her a quick nod and smiled, then followed Elric and Jack across the bridge. I looked up and saw dark, threatening clouds moving our way. A storm was definitely forming.

NINE

Alarming shrieks and menacing howls pierced the cave. We huddled closer to the fire, hoping the warmth and light would help fend off the ominous sounds of the encroaching darkness. Lightning briefly flashed, casting eerie shadow figures along the wall—dancing wildly on the stone surface. Smoke from the fire drifted through the small cavern, intensifying the spooky atmosphere. When we first entered the cave, bones crunched under our feet, making us hesitant to stay, but as the sun quickly disappeared, so did our options.

My eyes constantly trailed to the jagged mouth of the cave, silently debating whether the small opening provided us shelter from the fierce storm or turned into a tomb for whatever was making those terrifying noises.

A slight movement at the entrance took my breath away, but I quickly realized that Ciar was standing guard. His black body was perfectly concealed within the shadows.

I refocused my attention back to Shu and Menhit.

"Why is this area forbidden?" I whispered. The cavern had strange acoustics that made a mild-toned conversation seem like you were yelling across the valley. "Who built the bridges across the mounds if no one is allowed here?"

A high-pitched yelp rang out in the night, causing everyone to jump. The cry was closer than it had been a minute ago. Jack sidled up to Thyra, grabbing her arm and hugging it against him. I noticed Elric moving his bow onto his lap. He calmly pulled his quiver closer to his leg for easier access to the arrows.

But Menhit and Shu appeared completely calm, paying no attention to the creatures making the unnatural noises outside.

"Ah, yes, the bridges are not a recent construction, Healer, for they are as old as the creatures that inhabit this land," Menhit said in a soft voice. Her tone was so low that everyone automatically leaned forward, eager not to miss any detail.

"The mounds that surround us were created by the greatest of the gods, who brought forth his scarab servants to illuminate our world. But, as always, light must face an enemy, so darkness, the Underworld, followed. And, as long ago, battles within this wicked darkness continue to thwart the goodness of light."

I gasped. "Are you talking about Ra?"

Menhit raised a surprised brow. "Yes, but how do you know about Ra, the Almighty?"

Everyone looked at me with the same shocked expression, except Jack, who started to laugh.

"Anwen is a nerd," he smiled. "In our old world, she always had a book in her hand about some ancient culture."

Shu shook his head in disbelief. "Your old world wrote about our ancient people?"

This time around, Elric couldn't help but laugh.

"Anwen is full of surprises, my friend. It seems that she possesses knowledge about us that we might not realize about ourselves."

I shook my head in denial, and with a bit of embarrassment.

"No, really, they exaggerate—I don't know much about your world at all. Or at least the truth of your culture. I mean—everything I read back in my old world doesn't come close to the truth of everything I have encountered."

"She is just being modest," Elric added. "Do you not remember our conversation about centaurs and giants? Or even elves? How writers in your old world recorded information about the many people and creatures from our world?"

He turned to Menhit and Shu with a wide, proud smile. "Once Anwen mastered our language, she devoured everything in Healer Hrafn's library, and when she was finished with those books, Vardians would offer their own personal books for her to read. The subject was of no concern to her—any knowledge acquired made her a better Healer for our people."

Elric turned to me with a loving expression; his gentle words felt by all. "Her keen determination to understand her new home has endeared her to all of Vardia, especially me."

My eyes dropped to my lap, feeling the blush rise up my neck and spread across my cheeks. I was once again left speechless—and confused by his loving words. He was engaged to Sigrún. His words should have fallen on deaf ears, but unfortunately, they found a place in my heart.

Silence followed until Thyra gracefully coughed.

"Well, Shu—Menhit, are you telling us there's a battle going on outside right now?"

Shu paused before responding. His eyes moved from Elric to me, trying to understand our strange interaction. Menhit, however, appeared to have it figured out and smiled knowingly.

Really, was it that obvious? Nothing was said that would reveal our past relationship.

"Ah, my dear Thyra, battles have long passed, but the creatures still roam the land, and that is why shelter and a bright, warm fire shall always keep them away," Shu chuckled. "And as for the bridges, ancient men thought traveling over the mounds would keep the creatures from attacking them. But no one considered the sky to be just as dangerous. Day or night, no one is safe in this land."

"Again, the question has to be asked—why did Anwen's demon friend drop us in this nightmare?" Anu hissed. Her arms wrapped around herself. Her head shifted toward the cavern entrance. "Our deaths surely would put a damper on our mission to defeat Loki and Kenrick."

Anu turned to me. "Freyja sent the demon so that he could help you? By throwing us into a land that may kill us by sunrise?"

"That is not fair, Anu. I didn't know Kal's plan—and he's not a demon, and certainly not my friend," my voice rose an octave.

Suddenly, the fire's flames grew taller, and the light became brighter. The thin red and orange tongues whipped wildly back and forth until an odd crackling sound came from the heart of the blaze. A small glowing figure pushed its way out of the shaky fire fingers and landed in front of me. Smoke billowed from his body as he brushed the ashes off his skin.

When he finally stopped fidgeting, he looked up and smiled.

"Hallo, Healer," Kal exclaimed, his smile widening from one pointy ear to the other.

He lunged forward with his hand extended. But before I could react, Elric leapt in front of me with his bow raised, and an arrow nocked.

"Not one step closer, demon," he said.

Although Kal halted his advance, his smile remained.

"Come, come, Volun, you should know by now that I'm not the enemy—if I were, you'd be dead by now." Kal waved his hand in the air. "And this shelter wouldn't keep you safe from the beasts outside."

He looked back at me and extended his hand out again.

"I came only to give the Healer this." My gold necklace swung from his fingers. His eyes lowered in guilt. "My dear Freyja was very angry that I did not give it to you when I placed you here. Please accept my apologies."

I pushed past Elric and knelt in front of Kal, looking from him to the necklace. As I reached for it, Elric placed his hand on my shoulder.

"Do not touch his skin, or he may transport you away from us."

I looked up at Elric with surprise. His hand on my shoulder tightened, knowing that wherever Kal would have taken me,

Elric would be hard-pressed to be left behind.

With more courage than I actually felt, I took the necklace from Kal. Instantly, I felt a powerful surge of energy flow through my fingers and down my arm. A strange sensation spread through the rest of my body, causing my hand to glow with amber light.

The force of the energy connected to Elric and sent him to his knees. His hand on my shoulder glowed silvery white.

The group scrambled for their weapons but didn't know what to do with our sudden and strange reaction. Kal's surprised look turned to delight. He jumped up and down, clapping his hands.

"Oh, how exciting to see such a marvelous sight—no wonder dear Freyja was fraught over the necklace not being in your possession."

Thyra lowered her weapon, signaling for the others to do the same.

"Anwen? Elric?" She leaned forward cautiously. "Are you alright?"

The power surge faded. Elric lifted his hand from my shoulder, but with great difficulty. His eyes widened in shock.

"Anwen?" He whispered. "What just happened?"

"I—I don't know." I turned to Kal. "What did you do to us?"

Anu stepped forward, her expression a mix of boredom and curiosity. "Yeah, why did they get all glowy together?"

Jack pointed to my neck and then swept his hand to include all of my body. "And her words lit up. We haven't seen that in a while."

Kal acted as if he was insulted.

"Truly? You must be joking?" Kal said, shaking his head in disbelief before bursting into hysterical laughter. "You don't know the power of the necklace? Especially when the magic bonds with her friend?"

Kal doubled over, thrashing onto the floor, slapping his hands, and stomping his feet. "And Freyja trusted you to keep our world safe?"

His silly antics upset the group.

Shu stepped forward and raised his sword slightly higher. "Now hold on, fiery one. We may not know what your goddess has planned for us, but we answered her request with honor and solemnity. You do not have the right to criticize us for not knowing everything we need to succeed in this quest, especially when you were obviously scolded for not returning an essential item to the Healer. And apparently, an item that helps the Volun as well."

Both Anu and Jack began to shift between Lirrean and human while Thyra and Ciar closed in around Kal. Although their defense against Kal's callous words was appreciated, I knew the situation could escalate into something we would all regret. We needed more information from Kal at this point, and harming him or even scaring him off would do us no good.

Heeding Elric's earlier warning about not touching Kal, I carefully moved in front of him, blocking the group.

"Look, both Elric and I are fine . . . just a little stunned, like all of you, but that doesn't mean we should hurt Kal, especially when we need him to give us more information about our mission." I faced Kall. "You need to tell us everything you know. Do you hear me? I don't care if Freyja or anyone else told you differently, but in order for us to move forward, you have to be honest."

All eyes were on Kal. He tilted his head thoughtfully. Seconds stretched into minutes until he finally nodded in agreement.

"Alright, love, but I would take that necklace of yours and put it on right now." He stepped back from me nervously and darted to the far side of the cavern.

My brow furrowed at his odd behavior, but I heeded his request.

"There—now can we discuss why we are here?"

The words were barely out of my mouth when a deep snarl echoed through the cavern.

Kal moved further back and cowered behind a pile of rocks.

"Of course, Healer, but let us talk after the attack. If we survive, of course."

The sound of Ciar's sword as he pulled it from its sheath echoed in the cave.

We turned just in time to see a pair of red eyes peering into the cave. A large, fearsome creature struggled to get through the opening, squeezing and stretching its powerful body within the confined space. When it finally broke free, more followed until five giant creatures stood before us, eyeing us like we were their next meal.

TEN

The snarling creatures blocked the cave entrance—each awkwardly standing on its hind legs. Long pink tongues wickedly licked their vicious-looking teeth. These mysterious monsters resembled hyenas—only five times larger. Sharp teeth bared to tear into us—teeth the size of my hand.

Elric moved forward, bow raised and ready to fire his arrow. Without looking away from the creatures, he spoke softly to Shu. "What are these beings?"

"Ancient creatures that live double lives—roaming the land as our brothers during the day and then hunting as beasts at night," Shu said. "*Kaftar.*"

"Are you saying these creatures are human?" I murmured.

"Yes, but do not hesitate to load these monsters with your arrows."

With Shu's last statement, one of the beasts snarled, as if it understood Shu's words.

"Kal—get us out of here," Anu rasped under her breath, moving closer to the fire. "Now."

One of the smaller creatures moved to our side, sneaking quietly. Its eyes focused on Jack.

Thyra noticed and shifted him behind her, then pointed her sword at the beast.

The creature stopped its progression for a brief second, but then continued slowly. Its body touched the ground, ready to pounce.

I raised my hand unexpectedly, releasing a burst of energy that hit the wall in front of the beast. Rock shards flew at the creature's face, halting its movement. It snarled furiously and was just as stunned by the sight of my magic.

Menhit moved closer to Thyra and Jack, her back tense and stiff. "The young one is their target—children are their first choice."

From the corner of my eye, I saw Kal inch toward the fire. Elric also caught his movement.

"Kal, can you transport us out of here?"

Kal shook his head, stopping his movement when one of the creatures noticed him for the first time. The larger of the beasts lowered its head and bared its teeth.

Kal dropped his head into his hands and started to cry.

"I cannot—" he stammered into his hands. "I cannot transport a group, only one at a time."

"Take Jack, Kal, please, take him away from here," I whispered from the side of my mouth, afraid that the beasts could understand us now.

Elric moved toward me. “No, take Anwen first. She needs to be kept safe.”

“No,” I said to him, now angry. “I can take care of myself. I will not leave everyone to be slaughtered.”

The doubt in Elric’s eyes only strengthened my resolve. Yes, my magic was unreliable at first, but that was before Kal brought me the necklace. Any doubts that my magic wasn’t working faded as the tiny amber stones began to glow. Whatever the reason for my new connection to the necklace, it only gave me more confidence and strength.

I turned back to the pack, locking my eyes on the biggest of the beasts—the leader.

“Besides, I am aching for a fight, to hone my skills. Let us begin, you mongrels. Attack us and face your death.”

I heard Elric grumble with annoyance. Good. Maybe now he could see my fighting skills—abilities I had to learn on my own because of his absence and indifference.

“Come on, you filthy beasts,” I yelled confidently. “Come after me, you cowards.”

The largest of the beasts crouched and lunged at me, deadly claws on its huge paws ready to strike.

From the moment it pounced, my body responded instinctively. I didn’t wait long. Whispers grew louder. I felt the Shadow’s power merge with my other abilities. A faint reverberation hummed through my body, and when I raised my hands to block the beast’s deadly claw strike, a slash appeared across its chest.

Thrown by the force of the Shadow, the yelping beast

crashed to the floor. But it instantly got back to its feet and shook its head, not believing I was the one who struck the first blow. It turned its long snout toward me and smiled—at least that's what I thought it did.

Its long, pink tongue flicked over its teeth, smiling even broader. Its mouth stretched back, making its face appear more intimidating.

"What power for such a small girl," the beast muttered awkwardly. "I shall relish the thought of possessing that power as I tear into your flesh."

Changing tactics, it remained cautious, but the smile never faded from its face. Its confidence shone through as we moved around each other. Its movements were slow and relaxed, while mine felt restless.

From the corner of my eye, I saw another beast circling Elric, whose bow now hung behind him—one hand held a dagger while the other was splayed in front of him. The beast's movements mimicked the larger one, possibly sensing the same power surging through Elric.

The others were herded into one of the corners of the cave. One beast swayed back and forth in front of Thyra, Anu, and Ciar as Jack crouched behind them. Another beast prepared to pounce toward Shu and Menhit. Kal was curled up in a ball, eyes wide with fear.

"I don't have all day, beast, so let us begin again, shall we?"

Elric gasped at my reckless taunt, but that was all it took for the beast to attack.

Teeth bared, it shook its head and flung saliva. A terrifying growl erupted. The beast threw its body at me, hitting my side with its head and flipping me into the air.

I landed on my feet just in time because the beast shifted to my other side, grabbing the sleeve of my tunic and shaking me violently. The force repeatedly slammed my body against the wall. Its teeth now found flesh, biting into my right forearm.

The pain was unbearable. I struggled to pry its jaws off my arm. The soft whispers had turned into shouting, urging me to surrender control and let my powers take over. But I strongly resisted their pleas. I didn't want to feel that way again. Not like when the Lokrum attacked the Vardian camp. That loss of control scared me more than these beasts.

I raised my left hand and grabbed the beast's forehead. A surge of energy burst from my hand, flinging the beast away from me, allowing me to scramble back and get into position for another attack.

Blood dripped down my arm and pooled at my feet, but I couldn't focus on the pain. Not now, not while the others fought to the death.

Elric jabbed his dagger into his foe, and when the beast backed away, Elric struck again. The dagger punctured the beast's neck, while Elric's other hand released his energy into its chest, sending it flying across the cave. Elric ran forward, jumped on the beast, and stabbed it again, killing it instantly.

The death of their comrade sent the others into a frenzy. My beast let out a loud howl. It slashed its mighty paw at me, crushing me beneath it and knocking the breath out of my body. I sensed Elric's presence beside me. I tried to keep the snapping jaws away from my face. Elric's dagger struck the beast's side, but the creature kept fighting.

The voices of the Shadow grew louder. They tried to persuade me to let them take control. I didn't want to, but the sounds and screams coming from my friends made me realize I might not have a choice. They needed me to kill, but the thought of losing control again terrified me.

The beast sensed the fear growing inside me and pressed harder against my body. I could hardly breathe. The pressure became too unbearable to tolerate.

Elric pressed his hands against the side of the beast, releasing his energy, but the beast remained steady. A wheezy grunt slowly escaped its mouth as it struggled against the energy. I could feel the beast's need to tear me in half.

It lowered its face so our eyes were level. A flash of triumph gleamed as it brought its teeth close to my neck. Its foul breath brushed against my face, and hot drool slid down my cheek.

"You should have released your true self, young one," it growled into my ear. "Now, I will indulge in the taste of your flesh."

But before that could happen, the beast leaped off me as if I were made of fire. It gasped and cowered away. Its companions did the same.

The sudden and unexpected movement took Elric by surprise. We scrambled to our feet, waiting for the next round of assault.

But nothing happened.

The creatures gathered around their leader, wondering why

the attack ended.

It threw its head back and barked a few times into the air. The others looked startled at what their leader said. All turned to me, studying me. Suddenly, they all sat down, threw their heads into the air, and began to howl.

The noise was so loud that we fell to our knees, pressing our hands to our ears to block out the echoing pain inside the cavern. My thoughts shifted to the possibility of another strategic attack—one that could disable us with their deafening cries.

I struggled to my feet and leaned against the wall. The deafening howls, the voices, and the frantic Okri were all too overwhelming. I clutched my head in pain.

"STOP," I screamed, doubling over.

Surprisingly, the howling stopped.

I fell to the ground, praying to stay conscious. The pain eased, but my body started to shake uncontrollably. The room spun. My vision blurred.

Elric immediately moved to my side, took my head, and held it gently against his chest.

"It's okay, calm yourself," he whispered into my hair. His lips brushed my temple as his energy merged into my body. The familiar yet intense sensation crashed like a wave, leaving me breathless. I inhaled quickly but exhaled slowly, savoring his closeness.

My eyes opened to his piercing blue stare. He stroked his finger down my cheek. "Calm yourself, my love—all is peaceful now."

Gently pushing away from Elric's embrace, I sat up and looked around the cavern. But the creatures had vanished. Instead, four humans stood there with their arms outstretched toward us.

"The prophecy is finally upon us," the beast-human said. "The curse has come to an end."

ELEVEN

The sudden appearance of our attackers in human form stunned us. They stood tall and proud—and completely naked. Their dark brown skin displayed jagged white scars. Muscles rippled over their taut bodies. Long brown hair flowed down their backs. Except for one—a young girl with hair as black as coal stood right behind the leader.

Elric grabbed his bow from the ground and nocked an arrow. Ciar and Thyra, looking a little worse for wear, raised their weapons higher, uncertain of what was happening.

"What do you want from us?" Elric asked.

The beast leader stepped forward with his hands raised in the air.

"We craved the taste of your flesh, but now that the sign is revealed, you must come with us to our village. The sun is rising, so it will be safe."

"I don't think so—you just tried to kill us, and now you

want us to follow you into a whole village of your kind?" Anu crossed her arms in defiance. "You must be mad."

The beast leader lowered his arms and started to laugh. The deep, rumbling sound rumbled throughout the cavern.

"Silly girl, the powers within this cavern could easily stop us, but we are only following our nature—my people are starving, and your meat would have been relished by all." The leader now smirked as if someone had just told an inside joke. His smile reminded me of a cat just before it devoured the bird.

"Why should we go with you?" I asked. "It could be a trick to lure us out into the open with more of your kind ready to attack us again."

The young girl moved forward with confidence. Her slender figure radiated authority as she passed by the beast leader.

"My father does not *trick*. When sanctuary is offered, it comes with a pure and honest heart—you should know this because Odin has sent you to us."

I stepped back in surprise when Odin's name was mentioned. The beast leader furrowed his brow.

"Do you not know?"

I shook my head. "I—I am not sure what you mean?"

Elric moved closer to me, as if that was even possible. He was nearly on top of me. He raised his bow even higher. "What do you know of our mission?"

Shu stepped to the front of our group. He had already sheathed his sword.

"Your offer of sanctuary is accepted, night-stalker, but you must understand our hesitation with this sudden concession—

what can you offer us in exchange for your loyalty?"

The beast leader grimaced as his daughter let out a brief yelp of anger.

"How dare you question my father's loyalty, desert rat," the young girl rasped.

The beast leader raised his hand to prevent her from speaking further. He smiled.

"You know us very well, elf, and for that, you shall have what you are asking."

And on cue, the girl moved toward Shu, hesitantly extended her left arm, then with her right hand, dragged a long nail across her skin. Blood as black as her hair trickled down her arm.

Menhit pulled out a small glass vial and held it under the girl's arm until it was half full of blood. With blood still dripping from her arm, the girl sliced a small piece of her hair and held it out to Menhit, who took it and placed it in the vial. The girl then pulled out one of her canines and, instead of offering the tooth to Menhit, put it into the vial, closed her eyes, and muttered softly.

Both Menhit and Shu bowed, crossed their arms over their chests, and muttered the same phrase. Menhit placed the vial into her pocket and turned to our group.

I was at a loss for words, unsure of what was happening, but the satisfied expressions on the beast leader's face and both Menhit and Shu's were enough to show that some form of magic had bound their declarations.

"It is safe for us to follow the Kaftar to their village because they are now bound to their promise of protection," Menhit said.

"I do not trust these dogs." Ciar stomped his front legs and raised his sword higher. "Why should we trust anything that they say?"

Thyra nodded in agreement, raising her sword higher and pointing it toward the leader.

"Anwen, how can we follow these treacherous beasts into their own village—especially with Jack? Just having a child close to them will drive them into madness for want of his flesh."

Shu was about to speak, but I knew what was at stake. "Because they used a binding spell, is that correct, Menhit?"

She nodded and placed her hand over the vial in her pocket. "Yes, and if any of their people should renege on that promise, the children in their village will perish—and that includes the leader's own daughter."

I looked at each person in my group, hoping they would all agree with what we were about to do. My gaze lingered on Jack, knowing that he would be walking into a village full of these beast—creatures that relished the flesh of children more than anything else.

I felt Elric's hand on my arm, and my eyes met his. He leaned into me and whispered. "With my life, I will keep Jack safe—and I promise, with all my heart, I give my life to keep you safe, Anwen."

Magic surrounded each word as his vow of protection flowed through my veins. Warmth emanated from his hand onto my arm, causing tremors inside. The gods' spells flickered on my body, only for a few seconds, but long enough for only Elric and me to see the glow. Our eyes briefly met, mine filled with confusion and his with conviction.

I placed my hand over his and automatically said whatever came to mind. "As I with you."

The phrase came easily from me. I understood what his words of sacrifice signified, but confusion still lingered.

I turned to the beast leader. For the first time since being thrown into Sorayn, I genuinely felt confident—this place was the way to Saerún. And these people were part of our quest.

"All right, but first, what should we call you?"

Bowing his head slightly, he said, "Amastan—Leader of the Katak Band."

"Well then, Amastan, we will follow you to your village, but in return, I want you to tell me everything you know about Odin and this prophecy."

***

I stifled a yawn as we walked along the bridge stretched across the rock mounds. Even though we tried to grab a few hours of sleep in the early morning light, having Amastan and his warriors outside the cave watching over us proved to be too threatening. Sleep would just have to wait.

Amastan and his daughter, Zira, led our group while the other two men, Aksil and Merin, brought up the rear. They took turns carrying their fallen comrade across their shoulders.

Everyone followed Amastan except Kal, who decided he was better off serving them if he dove back into the fire.

My eyes tracked Elric's back as he followed Zira. His bow hung over his shoulders, showing he trusted our new companions, but his stiff posture and cautious glances at Amastan suggested otherwise. We all knew we might be walking into a trap, but what other choice did we have? The mention of Odin, especially the prophecy, stunned us, but it also piqued our interest. Elric once mentioned a prophecy related to what was happening to me. His father, a Volun-turned-Mage-turned enemy, had spoken of a prophecy long ago. So, he thought Herja might know something about it. However, she couldn't recall anything particularly relevant to Loki's plans, especially what he intended for me and the unknown prophecy.

And Amastan. Can we truly trust them with what they tell us? That they will not harm us? Or even harm Jack?

I felt a small hand press against my arm.

Jack smiled.

"You don't have to worry about me." He wiggled his hand into mine and looked out over the desert. "I may not have all of my powers under control, and I still have a lot to learn from Anu, but for some reason, this seems right. Does that make sense?"

He tilted his head in thought. "I feel like these people have an answer for us—something that we need." Jack shrugged. "I don't know, maybe it's some weird Lirrean intuition, but I feel their sincerity, but also—"

He paused.

"What, Jack?" I asked.

His brow furrowed. "I feel—I don't know, like they are afraid of something."

"Like what? What do you think they're afraid of?"

Jack shrugged.

"What do you feel?"

He looked up at me again and frowned more deeply. "You—I feel like they are afraid of you, like they know something inside you is different. No, not afraid . . . intrigued, excited about something they feel coming from inside of you."

Suddenly, Elric hesitated in his steps, and I ran into his back. He turned and caught my arm before I could stumble over the bridge.

"Sorry," I mumbled.

Elric held onto my arm, studying me a bit longer than he probably needed to. He seemed like he wanted to say something, but mumbled incoherently and kept walking.

Before I could comment on his strange behavior, Zira stopped next to her father and pointed to a tall rock formation in the distance.

"That is our home. We will arrive in an hour."

My heart jumped into my throat, and I now had serious doubts about walking into this village full of hungry creatures. Jack squeezed my hand again and smiled at me, trying to ease my worries. Where was the confidence that once came so easily to me in the cavern?

"I can't believe we are doing this," Anu mumbled. "I don't know about you, but I prefer to keep my flesh on my bones."

Zira turned and threw Anu a deadly look that ended with a low, throaty growl, but Amastan laughed.

"Be assured, changeling, that you shall leave my village with your flesh intact," he sniffed in her direction. "Even without the promise, your flesh would not have been our first choice."

Amastan's soldiers snickered. Anu huffed.

"Well, I am sure my flesh would be pretty tasty, thank you very much."

I began to laugh at how absurd her words were when a piercing howl interrupted us.

Jack grabbed my arm, stopping me. Everyone stopped and raised their weapons.

"I told you—this is a trap." Ciar spun around and brandished his sword at Aksil and Merin.

Amastan raised his arm, trying to calm Ciar's fears. "Calm down—the Watchers are always around our village. They're just announcing their leader's return."

Jack relaxed but continued holding my hand until we almost reached the village. The round mounds ended, so we climbed down to the ground. As soon as we started toward the strange-looking cliffs, a low growl sounded from my right. I quickly raised my hands. Thyra came to my left side and stepped in front of Jack. She, along with the others, formed a circle around him and faced the direction of the ominous sound.

Rock formations gradually grew taller on both sides as we followed Amastan and Zira. Merin and Aksil now walked alongside us. Narrow crevices sliced into the rocks. We kept moving toward the tall cliffs.

Tall, dark clouds slowly churned in the sky and blocked the sun, making it look like nighttime. I moved my head forward to get a better look into one of the crevices when a shadow with silver eyes blinked.

I stepped back, trying not to scream. Elric looked from me

to the crevice and raised his bow. Amastan saw his sudden move and stopped.

"You have to believe me, Volun. We mean you no harm. They are my Watchers—they don't turn into humans during the day. They're protectors of the village and will only attack if I tell them to—or if you attack us."

Hesitating, Elric and the others lowered their weapons. Menhit broke free from our circle and gestured toward the cliffs.

"Please, King Amastan, you won't need to offer reassurances again. Please forgive my friends, for they are not from our land—they do not understand what you have given me—what your daughter has sacrificed." Menhit placed her hand over the vial in her pocket.

Amastan nodded and led us deeper into the valley. Zira glared at Menhit for a quick moment, then realized I was watching her. She turned toward me.

"And you, are you afraid? Do you believe that you will be killed once we are in our village? Do you not trust us as well?"

I shook my head. "No, Zira. I believe in the power of magic, and even though I am not familiar with the binding spell in Menhit's pocket, I do not think you will break that promise. I feel that honor and trust are important to your people, as they are also important to mine. But to answer your first question—yes, I am afraid because saying otherwise would not be truthful. I have never met anyone like you before, but we are on an important mission, and the need to put that fear aside and trust those who can help us is vital to our journey."

My answer seemed to satisfy Zira and her companions, so

we began the last half-hour trek to their home. The rocky cliffs now became large fortifications. Amastan led our group into a semicircular formation that left only one way out. People poured out of small openings within the rocks. Amastan stopped and turned to us. His arms gestured to the taller cliffs in front of us.

Perfect holes, large enough to fit an adult, lined the side of the cliff. Chiseled steps descended from each opening to the ground. Several people peeked out of the holes and hurriedly descended. The scene reminded me of a busy beehive as we quickly made our way to the center of the village.

We stopped at the base of the cliff. It didn't take long for the crowd to gather around us. A long canopy of bright canvas shaded the front of a large cavern—apparently the entrance to Amastan's home.

Excited and hungry expressions stared at us. The Kaftar expected their king to open the buffet of food in front of them. Anxiety and fear coursed through my body. The Okri noticed. Their whispers caused discomfort, and then the Shadow joined them. My energy itched for release.

I clenched my hands, silently telling my internal companions to relax.

Elric noticed my discomfort and understood what was happening. He gently covered my hand with his, letting a cooling stream of his energy flow into me. I briefly closed my eyes and savored his familiar touch.

When the crowd started to cheer wildly, Amastan raised his hands to quiet them. Instantly, his gesture calmed the group.

"My people, although our mission last night was to bring

these travelers back to our village to prepare for a grand feast, it has been discovered that they have another purpose."

Amastan stood by his daughter and placed his hand on her shoulder. "A *maraq* was performed." Angry protests erupted during his speech.

"Please, calm yourselves—my daughter had to sacrifice herself for a greater cause." Amastan's piercing gaze swept over his people's faces. He pointed to me and continued, "Odin has sent us the elf-girl—she is here to set us free. She is here to break the curse."

TWELVE

"*Cursed?*"

I spun back around to face the king and the rest of his council. Their happy and satisfied expressions were completely opposite of ours. We were all surprised and somewhat skeptical of this new revelation—this totally unexpected and new aspect of our mission to save the world.

"And how, may I ask, can *I* be the answer to this ancient curse of the Kaftar?"

I noticed both Menhit and Shu shuffling their feet nervously.

"Did you know about this?" I asked them.

Shu gave me his most dashing smile and shrugged as if it wasn't a big deal that they might have known an important piece of information that could affect us all—especially me. He threw his hand up in the air, spinning it around.

"It is part of our legend, but we did not know it would be

important for this journey. Does it really matter, Anwen? Now we know that the Kaftar play an important role—that they hold one of the pieces of our puzzle in defeating Loki and Kenrick." He paused. "We should focus on that knowledge and move forward."

Everyone nodded in agreement, but I couldn't let it go. Anger boiled up inside me.

"Forget about the fact that you lied to me? To all of us? Don't give me that crap about knowing about a legend but not the connection. You're smart, both of you, and the fact that you held this back doesn't give me confidence that you are telling us the whole truth now. *Is* there more you're not telling us?"

Shu and Menhit exchanged glances, and that was enough for me.

"Tell us everything. Now," I murmured with quiet insistence. "We go no further if you don't."

Elric agreed. "I am with Anwen. If you do not tell us everything, we will leave you behind and go alone."

Menhit shook her head and frowned. "Please, we did not mean to deceive you, Anwen. Queen Gamila ordered us not to reveal anything during the council meeting. Shu was right when he said that we did not know how you fit into our kingdom's legends that have been passed down from generation to generation. It is a part of who we are as a people—what is part of a child's tale and part of our reality is not easily distinguished. The mark of Odin that you bear means something different to us than what it means to your people."

"I don't understand." I reached up and gently traced my

finger along the three triangles on the side of my face. "What does my mark have to do with breaking a curse for the Kaftar?"

Amastan raised his hand and signaled for us to sit around the central fire. Large, colorful cushions covered the floor. As we all took our seats, Amastan started his story.

"It is said that a peculiar group of dwarves from the dark mountains of Myrk in the Outerlands approached our sun god, the Almighty Ra. The small beings asked Ra for help in their quest. They carried a simple wooden box with them, waving it in front of Ra as if the box were made of pure gold. At first, our god was indifferent to these strange newcomers to his land, but when they opened the box to reveal its hidden contents, he became more than intrigued. Inside was a magnificently forged spearhead—long and triangular-shaped, with strange symbols engraved along the sides." Amastan paused briefly before continuing. "The metal was golden, iridescent, and beautifully crafted, but you could tell something was different about it—something very special. It pulsed with its own power. They explained to our Almighty Ra that it was a gift for their All-Father, the great warrior Odin, from one of his siblings, and they wished for the power of the sun to enhance the magic within the weapon."

Amastan looked at his daughter with a sad smile. "Ra was skeptical, but with further coaxing, he granted their wish. The weapon became so powerful that it never missed its target when wielded by its owner—so devastating that it could kill an entire army with one throw."

"*Gungnir*," Thyra whispered in awe.

"What?" I asked.

Without acknowledging my question, her eyes remained fixed on Amastan. "*Gungnir*—a spear wielded in many battles. Our All-Father's weapon."

"But how does this involve you?" I shook my head, not understanding the significance of the story.

"The spear holds the power of binding—one utterance could force someone to its will forever. Never to be broken," Zira added.

"That is how the Kaftar came into being—the spear was used to curse our way of life."

Anger radiated from Amastan. "My forefathers were used as pack carriers, hauling supplies across the land, but a few were fierce companions to their brave warrior masters, fighting alongside them—protecting and killing the enemy. A great battle was lost, and all the warriors were killed. But the punishment did not end there. My ancestors who survived were cursed with this spear—tormented to live double lives. Human during the day, animal by night."

"So, this great battle was with Odin?" I asked.

Zira shook her head. "No, it was not your Odin—the spear was commanded by someone else. Not a god. Stories passed down to us say that he was bragging about being given the power to wield the spear from the great All-Father. The devastating battle on our land and against our people was just a mere afterthought for a warrior with a superiority complex. We were objects to him, needing to be swept away with his hand."

I asked Elric. "Do you know of this battle? Of this story in

Vardia?"

Elric shifted his eyes from mine. He shook his head but didn't say anything else.

My eyes narrowed at his obvious lie. During Amastan's story, Elric grew more agitated—distant. His eyes stayed down, avoiding mine.

"Elric? Tell me the truth? Does Loki have this spear? Could this weapon be part of his plan to defeat us?"

Ciar, who remained silent for most of the council, stomped nervously as he eyed Amastan. His tension was palpable.

"No, Loki does not possess Gungnir. The spear can only be held by Odin or those blessed by the All-Father. The Lohrhan legend tells us that the spear was lost in a brief skirmish between Odin and the Lirreans. It disappeared forever. No one has ever seen Odin wield his weapon since then."

I felt like my head was going to explode from all the new information. There has to be significance in what everyone was saying—the lost weapon of the great All-Father. There was a reason why we were here, and a reason why Freyja sent Kal. It had to be the spear—the weapon that Anu's memories revealed. It's easy to assume that's why Kenrick and the Mage want the spear—for the power to control and kill.

"Kenrick and the Mage need this spear," I said. "That is how they want to destroy us."

"But you heard what Ciar said, Odin is the only one who can hold the spear. What good is it to Kenrick? Even the Mage and Loki cannot use it," Anu proclaimed.

"But Anwen can," Elric declared. "She has the mark of

Odin. He gave her the power to handle the spear."

"This must be why we are here—the spear needs to be found and given to Odin," I proclaimed.

Elric frowned. "Kenrick must know this legend, which makes you more vulnerable. He will go to great lengths, now more than ever, to capture you."

"I can protect myself," I scowled.

"I know you can. But I feel the magic inside you changing—evolving. If I can sense its lifeforce in you, surely Loki and Corvus can too. You are powerful, Anwen. You are a strong Healer. They will use that against you, and if you wield the weapon, you may never be the same again."

His voice was soft, almost hesitant, leaving no doubt about the meaning behind his words. Worry hid behind his eyes, which made me pause. Was he frightened of my powers? Did he doubt my loyalty to Vardia and all of Emberval?

"You do not trust me with the weapon," I stated, my voice just as soft as his. "You think I will turn against my family, my friends, because I can't handle the power."

Elric's expression confirmed my fear. His emotions surged so strongly, I had to step back from him. How could he not trust me? How could he think I would hurt my family?

Thyra placed her hand on my arm, startling me.

"We need to protect you from Loki because *he* will try to use you, Anwen. Yes, the spear is mighty and dangerous, but I see what Elric is saying . . . we need to protect you because you are connected to the weapon. Loki plans to use your powers along with the spear's power. To destroy us."

***

Dark orange, pink, and lavender outlined the clouds as the sun moved closer to the horizon. Shadows gradually crept over the rock formations as night began to take over the land. The sounds of restless chatter filled the valley. The Kaftar started their transformation.

Shivers ran down my spine as goosebumps spread along my arms. Turning away from the window, I moved to the far side of the room and stood in front of the fire. Interestingly, the smoke spiraled through a shaft, rising to the top of the cliff, where it dissipated into the sky. Each room had its own hearth. The engineering achievement amazed me. But cliff dwellings were scattered across the southwestern part of my old world. You made your home wherever you were, regardless of what the environment threw at you.

Another string of howls echoed through the valley, but this time, they were further away. The Kaftar hunted at night, and one could only guess what they would bring back for a feast.

Even with the blazing flames, coldness seeped into my bones.

The disturbing revelation of my potential, though not immediate, role in Loki's plans sent chills down my spine.

Could Elric's assumption about wielding the spear, if or when it was found, change me? Would the wisdom of that much power make me hurt those around me? Especially when I am supposed to be their protector?

But why would Odin give me his mark if he didn't trust me to do the right thing? To make the right decisions and help our world? Wouldn't the gods, especially Freyja, warn me about losing control of my powers?

A smirk appeared. Of course, the gods wouldn't warn me. They rarely told me anything helpful, even when their beloved realm was in danger of being taken over or destroyed by their brother.

Screams of pain echoed through the night—sounds of prey suffering in their final moments. The Kaftar were merciless. Another agonized cry sounded, but this time it was silenced instantly as death took the unfortunate creature.

Amastan assured us that we wouldn't be harmed and that his people would honor the pact made with the binding spell. But he also warned us that other creatures in the night might not hesitate to hunt us. Amastan led us into our rooms, instructing us not to leave our sanctuaries until morning light pierced the valley. We were all ready to retire anyway, but his words gave us extra reason to end the evening of revelations.

My room was small with minimal furniture, but cozy. Bright decorations filled the space. Beautifully crafted textiles in rich colors covered every inch of the room. Deep red rugs with unusual geometric shapes scattered across the floor, and large dark blue tapestries hung on the walls. A big orange blanket covered the bed.

Exhausted physically and mentally, I sank into a chair in front of the fireplace. I needed to come up with a new plan to find Odin's weapon. A frustrated sigh escaped me as I thought about locating the ancient spear—a spear that even a god could not find. How in the world am I supposed to track down the weapon that can defeat a god and a madman? And apparently, avoid falling prey to its hidden, yet dangerous, powers?

And who did Odin bless to use his spear, only to lose it? Would he give this blessing to another god, or was the person an ordinary man or woman? What happened to this person? And why did Odin bless them? Did they have a mission like me?

So many questions raced through my head. I was trying not to get angry, but it was challenging. Why was this information kept from me?

I felt so powerless.

An awareness surged within my chest. The whispering of the Shadow echoed throughout my body. Suddenly, the sensation pressed down on me as the whispering grew frantic and painful. The words came rushing in—urgent and excited.

What were they trying to tell me?

I struggled to understand what they were saying, but a knock interrupted my concentration.

I pushed the voices aside.

"Come in."

Elric peeked around the corner with concern, furrowing his brow.

"I sensed a disturbance. Are you feeling well, Anwen?"

He pushed open the door and stepped inside, quietly closing it behind him.

My heart fluttered when I saw him. His black tunic, pants, and boots, along with his slightly ruffled black hair, took my breath away. It was hard to believe how much he had changed since I last saw him, but I was different too. And even though he now belonged to Sigúrn, I couldn't help but feel he still had feelings for me, especially with the way he was looking at me now.

I cleared my throat and smiled. "I am fine. Just tired. I guess the Okri are feeling the stress as well. They are quite agitated tonight."

I moved slowly across the room to where he was standing. I saw a deep cut along his chin. When I reached out and touched the wound, he briefly closed his eyes at my gentle touch and smiled.

"You're hurt," I whispered.

He gently took my hand and brushed it against his lips.

"I am fine, Anwen, but something else is bothering you," he leaned into me. "You are hiding something from me."

He ran his fingers over my knuckles, gently caressing them. My eyes moved down to our intertwined hands. Naturally, he would know I was lying about the Okri. They were always with me, but they weren't the cause of my energy reaction. The Shadow kept murmuring, now annoyed that Elric was questioning them.

But there was also another voice, soft but commanding, filtering through the Shadow. Chills ran down my spine.

Push him away, Anwen.

Suddenly, I pulled my hand away from him and moved back.

"I just—I just thought we could talk," he started to reach for my hand again. "I know a lot has happened—I am concerned about you. You must have questions regarding Wynfalle, about my people's new home . . . about Sigrún. I know it may not be the right time to discuss what has transpired, but I would like us to talk about it."

His smile faltered when I didn't answer immediately.

"I know you were stunned—angry—about the whole situation, the announcement, but . . ."

"I—I am fine, really. You don't have to worry about me," I interrupted, turning away from him.

Space. That's what I needed right now.

I walked to the hearth. The forceful voice echoed again in my head, making me wince from the sharp pain. What was happening to me?

Tell him to leave.

I was confused about what was happening—and a little annoyed. I had to put a stop to it.

Who are you?

Feeling scared of this new presence giving orders, I nervously wrung my hands. What should I do? I didn't want Elric to leave. We needed to talk about the rift between us.

I felt an odd stirring inside me. My feet shuffled forward on their own. A strange throb spread through my stomach—like someone punched me from the inside. It wasn't painful, but it was uncomfortable. Panic began to rise inside me.

I turned around, hoping my voice wouldn't reveal my fear.

"I am fine," I said. Cold confidence surprisingly poured from my words, hiding how I truly felt inside. "You may leave now. Don't you have someone to scykra? Your bride-to-be, maybe? I'm sure she's wondering how her love is doing in this land."

My voice sounded harsh and unfeeling. The words forced out of my lips. Someone else was making me speak.

"I don't want to talk anymore about what happened between us. Please leave."

I cringed at the callousness of my words that fell from my lips, but I kept my composure. I felt like a robot as my hands dropped to my sides, secretly commanded by some unknown force.

Elric stepped back from me as if I had slapped him. His eyes scanned my face with intense pain. My words hit him hard, but I couldn't make myself tell him that it really wasn't me speaking. Wariness drew his shoulder blades together. He bowed his head with remorse.

He quickly turned away from me and opened the door, but stopped short before leaving.

"I thought you deserved an explanation for my actions, but apparently, you don't want to hear it. I apologize for my bluntness. I won't mention our past again."

And then he left, gently closing the door behind him.

My body instantly relaxed as the strange inner force let go of its hold.

My heart ached over what just happened between us. Elric wanted to talk about us, finally explaining why he pulled away from our love. But, this new force inside me stopped him. It stopped me from talking to him. Anger grew inside me.

"Who are you?" I snapped.

I spun around, looking for the culprit; my hands clenched

at my sides.

"How dare you take over my body like that," I said a little louder. "Show yourself."

The tiny hairs on my neck bristled. Shivers ran down my arms. The room suddenly felt electric, as if a lightning bolt had struck the ground.

A faint figure of Odin stood by the fire, arms crossed in front of him and looking very confident.

"You already know me, young one, for I have placed my powers within you."

THIRTEEN

Anger subsided with his sudden appearance. I couldn't believe that the great All-Father was standing in front of me, here among the cliffs of Sorayn. Our last encounter had been in the Wynfalle Mountains, right before Loki and Corvus' attack—when Odin gave me his mark for protection. His very presence commanded respect from everyone.

My admiration quickly faded, though, when I remembered him kicking Elric out of my room.

I unclenched my fists and crossed my arms over my chest. The anger was starting to grow inside me again.

"How dare you!"

Odin raised his right arm to his chest, pretending to be surprised by my outburst. His expression mocked me.

"Why are you unhappy with me, dear one?" Odin's wispy figure took a step forward. I instinctively stepped back from him. His towering form, even as just an apparition, radiated power and confidence. "Oh, is it because I made you turn away your lover, who was about to confess his indiscretions to you?"

My blood began to boil.

Odin straightened to his full height. "We do not have time for this, girl. You need to focus on the task at hand."

I stood my ground. "I *am* focused on the task, whatever that task is! No one will tell me all that I need to know—Freyja, you, and even my friends—the others know more about what I should be doing than I do!"

I walked to the window. "Why does this always seem to end this way? The gods who did this to me refuse to tell me what I need to succeed. It's like you're playing a game with my life—with the lives of everyone I care about. I'm tired of being the last to learn the details about my mission, and even then, I still have no idea how to save the world from Loki."

Defiantly, I crossed my arms again. "And, for your information, Elric is very important to me—I know that is hard for a god to understand."

Odin wandered around the room, looking more interested in the decorations and furniture than he was in our conversation—our one-sided conversation.

"They are really a resourceful lot, are they not?" He asked as he continued toward where I was standing. "The Kaftar were once just beasts, but they have adapted very well to their human existence. They embraced the frivolous materials of the species." Odin picked up a beautifully decorated pillow but then tossed it on the bed. "If the curse is broken, do you not think that the village will be divided? That those who would rather stay human than turn back into a beast will revolt?"

Standing a few feet away from me, his eyes locked onto mine and his words sharpened with anger. "I have come to warn you, Anwen. Do not let these beasts manipulate you or distract you from your mission. They are only using you to find the spear, no more and no less. They don't care about you or the kingdoms—they just want to find the weapon and take it from you for their own gain."

"And what about you? And the other gods? Are you not manipulating me—manipulating my friends into finding something that *you* lost? Something that will benefit you? Possibly to our own demise?" My words were harsh at first, but gradually softened to reflect my true feelings. "Are *you* not using *me*? Giving me the spells of the gods and now your mark—your power in order to save your existence, your way of life?"

Odin's face softened after my last words. He sat down and signaled for me to do the same. He must have sensed the chaos inside me.

"Aye, my dear one, you are not mistaken. The gods have used you—I have used you. There is no denying that your body became a vessel of salvation for us—a misguided decision that started with a heinous punishment made against our brother. But you have become so much more to us, to Vardia, and to everyone in this world. You are a Vardian Healer first and foremost. Think of your people—your grandparents, your brave parents. And Hrafn. They placed great faith in you. And even your Mountain Elf. He believes in you, although I sense an inner turmoil within him, something he cannot quite control.

Nonetheless, I know you are dealing with the pressures we placed on you, but we would not have given you these powers if we doubted your ability to handle such responsibilities."

Odin reached for my hand. Strangely, I felt a faint pressure as his ghostly hand hovered over mine. His brow furrowed with concern as he pulled his hand away.

"I trust that you will do as I say, my dear, but I also need to warn you about the darkness growing inside you."

I stepped away from him and stood up. "I don't know what you mean--"

"Do not lie to me, Healer. Choose your words carefully when you talk to the great All-Father. I know what you have been studying—I know that the dark elf, Herja, has mastered the Shadow, but you have not, and without true guidance, you will become no better than Corvus."

"I am nothing like that monster," I seethed. "I know what I am doing—I am taking control of my own powers."

Odin didn't respond right away. The silence grew awkward, but I held my ground. How could he compare me to Corvus? He knew nothing about the Shadow—or how it affected me. Maybe I hadn't fully mastered it, but I knew it wouldn't hurt me. It protected me.

Sensing the anger building inside me, Odin backed away to the fireplace with a sigh of defeat.

"Very well, young one. But heed my warning as well as the caution that Freyja has dutifully voiced to you. Stay true to yourself, stay true to the mission. I do not know if Gungnir will be helpful; I only know that a greater purpose is at work. It is with haste that you journey to Saerún. I am afraid I can tell you no more."

"But it makes sense, right? The Kaftar are the key to finding this spear of yours—to help defeat Loki? We have to trust them, or all is lost."

Odin began to flicker in and out of view. "Why are you like this?" My hand motioned toward his ghostly figure. "Why is Freyja not answering me? She is the one who told Kal to bring us here. We discovered that we need the Kaftar to lead us to Gungnir—your weapon that was taken from you."

Odin laughed. "My dear Healer, my spear was given to a mortal I once trusted. He was granted the power to wield my weapon so he could wage war on his enemies. He was very convincing when he came to me, begging for an advantage to eliminate those who encroached on his land and threatened his authority. Of course, you know I cannot pass up the chance to witness a great battle, especially between humans."

"Do you know where Gungnir is hidden? If so, why don't you just take it back and end this with Loki?"

"Alas, my dear, I only shared the beginning of my story—I was betrayed by this mortal. The spear was hidden from me—a magic I didn't understand took the one object I cherished above all others."

My hopes of finding the spear easily disappeared. "Who was this man?"

Odin gazed into the night sky. He cocked his head when the howl of one of the Kaftar pierced the darkness. He turned to me and shrugged. "A mere mortal who tried to be a great king. His name was Ramses the third . . . or maybe it was the second . . ."

My mouth dropped open. "Wait—are you saying that you gave Gungnir to the Pharaoh Ramses?"

I slowly, and with shock, sat on the edge of the bed, placing my head within my hands. I couldn't help but think that if I had a resume showcasing my experiences acquired within the past several years—foster kid, princess, granddaughter, healer, and now archaeologist—my career opportunities would be endless.

Then it suddenly hit me. My head straightened up.

"Wait—Ramses, all of them, lived in Ancient Egypt. Are you telling me that the spear is hidden in my old world?"

Odin laughed at my distraught state. He sat next to me on the bed.

"Healer, Dear Anwen, I understand I've placed a huge burden on your shoulders. But don't worry, the spear exists in this realm, and another, but sadly, the spear is not here. . ."

I looked up at him and saw that he was starting to fade away.

The spear was here, but not here? What kind of nonsense was that? Once again, the gods always vanished when I needed them the most.

The story that Amastan shared earlier made more sense now.

"So, the story of the dwarves coming here and asking Ra to donate some of his magic to the spear was true? And then the dwarves gave it to you, right? It makes sense that Ramses would want this weapon that his god helped create," I stated.

"The dwarves created Gungnir, but they did not craft this powerful divine weapon for me. They made it for Loki and my dear Freyja."

Odin gave a faint smile at my surprise and kept going.

"But Loki eventually gifted the spear to me—a sign of brotherly love and trust."

My anxiety was clear—Loki could wield the spear. Freyja could too. He did not need me. But why am I so important?

"Is there more to Gungnir than what you're telling or what even the Kaftar knows from their stories?"

Odin furrowed his brow in thought. "Gungnir is the most powerful weapon ever created, but as for its true origins, I only know what Loki has told me. It has proven to be an excellent and formidable weapon during many battles. When one holds Gungnir for the first time, the power of the sun and the light of its energy surround you, binding you with its power. It is fast; it can travel through the air as if propelled by the greatest of godly winds. It truly is remarkable." He paused. "There was something mysterious about the spear—symbols decorating the shaft could not be explained. I questioned Loki regarding their meaning, but even he was confused about their worth, truly, even their origin. Freyja seemed mystified by the symbols as well."

Suddenly, Odin rose to his feet, a troubled look on his face.

"The last time you saw Freyja was after a great battle in one of our realms—a battle that still continues right now. I must go because my brethren are calling me. Know this, dear one, the spear must be found if this realm is to survive. I know Freyja has a special place in her heart for this realm. But in my defense, I am not without feelings. I truly believe humans need to fend for themselves, but I never wanted Loki to destroy the realm that means so much to my beloved Freyja. The spear has long been forgotten, and now it seems to be the one object that could save your people. It's located in a place I cannot reach—a land filled with memorials of all the ancient gods. Where the memory of great magic is just a flicker in one's mind—the end and the beginning of all.

"The Kaftar have been known to travel to and from this sacred realm—the In-Between—searching for the one object that will save their kind from the cursed life. Amastan is correct. Even if they found the spear, they would not be able to wield the mighty weapon—only those deemed worthy to receive the power of the gods. Amastan will have no choice but to show you the way, and he will be wary of your knowledge of the In-Between. Find the spear—it will guide you. But, Healer, do not give in to Amastan and his promises. He will deceive you and then destroy you."

"I don't understand? Where is this In-Between Realm? How will I know where to go?"

"The answer is written on the stones, follow your heart, trust your magic." Odin turned and walked toward the fire. "You must go on this journey alone. Leave the others behind. Once you have the spear, take it west to the Sea of Saerún. And Anwen, be very careful with whom you trust. I sense treacherous thoughts within your group."

"Wait!" I stood up. "What do you mean?"

Odin's image faded away, but I didn't call him back again. I knew it would be a waste of my breath. The gods had a way of giving you pieces of information here and there, but they never truly revealed the whole story.

An intense howl echoed through the night, sounding frustrated and hungry.

I jumped up and ran to the window. Several of the Kaftar beasts circled below the cliff dwellings. One of the animals looked up, and our eyes met. This sparked a frenzy of movement as he jumped and growled, hoping his huge legs could help him climb the slick rock up to my room.

I stepped back and leaned against the wall. I thought Amastan's warning to his people would be enough to keep our group safe, but apparently, he was wrong.

A secondary growl sounded, followed by another, then a deathly cry.

I quickly turned to the window just as Amastan's beastly body loomed over his kin's body. He killed the instigator.

Amastan looked around at his people, who were gathering around him. My heart started to race. Fear for Amastan, our protector, grew. But within seconds, his people turned away from him and ran off into the night again. Amastan looked up at me, nodded his head, and followed his people for the hunt.

My body started to shake. With unsteady legs, I walked to the fire and sank into the chair. What was I supposed to do? How could I convince Amastan not to come with me into the—what did Odin call it—the In-Between Realm? Amastan knew where to find the spear, yet he failed to mention the realm. Why?

And the others. How could I convince them to let me go alone? Convince them to be left behind with the Kaftar? Once I found Gungnir, then I would deal with Amastan and his people.

But should I ask them to stay here? It wasn't safe. If anything happened to them, I would never forgive myself.

Nonetheless, Amastan would protect them. He needed the spear to free his people, which could work in our favor.

I could give him the spear first. When I return, he might end the curse right away. But I knew that would be a mistake—once they're back to their beastly form, there's no stopping Amastan and his people from killing us.

Maybe that would be the incentive. He would think that we trusted him, believing he would never harm us, and then he would tell his people about my gullibility. Amastan would promise his people the feast of a lifetime if no harm came to my friends until the spear was returned.

I leapt out of the chair and ran to the door. Telling the group was the only way to ensure everything would go as planned. I had to act quickly because the sun would be rising soon, and the Kaftar would be changing back into their human form.

I had to persuade the others about the plan, sharing everything Odin told me. I knew it would be difficult, especially to get Elric and Jack to agree to let me go alone. But I had to convince them, for the sake of our world's future.

FOURTEEN

"No, absolutely not," Elric exclaimed, throwing his hands up again. "I will not let you go alone to find Gungnir."

With every pause in my arguments, Elric expressed his opposition to my traveling alone to the In-Between Realm.

"You will not *let* me?" I whispered harshly. "You are not my keeper. You have no right to tell me what to do or not to do, do you hear me?"

I pressed my finger into his chest to stress my point. "We are not together anymore, so you have no say at all."

The glow from both of our hands cast eerie shadows on the small bedroom walls. My words clearly hurt him, but I needed him to understand. Time was slipping away. The sky was streaked with orange and lavender.

Thyra stepped between us, placed her hands on our chests, and pushed us away.

"Please, take control of yourselves. We do not have time for your quarreling," she said, pushing me away even further. She turned, grabbed my shoulders, and looked me in the eyes. "You cannot go alone, Anwen. Elric is right—you need someone to help you. And this In-Between Realm? I've never heard of it. Why didn't Amastan tell us where it was? The great All-Father couldn't give you any more information?"

Anu scoffed. "Of course, he didn't; that's what the gods do. They let others do the dirty work while they sit back and watch everyone die."

Ciar started pacing back and forth. His hooves scraped the floor like fingernails on a chalkboard. My nerves were on the verge of shattering.

"I do not like this change in our mission. Finding the spear within these rocks was one thing, but now, we must send the Healer into another realm that does not exist? If she is the only one holding this weapon, someone should go with her. Protect her."

Elric agreed and closed the gap between us.

"Anwen," he whispered to where only I could hear. Concern marked his face. "Please, I understand Odin has given you a task, but be sensible, my love. You shouldn't go alone. I know you're thinking of us, not just your safety. You don't have to protect us, little one. We would die for you."

"No, no way, I don't want your death on my conscience. Odin gave me this task, and I will do it alone. I will return, and then we can take the spear north to Saerún."

Elric kept trying to change my mind.

"We both know that our magic works better when we are

together, especially in Sorayn. What if your magic does not work in the In-Between Realm? You need someone to help you."

"At least understand our concerns. We do not want you to be stranded if your powers are non-existent," Menhit murmured. "Both Shu and I do not understand why Odin insisted that you go alone to this mysterious place. The spear seems important to the mission . . . our mission . . . so let us go with you. To help you and to protect you. You are the only one who may wield this weapon, but you are also the key to finding the monks. Without you, there is no mission, there is no saving our world."

I stepped back, my eyes scanning each member of the group. I was losing my footing. Everyone made valid points, but the truth was—I still had to go alone.

Anu snickered. realizing my frustration and enjoying it. I glared at her.

"Come now, we need to make a decision, and the decision should be that I will accompany Anwen into this strange In-Between Realm." She draped her arm around my shoulders. "Herja said that something inside of me can help Anwen, so maybe this is what she meant. So why not me?"

Elric's face reddened as he looked away from me. "Of all the crazy, unbelievable plans."

I turned to Jack. His expression plainly showed how he felt about my plan—I was leaving him again. I sensed the anger building inside him.

"Anwen, you said Loki gave the spear to Odin. Loki knew it was powerful, so why did he give it away?" Shu asked.

Menhit shook her head thoughtfully. "Something new was

discovered, perhaps? A new power that he did not know about? Maybe that is why he needs Anwen. She is the only one who can hold the spear, command it, and in return, Loki may have found a way to control Anwen."

I crossed the room to the fireplace and watched the flames for a brief moment. The frantic wobbles reflected my own nervousness. The plan I had just outlined for my friends was risky and dangerous, but we all needed to be on the same page. We all had to agree on the plan to succeed.

Menhit's statements made me pause. Were there powers within the spear that Loki didn't realize? Was I truly the only one who could hold the spear, and was that why he was using me?

A gentle touch on my arm pulled me away from my thoughts. Jack stood beside me; his eyes were glassy from unshed tears.

I held him in my arms, squeezing him tightly against me. His anxious hiccups echoed into my soul.

My eyes scanned the group again.

"I don't want to argue anymore—the sun is about to rise, and as soon as Amastan transforms back into his human form, he will be here asking questions about a plan to find the spear. I will be truthful with him regarding Odin's request, but I stand firm. I am going alone. However, the rest of the plan must be followed. When I return with the spear, we'll need to be ready to fight our way out of here and continue our journey to the Sea of Saerún."

I paused when my eyes landed on Elric. The swirls of his tattoos showed from the collar of his tunic. Silver churned chaotically. His magic roiled with his anger—for leaving him behind while I risked everything.

I was confused by his reaction. If he truly loved Sigrún, then why would he care if I traveled alone for that part of the mission? He should be happy that he didn't have to protect me and put himself in danger.

Elric turned away from me, hunching his shoulders.

Did my mind block waver? I didn't think it would, but his reaction was so immediate.

Thyra placed her hand on my shoulder again.

"Very well. We will do as you ask." Elric spun around at her words, feeling shocked and disappointed. "We trust your judgment. And if the great All-Father has placed his faith in you, ours should not waver. Go . . . find the spear as quickly as you can, and once you return to us, we will fight our way out of this valley and continue our journey north."

Everyone nodded in agreement except for Jack and Elric.

Anu rolled her eyes.

The sun peeked over the valley walls.

"They are coming."

***

Amastan and several of his warriors stood at the entrance of the room. His complexion looked refreshed, ruddy, and glowing. A shiver ran down my back as I thought of the doomed prey that caused his rejuvenated appearance.

His hesitation did not go unnoticed.

"Please, King Amastan, join us," I said. "I assume that the

hunt is over and all your people are well again?"

"Yes, Healer, my people are quite satisfied at the moment," he said. "The gods provided food for us, and we are grateful."

He paused before continuing. "I hope you weren't frightened last night. Several of my people needed to be reminded of our obligation to your company. The frenzy of the hunt can make them rambunctious and cause them to forget their priorities."

I nodded, knowing he was talking about the incident outside my window. "Of course, no harm came from their efforts."

"Indeed," he murmured.

Elric and the others looked confused by our exchange. I turned to them and smiled, hoping to calm their rising nervousness.

"King Amastan made sure his people followed his orders in keeping us safe, that is all. Just a minor scuffle that was quickly stopped by the king."

Elric stood next to me and placed his hand on my arm. "King Amastan, Anwen has been discussing our next steps to recover the spear. I think she has an interesting plan to share with you."

I felt his energy bleed from his hand and into my arm. Instead of his usual gentle and comforting energy, his power forcefully pushed through mine, causing my breath to catch. I forced a smile.

"Yes, Odin appeared to me last night and laid out a plan of action."

Amastan gasped in surprise. "Of course, let us discuss, but

first . . ." He turned to his soldiers. "Find my daughter, bring her to me. A new day will dawn for us, and the curse shall be broken soon."

The soldiers returned within a few minutes, with Zira leading them as she hurriedly rushed to her father's side. Her excitement was clear.

"I've been told that there is a plan ready to be implemented?"

I nodded, hesitating before I shared the unpopular strategy.

"Odin gave me directions on how to find the spear."

Amastan's smile widened. "Excellent, how can we assist?"

I cleared my throat nervously. "Well, I must be taken to the In-Between Realm and enter by myself to find Gungnir. Odin told me where to find it."

So, I lied about that last part. What better way to persuade Amastan and his people to let me enter the mystery realm alone than if I knew exactly where to find the spear?

Simple. No problem.

I could not have been more wrong.

FIFTEEN

Still bristling with anger, Amastan huffed in frustration as he led me to the In-Between Realm portal. His council argued and offered excuses for withholding the spear's location, but their words fell on deaf ears. It sounded hollow, but there was nothing anyone could do about it now. The plan was laid out and approved. Amastan wasn't happy that I would be traveling alone to find his prized savior spear, but since Odin ordered the strange request, he set his arguments aside. He wanted the spear, and if my plan was the only way to get it, then he had to follow my rules.

But unfortunately, I had to follow the rules of the realm. Thyra and Elric were right in their observation about the mysterious realm. And obviously, the great Odin decided to hold back some of that information—magic wouldn't work. So, needless to say, Elric and the rest of the group were not happy. I wasn't excited about this new revelation either, but what could

I do? We had to stick to the original plan.

My eyes traveled up the high cliff walls. We shuffled sideways through the narrow crevice of rock. Several hours spent struggling in the confined space were enough to make me rethink going alone. With my hands sprawled along the smooth walls, I fought to pull my body through another tight space. My thoughts turned to Odin and Freyja. The silence from both of them worried me—about their situation as well as mine. Doubt rampantly raged inside me. I constantly worried about Loki and Kenrick's true motives—I didn't need to worry about Odin's, too.

"Are we there yet?" I grunted as my body finally squeezed through the rock, only to find another narrower crevice ahead. I needed to focus on the task at hand. "Surely, there must be an easier way?"

Amastan vanished around the corner, but I heard him snicker and then grunt in pain.

"The way to the portal is not easy, Healer, I can assure you, but we are almost at the entrance."

I grimaced with his answer, as well as facing another narrow sliver of an opening. Amastan wiggled through without a sound. Bleeding cuts and scrapes belied his stoic efforts. At least I was smaller than him and managed to get through the rock maze without injury. Amastan, on the other hand, took a beating. Bones cracked and splintered so he could fit through the narrow spaces. Something that was natural to him, although slightly painful—turning from human to beast was worse.

Suddenly, several small rocks rolled down the wall. A soft

crunch of pebbles sounded behind me. I carefully turned my head in the tight space, straining my eyes to see who or what was making the noise.

"Hello?" I murmured, but couldn't see or hear anything. I tilted my head to listen for another sound, but was met with silence.

"Healer, are you alright?" Amastan's distant voice whispered back to me.

I looked back again at the spot where the mysterious sound came from.

Paranoia must be setting in.

"Yes, I'm fine."

I shuffled through the crack and came face-to-face with Amastan. He was looking through an opening in the rock wall, and he crinkled his brow.

"Did you hear something?"

"No—no. I couldn't see you, and I had a moment of panic."

I offered him a slight smile and pointed toward the jagged hole.

"Is that the entrance?" I attempted to ignore his doubtful expression.

I walked past him, brushing dust off my tunic. I bent down and looked inside. Immediately, I turned to him. "This goes straight down—and it looks deep. How do we get down there?"

"You jump, Healer. It is only about 40 feet."

I straightened up quickly. Amastan smiled widely.

"Forty feet?" I threw my hands up. "I can't use my magic here, remember? And I'm not an animal that can easily jump that far. I'll be seriously injured or die!"

Amastan's smile widened as he placed his hands on my shoulders.

"I would not have traveled all this way if I didn't know you would survive the fall, Healer," he let go and kneeled before the hole. "Magic is not necessary, nor a rope. You have no worries. Trust me."

I tried not to let doubt show in my eyes, but Amastan saw it anyway. He stood up and turned away in annoyance.

"Trust is essential between us, Healer, and I have placed quite a bit of it with you and this concocted scheme of Odin's." He paused. "My people need to be free; we have suffered enough because of both of our gods' cruel games. I wouldn't have shown you this sacred place if I didn't trust you. I wouldn't have sacrificed my daughter for a simple feast for you and your friends. We could have slaughtered all of you, but this is a quest I never thought I'd be part of. The idea of saving my people from the ongoing hardships of transformation—it takes a toll on our bodies and minds. So, please, trust is all I can give you, and I would appreciate the same in return."

I swallowed my shame. He was right. I needed to trust him, as he carefully placed his faith in me. The key to his people's salvation from this cursed plight was the spear, and I was the only one who could find it and bring it back to him.

"You're right. I am struggling with my own doubts about this journey, and with that doubt comes questioning of your intentions. But please accept my apologies. I do not wish your people to suffer anymore." I looked back at the hole, trying not to show fear. "What do I do now?"

Amastan shrugged his shoulders. "Simple. You jump."

I held back a sarcastic reply as my feet shuffled toward the entrance. I knelt and peeked inside again. Darkness engulfed everything as an unexpected smell of damp earth wafted up through the shaft. I pulled back slightly at the intrusive odor. Another soft crunch of rock sounded, but when I turned, nothing seemed out of the ordinary. I looked up at Amastan, but he was still staring into the hole, not reacting to the movement. A chill of cold air brushed the back of my neck, sending a shiver down my spine. The moment was broken when Amastan suddenly knelt beside me.

"I know it looks dangerous, but trust me, this fall isn't really a fall; it's a strong pull that floats you down safely," he whispered softly, as if speaking normally might break whatever enchantment he was explaining. "I don't know how else to describe it, but you'll be safe. From there, you'll see a small tunnel, and you must enter it.

"Once you follow the tunnel, you will come out into a cavern with a brightly lit spring. You need to swim deep through a cavern, and when you emerge on the other side, you'll face an obstacle."

My brow furrowed. "An obstacle?"

Amastan shook his head. "The obstacle always changes, so I can't tell you what you'll encounter. Once you've figured out how to cross into the realm, your hunt for the spear will begin."

"Wait—this isn't the portal to the other realm?"

He shrugged indifferently. "Well, not exactly. This is the

entrance to the cavern. The realm entrance is on the other side of the spring. You must be successful, whereas my people have not."

Panic began to surge again. "But you said your people have been to the realm . . . you said you have tried to find the spear yourself."

"My people discovered the entrance many years ago, that is true, and several groups of warriors have succeeded in gaining access to the realm, but they never returned. So, I was not lying when I said that we have not been successful in finding the spear."

Not wanting to argue anymore about the nuances of correct word phrasing, I took a deep, calming breath, but couldn't help throwing one more jab.

"Well," I said as I swung my legs into the hole, dangling them precariously. I edged my butt to the edge while I held onto the sides of the rock. "I shall choose my questions more carefully in the future when I need actual answers from the Kaftar."

Amastan smiled ominously. "Yes, my dear Healer, that is an excellent observation—one that you should remember when you are within the realm, trying to find my spear. Many people are relying on you."

I glanced sideways at him, wondering if his statement was a threat.

I scolded myself—of course it was a threat. I was the only way to get what he wanted most. If I don't deliver the spear, my friends will die.

I nodded in understanding as I turned to look into the hole

again. I pulled my bag closer to my body and swung my bow onto my back. The dagger strapped to my waist reassured me.

Chills ran up my legs as darkness swallowed them. I moved a bit closer to the edge. Fear flickered inside me, but quickly faded with adrenaline.

I dropped into the unknown abyss.

My hands reached out to the sides, hoping to feel the walls, but only grasped at air. I tried choking back my screams, but I couldn't hold them. A short cry of panic escaped. My legs thrashed as I tumbled head over heels down the shaft.

I wasn't sure how long I kept falling. My sense of space, time, and what was up and down was disoriented. Hope for any light from the bottom seemed impossible as the dark void continued to swallow my plunging body.

"Help me," I managed to sputter. Nausea overwhelmed me. My hands reached for the walls, but they touched empty air again. I looked down, or what I thought was down, as a pinpoint of light emerged from the darkness.

Fear gripped me again. My imminent death became clear. Amastan must have been lying because the small circle of light was now widening, and to my horror, I was accelerating. My hands and feet flailed, trying to find something to stop my deadly fall, but all I met was air with each movement. Strangely, and even more unsettling, the Okri and Shadow stayed silent. My magic truly vanished—my powers deserted me.

This was the end.

My journey to save my people ended with my body splattered at the bottom of a stupid shaft. My grandparents, Jack, and Elric will be devastated.

Would he mourn my death? With my end, it would be up to him to save our people. Could he save our world without me?

The light at the bottom turned a shimmering blue, rippling up the sides of the rocky shaft. Another scream escaped. The ground sped up to meet me. Closing my eyes, I threw my hands up to my face for protection, not that it would have helped, but the instinct to use my energy pushed me into action.

Suddenly, my body jerked to a stop—similar to a roller coaster lurching to a halt after an exhilarating ride.

I gradually opened my eyes and moved my arms away from my face, afraid of what I might see.

Was I dead?

I wriggled my fingers in front of my face. I didn't feel any pain, but surely, I was dead. No one could have survived that fall.

But as I stretched my arms away from my body, I saw the ground several feet below me. I turned my head to the side and was surprised, and of course, extremely thankful, that the blue shimmering light was not just light, but a web of some sort. The soft tendrils spread like a spider's web, clinging to the sides of the shaft. Thinking it would be sticky, I moved my arms and legs around, but the iridescent threads did not cling to my clothes. It was like a trampoline, bouncing above the ground.

"Interesting." My voice echoed through the shaft.

My relief was short-lived as the tendrils snaked from the walls and wrapped around my arms and legs.

Screaming, I tried to rip the threads away from my body,

but they were too strong. I struggled against them and was shocked when the tendrils suddenly hurled me to the ground, freeing me from their grip and vanishing into the walls.

I scrambled to my feet, crouching into a defensive stance, but the tendrils did not reappear. Quieting my breath, I surveyed the shaft and found the small hole that Amastan mentioned. I strained to see above me, but darkness cloaked the shaft. The light from the entrance vanished. I rolled my eyes at the misjudgment of the shaft's height—it's definitely more than 40 feet.

My eyes shifted toward the hole. I half expected a white rabbit to appear, guiding me deeper into the magical world of Wonderland.

A weary sigh escaped—unfortunately, no rabbit appeared. I was alone.

I peeked through the hole, expecting to encounter more darkness. But, to my surprise, the hole revealed a bright light at the end.

Crawling a short distance through the restricted tunnel, I emerged into a cavern almost like the one in Wynfalle Mountains—the Sacred Spring. Strange-looking torches, lit by white flames, lined the walls. Stalactites and stalagmites converged in the center, forming beautiful, glistening columns as far as the eye could see, while rainbow-colored crystals decorated the walls, shimmering like sun-kissed water just before sunset.

I couldn't believe this oasis was hidden beneath a harsh desert sun.

The dark water beckoned me closer. My feet moved on their own. Carefully, I stepped to the edge of the shimmering spring. Supposedly, the true entrance to the realm was on the other side of the cavern—swimming was the only way across.

I reached down and gently moved my hand through the water. It was cold but bearable. Amastan told me to trust him, and that's what I have to do now. There was no other way to get to the other side.

Unraveling my head scarf, I placed it in my bag along with my dagger, boots, pants, and tunic, leaving only my sheer undergarments covering my body. They were still going to get wet, but at least the extra clothing wouldn't weigh me down. I quickly braided my hair for easier manageability in the water. My bag, bow, and quiver were secured.

Now, standing at the edge of the spring, my nerves started to come apart. The idea of swimming scared me. No, the idea of getting into the water scared me. I couldn't swim, and even when Amastan explained how to reach the realm through the water, the thought of showing my weakness to him wasn't an option. I had to make it across and swim to the other side.

Jumping up and down, swinging my arms over my head, I hoped to speed up the adrenaline flowing through my veins. I needed to succeed—I couldn't let fear stop me. The mantra kept repeating in my mind as I placed one foot in front of the other and slowly moved deeper into the pool. The coldness seeped through my sparse clothing. The water lapped against my stomach and then over my breasts.

Taking in my last breath and sending a prayer to Freyja, I

dove underwater, telling myself to keep my eyes open and not shut them out of fear. The water was dark, but a faint light at the bottom guided me to another opening in the rock. I went deeper, not stopping with curiosity when I saw the faint light was another ghostly flame. Pushing through the entrance, darkness enveloped me, but there was another light at the end of the tunnel, calling me hopefully toward the surface.

My held breath was fading as I pushed off the wall and tried to swim faster. But I was losing the fight. My body floated to the rocky ceiling; I struggled to swim. What was left of my confidence was quickly vanishing. Lack of oxygen combined with my fear of drowning slowed me down.

The sharp edges of the rock scraped against my skin as I dragged my body along the top. The point of light was growing larger and brighter. But every muscle in my body protested every effort to stay alive. My lungs ached. Water entered my mouth.

The struggle transformed into peaceful silence. My body no longer felt like my own; all worries drifted away.

I ignored the rough hands gripping my wrists and then my waist, pulling and shoving me toward the light.

Death needed me, I guess.

SIXTEEN

A heavy weight around my waist and quick pushes of pressure on my chest forced my eyes open. Water poured from my lungs. Hands roughly turned me onto my side. Water splashed everywhere. My eyes snapped open in fear, and to my surprise, smooth, sparkly stones caught my gaze. The heavy pressure was gone, but movement beside me startled me into scrambling away. Though this mysterious person saved me from drowning, I couldn't understand who would live in this realm.

But the hands reached for me again, causing me to turn toward my savior. I raised my hands, knowing my magic wouldn't work, but old habits were hard to break.

"Anwen, stop struggling."

Surprised by the sound of the voice, I sat up and looked in amazement at my rescuer.

"Elric?" I sputtered. "How—how are you here? How did you pass Amastan?"

My mind was playing tricks on me. It had to be an illusion. How did he manage to deceive Amastan and follow me down the shaft? Magic wasn't an option, so how was he here?

I shifted awkwardly. He looked so alluring with his wet hair, clingy tunic, and bright, beautiful eyes staring at me with concern. My heart skipped a beat at the way his eyes drifted over my body. How could he look at me like that? He had no right to look so good to me, not now and definitely not ever again.

Anger flared. My eyes scanned the surrounding area, suspecting it might be a trick and that Amastan was coming after me too.

Elric leaned back on his heels. He shook his head as if he understood what I was thinking.

"I am alone—Amastan didn't accompany me, nor did the others," he said as he looked down at the ground and picked up one of the shiny rocks. He studied it for a few seconds before throwing it into the water. I followed the rock as it skipped four times along the surface before floating into the dark blue depths. I scrambled to my feet. The memory of my easy acceptance of death in the watery grave pierced me like a dagger.

How could I have been so weak? My behavior disgusted me. How could I succeed in the In-Between Realm if I couldn't even swim through a watery tunnel? A hollowness grew inside me—my mission was doomed.

Elric shook his head in frustration. He followed me up from the ground and turned away from me in anger. The toe of his boot kicked a few stones. An odd sensation swept through me as an unknown presence echoed within my thoughts, gently pressing against my mental barrier. The hushed mutterings confused me.

But the voice was momentarily forgotten. I turned on Elric.

"You didn't answer my question! How did you pass Amastan without being noticed?"

Elric threw a few more rocks into the water before he stood up and turned to me, hands on his hips. Guilt replaced anger now.

If I tell you, please do not be angry with me.

Wait—what?

His soft voice caressed my thoughts.

"You're . . . you're not using your mind block . . . I mean, I can hear you . . . which means . . . " I stuttered in embarrassment. I backed away, surprised and horrified at the same time. "You—you can hear *me*. This cannot be happening."

Where the hell was *my* mind block?

Suddenly aware of my scantily dressed body, I quickly tried to pull the sheer fabric over the bare patches of my skin while my other hand scrambled around the ground for my bag. As I pulled the tunic out, I twisted around so that my back was to Elric and clumsily pulled it over my head. The fast movement or simply the humiliation of the whole situation caused my legs to buckle. My arms, caught within the sleeves, couldn't stop my fall to the ground.

Elric quickly and effortlessly caught my waist and pulled me to him, pressing his body tightly against mine.

I struggled against him, but now I'm even more annoyed because our bodies fit perfectly together.

A hot blush spread across my face—of course, he could read my thoughts now. Ugh!

A peaceful feeling replaced my aggressiveness. His energy once again provided the necessary calmness in a time of need. But his power also felt different from mine.

"How—how are you doing this? Magic doesn't work here. It shouldn't work here," I whispered. His arms tightened around me. Finally, he released me, but he was still so close. His energy dissipated, leaving a hollow emptiness inside me.

He studied my face, trying to decide if I was going to lose control again, but sensed my questions were masking the anger. He smiled faintly.

"I couldn't let you go alone—you are too important to me, to all of us. My plan was to follow you from a safe distance so you and Amastan wouldn't notice me. But you kept stopping now and then, like you sensed someone nearby, so I decided to try my magic, to see if what the All-Father and Amastan declared was true."

I pulled back a few inches, frowning. "But obviously, they lied to us, which makes no sense."

Elric moved even further away from me, now scanning the area around us. His body tensed. His warrior instincts must have kicked in as he carefully examined our new, mysterious surroundings.

"No, Anwen, they were correct. Your traditional magic does not work—but the Shadow does."

"I don't understand . . ."

"The Shadow helped conceal my body from you and

Amastan," he held out his hands and shrugged. "I didn't think it would work, but it felt different in the valley. As we got closer to the cave entrance, it called to me. It told me to use them, so I did. I waited until Amastan left the entrance, and then I jumped into the hole. Soon after that, I heard your thoughts and felt your fear. And then the emptiness."

"I was drowning," I whispered.

Elric closed the gap between us and gently squeezed my shoulders. "I felt the energy leaving your body. I—I couldn't lose you. Not again. I could not let you hunt for the spear alone, no matter what Odin said to you. We need each other, we always have. The Shadow called to me because I believe they knew you would need me—that we would be stronger together."

I tensed at his words. The Shadow called to Elric, but they stayed silent around me.

"I didn't realize you were so familiar with the Shadow or they with you."

I cringed at the resentment in my words. Clearly, Elric used the Shadow. He was from Wynfalle—the heart of the Shadow, the home of Herja. His tattoos were the symbols of the Volun—the markings of his ancestors.

Elric didn't respond to my jealous words. He smiled as his thumb gently brushed my cheek.

"I know enough. I used to watch my father train with Herja. But this was different—I felt the Shadow through you, Anwen. The pull was strong—I'm not sure how to explain it. Sigrún's father told Herja to stop using the Shadow after my father . . . died. But the Shadow will always be part of me, part of my family's legacy."

The mention of Sigrún hit me like a lightning bolt. I stepped back from Elric, needing to stay focused—and to suppress my feelings.

I straightened my tunic and pulled the rest of my outfit from my bag, dressing in silence. When I finished, I gathered my courage. Rules needed to be established.

"So, this is how it will go. Rule number one—you will stay out of my mind, and I will stay out of yours. We will only use it in extreme situations if something should come up. Rule number two—you're here, unfortunately, and there's no way around it. I could send you back, but I believe the Shadow, not you, will be helpful when we need to work together. When the Shadow is required, you will assist—no questions asked . . . and finally, Rule number three---" I exhaled nervously. "No more mentions of your fiancé or any feelings. We're here for one purpose: finding the spear. Anything related to your people and your new life is a distraction."

Dismissing him, I headed toward the cave exit and stopped right away.

"Oh, and Rule number four—don't assume that just because the Shadow pulled you to me, it means I need you or your help. I am fine on my own—something I've been doing for a very long time."

I expected Elric to voice a few grumbly thoughts, but his silence persisted. I walked to the edge of the opening and stopped instantly in awe.

Elric approached from behind and gasped.

We couldn't help exchanging surprised looks.

"Well, I have a feeling we're not in Kansas anymore."

SEVENTEEN

Those were the only words I could think of to accurately describe the landscape before me. The world burst with bright, vivid colors—almost as if every blade of grass, flower petal, leaf on a tree, and stone against the bluest sky had been painted with fine brushstrokes. My eyes took in each distinct detail of everything around me. The arrival of Dorothy in the great land of Oz, with its lively hues, was the only possible description.

Or maybe it was the fact that we just came from the most barren of lands and landed in the middle of a painter's palette.

"It's amazing," Elric whispered beside me. He stepped forward, out of the shadow and safety of the cave, and tilted his head up. "What is it?"

I followed his gaze to the mammoth wall rising from behind the trees, no more than fifty yards or so.

"Whoa," I muttered.

The greenery extended upward at least five stories and

stretched as far as the eye could see. It reminded me of the Great Wall of China.

I started to walk closer to the hedge-like barricade when I felt Elric's hand clasp around my arm.

"Wait—we need to talk about our plan before we approach the wall."

His hand was light and gentle on my arm, but I didn't pull away.

"I just want to see it up close. It seems to go on for miles with no entrance," I said as I shielded my eyes from the blaring sun and looked up again. "What do you suppose it's for?"

In other words, was it about protecting someone from a specific threat? And if that's the case, which side were we on?

I turned to grab my bag from the ground and cried out.

Elric spun around, nearly knocking me over in his rush to place himself between me and the apparent danger signaled by my scream.

The cave entrance had disappeared, replaced by a smooth rock surface.

"Where's the cave?" I exclaimed as I moved around him. I placed my hands on the wall, hoping it was just a hologram. But it felt solid. I slapped my hands against it, trying to stay calm. My forehead pressed against the cold stone with dread. At least we still had the option to turn back and look for another way to defeat Loki and Kenrick, in case we couldn't find the spear. But now that option was gone.

Our journey has begun. There was no turning back. I lifted my head up.

"Well, it looks like we're now forced to move forward, with no way to go home."

Elric shrugged indifferently, as if in his mind, going home empty-handed was not an option at all.

"So be it. We have to find a way in," he said matter-of-factly.

"And how do you propose we do that?" I asked, now annoyed by his practicality. "It all looks the same."

Elric smiled at me. "Yes, it does, so we shall walk along the wall and find an entrance."

"There has to be a door nearby, right? Otherwise, why would the cave put us here?"

Elric walked alongside the wall, staying at least ten feet away. His gaze slowly scanned the green barrier. "Just because we entered this realm at this exact spot does not mean we are within reach of the spear, Anwen. If it were that easy, Amastan would have found Gungnir a long time ago."

Bristling at his patronizing tone, I hurried to catch up. "I knew it would not be easy. I was just making an observation."

Elric stopped and turned to me. "I am not being insolent. I was simply answering your question."

He kept staring at me, his brow furrowing even more in thought. "May I offer a few rules of my own?"

Tilting my head, I sighed impatiently and waved my hand to the side. "Of course, offer away."

"Firstly, my observations and opinions used to matter, and when I offer one as such, it does not deserve condescension. I am not criticizing you, and secondly," he paused, unsure how his next rule would be received. "Secondly, I am not your enemy, so

I would appreciate it if you did not treat me like one. No matter the hard decisions I have made in the past concerning our relationship, it does not mean I do not care for you."

Our eyes met, and my breath caught in my throat. I wasn't expecting the pain flickering in his eyes and the guilt from those choices. I quickly looked away, not ready to explore those reasons just yet. The loss of his love still burned with anger, and I wasn't prepared to forgive him.

He may not be my enemy, but he definitely wasn't my friend. Not at this moment.

"Well, I guess that seems reasonable enough," I said with as much indifference as I could muster. It sounded forced. His words affected me more than he could know. But I refused to feel guilty for my earlier words.

I swept my arm in front of me again. "Great, now that we have both established the rules, let us begin again."

We started the journey, staying close to the wall but far enough away just in case something jumped out at us—or whatever Elric thought might happen. We walked for several hours, with silence as our companion, and we began to relax a little. Our scenery changed dramatically. Gone were the vibrant colors of the trees and flowers, and even the slick, smooth rocks around the cave. Now, two colors followed us along our path—one side green and the other a dark brown.

"I am curious, Anwen," Elric interrupted the silence. "What did you mean when you said we were not in, what was it? Kansa?"

I couldn't help but laugh. It was hard to say the word

Kansas in our Vardian language, Skovmal.

"No, not Kansa, but Kansas. It is a state back in my old world."

"So, it has meaning for you?" he asked. "You were hoping to see this place again?"

I shook my head and smiled at him.

"No, it was just a reference to an old movie about a girl from Kansas who was transported to another world. She spent the entire film trying to find a way back home. She missed her family."

Elric furrowed his brow. "So, you were hoping to be transported back to your world?"

"No, not at all. It was just a reference to her landing in the new world, the land of Oz, and how clear and beautiful the colors were. You see, the movies in the old days used to be black and white, and this movie, *The Wizard of Oz*, well, it mixed both black and white footage with color."

"Interesting. A wizard, you say?"

He tilted his head toward me, looking very intrigued now.

"I would like to see this movie," he declared firmly.

I laughed again at the seriousness of his tone. "Well, unfortunately, I didn't have it with me when I came to this world. So, I am afraid that you're out of luck."

"One day, we will travel to your world and bring this movie back with us."

I stopped and stared at him, but before I could ask about this strange revelation and the 'we' involvement in his plans, a strange and eerie shriek echoed from the rocky side of the path.

"What was that?" I whispered, looking up at the sky and crouching as if it might fall from the sky.

Elric swung his bow over his shoulder and nocked an arrow. His swift movement elicited the same reaction from me.

A fierce wind tore through the valley. My feet sank into the dirt as I struggled to keep my balance, while my eyes kept scanning the sky for whatever made that terrifying sound.

For a brief moment, the wind ceased only to surge through the valley again. It repeated this strange cycle, blowing and then stopping, until I could take it no more.

"Why is the wind so erratic?"

Elric stayed silent but signaled for us to step back, closer to the leafy wall. His eyes carefully scanned the cliffs ahead.

"Is it a bird?" I whispered. My eyes quickly darted nervously to the green wall. The voices that had been silent moments ago were now murmuring anxiously.

"Elric, don't move back any further," I warned as the voices grew louder and more painful.

He stopped without hesitation and nodded in agreement. The same pain showed on his face.

Could he hear them as well?

Suddenly, Elric pushed me to the ground. His body briefly covered mine, but he jumped back up and aimed his bow at the rocks, releasing his arrow.

Trying to catch my breath, I yelled, "What are you shooting at?"

By the time the question escaped my mouth, a winged creature jumped from the ledge and landed at the edge of the rock wall. The eagle-like bird stood over 10 feet tall. His mottled white and brown feathers gleamed in the sun as he lifted his orange beak toward the sky, screeching in dismay. His large claws dug into the ground, grabbing dirt and boulders, then he leapt into the air.

Elric grabbed my arm and forcefully pulled me to my feet.

"Run, stay close to the wall." He aimed another arrow at the bird and released it, hitting it directly on the wing. The arrow struck its target, causing the creature to drop his rock bombs just short of our position.

Elric turned and shot another arrow at its torso, but it deflected it with a swipe of its healthy wing. We kept running, thinking we had wounded it enough to make it stop attacking, but suddenly, the ground shifted beneath us, and we tumbled to the ground. I immediately turned back around to see the most terrifying sight—this enormous bird transforming into an even larger man.

Elric grabbed my waist and lifted me up. His face was filled with terror at what we were witnessing.

"*Hraesvelgr*," he whispered.

"What!?"

He turned to me and calmly said, "The Corpse Swallower. We cannot escape him."

With his words, he placed his bow on the ground and bowed his head in defeat.

I couldn't believe he was giving up. I faced the running giant, who was now slowing down and stopping in front of us. A smirk spread across his face.

"So, elf, you know what I am," the creature muttered happily. "You know you can't win."

My body tensed up. This creature recognized what an elf looked like.

"You are well-groomed, clean. Your flesh looks tender and pink." He sniffed the air. "I shall enjoy the taste of your fear and your cool acceptance of defeat."

I raised my bow, but Elric quickly grabbed it roughly from my hands and laid it on the ground.

He turned back to the giant, who was now watching his slow approach. Elric reached for my hand and held it tightly.

"What are you doing?" I murmured sharply. "He is going to eat us! We need to fight!"

Elric's eyes never left the giant's figure. He pulled me closer, our sides now touching. His grip on my hand tightened, sending pain up my arm.

We had to fight, not cower in fear and let this giant eat us. I tried to yank my arm free. Suddenly, coldness flooded through me.

It happened so quickly and with such jarring intensity that my body would have collapsed if Elric hadn't wrapped his arm around my waist.

His Shadow consumed me, along with the familiar and velvety energy of Elric. The cool, yet smooth feeling stole my breath as it merged with my magic. The Shadow within me fought but was soon overwhelmed by Elric. A soft moan escaped my lips, and my eyes dilated. The brightness of the sun became overwhelming. I raised my free hand in front of my eyes to block the intense glare. Elric's body tensed as his arm mimicked mine, lifting to shield his eyes.

Pushing through the strange sensation flowing through my body, I realized my hand and then my arm were slowly disappearing—we were becoming invisible. The memory of Herja using the same Shadow spell in the Wynfalle Mountains came to mind.

The giant stopped and furrowed his broad forehead. His black eyes looked from side to side, scanning the area where we still stood, but he couldn't see us.

"I know you're still here, elf. I can smell you."

He lifted his head to the sky, then crouched low to the ground, his mouth gradually turning into a pointed beak.

"Your magic should not work here, but for those who are granted the gift of retaining their power, they shall pay a high price," he squawked.

The giant changed into an eagle and took off from the ground. Thinking he was about to give up and fly away, I lowered my arm to my side.

The eagle spotted the shimmering movement and dove toward us. His deadly claws glinted in the sun.

Elric, still gripping my arm, fell back against the foliage wall. I stumbled backward with him as the eagle extended his claws toward us.

Thorn-covered branches pricked my back, and I screamed out in pain. Elric let go of my hand, causing me to fall deeper into the wall. I tried to regain my footing, but a vine latched onto my arm, its barbed sprouts digging into my flesh. Another vine curled around my neck and then around my torso, squeezing the last breath from my lungs.

The last thing I remembered was Elric's scream as darkness pulled me under.

EIGHTEEN

I sprang from the ground with a wild gasp. My arms flailed as the last remnants of the deadly vines loosened their grip and slowly retracted into the wall. My hands rubbed my throat, trying to draw more air into my lungs.

When the black dots disappeared from my vision, I focused on a kneeling Elric, hands splayed on the ground. His back arched as he struggled for air.

"Are you okay?" I asked, crawling to his side.

He sank back with a groan. His breath was irregular, but he nodded, not able to speak just yet.

I scanned the wall, raising my hands in defense and waiting for the eagle creature to burst through the foliage, but nothing moved around us.

"Where are we?" I asked, glancing around nervously.

A wall similar to the one we passed was mirrored on the opposite side, leaving a solitary path down the middle. The walls were so tall that only a narrow strip of blue sky was visible above us. Deep shadows pressed in as the sun's rays lit the center of the path.

"How are the walls taller on this side?" I asked, perplexed.

What I thought was the mirror image of the foliage wall that pulled us through was actually something different. Although the same vines hung from the wall, a faint, ghostly breeze swayed them to the sides, revealing painted images.

I felt a pull toward the figures. My hands extended to the rock.

"Don't touch it, Anwen," Elric called out as he leaped to his feet, grunting in pain. I turned just in time to catch him before he fell back to the ground.

"Elric!" I yelled, tightening my hold around his waist. He muttered under his breath, and I felt his pain surge through his body.

I carefully lifted his right arm and saw several stains spreading down his tunic.

"What happened?" I tried to pull his tunic up, but he pushed my hands away.

"I am fine, just help me up."

I grabbed his waist again as he struggled to his feet. Once he was stable and able to stand on his own, I went back to lifting his shirt.

My examination uncovered multiple puncture wounds just below his ribs.

When Elric noticed the concern in my eyes, he laughed.

"I am fine. Really," he grabbed his shirt and pulled it down.

"The winged fiend just pricked me; it is of no concern. I shall heal within the hour."

He spun away from me and resumed picking up his dagger and his bow. I noticed a bead of sweat running down his temple. My mouth opened to ask if he was truly okay when he straightened and turned to me, his smile leaving me breathless as usual.

"My moment of weakness has passed. The Shadow feels stronger here for some reason."

He dismissed my concerns, then focused his attention on which direction to take.

"It looks as if we only have two choices, left or right," he said as he studied the path in front of us. "What say you?"

He fixed his brilliant blue eyes on me. I studied him for a few seconds, trying to see through his act of gallantry, or his foolishness, but he seemed fine for now. Besides, if he was going to be stubborn about me helping him, then so be it.

I turned around and narrowed my eyes, hoping to spot any signs that would lead us to the best option.

The gentle breeze that earlier drifted down the path faded away, and the sweltering heat of the air pressed down on me. Sweat trickled down my back.

The wall called to me again. I slowly approached it, instinctively lifting my hand to brush the vines away from the painting beneath.

Elric noticed my intentions and moved to stop me. I swung my hand at him, halting him in his tracks.

"Remember, I can use the Shadow as well," I muttered as I

resumed my movement and lifted the vine away.

"Anwen," Elric said angrily.

Ignoring him, I leaned closer to the painting. Brightly colored figures raised their hands toward the sky. Symbols lined the top of each scene, while various-sized swirls and circles filled the background. I kept pushing more vines aside—a story was revealed.

More figures appeared but were now kneeling with their heads and hands touching the ground in front of them. I continued along the wall, revealing more of the scene.

"It looks like someone just painted these. Look how vibrant the colors appear," I whispered. "But, what does it mean?"

"Anwen, can you please release me?"

Without turning, I swished my hand through the air, dispelling the magic that restrained him. "What are these symbols—is it a language? It looks familiar."

Elric leaned closer to the painting. He shook his head dismissively, showing indifference toward my find. Instead, he seemed nervous and jittery.

"I don't know, but we have to keep moving. We need to find a safe place to rest."

I ignored him as I kept moving the vines aside.

"The figures might be bowing or praying? I'm not sure—" I suddenly paused. "Look!"

My heart nearly stopped. My hand reached out and traced the familiar symbol.

"Odin's mark," Elric whispered.

My other hand reached up and touched the three triangles

near my ear. The mark Odin gave me—the mark of the All-Father's blessing. Beside the three triangles was another triangular shape, with a bright stone at its center, illuminating all the followers.

I turned to Elric, hoping he would have more to say about my find, but his attention was now fixed on the darkening trail. His eyes examined the deep shadows forming around us. A distant rattle echoed—light and soft, but still foreboding. A shiver ran down my spine, and the hairs on my neck and arms stood up.

Elric's eyes widened in alarm. "We need to go."

"Yes, yes, that sounds like a good idea," I gulped as we turned in the opposite direction.

Elric nocked an arrow as I drew my dagger from its sheath. My other hand spread out in front of me, just in case.

"Stay in the center of the path, where the sunlight shines," he said.

I nodded in agreement. My eyes struggled to adjust to the growing shadow on my left.

"At least we know we are heading north," Elric whispered over his shoulder.

My heart pounded in my chest. "Sure, and that helps us in what way?"

Elric clicked his tongue in irritation at my condescending tone, but didn't say anything back.

Guilt replaced my fear, so I silently muttered a quick "sorry."

We walked until I thought my feet would fall off, but luckily, the rattling disappeared.

The path was now covered in darkness, so both Elric and I called on the Shadow to help light our way. Oddly, the dark mist hovering over our palms emitted a strange, silvery glow, yet it was bright enough for us to see the path.

I raised my hand up toward the wall, hoping to see more of the paintings, but the vines were too thick.

My mind was on the images and not on walking when Elric suddenly stopped. I grabbed his tunic with my hands and then pressed my palm to his back to keep from falling into him further. The contact with his tattoos, even though a simple cloth kept me from touching them directly, overwhelmed me. My senses flared with heightened awareness.

All of his thoughts merged with mine. I felt all of his emotions flooding into me. The intensity was so overwhelming that I roughly pushed him away, causing him to drop to his knees. I doubled over to catch my breath.

Stunned but not angry, he quickly jumped back up and put his hand on my shoulder with concern.

"Are you alright?" His words quivered as he attempted to steady his breathing and maintain his composure.

I pulled away from him—his touch still made my breath stutter and overwhelmed my senses. The force of his touch, or more precisely, of my hands on his tattoos, was shocking. The feeling was new—intoxicating. Consuming.

I faced him, hoping my emotions weren't as obvious as his. With only the faint light still flickering in one of his palms, I saw his eyes were dilated and his face was flushed. He probably felt the same rush of emotions.

"Yes—of course," I exhaled, hoping to calm my jumbled thoughts. "I tripped and when I touched your back---"

"I—I thought I saw something ahead, and . . ." he struggled to find words. It had been a long time since we genuinely connected—something I deeply missed. And from the look on Elric's face, he missed it too.

He shuffled his feet nervously. "It was quite amazing, wasn't it?"

A small smile lifted the corner of his mouth. My breath faltered. How could someone so handsome make me so angry? I closed my eyes, willing my heart and my thoughts to stop racing.

Refusing to give him a truthful answer, I sidestepped around him, needing to take the lead for a while and to make sure I wouldn't trip and touch his back again.

I took a few more steps down the path, but unfortunately, not paying attention, my light suddenly illuminated a face.

Elric pulled an arrow from his quiver, and within seconds, it was nocked.

"Wait," I cried out as my eyes adjusted to the object in front of us. "It's a sculpture, not real."

Keeping his bow up, he slipped beside me until he was sure that we were not in danger. His bow drooped as we both looked into the most striking eyes and beautiful face I had ever seen.

The figure was vividly painted with striking features. The top half was clearly female, but that was where the female anatomy ended. Green scales formed her lower torso, wrapping around her body. The contrast between her peachy, naked skin and the bright green scales was a stunning work of art. Peering up into her face again, my eyes wandered to her hair.

I quickly stepped back and away from the figure.

Snakes, so life-like, twisted around her head. Mouths opened, with tongues stretched out as if to taste the air to locate their prey. I couldn't look away from the hideous mass; my breath caught in my throat.

"What is this beast?" Elric murmured.

"It looks like a sculpture of Medusa, a mythological creature from ancient Greece, but she looks nothing like what I have seen in my old world," I muttered as I peered up into her light red eyes. "She was portrayed as an ugly beast, not this beautiful figure here."

Elric hesitated to step closer to the sculpture, almost scared to look at it.

I smiled at him. "She won't hurt you, but the one of legend could turn you into stone in an instant. One look into her eyes, and you were petrified."

I walked around the figure. "But why is it here, of all places?"

Elric turned away, seemingly ignoring my warning. "This creature is an omen. We must move on, away from here."

His energy gathered in his palm again as he lifted it to look farther down the path.

We both cried out in surprise.

Medusa wasn't the only sculpture littering the path. Even though many looked broken, their faces were still recognizable.

As we walked through the marble graveyard, I pointed out the figures I knew.

"A cyclops, a sphinx, and this one is a minotaur."

I paused in mid-sentence. "Whoa. Well, this one is out of place." I turned to Elric. "This one is Ancient Egyptian—Bastet."

Elric's head swiveled back and forth, trying to understand the strange sight. When we reached the end, he stopped and turned back to look at the figures. His attention was drawn downward to one of the statues. He picked up a heavily dented and worn shield. More weapons littered the ground around us, as if the soldiers just left in a rush.

"This is very strange—why would these statues be in this realm, and of all places, in the middle of this path?" he whispered as he held the shield up. "And the weapons?"

"I don't know—"

A noise pierced the darkness—unfamiliar but an ominous feeling hung in the air.

"We should keep moving," Elric whispered. "Use your energy to continue to light our way."

He swung his bow over his shoulder again.

"I believe we are being hunted."

I raised my hands higher, trying to see through the sculptures. "By what?"

Suddenly, a sharp hiss cut through the darkness.

Elric grabbed an arrow and aimed his bow at the sound while stepping backward. His eyes searched the darkness.

I did the same as we kept moving backward. My heart

pounded wildly, afraid that the night would finally uncover the source of the sound.

But nothing stirred.

Instantly, the hairs on my arm stood up, and the voices of the Okri screamed inside my head.

Something flew through the air and struck the ground in front of us. I jumped back and fell on my bottom. Still with my hands raised, the Shadow charged toward the attacker.

I scrambled to my feet, grabbing Elric's arm. "RUN!"

We both jumped back as an enormous serpent writhed and glided through the air above us, opening its mouth to strike.

"You cannot escape, trespassers," it hissed. "Night has fallen. Your sun god cannot help you now."

NINETEEN

Shadow magic erupted from my hands, hitting the ground in front of the taunting snake and sending it flying backward. Elric launched an arrow into the darkness, hoping it hit its target. We didn't wait to see if it did. Stumbling in the dark, our only hope was to find shelter from the snake monster.

The ground trembled as the snake's screech echoed through the night. The path started zigzagging, making it hard for us to navigate in the dark. Several times, I brushed against the vines, scraping my outstretched hands on the tiny thorns. Elric pulled me aside more than once. Determination to keep going surged through me as I pushed off the wall again. My sense of direction faltered. I reached out to Elric to push him forward with urgency, but instead of running, he stopped, gathered more of his energy, and pressed his hand against the side of the wall.

"Look." He glanced over his shoulder at me. He swung his bow around his back and pulled back some of the vines. "There is something here."

I looked closer, noticing the narrow ledge sticking out among the vines. I pushed the branches aside and saw another ledge just above the one Elric found.

A distant rumble shook the ground.

Elric looked up at the wall. "We need to move to higher ground—"

He began tearing away the vines. Thorns cut into his skin. Blood dripped from his hands, but the pain was worth it as more steps came into view.

Grabbing my waist, he pushed me toward the wall. "Start climbing, quickly."

He didn't need to tell me twice. I grabbed the first rocky outcrop and lunged up the wall. It took several tries to find a rhythm with the steep climb and the advancing darkness, but we both made it up the wall.

I turned to check on Elric, but he grabbed my leg and pushed me upward. "Do not look down—keep climbing. I am right behind you."

My hands throbbed from the cuts and prickled with pain, but I kept finding my way through the vines. Luckily, as we climbed higher, the thorny branches turned into soft stems. Soon, I felt the coldness of bare rock against my hand.

"I—I think we must be getting closer to the top," my voice was barely audible.

Finally, after what felt like hours of climbing, I reached out and grabbed a larger ledge, pulling myself onto the flat surface. Elric quickly followed, landing exhausted beside me.

Peeking over the edge, my eyes scanned the darkness below.

"I don't hear anything," I whispered over my shoulder. "I think we lost it."

Elric sat up with a grunt, holding his side.

I quickly moved toward him and pulled his hand back. He tried to push me away, but I clicked my tongue in irritation.

"Let me look at your side, Elric," I muttered. "You're no good to me wounded."

His hand dropped in defeat. The light in my palm flared at his side.

"It should be healing by now—why haven't you healed?"

I quickly raised my hand, illuminating his face so I could see him better. The paleness of his skin, his bloodshot eyes, and the tightness around his mouth showed me he was in severe pain.

I placed a hand on his forehead, then his cheek, feeling the heat of his fever.

A distant rumble shook the wall. Grabbing Elric and the side of the ledge, I searched the darkness below.

"I think he slipped past us." I kept scanning down the sides of the wall. "I think we are safe for now."

Elric grimaced as he leaned over the side to look.

"But he will be back," he said. "We need to keep moving."

"No, not yet. You need to rest." I pulled him back and started to lift his tunic. "You need my help."

He grabbed my hands and held them still. "No, you need to save your energy."

I scoffed. "Don't be ridiculous. Why would I need to save it? I am fine. Besides, the Shadow can help you."

My hands fought against his grip, but he was too powerful.

"Anwen, I'm not sure about that—we know our energy works together, but every time we use it, it feels weaker, don't you feel it?"

I stopped my struggle. "I—I don't feel different at all. Actually, if I must confess, I feel stronger. When I touched your back, the sensation was unlike anything I had ever experienced before. Our connection had always been strong, but here? I thought you felt the same rush?"

He paused as if lost in thought, furrowing his brow in confusion. But he quickly shook his head more firmly, seemingly reaching a decision. "It was wonderful, and I agree it was more intense, but I can't explain it. It was different." He clutched his side in pain. "No matter. Leave me here. I will only slow you down. You have our people to think about. I cannot let you waste your efforts on me."

"Waste?" I looked into his eyes, confused about why he said that, considering all we had been through together.

"Waste?" I repeated more softly.

His eyes held so many questions.

Could I trust him again after his betrayal? With me? With the people of Vardia? He chose the Mountain Elves—the people who lied to him, disowned him, and banished him. He had no right to look at me with such tenderness. And love.

I bristled at his audacity.

"Well, it was your decision to follow me into this realm, and now, I can't just leave you here. You should know that I am not heartless. Besides, no matter what you say, having you around seems to work for us here. I need you to help me, and with you wounded and not healing, that will only slow my progress in finding the spear."

He smiled. "So, I am a means to an end now?"

"No—that is not what I meant," I stammered, struggling to find the right words. He was irritating. My hands went back to what they were doing. His hands, however, kept blocking my efforts.

"So, you still care about me?"

I stopped, giving him a pleading look. My heart wanted to tell him I still loved him, but instead, I leaned forward so close that he thought I was about to kiss him. The struggle to say the next words tore my soul in half.

"My heart closed to you the moment you picked Sigrún. Don't think for a second that healing you has anything to do with love."

Elric leaned back and reluctantly released my hands. The words stabbed him like a dagger. He looked away from me.

"Fine, but don't overexert yourself. The beast might return. I'd hate to render you useless for your quest."

I fought back the tears, but knew that my hurtful words had to be spoken, even if they sounded unconvincing to me. Elric took them at face value.

I pushed his tunic up and placed my hands over the blistering holes in his side. I closed my eyes as black tendrils wriggled through my fingers. Magic seeped into his skin.

But what should have been an easy fix became almost too much for me. I concentrated more, focusing harder on his wound.

Something was fighting against me.

Elric grunted in pain and grabbed my hands. His eyes turned red, and his voice deepened ominously.

"Please, stop. It's not working. Only . . . making . . . it worse."

He sighed in relief when the energy ceased, leaning his head back in exhaustion. His pallor deepened, and his body trembled.

I shook my head in disbelief. "How is this possible? Your wound should be healed." And his eyes. What was wrong with him? Why did his eyes turn red?

I wanted to ask him, but he was struggling just to stay conscious.

A few minutes passed before Elric steadied his breathing. He reached out his hand to me, but I was still too stunned by the strange change in his eye color. I pulled away to avoid his touch.

He lifted his head when I didn't respond to his gesture. I cautiously examined his eyes. They were unfocused and confused, but not crimson. Pale blue eyes stared back at me.

"Anwen?"

"Let me check your side again."

Ignoring his confusion, I knelt beside him. My energy didn't heal him, and it looked even worse. I tore a long strip from my tunic and pressed it against his wounds before wrapping it around him.

His hand stopped my movements. "Look at me."

I hesitated, and he noticed. "Anwen—please."

My eyes met his.

"Did I hurt you?"

His question surprised me.

"What? No, of course not. Why would you hurt me?"

He turned away so I could finish bandaging his wound.

"I—I don't know. The way you looked at me, and with what I have been experienced, I've been---"

I stopped when I heard the deep worry in his voice. "What's been going on? You have been *what*?"

I leaned back, pausing as he looked away from me again. "Elric? You have to trust me."

"It's not you, Anwen. It's *me*. I shouldn't be here. I'm putting you in danger."

My hand gently rested on his cheek and turned his head so he would look at me.

"Please, tell me what's wrong."

Elric struggled to sit up, and I pushed him back down. Sighing in defeat, he laid his hand on top of mine.

"I've been blacking out lately. It started when our group traveled back to Wynfalle. I was searching through the rubble—one minute, I was holding a lost memento, and the next, I woke up in one of our tents in the valley. Tyr said I was found unconscious near the Sacred Springs."

Confused, I shook my head. "Maybe a rock fell and hit you, or you could have passed out from exhaustion."

My thoughts returned to our first arrival at Wynfalle—Elric's punishment, the king's murder, and all the death when the mountain collapsed from Kenrick's attack. Any of those experiences could have caused Elric to relapse.

"But I wasn't in the Sacred Springs. I wasn't that far into the mountain. I was searching in the children's quarters."

He brushed his hand across his face, trying to wipe away the memories.

"So, Tyr found you in the springs. Maybe he made a mistake," I suggested, though I knew my excuse sounded weak.

Elric's expression told me the same thing.

"So, you started to black out after that? Maybe it's the trauma, or exhaustion? Why do you think you would hurt me?"

"I am not sure. It's a feeling sometimes when I think about you."

"You think about me?" I asked, now turning away from him. "Why?"

I started to stand when his hand gently grabbed my arm.

"I think about you all the time—but I have obligations to my people now, but when I saw you again---" He released my arm. "It was like something inside of me was making me stay away from you, but also something was pulling me to you."

I needed time to think, to understand what he was telling me. I could not deny that when I tried to heal him, his eyes changed—like something inside him was hindering his recovery. What actually happened to him in the mountain? I believed him when he said he was searching in the children's area, not the springs. Why was he found there?

"You need to rest now. We will wait until the sun rises, and then we will head back down the wall."

Elric agreed, laying his head down, closing his eyes, and quickly drifting into a restless sleep.

The distant rumble kept me awake—the serpent continued to hunt for us through the darkness below. We only had a limited number of hours once the sun rose, assuming the days were like those in the real world—so little time to find the spear before night fell again. And when darkness covered the realm, we would be hunted once more.

Elric mumbled incoherently in his sleep. I leaned closer to him, observing his features twist with mysterious distress. What was he dreaming about to cause such pain?

His eyelids pulsed rapidly back and forth. His distress worried me, so I laid my hand on his arm, hoping to quiet the demons in his dreams, until finally, he calmed.

TWENTY

Sunlight caressed my face, gently encouraging me to start the day. My eyes fluttered open despite the lovely dream keeping me from the morning light. Elric sat across from me, cross-legged, and watched the sky transform with the most breathtaking colors. At the sight of him, and so fresh out of my dream, I felt my own tinted blush rush up my neck and flush my face—Elric occupied my dreams as well as my reality.

"I didn't mean to sleep," I said defensively, even though no accusations were directed at me.

As if he didn't hear my confession, he closed his eyes, basking in the growing warmth of the sun. His meditations gave me a brief chance to observe his profile—a long, straight nose, a strong jawline, high cheekbones, and smooth, pale skin. Even after days of traveling, rough stubble refused to blemish his face. Long, dark lashes swept over the soft skin beneath his almond-shaped eyes.

What was I doing?

I tried to look away, but the dream that pulled me back stayed with me—Elric professing his undying love, his arms around me as we surrendered to our passion. My heart pounded as I recalled all the details, the words, the feelings.

I rubbed my eyes vigorously, trying to erase the details even more from my memory.

"I tried to stay awake," I offered another casual excuse for my unplanned nap.

"I am not accusing you of anything, Anwen," Elric said as he opened his eyes and smiled at me. "We both needed time to rest because we have a full day ahead of us."

Despite my earlier reservations, I returned the smile and said, "You seem better."

He smiled even wider, revealing his elusive dimple. My heart skipped a beat; I couldn't help but stare at his mouth, sensual and inviting. His smile deepened, and when my eyes met his, the intensity took my breath away.

"Thank you for helping me last night," he murmured.

Embarrassed about being caught staring, I looked away, searching the horizon instead. "I didn't really help. I couldn't heal you. Which reminds me---"

I moved to his side and, without asking for permission, lifted his tunic and unwound the fabric. An angry reddish-purple rash encircled the wounds.

I clicked my tongue. "We need to hurry up and find that spear so you can get proper help."

Reaching down to the bottom of my tunic, I ripped off

another long strip for his bandage. Elric placed a hand on my cheek.

"Thank you," he repeated softly.

The feel of his thumb stroking my cheek brought me back to my dream. I closed my eyes, hoping he wouldn't see how his touch affected me. After a few seconds, the reality of where we were and what we had to do pulled me out of my own dangerous thoughts.

I pulled away and directed my gaze towards the horizon again. I frowned at what I was noticing for the first time.

"Did you see this?" I asked, surprised.

Elric chuckled softly at my new discovery. "Yes, I have been studying our surroundings for quite a while now. It is quite interesting."

"Interesting?" That was an understatement. "What is it? Where are we?"

Elric struggled a little to stand up, but he managed to pull me up with him.

"It looks like we are inside a labyrinth. A very strange one at that."

It was like the merging of an ethereal fantasy world with the cold structures of science fiction—both genres fighting over the same patch of valuable land. Large steel structures stood tall and silent, various shapes and sizes packed tightly together, gaining strength and stability from their close proximity, while enormous canopied trees and vibrant greenery encroached upon the steel monoliths. Without a doubt, the green giants were winning the battle.

I pointed toward a haze farther away. Its stormy, misty shape swirled fiercely as if caught in a battle of its own.

"What do you think that is?" When the last word left my mouth, the storm inside the haze calmed. I pulled my hand back, as if the strange cloud heard me, and soothed its rage for my benefit.

Elric noticed and turned to me. He glanced behind us, taking in the towering cliffs and rock formations, then looked at the wall we were standing on. It extended for a while before plunging into the canopy of the trees. He looked below us, noticing that the path was still shrouded in darkness.

"Let us travel along the wall and walk as far as we can," he suggested. "I don't like the shadows lingering below us, at least until the sun rises above."

My eyes tried to make sense of the darkness below. Suddenly, a sharp pain erupted in my stomach—a sensation that was hard to ignore. My hands clutched the edge of the wall, fearing that my body might suddenly topple over the ledge. The discomfort persisted until it transformed into distorted whispers, stirring the voices inside me into action. They were unclear and jumbled but grew more intense, making my heart race and leaving me nearly breathless.

I quickly looked away from the shadowed path. Luckily, Elric didn't see or notice my episode.

Absolutely, let's walk along the wall for a while. Elric didn't need to know about the turmoil raging inside me—that the voices wanted me to climb down into the shadows.

"Yes, that sounds like a plan." I grabbed my bag, swung it

around my head, and tucked it under my arm. "We need to move quickly. At least in the forest, we will have a better sense of our surroundings."

Turning around on the ledge, I headed toward the trees, not bothering to see if Elric followed. My nerves were on edge, but as the sun rose higher in the sky, the murmurs grew quieter and a sense of calm—despite our mission—settled within.

I tried to resist looking over the edge of the wall again, not only to forget the mesmerizing whispers from below but also to focus on the narrowing of the ledge. At the spot where we spent the night, the ledge was at least five feet thick, but as we moved closer to the forested part of the maze, it became smaller and more deteriorated.

After walking for several hours, Elric's small grunts of pain grew more intense until his discomfort became unbearable.

"Why don't we rest for a few minutes so I can check your bandage?"

When I turned to confront him, I couldn't believe how much he had changed. His condition was getting worse.

Elric managed a quick nod, but as he began to kneel, his hand slipped on the pieces of crumbled wall, nearly causing him to fall over the edge.

I grabbed his arm and pulled him back toward me. Holding his waist, I gently sat him down.

"I just need to rest, that is all." His hands trembled as he gently set his bow aside. He saw the concern in my eyes and offered a weak smile, but I kept holding onto him. I placed a hand on his cheek and then his forehead—heat radiated from his skin. Fear gripped me.

I blinked away tears. The idea of losing him overwhelmed me.

"I—I don't know what to do. I can't heal you, and if we don't find help, you should have said something earlier. I wasn't paying enough attention . . ."

I couldn't keep going when I saw his expression.

What I saw angered me.

He wasn't worried about his health or wellbeing; he cared more about me. He didn't need to speak—his thoughts echoed inside my mind.

My body shook. I started to break down.

"Don't you dare give up . . . not now."

Even though Elric hurt me, I still needed him.

His fingers wove through my hair, pulling me closer. His lips touched mine, gentle and reassuring.

"I am of no help to you like this, Anwen. I won't be a burden on your quest."

Panicking, I looked toward the forest.

"We are so close to the trees. If you can make it there, I can try to find something to help with the infection and stop the bleeding."

"Nothing will help. The talons of the Hraesvelgr are lethal. There is no cure for the venom."

I stared at him in disbelief.

"Why didn't you tell me you were poisoned? I'll find something in the forest. There has to be something to help you." Anger resonated in my words.

Elric drew in a shaky breath and closed his eyes as the pain twisted through his body.

"Anwen . . ." His voice trailed off. He was giving up.

"No, do not use that tone with me." I struggled to lift him up. "I will use magic to carry you. Please, help me."

"Why are you doing this? After how I treated you."

I kissed him gently and whispered, "Don't you know?"

His face paled, bewildered by my unspoken words. A struggle unfolded inside him—he withdrew his thoughts from me, shutting down. He pushed my hands away, leaving me more confused.

The quick, unbalanced movement caused the wall to crumble, and he lost his grip from the ledge. My hand shot out, trying to grab his arm as his body tumbled over the side. I caught the neck of his tunic, but the heaviness of his body ripped it from my grasp.

Hopelessness enveloped me as his body silently crashed to the ground. No yells or screams escaped his lips.

No, this cannot be happening.

All I could think about was doing the unthinkable.

I threw my body over the ledge.

TWENTY-ONE

My hands reached out, propelling my body like a torpedo. I had to save him, but I wasn't sure how. With that thought, black webs shot from my palms, latching onto the sides of the walls in a crisscross pattern. Elric's body, now unconscious, flipped and flopped head over heels until the web-like tendrils caught him. A sigh of relief escaped once I knew he was safe. The tendrils gently placed him on the ground.

My safety never crossed my mind, but as soon as I envisioned the ground rushing up to meet me, a gentle pull upward halted my fall. I floated like a leaf softly swaying in the breeze. Soft yet firm vine-like tendrils grew from the wall, gripping my body and lowering me to the ground.

Surprise, not fear, swept over me as the last hand gave me a gentle squeeze and then faded back into the wall. I blinked several times at the vine-covered wall—waiting to see if one of the green tendrils would come to life again. A soft moan near my feet pulled me out of my shock.

The last of the black strands released Elric and faded into the shadows.

"Elric?"

I sat beside him, resting his head on my lap and gently stroking his face. I searched the shadows crowding the path, aware of the danger lurking in the maze. The sun's warm touch brushed our skin. A small sliver of light indicated the middle of the path. Elric's eyes remained closed, and his breathing was uneven.

I pleaded at the wall, hoping whatever helped me would reappear.

"Please—he's dying. Can you help him?"

Whispers played inside my head—the droning mottled with incoherent words. Only one word was clear—shadows.

"What are you saying? I don't understand."

The whispers grew louder, and although their words remained jumbled, they were filled with such emotion. The words echoed in my mind, raw and deeply urgent, until my brain finally grasped the meaning.

Drag him to us. To the shadows.

I hesitated.

What if this was a trap? I didn't understand what the voices meant; for all I knew, it could be another monster, tricking me. We could end up being someone's dinner.

"How can I trust you won't hurt us?"

The whispers stopped suddenly. My body jerked forward as the voices vanished, leaving a sharp void inside me that made me gasp for air. I pushed Elric away and tried to stand, but I tipped to the side, my hands clutching the dirt beneath me.

A frustrated cry escaped. A hollowness settled in my gut. A sense of futility overwhelmed me while desperation flooded my mind. It felt as if a part of my soul was ripped from my body in the most inhumane way.

"Please---" My voice broke, and the pitiful plea hissed from my lips. "What did you do to me?"

Trust. Us.

Their words had the effect they intended.

I lifted my head. "Yes."

Shadows. Come to us.

I dragged Elric's body into the shadow of the wall. As soon as we were fully hidden within the darkness, a familiar sensation crept up my side. I glanced at Elric, thinking he was awake now, using his powers, but he was still unconscious. Panic surged within me as the cold feeling slowly moved up my chest, but what I thought was a familiar sensation became something very different and more invasive. Not only was my physical body vanishing, but I felt my existence fading. I was losing myself to the darkness.

***

I was aware of the warmth—from my toes to the tip of my nose. I snuggled deeper into the cozy comforter, savoring the softness of the bed surrounded by the scents of fresh lavender and sweet vanilla. If this was a dream, I never wanted to wake up.

The crackle of a fire caught my attention. My eyes

stubbornly fluttered open.

My first thought was that the ceiling looked strange—cold, dark, and lumpy. A sharp contrast to how I was physically feeling.

I pushed up on my elbows lazily, but then, noticing my surroundings, jolted to a sitting position. I couldn't believe the fully furnished room—not just any room, though, but an extravagant one.

And curiously, I was lying in a very large bed, fully wrapped in a warm, golden-colored comforter. The flames from the billowing fire reflected on the satiny fabric, making it look like a pool of melted gold. My hand gently stroked the shimmering surface, wondering who could have made such a beautiful piece. Confused, I brought my hands closer to my face—stripes of clean linen bandages covered the vine-torn skin.

As my eyes wandered across the room, memories of a similar situation came to mind—waking up in a room just like this one, a room that belonged to my mother in Vardia.

But I knew this wasn't Vardia, and definitely not a room belonging to my family.

Now, feeling too hot, I threw off the comforter and swung my legs over the side of the bed. The floor was covered with rugs, but underneath was rock. In fact, as I looked more closely at the room, the fancy furnishings seemed carefully arranged to hide the dullness of my surroundings.

Sweat streamed down my face in the stifling heat. I swiped the back of my hand across my forehead while thinking about putting out the fire.

Instantly, the flames shrank to where only a few logs retained the deep orange heat.

The hairs on the back of my neck stood up. I tensed, scanning the dark corners of the room, listening intently. Something nagged at the back of my mind—something familiar, something I should have recognized. My eyes adjusted to the darkness.

I was not alone.

"Hello?" I turned my head around to scan the entire room for movement. No one answered. "Where is my friend? Where is Elric?"

A faint glow from the fire caught my eye. I slowly stood up, placing my hands at my sides. I didn't want to appear threatening.

"Is he alright?" I asked, hoping to see another move.

Another shimmer caught my attention, but it was near the corner of the room.

I started to walk toward it.

"Please, is Elric okay? I need to see him."

A sudden gust of air pressed against me, making me breathe in quickly.

Soon.

The faint whisper echoed through the room. A surge of energy flooded my body, and I doubled over, gasping for air. When I straightened up, I felt like I had just finished running a marathon. My heart was pounding twice as fast, and a rush of adrenaline coursed through my veins.

The experience was exhilarating, and even though none of

my questions were answered, I didn't fear these beings or worry about my safety. I couldn't explain any of what happened to me, but I knew I had to be patient with them. Somewhere deep inside, something was telling me that all of my questions would be answered soon.

I sat on the bed, hoping my patience would hold until this new revelation sank in. But as minutes stretched into hours, my patience unraveled. Tired of pacing back and forth, I sat back down on the bed with a sigh. My thoughts kept drifting to Elric, and my anxiety about being away from him for so long started to grow.

A quiet click sounded in the room. The door opened slightly, creaking softly. Thinking that someone was about to walk through it, I waited. But no one appeared.

I tiptoed to the door and slowly pulled it open wider, revealing a passageway.

"Hello?" I whispered, cautiously peeking around the door.

Not a single person was in the passage, so I waited, but no one appeared.

I glanced around, unsure what to do when a torch mounted on the cavern wall suddenly flickered to life. I stepped toward it only to have another torch sputter with flames.

"I guess you want me to go this way?" I asked out loud.

A third torch lit ahead of me, answering my question. Several more lit as I followed the passageway, not sure where the invisible being was taking me. The cavern appeared empty, but, strangely, I felt the pulse of life all around me.

The torches stopped their domino effect, leaving me in

front of another door. I searched the passage, thinking I would finally come face to face with my mysterious guide. But no one appeared. This had to be my destination.

I pressed my ear against the cold wood, hoping to hear anything, but silence once again prevailed.

Taking a deep breath, I turned the knob and slowly cracked the door open.

The first thing I noticed was the stifling heat, just like my room. I hesitated briefly before pushing the door all the way open. I immediately saw Elric lying on a bed.

With a quick cry of relief, I rushed to his side.

The comforter was loosely tucked around him. I placed my hands on his cheek, hoping his temperature would be normal, but he still felt hot. His skin was flushed with fever.

"Elric?"

I pulled his blanket back to reveal his wound, not caring that he was naked. Fresh bandages covered his injuries, but I could tell that the puffy, red rash was no longer spreading.

Besides his nudity, I also noticed his tattoos—changing from black to silver, swirling chaotically, but also covering more of his skin. The mystical swirls adorned his chest and seemed to extend further onto his shoulders and down his arms.

Unsettled, I threw the comforter over the chaotic scene, hoping the unseen being didn't see the unusual chaos.

"Thank you for helping him. Will he be okay?" I asked.

Time seemed to stand still.

Yes.

"Thank you," I repeated.

Rest.

"Who are you?" I asked, uncertain if I wanted the being to go. I had so many questions. "Why are you helping us?"

A flicker of movement appeared near the door as several figures emerged from the wall, but they were not flesh and bone—only two-dimensional, black as the shadows they came from.

One stepped further in the room while the other figure hesitated, staying near the wall. Their features lacked any distinguishing characteristics.

Do you not know?

The figure's voice invaded my mind. It stopped a few feet away from me, its head tilted as if confused.

"Know what? I don't understand," I asked.

The other figure walked slowly to their companion.

You called us many times, so we answered your plea.

I was more confused by their answer. I looked down at Elric, but he was still unconscious.

"You mean Elric called you?"

No. You called for us, so we answered your plea. Just as you once answered ours.

I shook my head, still not understanding what they were saying.

"I apologize for sounding so dense, but I am not following what you are saying. How was it that I called you? I don't even know who you are."

The anxious figure turned away while the other remained.

"I won't hurt you," I said to the one moving away. "I just

need some answers. You see, my friend and I are on a quest. We are searching for something in this realm. Something to help my people. We were told it was hidden here a long time ago—it belongs to a very important god."

Yes, we know.

The figure closest to me spoke, but the one by the wall made a soft hissing sound.

My sister does not believe we should talk to you. The Others will be angry that I have communicated with you.

"What is your name?"

Silence filled the room. Seconds stretched into minutes. I believed they had left.

They call me Son.

His sister hissed again.

"Thank you for trusting me, Son. Do you know what object I am talking about? Can you help us?"

The Others are summoning us—we must go.

Son floated toward the wall. His sister disappeared.

Son hesitated.

You asked about us and why we helped. You called us because we are within you. We are part of you, Healer. We guide you when needed. Do you not know who we are now?

I wrestled with the most outlandish answer. The conclusion was improbable. Yet, the proof was right in front of me.

I shook my head in denial.

"It can't be true."

Son's declaration coursed through me—the revelation wrapping around the denial and pulling so the truth could shine through.

I quickly checked to see if Elric was awake, but he remained unconscious, breathing softly, with no sign that he heard Son's admission—the people responsible for his powers and a fraction of mine were standing in front of us.

The Shadow was more than just magic—more than lessons and practicing from a book. The Shadow were people—living beings full of powerful energy.

And before I had a chance to answer, Son disappeared.

TWENTY-TWO

A gentle caress tickled my arm. Elric lazily stroked the underside of my forearm—just above the spell belonging to Hermod. The sensation instantly brought a smile. Elric's eyes were still closed, but a smile curled along his lips. My body was snuggled against his side, my arm across his chest, and our legs entwined. I started to pull away, but his arm tightened.

"There is much that you need to tell me," he declared.

He glanced around the room. He let go of me, leaving me suddenly sad from losing his touch, and swung his legs over the side of the bed. I could tell by the confused furrow of his brow that he was trying to piece together the past events.

Elric realized that he didn't grunt in pain. His hands moved to his side and found that his wounds were nearly healed, leaving almost no scars.

He realized he was naked.

He raised an eyebrow in surprise, but all I could do was

offer a mischievous smile. He gathered the comforter around his body and paced around the room. His clothes were neatly folded and placed on a chair by the fire. Without hesitation, he dropped the comforter. I quickly turned my head away, but not before noticing how much of his body was covered with his markings. Once he was dressed, he circled the room, taking in everything around him.

He stopped and stared at me, now almost angry. "I should be dead."

"Well . . ." I said carefully, unsure how to explain the little information the Shadow had left me. "Yes, *you* should be dead. *I* should be dead, but we were saved."

Confusion creased his brow once more. "Who saved us?"

I hesitated, trying to find the words to explain to him without sounding crazy.

When I didn't answer quickly, he grabbed my shoulders. "Who?"

"The beings," I whispered. "The Shadow beings."

Elric quickly stepped back, surprised.

"I know. I still don't understand, but Son said that they were part of us and that I called for them. I can't explain it, and I'm not sure I fully understood what he was telling me."

Elric kept staring at me as if everything I said was nonsense. His confusion was almost funny.

"Son?"

"That's his name," I said, now feeling exasperated. "Don't you get it? They are the Shadow, the magic inside us. They saved us from the fall. They healed your wounds." I pointed to his side and then swept my arm to the side. "They brought us here to their home."

With my words, Elric gripped the bedpost and carefully sat down on the side of the bed. "I—but—are you sure, Anwen? That these beings you talked to are the Shadow?"

I crawled to his side. "That's what he told me. They had to leave before they could answer any more of my questions." I paused. "Why do you seem so stunned? Isn't this good news? Apparently, they know of the spear, too."

Elric shook his head. "What did Herja reveal about the Shadow to you? Did she tell you how she gained the power?"

How could I explain that Herja barely told me anything about her powers? That most of what I've learned came from a book supposedly forbidden to me, and, of course, without Herja's permission or guidance.

How do I express the whispers that comfort me more than the Okri? Or even the powerful energy of Hrafn?

No, Elric would lose it if he found out I was learning the Shadow on my own.

Soft whispers calmed me.

Should I be honest?

Suddenly, the whispers grew louder inside me.

Do not tell him. Not yet.

But how can I not be truthful? I argued.

They did not answer.

Elric waited for my response. His patience wore thin as he backed away from me. He finally realized why I was still not responding to his questions.

"Are they talking to you now?" He asked. His eyes searched mine. "What are you holding back from me?"

When I didn't respond, he leaned in and placed his hand on my cheek.

"Do they whisper to you often? Does the ache of their voices leave you breathless?"

My eyes widened, and I nodded into his hand.

His energy flowed into mine, almost like a truth serum. I couldn't help myself. The need to tell him everything unraveled inside me.

"I hear them all the time—the whispers soothe me when the Okri are agitated," I declared. "I cannot explain it. I feel complete with my magic for the first time in my life."

Elric's finger caressed my cheek. "You have the book, don't you?"

I pulled back, shaking my head. "Yes—I mean—no."

My words trailed into silence.

"I don't understand what is happening. The Shadow are telling me to lie to you, and lie about everything that has been going on since you left, but I am conflicted."

Elric approached me but didn't touch me this time. "Because why?"

Because she cares for you.

My head quickly turned toward the door.

Son appeared. His featureless body was mostly solid, although I could still see the wall behind him.

She is loyal to you.

I turned back to Elric, who was still staring at me, and not even bothered by our new observer. Did he hear it?

"I need to talk to her. Alone," he demanded calmly. He looked up at the figure when it didn't answer. "Please."

Son hesitated for a few seconds before disappearing.

I couldn't believe it. Elric looked so confident, especially when he spoke to the Shadow.

"Well, it looks like you have some explaining to do as well," I tilted my head and placed my hands on my hips defiantly. "What is going on? And why did he leave at your command? This is their home, and you seem too calm about what I just told you."

Elric closed his eyes, irritation evident on his face.

"You can be so stubborn sometimes, Anwen."

"Well, you of all people know that I have to be—and you're not the most forthcoming person either!"

He opened his eyes, a smile curling at the corner of his mouth, then sighed and sat on the bed. His hand rubbed his face in frustration.

"Herja doesn't know that you have the book."

A grumble of surrender escaped.

I sat next to him on the bed, my hands clasped together in my lap. I was exhausted from turning everything into a problem, tired of the struggle between trust and anger.

"No, she doesn't, and . . . well, she hasn't really taught me much about the Shadow—just a little here and there. But when our people started getting sick, and when grandfather fell ill, I had to learn about the Shadow myself. Anu helped a bit, giving me advice whenever she could, but mostly it was just me and the book. No one knows I have it."

Elric stared across the room, almost in a daze. "How did you find the book?"

"It called to me," I whispered. "I found it in the rubble when I went back to Herja's room at Wynfalle."

"Interesting," he said softly. "It called you."

I waited for more information, but he continued to stare at the wall, lost in thought.

"I didn't mean to be deceitful," I offered solemnly. "I—I just felt protective of it. I wanted to keep it and learn from it. Herja had the task of helping Vardia—I couldn't ask her to continue helping me. She was so exhausted."

My words trailed off, not sure what other excuse or apology I could offer. Herja's opinions—her trust—meant everything to me. I couldn't stand it if she found out about my deception.

Elric shifted on the bed and faced me.

"Herja knows about the book, Anwen. She always knows where it is, so you don't need to worry about her. If she truly didn't want you to have it, she would have taken it from you."

My face twisted at his words—he read my thoughts.

"So, she knew? How? And why didn't she say anything to me?"

"I'm not sure why she chose not to confront you—she probably had her reasons."

Elric didn't say anything else as he drifted back into deep thought. "That would explain what I saw in the forest outside our camp. Your meditation. Your moves and your energy. And the amulet."

"I don't understand," I proclaimed.

"Your energy felt different, but that would explain it—how the Shadow guides it for you. The Shadow protected you—that explains your ability to destroy the amulet. To focus that much energy and destroy such a powerful magical object—something inside you triggered the Shadow to help. Your control of the Shadow in such a short time, Anwen, is impressive, especially with Herja not guiding you properly."

"Herja hasn't told me any of this; she's been hesitant about sharing anything with me regarding the Shadow. If she knew about the book and that I was using it to learn about the Shadow, why didn't she say something?" I paced the room, now agitated. "And the amulet? It was pretty horrific, if you must know the truth. I really didn't know what was happening—I felt powerless, and that scared me. I didn't feel like I was in control at all. And the soldier . . ." I shuddered, remembering the pieces of flesh lying around me. "I never want to feel that helpless and out of control again."

Elric opened his mouth to say something but suddenly stopped. He kept staring at me, as if weighing whether to trust what he was about to reveal.

Losing patience, I stopped pacing and faced him.

"Now is not the time to hold back from me. I am trying really hard not to enter your thoughts—but you are making it very difficult. I know I have not been forthcoming with information, but you must understand—the way you left Vardia and me, and then you show up all lovey with your mountain kin? Your loyalty was questionable—not only to the other Vardians but to me."

I sat beside him on the bed and put my hand on his leg.

"Please, I am trying to be honest about everything that has happened, based on what I can remember that matters. Whatever you can tell me about the Shadow—the beings and their magic—will help me. Help us."

When Elric didn't respond right away, I pressed harder on his leg.

"Please, Elric. What can you tell me about the book? If Herja knew I had the book, why didn't she stop me? Surely, she would have wanted to know what I was doing."

A small smile pulled at the corner of Elric's mouth. His hand brushed a strand of hair away from my cheek.

"Herja always knows the location of the book."

The quick brush of his hand on my skin quickened my heart. "I still don't understand."

Elric took my hands in his, folding them together. "Herja is connected to the book—she *is* the Shadow."

TWENTY-THREE

Herja *is* the Shadow? And she is connected to the book?

What in the name of the gods does that mean? Have I been toting her around in my bag all this time?

I began pacing the room, wringing my hands in anxiety. The whispers grew louder into a steady drone.

"Please sit down, Anwen. Your energy is chaotic." Elric winced as he rubbed his temples. "And you are aggravating my Shadow."

I stopped.

"It has been quite a while for him to elicit this reaction inside me," he complained.

"Okay, fine," I complied. "Please tell me what you mean about Herja and the book."

Elric sighed in frustration—not with me, but with Herja and the situation.

"I was truly hoping she had started training you by now,

beginning with sharing her own journey with the Shadow. From what I've observed recently, I thought Herja was guiding you—that she allowed the Shadow to be with you." He paused, seeming to figure out where to start his story. "Our gods chose us to connect with the energy around us—to work with and guide our magic. The energy floods everything in our world, and we thrive off that power. But the Shadows are not energy, or rather, the energy we think of in the usual sense. The Shadows are living beings; they are inside you and me, and just as we use the energy around us to strengthen our magic, the Shadows use our powers within us to bolster their magic."

"Almost like a host," I interrupted.

"Well, yes, and, like the gods, they choose the person to give their gift to. But also, like with our magic, the Shadow must be controlled. If used the wrong way . . . " His voice faded as he turned away from me.

I knew what he was about to say—his father took that risk, and it changed him. He turned into a monster.

"So, tell me about Herja and the Shadow." I curled my legs underneath me, hoping Elric would share more information.

Elric brushed his hand against mine before placing it beside his leg. Even without touching, our Shadows instantly connected. The idea that our energies were linked in that way excited me. Was this new aspect of our powers due to our location or because of evolution? Something bigger was happening between us, within us.

"Herja is the oldest elf, Anwen. She is *the* elf—the first elf. When the gods created our people, they created Herja."

"Wait, what? How is that possible? She cannot be that old. That would make her---" I couldn't understand how much time had passed and how unlikely it was that Herja could be the very first elf. But it made sense because of her connection to the Lirreans.

Elric smiled.

"It is quite unbelievable, I know. So, when our All-Father gained knowledge of magic, he also connected with beings called the Shadow. He was captivated by their powers, their seemingly impossible abilities—almost like gods. But they refused to acknowledge him or grant him the gift of their power.

"He was angry, and they saw how powerful he was, so they made a deal with him—they would only work with Herja, and in return, they would give her all their knowledge."

"So, Odin just handed them Herja? Did she even want this power?"

Elric hesitated, unsure how to phrase the next part of his story.

"No, she did not, not at the beginning, but you have to understand—the gods created Herja, and she knew she had an obligation to do their bidding."

"So, Odin forced her to go to the Shadow?" My heart twisted at the thought of her sacrifice.

"Yes, he did, but it was not without acknowledging the trust he placed with the Shadow as well as with Herja—the trust that she would return safe and with more knowledge, more power than any of the gods could have imagined." Elric moved to the fireplace. He watched the flames shift from orange to a deep crimson—possibly a sign of his inner turmoil. "When she returned, the change in her was remarkable—both physically and mentally."

I thought about Herja's appearance—her silver hair, the runic symbols on her body, and her silver eyes. She didn't seem like the other elves anymore.

"She didn't give the knowledge of the Shadow to Odin," I explained, now understanding. "That is why he is afraid of her—maybe why most of the elves are cautious around her. She became a god."

"Herja negotiated with Odin. She would give him a small portion of her knowledge and, in return, she would choose one of her own kind, another elf, someone worthy, to accept the power and responsibility of the Shadow. It was her decision, not the gods', to give us the gift. The temptation to acquire just a fraction of the Shadow's power was enough for Odin to accept Herja's terms. So, Herja gave the Shadow to my family—my great-grandfather, my grandfather, and then my father."

"And you," I said. "She chose you."

I took his hands in mine. Our energy instantly connected again, sending an electric pulse through my body—the increase in intensity and strength noticeable.

"Yes, but she also chose you, Anwen."

"No, I think I walked into that one on my own," I confessed. "Freyja, not Herja, told me about the Shadow. I kind of demanded it."

Elric smiled and squeezed my hands.

"Herja doesn't take kindly to being told what to do, so if

she didn't want you to have her knowledge, she would have told you. There's something different about you. I can see it and feel it, and I know for sure Herja also noticed. And as for the Shadow, they wouldn't have called to you if they didn't believe you are worthy."

The distance between us narrowed even further.

"And the book—it was Herja's journal from when she was with the Shadow. It contains most of her knowledge about the beings. This is the book you've been reading—Herja's thoughts, her experiences."

That would explain the emotions I felt when I read or even touched the book. I was experiencing Herja's life experiences—the thrill of learning about the Shadow but also the sadness of leaving her people behind.

"So, where does this leave us with the Shadow? I may have called for them, but I'm pretty sure they've been following us ever since we entered this realm."

Elric glanced at the door, even though he knew they could appear out of the walls.

"I can feel them—their whispers and their connection to my energy, but it seems they have a stronger hold on you, and you with them. What do you think they want from us?"

My eyes probed the darkness, trying to distinguish between the natural shadows and the being. I knew it was there, watching us—and it seemed cautious about something.

I walked toward the Shadow.

"Son, is that you? You heard everything Elric told me, yet I sense your hesitation in talking with him."

Elric stood behind me, but suddenly gasped.

"Why are you using your power on me? Are you afraid of me?" Elric stuttered in pain.

Son moved forward, his figure shifting in front of us—like a television set losing its sharpness; the form was indistinguishable and blurry with faint, dark lines. My heart stopped when silver-orbed eyes appeared within the hazy figure.

The whisper grew into a loud sound when Son tried to explain his feelings. My hand raised to signal him to stop. "Please, I cannot understand you. Talk slower and more clearly."

Son suddenly released his power over Elric, causing him to stumble forward. My hands caught Elric around the waist before he fell.

"What is wrong? Did we say something to upset you?"

We trusted Herja. She was our friend, but she misplaced her trust. Brynjar betrayed the gift he was given.

Elric and I were both surprised that he knew about Elric's father.

All Shadow are connected. We feel the gift in everyone who has received it. Because Herja shared her knowledge with Brynjar, his betrayal affects her the most; with his deception and misuse of our gifts, our suffering is great.

"What do you mean that you suffer?" Elric asked. "How did my father's betrayal hurt you here?"

Your father used our gift without fully understanding the consequences, and he paid the ultimate price.

"But what did he do?" I asked.

Son tilted his head.

You truly do not know?

"No," I answered, but I sensed Elric's reluctance.

"My people were afraid because of what my father did, so they banished me from Wynfalle and kept themselves apart from the rest of our world," Elric pleaded. "Please, tell me what you know about my family."

Another Shadow appeared beside Son but remained silent. It gestured to Son, who started to back away from us.

You need to understand that your people were afraid of the Shadow. They didn't understand us, but they trusted your Seer. They trusted the Volun. When your father chose to betray that trust—especially by using our gift—the faith was shattered. The past cannot be changed. Herja decided not to reveal your father's betrayal for a reason, so only she can explain what happened that night.

Elric moved closer to the beings. His anger ignited. His fists clenched tightly.

I could sense his struggle for control.

"No—I will not let you keep suppressing my father's troubled past. Silence on this matter isn't an option. Why did my father change? Was it because of my mother?"

The Shadow inside Elric seethed; the silver tattoos along his collarbone pulsed with his feelings.

My Shadow, as well as the Okri, hummed inside me, wanting to quell the turmoil inside Elric.

My arms circled his waist, drawing him closer to me. My calming energy flowed into his body.

His eyes briefly closed, and his markings darkened once more.

The Shadow noticed our unusual interaction, causing

confusion.

Your Shadow should not rage inside you unprovoked, Volun, for it is against our teachings, but the Healer has quelled your anger. How is that possible?

Elric stayed silent. His emotions still not under control.

"The energy within our magic melds together; it calms us when needed, but our traditional magic doesn't work so well in your realm—and you already know that. Our Shadow magic is stronger here, and now it makes sense why that is."

Son contemplated my response.

Elric's questions needed answers. What we discover here could aid us in our realm—help us defeat Loki.

How did Brynjar become so powerful that a god joined forces with him?

Son's blurry figure became sharper—the haziness transforming into darkness.

Your father used the Shadow to defy death—to save a life that he callously took.

"Whose death did he cause?" Elric whispered. His voice trembled with dread, as if he already knew the answer to his question.

Your mother died because of your father. When he realized the consequences of his actions, he ventured into your Underworld and fought Death. He was not strong enough, and when he lost the battle, the penalty was severe. He became who he is today—Death in the living realm. And his use of the Shadow in unspeakable ways has led your world into the state it is in now.

Son glanced at the wall.

I must leave you; our council is gathering.

The urgency of his words caused the Okri to cry out. Their panic worried me.

"Wait, what is happening? Why is your council meeting?"

To decide your fate.

Elric was still in shock and didn't respond to Son's words right away.

Defeat overtook his body—the revelation about his family was too much for him.

"Whoa, what do you mean *our* fate? Are we in danger?" My insides twisted. All the voices screamed in unison. My whole body began to shake. "I thought we were allies."

Son sensed the chaos within me.

He placed his hand on my arm.

A chilling surge raced through my veins. My body jerked at the contact, but then the coldness transformed into a soothing flow of warmth and calmness. The voices faded away.

Your mission in our realm will be twofold. We will help you get your spear, but you must help us.

Son drew Elric's attention again.

"What do you need us to do?" Elric asked hesitantly.

Destroy Brynjar and release his Shadow.

TWENTY-FOUR

Steal the spear. Save the world. Release the Shadow.

How can we continue adding tasks to our mission? So many people depended on the success of this quest—a life-changing, dangerous challenge—that I couldn't help but think there were cameras hidden in secret corners within the walls, waiting to be discovered so the joke could be uncovered.

Our chances of success were shrinking. Victory appeared so distant.

Elric's continuing silence worried me. His cool gaze fixed on the fiery coals of our fire, but his emotions were intense. The struggle between saving our world and his hatred for his father played out in his mind—and in mine. I didn't block out his thoughts—I wanted to feel his pain. That was the only way he would communicate with me right now, and I needed to help him.

Hoping he would open up to me, I knelt beside his chair

and grasped his clenched hand.

A flicker of flame retreated into the ashes, leaving behind a pulsating blob of red and orange. My heart ached for him, but I knew that any words spoken would only feel empty at this moment. He was mourning a loss that occurred hundreds of years ago. Finally uncovering the truth did little to ease his pain.

"Please talk to me," I pleaded.

He immediately blocked his emotions, and his sudden absence from my mind resonated through me. My hand gripped him in pain, trying not to double over from the abrupt emptiness. But my discomfort was clear.

Realizing he was the cause, Elric took his hand away from mine.

"I am truly sorry for making you feel my pain, Anwen. I didn't realize that my emotions were affecting you so deeply," he said solemnly.

I grasped his hand once more and placed it on my cheek. Tears welled in my eyes as he opened his feelings up to me again.

"I understand that anything I say won't bring your mother—or the father you knew—back. But I do know what it's like to lose loved ones to acts of hatred and violence beyond words. I can't imagine what happened between your mother and father that led to her death."

Elric curled his hand around my face, gently running his fingers along my jaw. His eyes shimmered with many unshed tears, and so many unspoken words hung between us.

I thought he would open up to me, but instead, he pulled away.

He lifted me off the floor but didn't touch me again. His eyes searched mine in desperation.

"Once we are home, we will confront Herja. We will demand that she tell us everything she knows about your parents." I shook my head. "There has to be more to the story. Why did your mother die, and why was your father at fault?"

Suddenly, I remembered something that Hrafn said to me in Arcadia.

"Wait, Hrafn told me a story about someone trying to defy death and the consequences of that. He must have been talking about your parents."

Elric looked stunned.

"He told you this?"

"Yes, in Arcadia. In the garden, right after Elwyna---" I paused at the memory of her death. "Right after she died. We talked about death in general. I was upset that we couldn't use our powers to stop someone from dying, and he explained to me our limitations and the consequences we must face in trying to defeat death."

So, Corvus was the one Hrafn was talking about when he mentioned the battle between life and death. What the Shadow told us now made sense—Brynjar did not win the battle with death. He became Death. That knowledge and power, combined with Loki's, would definitely create an unbeatable alliance.

Freyja revealed that Corvus was using alarming and uncontrollable magic. Could this be what she meant?

Whatever happened to him in the Afterlife, with trying to save his wife, could he use that magic in our world? And what about his Shadow magic? According to Son, the Shadow inside Corvus needed to be released. What exactly was Corvus doing with his power?

The strange and deadly magic that Corvus displayed was not from our world. But what did Kenrick contribute? I remembered the deathly pale man and thought he was insane. Maybe Corvus was using his power on Kenrick.

My thoughts echoed loudly between us. Elric's dismay swept across his face.

Elric paused before he spoke, his words unexpectedly hollow and distant.

"It doesn't matter now; whatever magic my father is using, he has to be stopped. What has already happened won't bring my mother back, and what he continues to do will only lead to more death and destruction in our world."

He turned away from me, trying to hide his emotions again.

"We need to concentrate on our mission—locate the spear and get out of this horrible place."

Knowing Elric could read my thoughts, I couldn't let it go.

"What your father did in the past could help us. This could turn the tables on Corvus and Kenrick. If we knew more about what they were after, other than the spear, and what they plan to do with it, it could save our world—save our families."

I sensed something inside Elric; a change occurred. Fear and anger merged—hatred grew.

My hand reached out and touched his arm, turning him to face me.

"I know how hard this is for you. It is just as hard for me.

This connection—my feelings." I swallowed a large lump in my throat as I felt a new surge of grief overwhelm me.

Elric grabbed my shoulders tightly with his hands. I winced at his strong grip, but he didn't let go. His emotions overwhelmed me, shifting from anger to sadness to grief. He shook me slightly.

"You can't understand what I'm feeling right now. Just because we have a connection doesn't mean you know what's really wrong with me."

His final words struck me hard.

"Wrong with you? I don't understand."

"He did this to me—to you. That is why I could not let you go on this crazy mission alone—why I can't stay away from you for very long," he pushed me away gently, but with enough force to prove his point. His face twisted with pain as his eyes searched mine. He struggled to relinquish the truth.

I moved closer to him, reaching out, but he took a few steps back and raised his hand to stop me.

Confused, I shook my head.

"Please, tell me what is causing you so much pain. I want to help you. I—I love you, Elric, and no matter what has happened to create this rift between us, that will never change for me. Please." I took a few steps toward him again and pressed his hand against my heart.

He may not love me anymore, but I had to tell him the truth.

"Did you hear me? I love you, and that will never change. We have a connection."

"My father killed my mother, and I know why he did it. She

was trying to protect me—protect me from what he was doing to me."

He paused, shifting his eyes away from me. A quiet resolve settled within him.

"My mother discovered that my father was performing dark spells on me, experimenting on me, and using the Shadow in ways that would never be allowed. When she found out, she was going to reveal his deception to Herja. My father killed her before she could say anything."

My hand flew to my mouth in horror.

"Oh, Elric," I cried out. I sensed the guilt within him. "I don't know what to say, but it wasn't your fault. None of this is your fault."

Even though he didn't say anything, I felt his guilt about my family and their death.

But there was more. He was keeping something from me.

"The Shadow is strong in you, Anwen, and for some reason, we share this bond. I don't know what my father did to me, but he's using me to reach you. I've felt it for a while now." He turned away from me and walked to the mantel. "Corvus came to me in the mountain. He told me all of this, that I caused my mother's death, which was why my people banished me. I guess he needed to confide in me for some reason. But he also triggered something inside me."

I stayed silent, knowing anything I said would only make him stop talking. I stood behind the chair, gripping the back for support. The pain of his confession was clear with each word.

"I tried to stay away from you, making excuses for why I

should never see you again. I had to push you away; make you see that I was not the person you thought I was. Marrying Sigrún seemed like the solution to keep you away. Keep me away from Vardia." He turned to me again and faintly smiled in defeat. "But it seems our connection is too strong, and my will to stay away from you is too weak. Our destinies are entwined. You have a particular hold on me, Anwen. My feelings for you cannot be stopped. My father never dreamed that we would find each other and fall in love, but it is now working to his advantage, and I feel that we have started down a path that cannot be changed."

My heart fluttered, and I struggled to keep from being distracted by his declaration of love.

"What did your father want from you? What did he tell you to do?"

I immediately felt the tension grow between us.

His worried expression told me everything I needed to know.

"He wants me to bring you to him so he can take your Shadow."

TWENTY-FIVE

Although I knew Corvus wanted my power, I still couldn't believe he was brave enough to ask Elric for help in doing that.

"Just my Shadow? What about the other powers—the power of a goddess and an elder Healer not on his list, too?"

The humor in my voice tried to lighten the mood of what Elric was telling me, but he only scoffed.

"You must take this seriously, Anwen."

"Well, I have to find some humor in what you are confessing, which is ridiculous. You would never hurt me."

My faith in him only increased his anger.

I put aside my jokes.

"So, my kidnapping and death in exchange for what?"

His guilty look revealed what I needed to see.

"The safety of your people in exchange for me," I answered for him.

I shouldn't be surprised, really. Or even upset about making a deal with the enemy. I finally found my family, and if the same offer was made to me, would I make the same choice? Trade one love's life for the whole?

It seemed simple enough, but when it came down to it, I wasn't sure what I would do. One sacrifice, in my mind, was too huge. There had to be another option.

"Never think for a second that I would trade your life for anyone else's. No matter what I am asked to do, you are my only concern," Elric insisted.

"Your only concern? What about my family? Your Vardian family? I shouldn't be your only concern—they're the ones who need saving. I can take care of myself."

He leaned toward me, furious with my words.

"You are being ridiculous. Do you think I am so callous toward Vardia that I would forget everything they've given me?"

He scowled as he took a step forward, but I backed away. I lifted my chin in defiance.

"Obviously, you made the agreement; that's why you're here. Corvus believes you've traded one family's survival for another's, to hand me over to him," I said coldly. "So, what's your plan? Were you really going to hand me over? And then save me? And what about Loki? Does he even know about your father's side plans?"

His jaw clenched in response to my accusations.

"How are you planning to do it? Is that why you followed me here? To catch me? And where will you make the exchange? In Saerún?"

My previous amusement now vanished, replaced by rage.

Why didn't he tell me all of this before? Was his trust in me that weak? We could have devised a better plan than putting our families directly in harm's way.

Our emotions and energies clashed repeatedly in a steady rhythm, testing our strength and endurance. We both had crucial questions, but each intense, magical strike, no matter how forceful, never provided the answers we sought.

My energy wavered, and my thoughts were overwhelmed by our internal battle.

I needed some space. I needed to leave this room.

When Elric was about to speak, I raised my hand.

"Your father came to you on the mountain. He must have suspected that you would agree to this; otherwise, the risk of discovery would be too high, and his plan would be exposed."

I realized something was wrong as soon as the words came out of my mouth.

Elric looked at me with a somber expression.

"What did you do, Elric?" I asked.

"You of all people should understand what I had to do."

I shook my head in confusion. "I don't understand."

Unfortunately, several Shadow appeared at that moment. Son was not among them.

We are here to escort you to our High Council.

I drew in a deep, full breath, almost grateful for the interruption.

Elric nodded in agreement. Clearly, he shared the same sentiment.

The beings hesitated as they watched us.

Is there something wrong?

We both shook our heads.

"No, we are ready to hear the High Council's decision. Please, lead us to them." He gestured toward the door. "Time is running out."

The door opened, and Elric followed the beings without looking back.

I bristled at his dismissive behavior, but he was right.

Time was running out. And I needed Elric to tell me his plans.

***

Flames flickered along the tunnel walls. Just enough light clung to the rough rocks for the Shadow guides to be seen.

My head started to ache—trying to calm the anger bubbling inside me was almost impossible.

Obviously, my turmoil did not go unnoticed. The faint whispers returned. My Shadow trembled inside me, leaving me almost breathless. My steps faltered enough to make our guides stop.

The shadow figure reached out to me and covered my arm. I felt the trembling inside start to fade.

It seems that your Shadow is agitated.

Elric grasped my hand with concern.

"Are you having difficulties, Anwen?"

Instantly, the strange feelings melted away, as if our Shadows briefly connected and called a truce.

"No, I am fine. For a brief moment, the Shadow voice

responded more physically than it normally does." I gave him a faint smile. "It was an interesting sensation. I am better now."

My answer seemed enough, but as we kept walking down the tunnel, Elric kept glancing at me.

The tunnel sharply turned left and suddenly opened into a vast cavern. The size took my breath away. The Shadow guides pointed to a narrow path that wound around the cavern's sides. Oval-shaped windows lined the rock, with each opening showing the shapes of more Shadow.

Elric and I exchanged anxious glances. Will the shaky path support our weight?

The guides sensed our hesitation.

You must follow. The path will not be a problem for you.

We began our careful descent behind our escorts. Pieces of rock fell over the edge. My hands brushed along the side of the wall, trying to find any solid grip in case our weight was too much for the narrow path.

Elric followed my lead but also grabbed the back of my tunic. I frowned at the sudden pull, but he responded with a sharp click of his tongue.

"Just in case, Anwen. I cannot lose you."

I felt vulnerable on the trail when the trip lasted longer than expected. Every muscle in my body tensed from stress. It was difficult to see the bottom of the pit.

How deep were we going?

Finally, we reached our destination. My body relaxed as my feet touched solid ground, prompting a thankful sigh.

But Elric continued to hold onto my tunic.

"You can release me now," I reminded him.

He quickly let go of my shirt, exhaling a breath of relief.

I examined our surroundings, curiosity getting the best of me. We were deep inside a mountain. The opening loomed above us. Strangely, a familiar purple haze swirled and twisted, intermittently blocking the meager sunlight that entered from the top.

I swiftly seized Elric's arm and pointed at the cloud, muscles tight with the realization of the moving mass.

Our Shadow guides led us to a long dais in the center of the cavern where four Shadow stood. Son was among them but didn't acknowledge us.

Our guides flanked us, crossing their arms in front of them.

Are you a friend of Herja?

The whisper was gentle yet strong, with a feminine tone.

Elric and I answered at the same time. "Yes."

Another Shadow moved closer and pointed. His voice was gruff.

You are not like him. You are different.

I was surprised by the contempt in his words.

"I—I—am not sure what you mean?" I stuttered.

Elric moved forward slightly and was about to speak when the gruff figure flicked his hand, stopping him.

We will question you as well Volun, but now she must testify.

Testify?

My confusion was apparent. Son stepped forward.

Tell Father why you are who you are.

Well, that definitely didn't make it any clearer why I needed to testify.

My anxiety increased. The noise of the Okri grew louder. Maybe it was the hostility behind Father's words, the mounting pressure of finding the spear, or the anger toward Elric boiling underneath everything—then, the unexpected happened.

The spells of the gods ignited within me, bursting with a vibrant radiance and lighting the dark cavern with an ethereal glow. The Shadows' amazed gasp echoed through the space. Elric remained passive.

The figures began to change—their hazy, wavy features starting to solidify into clear lines. The female, presumably Mother, was the first to fully transform—becoming a beautiful woman with dark features and gray eyes. Her long, silvery hair floated around her as if made of smoke.

Father changed next—brown-skinned with even darker eyes. Both of their bodies floated in place.

I gestured at my body, hoping my words weren't as muddled as my insides.

"As you can see, there are many things different about me." I paused. "I am not sure what I need to testify about, but I can agree that I am different. The gods made me a vessel for their individual magical spells, and on top of that, I am a Healer for the Vardian People—my father was human while my mother was elf. Our mission is to save our realm, but we may need your help. It is true, Herja is both our friend and ally. She bestowed the gift to Elric—he is from the Wynfalle Mountains, just like Herja. But Herja did not give me the gift—the Shadow called to me. Maybe that is why I seem different to you. But please know that Herja knows about my gift and has given her blessing."

"Anwen was tasked with finding the spear, Gungnir. We came to your realm to locate it and take it to our All-Father, Odin," Elric finished. "We did not realize this was the home of the Shadow. Please accept our humble apologies for causing you distress."

Mother floated in front of Elric and placed a hand on his chest.

Please, let me see them.

Elric must have understood her request. He shed his tunic without hesitation, revealing his tattoos to everyone. Mother closed her eyes and, with a gentle touch of her hand, the dark patterns shifted to silver, swirling and twisting brighter than ever. Elric closed his eyes, trembling at the overwhelming chaos.

I stepped forward but was stopped by Son.

Mother is helping him.

The intensity of Elric's emotions overwhelmed me. My heart felt ready to burst from my chest. His thoughts mixed with mine—anxiety, surprise, and wonder.

But he wasn't in pain.

Mother suddenly opened her eyes and withdrew her hand, but it hesitated over his heart, as if she didn't understand something. Confusion flickered across her features.

Elric opened his eyes, but the tattoos continued to swirl uncontrollably.

The Shadow tried to protect you from him. But his familiarity with his gift far exceeded yours, Volun. You tried to hide them from your Vardian family, but it only made them stronger and more protective. Your father traveled a path that was forbidden to the Shadow, and he tried to take you with him. Unfortunately, he succeeded—your father still controls a part of you and your Shadow. There are consequences for his actions—that is your curse.

Elric bowed his head. "I understand."

I looked from Elric to Mother in confusion.

"What consequences?" I asked. Elric's frown deepened, contemplating Mother's words.

She laid her hand on my face, covering the three triangles.

Your Shadow is very protective of you as well, Healer. She did call to you, and Herja gave her to you. She is your gift and knows that your family means a lot to you—that's why she protects them too.

Mother paused with a strange expression—first confusion, then surprise.

She quickly pulled her hand away from my mark.

There is something else protecting you. I feel it inside you. Something ancient. You have felt this power, but confusion and doubt block the change.

"I don't understand." I glanced at Elric, hoping he knew what she was talking about, but he was just as puzzled.

Mother turned away, and when I tried to speak again, Son rested his hand on my arm, stopping me.

"I need answers now, not just more silence and insinuations," I pleaded. "Please, I do feel something guiding me, trying to show me something important, but it is hard to make out, just out of my reach."

I pulled away from Son's grasp, only for it to be replaced by Elric's hand.

"My dreams---" I paused. "Or memories—they feel more

like memories . . ."

This revelation caused me to stop.

Father placed his hand on Mother's shoulder.

Although no words were mentally spoken to us, their message was clear.

She hesitated. Her eyes never left mine.

Ancient beings guard the spear, and many obstacles block your quest. You're not the only one hunting for the weapon; most notably, a serpentine evil named Apep. Brother of the sun god Ra, he was banished to the realm of the forgotten. Apep knows you seek the weapon, and he will follow you to the very end. He understands the spear belongs to your god and will do everything in his power to stop you.

"Who are the Ancients? How do we find them? How will we defeat our enemies if we cannot use our traditional magic?"

So many questions, but I was afraid most would go unanswered. Again.

"Are the obstacles the forgotten gods?" Elric asked.

Not all need to be gods to be powerful. This is our realm, and we only permit gods here when they lose their power in their own worlds. They are harmless to us.

"But what about the snake? We were on the receiving end of his anger, and his power seemed all too real to us," I replied sarcastically.

Mother laughed, prompting the others to mimic her. Echoes sounded like the rustling of dry leaves all around us. Goosebumps spread across my arms.

The forgotten gods and creatures are harmless to us—but deadly to trespassers.

Mother raised her arms, spreading her fingers apart and swirling them toward the mountain opening.

The purple haze sped toward us, stopping suddenly above our heads.

From this point onward, you must use your Shadow. We will not interfere. This is your journey and yours alone. Seek and take what you came for. Our realm will be hidden from you once you leave—but that does not mean we are lost to you forever. Cross the River of Shades—the barrier protecting the old City of Spires will lead you to the sacred water. Stars will guide you back to your realm, and the spear will finally be reunited with its owner and at peace.

The haze moved unpredictably, twisting and looping around us.

Elric and I moved closer together.

His arm snaked around my waist and pulled me even closer. His hands pressed against my back as he turned me toward him.

"Whatever happens, do not let go," he whispered into my ear.

My hands wrapped around his neck, pressing my cheek against his chest.

Mother's arms were swirling in front of her, guiding the cloud and making it move faster around us.

Heed my warning, young ones. The spear is ancient and holds more power than you can imagine. Guard it carefully and do not let it fall into enemy hands, or all realms will be in danger.

Mother's gray eyes churned with the rhythm of the haze.

Do not be quick to doubt your abilities, Anwen. You carry the blood of the Ancients within you. Trust it . . . trust your powers.

The haze enveloped us, and even though we tried to hold onto each other, it easily pulled us apart. A scream built in my throat, but the fierce haze tossed me into the air, squeezing the breath from my lungs.

My fingers frantically clawed at the air, trying to make contact with Elric's body but only hitting emptiness.

The Shadow's betrayal settled within me.

They lied—they were not helping us. They were killing us.

My hands swept through the air again, trying to find Elric. When I summoned my Shadow, I was met with silence. I sensed her presence, but she made no move to help me.

Frustrated, I yelled for Elric. The haze jerked my body upward. It whipped me back and forth. But surprisingly, I felt no pain.

Were the Shadow truly killing us?

I was afraid, but should I be?

The fight left me, and my body relaxed.

Voices echoed in my mind—urging me to let the haze take over.

The chaos faded. The mist gently swirled around my body—not frantic like before, but peaceful and calm. My fingers brushed the soft, feathery wisps and the frothy, cloud-like mist.

Flighty fingers of air brushed against each swish of my hand, until suddenly, they landed on warm flesh.

Elric appeared before me, and my eyes widened with surprise.

He floated closer and drew me into his arms.

I couldn't speak. My heart stopped when I saw him. He

looked like something out of a dream.

A mischievous grin spread across his face as he leaned in close to whisper in my ear. The words were too faint to be understood.

Turning toward him, Elric claimed my lips with a fiery kiss.

TWENTY-SIX

Something rough and wet pressed against my ear. Short bursts of air brushed my skin. I brushed the nuisance away. Fuzzy, incomplete images raced through my mind as nausea tormented me.

Suddenly, a sharp pain shot through my ear. I opened my eyes and saw a scowling, pointy face.

I snapped upright, feeling a sharp ache shoot across my scalp.

Holding my head to stop the throbbing, I spotted the cause of my misery.

A rusty red squirrel with a wide, bushy tail stood in front of me. Its paws rested on its sides as if patiently waiting for me to wake up. When I didn't respond, irritation flicked through its tail, flipping back and forth. It chirped loudly at me, clenching its paws and waving them in the air.

I tried to suppress a giggle at the funny sight, which I am

sure didn't help the situation. He stomped his little feet in anger.

"Whoa there, little one," I said, raising my hands defensively while trying to hold back my laughter. "I mean you no harm."

My gentle tone didn't calm his raging fit. He started pacing in front of me, flailing his paws and wagging his tail.

"Hey, I'm really sorry if I landed in your tree, but I had no control."

I quickly searched my surroundings. The trees were huge, just like the ones back home in Vardia.

"Elric?" I shouted as I grabbed a limb and scrambled to my feet.

The screeching squirrel forgotten for a moment, I carefully reassessed my situation, hoping to see where Elric might have landed.

A flash caught my eye. Elric swung down from a higher branch and landed in front of me.

"Good, you're awake," he said. "I believe the Shadow placed us at the entrance of the forest."

He pointed to something behind me. "The wall ends here, but the trees are just as much a barrier as the stones. I think we'd be more comfortable climbing and walking among the trees than walking along the wall. Don't you agree?"

Elric's smile deepened. The trees seemed like a better option, but I stayed skeptical about our current situation, even if the Shadow moved us a bit closer to the spear.

Suddenly, the squirrel jumped on my back, but before I could grab the furball, it leapt onto Elric's shoulder, chipping frantically and waving its paws in the air.

"What's his problem?" I asked, brushing the leaves and dirt off my tunic and straightening the bag across my chest. "He's agitated with me for some reason."

Elric glanced at the squirrel and whispered in its pointy ear. The squirrel immediately stopped its chattering.

"What did you say to him?" I asked in amazement.

The squirrel jumped off his shoulder onto a higher branch, scurrying away silently.

Elric shrugged indifferently. "His agitation was with the dark cloud, not with you. It has been many years since he has seen people like us."

I snickered. "So, you speak squirrel now?"

A slow smile appeared again. He shrugged his shoulders. I took a deep breath. My heart fluttered at how his smile teased me. "Why, of course. Don't you?"

Before I could call his bluff, the wind suddenly picked up, blowing leaves and twigs around us. The gust's force lifted the branch we were standing on just enough to make me stumble.

"We need to find shelter," he said, grabbing my hand and pulling me toward him.

We hurried to the trunk and began climbing down. The branch-like steps made it fairly easy to reach the ground quickly.

The wind hit us hard. My legs buckled to keep me from falling forward. Elric grabbed my hand again.

"This way."

He guided me along the clearly marked trail between the big trees.

After a few minutes of fighting the wind, he turned back to

me and shouted, but the wind carried his words away.

I shook my head to let him know I didn't understand him, so he kept pulling me down the path. Eerie creaking and groaning echoed through the trees. I tried to look up to see where the strange noises were coming from, but the wind's force kept my eyes from opening more than just a slit.

Something bumped into my leg, making me stumble. Elric grabbed my waist and pulled me close.

"There is a hole in the tree in front of us—we will find shelter there," he yelled into my ear so I could hear him. I nodded in agreement and tucked my head into his chest.

Within a few minutes, we crawled through the hole and settled inside.

My eyes struggled to adjust to the darkness. A thin layer of dirt covered them, and it was painful. I frantically rubbed my eyes, but it only made it worse. The glass-like grit scratched my eyeballs, but I couldn't stop rubbing them.

"Elric, my eyes, I can't see very well," I muttered in alarm.

He stopped my hands from their frantic assault. He placed them in my lap and then slowly ran his fingers over my closed eyelids while muttering a spell under his breath.

A tingling heat radiated around my eyes as his fingers continued to softly rub away the pain. When the sensation subsided, he stopped his massage but kept his hand on my cheek.

"Sand cut your eyes, but they shouldn't cause you pain anymore." He leaned his head close to mine. His breath brushed my cheek. Memories of us falling in the strange haze and his hands around my waist flooded over me.

And his kiss. My heart skipped a beat at the memory.

"You kissed me," I blurted out. "In the haze."

I could sense his smile, the gentle pressure of his hand winding around my neck and pulling me to him. His lips found mine, and it was like we never were apart—the feelings that we both pushed away for our own different reasons rushed through us.

I pulled him closer, and his kiss deepened. I couldn't get enough of him. My fingers weaved through his hair, eliciting a soft groan from Elric. When his mouth left mine, I whined in disappointment, but he soon trailed his lips down my neck. I tilted it to give him better access. His hands began to untie my tunic laces. Our desire to be together drove us.

Suddenly, he stopped and pushed me away from him. His hands shot up to his head, clutching the sides as if he were in pain.

"What's wrong?" I said breathlessly.

His breath came out erratically before calming. His hands rested in his lap in exhaustion. He leaned his head back against the tree.

"I'm so sorry, Anwen . . . I . . ." he whimpered as the pain flared up again, and it seemed apologizing to me only fed the flames of agony.

His pain had to be connected to Corvus and what he did to him. I remembered what Mother told Elric—Corvus still had a hold on part of him.

Was Corvus controlling Elric now?

Elric needed to see Herja, and the faster we located this

ridiculous spear and took it to Saerún, the sooner he could be healed.

I crawled next to him and took his hand in mine. "Just rest, no apologies."

He rested his head on my lap.

My hand hovered over him; fear held me back from touching his hair. I wasn't sure if my touch might trigger the pain again, so I waited until his breathing slowed and steadied. Gently, I stroked his face, which caused the lines of his brow to soften. When I sensed him slipping into the dreamworld, I let sleep take me as well.

TWENTY-SEVEN

A sinister silence replaced the howling wind. Unease grew inside me. The feeling of loss filled our empty sanctuary. Instinctively, I hurriedly placed my hands on Elric's chest, relaxing as I watched his breathing become slow and steady.

The hairs on the back of my neck stood up. Fear ran through my body. I looked into the darkness for anything unusual. As far as I knew, no one had entered our space, but something was here with us. Sweat formed on my forehead as the temperature inside the shelter rose.

I felt someone watching me.

Slowly, I pulled my hand away from Elric's chest and held it out in front of me. Summoning my Shadow, a faint glow sparked from my palm. Illuminating the shelter with the light, I looked for the intruder.

Nothing seemed unusual, but the feeling stayed. When I lowered my hand and extinguished the light, I heard a faint rustling in front of me. The strange sound was so quiet that, at any other time, I might have missed it. But with my senses heightened, I quickly reached out in the direction of the noise, not caring what I might find.

The soft glow revealed a woman in a strange, long brown gown crouched before me, staring at me angrily.

I reared back but managed to hold back a full-blown horror movie scream. Instead, a pathetic whimper escaped my mouth.

The woman didn't flinch but continued glaring at me. I was too scared to move or even speak, unsure of her next move or why she seemed hostile. But as I stared at her, I realized I had completely mistaken her for a woman.

She looked distinctly feminine, but somehow, she was oddly connected to the tree. Long tendrils of delicate bark ran along her body, forming flowing waves of wooden hair. Small branches still linked to the tree wrapped around her, creating an intricate gown of brown and green. Her bronze-colored skin shimmered like dew beads on grass.

Her eyes drifted slowly to Elric. Her expression immediately shifted. The longing in her bright green eyes made me feel a surge of jealousy. Her eyes flicked back to me—rage etched into her features. A slow, mocking smile spread across her beautiful face.

The tree woman narrowed her eyes.

"He does not desire you. I saw him pull away and dismiss you. You must leave."

Her command surprised me.

"I don't know what you mean," I stammered. "We needed

shelter from the wind and saw your tree." I looked down at Elric. "He is sick, that's why he pulled away from me."

The tree woman leaned down and touched Elric on the cheek. I immediately swatted her hand away, which, in hindsight, probably wasn't the best idea.

She grabbed me by the throat and lifted me off the ground. Elric rolled aside, but surprisingly, he did not wake up.

"No, you are an intruder. He will stay with us. He belongs here with us."

My hands clawed at her branch-like hands, but her grip was too strong. I felt darkness crowding my vision, and I couldn't cling to consciousness much longer. As the thought of death settled in my stomach, I couldn't help but think with anger that, of all the ways I could die, strangulation by a tree was not one of them.

My life was not going to end this way.

I reached for her face and called to the Shadow. As I felt the power build inside me, my hands made contact with her head. The gruesome sound of wood splitting exploded from within the trunk, propelling the tree woman toward the wall.

I quickly scrambled to my feet and thrust my hands forward, ready to fight her, but the force of my power left her stunned and nearly unconscious.

Elric moaned at my feet. I leaned down without taking my eyes off the woman and shook his arm.

"Elric, get up. We have company." My voice sounded rough and breathless.

He lifted his head, shaking it a few times. His eyes looked

up to mine. They were unfocused and confused.

"I think she put a spell on you," I said, nodding toward the woman who was starting to regain her composure. She slowly rose but made no move toward us. Her eyes were fixed on Elric. He finally managed to stand beside me, looking from me to the now docile creature in front of us. His brow furrowed as he tilted his head in confusion.

"Who are you?" he asked. "Why are you attacking us?"

A broad smile instantly spread across the tree woman's face.

"I don't want to hurt you, my love. It's the intruder who needs to go."

Her words oozed with affection, but the meaning was crystal clear to me.

Go? Right. She wanted me dead.

Elric looked at me, confusion still clear in his eyes.

"Her wish for me to leave is actually her wanting to kill me," I muttered under my breath.

Elric faced the tree woman in anger, now understanding what the creature intended.

"If you harm her, then you'll have to deal with me. We only needed the tree's shelter from the storm. We will leave. We do not wish to harm you in any way."

Laughter erupted from the creature. Her wide smile exposed sharp, finely pointed teeth.

"You cannot leave, my love. You willingly entered my home. I *am* the tree, and for seeking shelter, you have given yourself to me. You belong to all of us now."

The wind started to howl, and the tree shook, but I had the

feeling it wasn't another storm coming. The air felt suffocating, and the space inside the tree began to shrink. Small, thread-like vines snaked their way toward us. I swatted one away, stopping it from wrapping around my arm. A thin line of blood seeped from the vine's cut.

I pulled my arm close to my chest, cradling it.

Elric slapped one of the vines twisting toward my face, and like me, a small cut appeared on his wrist.

More vines grew from the tree as the woman began to move.

"You cannot escape. We need you," she whispered calmly.

Knowing that the only way out was to use our magic, we both reached out at the same time, releasing our Shadow.

Black tendrils wrapped around the wooden vines, snapping them like toothpicks. The creature's face twisted with rage, and a deep growl erupted.

I swung my arms to the sides, back and forth, while murmuring a spell. The Shadow cut through the remaining vines easily, creating a small tunnel toward the door.

The creature cursed and screamed. Suddenly, the opening disappeared.

Elric rushed past me, extended his arm toward the creature, pinning her to the wall and immobilizing her with his Shadow. He then pushed his other arm outward, causing the Shadow to burst from his hand and slam into the wall, opening a path to the outside.

We hurried through the hole and ran down the path. The creature's tormented howl echoed through the forest. Fear ran through me.

Suddenly, a loud screech pierced through the trees, answered by several angrier cries.

"Elric?" I yelled.

He stopped and surveyed the forest. His eyes and ears were focused on finding the culprit making the horrible sound.

I could feel the hair standing up on the back of my neck. Another screech sounded to our right. And then another to our left.

"Where is it coming from?" I asked. "What is it?"

Elric's eyes continued to scan the trees. "We are being hunted."

As soon as he said the words, an arrow shot out and hit the ground in front of me. I jumped back, but not in time, as another one was launched and struck my shoulder.

Elric jumped in front of me and muttered a spell, spreading his arms to the sides. The Shadow created a shield around us. More arrows rained down on the bubble.

My eyes moved to the small projectile lodged in my shoulder—it wasn't an arrow. It was a long, thin piece of bark, carefully shaped into a deadly spike.

"Elric, it's the trees. We're being attacked by the trees."

He frantically looked around for an escape. Another round of arrow shots ricocheted off his Shadow shield.

"Do you have a plan?" he asked more calmly than the situation called for. His eyes drifted to my shoulder. "Are you alright?"

I nodded quickly. "Don't worry about me. We need to get

out of here."

He smirked and said sarcastically, "Really? And why would we want to do that? Like, I really desire to be the love slave to a forest of trees?"

Pain shot down my arm. I grasped the wooden arrow, clenched my teeth, and pulled it out. "Yeah? Well, I really don't want to be a human kabob and watch that happen."

I raised my hands to help him as we gradually moved down the path. The arrows suddenly ceased their barrage. An eerie silence fell over the forest. Not a single movement, not even a faint breeze, stirred the trees.

The sounds of splintering bark pierced the silence. The terrifying noise was all around us.

Movement at the base of each tree caught my attention. Figures formed as intertwined vines and leaves.

"Elric . . . the trees," I mumbled softly.

Tree women emerged from the trunks. Long, hair-like bark strips trailed behind them until a faint but harsh crunch separated them from their homes. They surrounded us, each wearing a delicate gown of green leaves. Their skin took on the bark color and texture of their tree homes—brown, thorny, orange, smooth, white, mottled, black, and even rainbow. Their physical appearance was certainly spectacular and charming, but their eyes revealed their true intentions—black and malevolent.

One of the women stepped forward, her hair and body accented with streaks of white.

"You wounded our sister." Her voice was deep and scratchy. "For that, you both shall pay with your lives."

Without looking at me, Elric whispered, "Disarm your Shadow."

"What?! No, they will attack us without our shield," I whispered harshly.

But despite my objection, Elric's hands dropped to his sides, leaving me alone with our only defense. After a few moments, I let it go as well, scowling. He wasn't the one who was shot with a piece of wood.

Lavishly, Elric bowed his head and placed a hand over his heart, believing he was speaking to one of the elder trees.

"With all due respect, your sister attacked us first. We are lone travelers in this strange land, and we only wanted to find shelter from the storm. We asked to leave your sister's sanctuary peacefully and without trouble, but she chose to fight us instead."

Angry murmurs rippled through the crowd of tree women. My Shadow twitched my fingers, signaling she was ready to continue fighting. I hid a smile at this newfound understanding, this new bond with my magic.

When the elder tree didn't respond right away, Elric flashed her a brilliant smile. If it made my breath catch, I knew the tree women would swoon.

Elric was charming the creatures who wanted to kill us.

TWENTY-EIGHT

Elric extended his hands to his sides. His smile grew wider and warmer. I was even captivated by its sincerity and trusting nature.

"We are not here to harm you. We only want to continue our journey. Surely, you wouldn't harm innocent travelers on a mission for the gods?"

Elric's declaration surprised me, unsure if mentioning the gods was such a good idea.

The tree women hesitated. A few stepped back toward their tree homes, surprised but fearful.

The elder tree moved closer. Her face was unreadable, but her eyes cautiously surveyed her forest domain.

"What do you know of the gods?" she hissed with contempt.

Now, rage consumed the tree women—no longer were they tempted to cower in their trees. I glanced at Elric, wanting him to change his course of action.

Mentioning the gods was definitely a bad idea.

I stepped forward to speak, but Elric faintly waved his hand back, using his magic to stop me.

With his smile even broader, Elric chuckled as if the Elder just told him something funny.

"Do you not feel their presence, my lady?"

The elder's expression shifted with his words. Now, recognition haunted her.

Elric continued. "We only need safe passage, nothing more."

She paused and resolutely nodded her head. Her lips tightened in displeasure.

The others, however, refused to comply. A burst of angry snarls and bared teeth responded to her choice.

She raised her hand. Silence immediately followed.

The elder approached Elric, examining him carefully. Her head tilted slightly, and with her eyes closed, she took a deep breath. She slowly opened them and then turned to me.

"You may go, but she stays."

Elric raised an eyebrow in irritation. "And why would I leave without her?"

She smiled at me without turning her head to answer his question.

"Because she can be used for bargaining against her kind."

My kind?

I smiled calmly at the elder, hiding the fear building inside.

"And why would you think I would stay with you?"

The elder threw her head back and laughed. The others

automatically screeched with her. The grating sound sent chills down my spine.

Elric's energy increased. His Shadow itched to be unleashed.

This was bound to end badly.

The laughter suddenly stopped. Malicious intentions from the tree women radiated through the forest.

"Do not think me a fool—the essence of the gods resides within both of you. They are not here to rescue you. The Shadow has forsaken us. They promised us gods to placate our desires and to propagate. It has been too long for us. And you---" she paused and looked me up and down with a satisfied grin. "You are different from your companion. Obviously, he possesses vast and impressive power—I imagine he would bring great satisfaction to my sisters. But you—you are special to the Shadow, and this makes you valuable to us. They will send us more companions if they know we have you."

She turned her focus to Elric and smiled sinisterly. "I changed my mind—he will stay as well. You will witness his usefulness as my sisters have their way with him. Sadly, it will be unfortunate that he shall not survive his duties."

A group of tree women moved toward Elric, hunger and desire visible on their bark faces—probably anticipating a blissful night of tree baby-making. Another group, including the elder tree, focused on me. Sharp, knife-like tendrils shot from each of their hands, aiming to incapacitate me.

My Shadow knew exactly what to do. Black tendrils shot out from my palms, slicing through the bark like daggers and leaving the tangled limbs thrashing in the air. Painful shrieks erupted, but they kept on attacking.

Elric's Shadow halted the attack, protecting us just in time. The limbs bounced off with a crackle, turning to ash. Louder angry cries resonated through the forest.

"You need to run, Anwen," Elric yelled at me. Shrieks of rage continued to swell. "I will hold them back."

"NO! I am not leaving you. You cannot fight them alone."

More trees grew around us, making it impossible to run. They became more aggressive, using their arms as swords and striking our shield.

My mind raced with ideas on how to defeat them. More tree women rushed down the path. My eyes scanned the angry mob, hoping to find an answer among them. We had to get out of here quickly.

My eyes fell on the elder.

She remained impassive as she stepped back from her sisters, letting them continue their assault without her. She stood regally with her hands clasped in front of her—a triumphant grin spreading across her suddenly serene face.

Several tree women stood around her, shielding her. My mind raced with this knowledge. She was an older tree, and this forest was almost like a kingdom.

Obeying their elder. Obeying their queen.

Elric, the elder must be their queen. I believe they will stop attacking us if we capture her.

The sudden contact with my thoughts startled Elric, but he quickly recovered and nodded in agreement.

Continue with your shield. I will grab the evil witch.

He grasped his dagger and jumped straight up to grab a branch. Swinging his legs over, he quickly scrambled across the branch with one hop to the next.

Before the guards understood his intentions, Elric landed directly behind the elder. He held a dagger to her throat and grabbed her arms behind her back.

"Stop the attack now, or your people will lose their queen."

The guards lunged forward to defend their sovereign, but Elric tightened his grip and jabbed the dagger's tip to her throat. A tiny drop of gold liquid escaped and gently slid down her neck.

The warriors halted when the queen cried out in pain.

"You will let my companion pass through your land free of harm, or I will not hesitate to kill your queen," he yelled out.

Their will to fight faded at the thought of losing their beloved ruler.

I lowered my shield, but kept my guard up. My Shadow kept watching for any small movement.

I walked up to one of the tree women, protecting the queen.

"No," I declared, keeping my eyes fixed on hers. "You will let both of us go, or I will unleash the Shadow and burn every tree in your land, including your queen."

Elric raised an eyebrow at my threat. I wasn't sure if I could follow through with it, but everything was at stake—my family, my world, and Elric. Choosing my family's lives over killer trees was easy. Their deaths were inevitable if we didn't complete our mission.

"We told the truth when we came here to do no harm. We

are searching for a way home to save our people—to save our gods. I apologize if you have been kept from contacting your own gods, but this land was created by the Shadow. Do you truly dare go against them by taking me hostage and killing a revered Volun?"

The silence across the forest was deafening, almost surreal. I quietly swallowed the nervous lump in my throat.

"I do not want to hurt you. The Shadow does not want to harm you. They gave you sanctuary. But, if you do not let us go, I will have no choice but to call upon them and destroy your forest."

Suddenly, the purple haze swept through the trees and zigzagged down the path. The tree women yelled as the aggressive cloud spiraled around them, forming a stormy ball above my outstretched hands. I felt the power of the Shadow emanate from within the cloud.

A small tendril snaked down from the ball and twirled around my outstretched arms. Another tendril followed, swirling around my body. The energy was overwhelming, but I stood my ground. A gust of wind raced down the path, knocking the tree warriors off their feet.

"I demand safe passage or all will perish." My voice was different—deeper and menacing.

The tree warriors were unsure how to proceed—conflicted about fighting, worried about the cloud circling their home, and scared of losing their queen.

But Elric's grip only tightened around the elder, waiting for a decision.

Defeat flickered across the queen's face, but it was only momentary. Soon, indifference took its place. She surveyed the group of warriors.

"Harm will not befall you, and safe passage is granted through our kingdom."

The tree women silently walked back to their tree homes. Not a single glance in our direction.

Elric released the queen and stepped back. He respectfully bowed his head.

She paused before bowing her head and walking into the darkness of the forest.

The magic ball continued to swirl in agitation until each woman disappeared into their tree. When everything was quiet and the threat was gone, the haze quickly rose through the trees and out of our sight.

I began to speak, but Elric grabbed my hand and pulled me down the path.

"No talking. Let's get out of here."

I couldn't agree more.

TWENTY-NINE

Any slight rustle or sound made us walk even faster until we couldn't take it anymore. As soon as the edge of the forest appeared, we sprinted with everything we had. When the forest was well behind us, we stopped and dropped to the ground, not caring if other dangers lurked nearby. We deserved a break.

But after a few minutes, the lack of sound, even the faint whistle of a breeze, made me more aware of a possible threat.

I propped myself up on my elbows and looked around. Another wall was not too far away, but this wall was different.

I quickly sat up. "Look."

Just as massive as a brick wall, the industrial-looking and very formidable wall stood out against the dark green foliage of the woods. Thick, spike-covered panels coated the surface. Spots of rust spread across the wall like a skin disease, but I knew looks could be deceiving. Animosity and strength radiated from its steely, spiked eyes.

When Elric saw the wall, he instantly scrambled up. He was lost in thought for a few seconds but then reached out his hand to me.

"The Shadow said to follow the barrier, and it will lead us to the river." He strained to hear the rush of water nearby. "But I don't hear anything."

He pulled me up but continued holding my hand. He looked down at our intertwined fingers, pausing before bringing them up and placing a kiss on the back of my hand.

"We need to get some proper rest before we face another dangerous part of our journey," he whispered. His lips hovered above my hand, as if sensing for any sign of pain, but then he quickly let go, leaving me craving more.

He bent down, grabbed his bow, and swung it over his back. He surveyed the horizon and pointed to a small, circular enclave of rocks.

"Let's head for that outcropping and rest for a while."

I didn't have the strength to argue. The mere thought of food made my stomach rumble. It had been a while since we ate, so I followed him quietly to the shelter.

The black rocks sparkled in the bright sun, reflecting a rainbow of colors. While Elric crawled beneath one of the outcrops, I reached across the top to touch the strange crystals jutting out from the surface.

"They're beautiful," I whispered. "Like a crown of jewels."

They resembled the crystals in the cave that linked to this realm.

Elric didn't respond, so I squatted down beside him and sat

next to him. He pulled out a few pieces of elven bread, handing one to me.

He gazed into the distance, silent. My eyes followed his to the strange wall a short way from where we sat.

I couldn't focus on this new obstacle yet. I already had too many questions bouncing around inside my head—especially regarding Odin and his relationship with Herja and the Shadow. Why didn't he say anything to me or share more information that could help save my world from Kenrick and Loki? And my ancient blood? What did that mean, and why didn't Freyja mention it to me?

My faith in the gods was fading.

And then there was Elric.

His special connection to the Shadow—and what his father did to him. What experiments did Corvus put Elric through?

But one question took precedence over everything else—the purple haze and how it came to me so easily. I glanced sideways at Elric and saw him frowning. Was he thinking of this new power as well?

I cleared my throat and decided to jump right in to talk with him about it.

"So, what do you think happened back there?"

He didn't answer my question but kept staring at the wall. I was about to speak again when he finally responded.

"The tree dwellers—they were very odd."

"They were dryads, I believe," I said. "They usually are harmless, from what I know about them, but they seemed really angry at me . . . and their gods."

I smiled and leaned into Elric, lightly brushing my shoulder against his.

"They did like you, though. In literature, they were known to mate with the gods."

Elric frowned. "How do you know this?"

Before I could respond, he raised his hand to stop me. "Don't tell me . . . you read about them in your books back in your old world?"

I hesitated before answering him. Something was really bothering him.

"Well, yes, but these dryads behaved differently. They seemed determined to harm us regardless of what we said, even when we told them we weren't going to hurt them. Their character and actions didn't match what I read about in the books."

Elric turned to me. "I am worried about our mission, Anwen, and the obstacles we keep running into. Time is running out for our people. But mostly, I am worried about your safety, especially as we get closer to finding the spear; it's much harder to protect you."

"I don't need protecting," I declared, trying not to sound harsh. "You are off the hook on that front. Besides, I feel different here, more in tune with my abilities, or at least they are becoming better adapted to this realm. I can take care of myself."

"I fear for you, and for what happened in the forest."

He must be thinking about the purple haze.

I tried to put into words what I felt when the haze descended and enveloped my body. But I couldn't. Not yet. The reason they came to me so easily was right beneath the surface. A revelation I couldn't quite understand yet.

"Look, it was just an odd thing that happened, nothing more." I tried to sound like it was nothing to me, but I could tell he was reading me like an open book. He knew I was lying.

"I understand if you don't fully trust me. I can see your hesitation sometimes when you look at me, especially when you're revealing your true feelings and concerns."

His hand cupped my face, and then his finger drifted over my marks.

His words struck my heart like a hammer. They were filled with sorrow and regret.

"I understand your feelings for me are conflicted. I sense your reservations about my loyalty. But know this: my feelings for you have never changed. I trust you. That has never wavered. My hope is that one day you will find it in your heart to forgive me for causing you so much pain."

All I wanted to do was to wrap my arms around him and tell him everything I was feeling right now. But something held me back, and all I could do was give him a small, sad smile. Nothing more.

He acknowledged my meek gesture with one of his own.

"As for the haze, well, I can only tell you what I felt—raw power. I was scared when it surrounded your body, but I didn't feel fear or hesitation in accepting its power within you. And that is what scared me more." He shrugged. "As for my abilities? I, too, feel the change inside me—something awakening within, for lack of a better word. I don't know what that means, but until we get back and talk to Herja, we'll let it guide us."

I grasped his hand and smiled, trying to show calmness.

"Please, don't worry, okay? I am fine. *We* will be fine. And we will use our powers to find the spear and go home."

My words felt empty, but I kept smiling until he nodded in agreement. Doubt kept flooding both his mind and mine.

But I was in control—that much I knew to be true. The feeling of losing control, of losing myself, never occurred while battling the dryads—not like in the fight with the Lokrum soldier. For the most part, I felt more in tune with my Shadow, and even, strangely, the mysterious haze.

"We probably should continue soon," I said, letting his hand slide from mine.

Standing, I stretched my back and then extended my hand to him.

"Are we okay?"

My meaning drifted over us—he needed to trust me, just as I needed to trust him.

Elric grasped my hand.

"With one condition," he whispered. "Be truthful with me. If you feel like you cannot control your new powers or if you do not feel comfortable at any time, please tell me."

"Of course," I said, knowing even those two words sounded like a lie.

***

Sweat soaked my tunic. The sun blazed overhead, unforgiving and relentless. What we thought would be a quick trip to the river turned into several days of walking through the rocky valley between the forest and the steel wall.

Several times, we paused and wondered if climbing to the top of the wall would help us locate the river, but something always held us back. Strange noises drifted down from the other side of the wall—odd creaks, ghostly whispers, or unsettling shrieks.

Enough alarms sounded from each noise, making the decision to continue along the neutral path between the two evils—the forest and the wall—an easy one.

But we couldn't deny the certainty of facing another adversary before finding the river, and then the spear—the Shadow made that very clear. The dryads were our first rival, so who would be the second? Apep? Or something else?

So far, nothing sounded like a hissing, evil serpent, or rushing water could be heard. We were both unsure where to go next, other than moving forward on our supposedly safe path.

As the third day dragged on, the silence between Elric and me was as deep as the quiet surrounding us. What once felt like a safe path now seemed too open, too exposed. I tried to start a conversation several times on the first day, but only got short nods or one-word answers. Anything longer than a sentence felt tedious and forced, so I stopped trying and instead focused on our surroundings and the task at hand—anything more personal or in-depth would have stirred up too many emotions.

When the sun set on the third day, Elric pointed to a group of rocks.

"Let us rest for the night over there."

I agreed and walked the short distance to the rocks, picking a spot away from him. My mind and body were exhausted from the lack of action today.

Pulling my right boot off, I began to massage the arch and heel, grimacing as my fingers brushed over several bulging blisters. I closed my eyes. I didn't care for food at this point; my body was overwhelmed with exhaustion.

When I realized I had drifted off, I startled awake to find Elric staring at me. He cleared his throat, briefly diverted his eyes to the sky, and then looked down at his bag.

He handed me a slice of bread, saying nothing and making no eye contact. He leaned back against a rock, closed his eyes, and chewed his bread slowly.

Sighing, I figured the silent treatment would go on for the rest of the evening.

With the unsettling silence of the night, along with Elric's contemplative silence, I could barely keep my eyes open anymore. I quickly ate my hard bread and curled up on my side, hoping the thought of sleep wasn't just teasing me into another restless night.

I let the tension and fatigue of the day drain away. Much-needed sleep took the opportunity, and I fell into a deep slumber.

When I finally believed nothing could wake me from my deep sleep, a light touch on my face disturbed me. My first thoughts were of the pesky red squirrel from the forest, but then I smiled.

Elric.

An intense, bright light enveloped me. I quickly dropped to my knees and raised my hands, calling the Shadow in one smooth motion. But strangely, nothing happened.

I called out again, but the absence of any Shadow presence worried me. As I looked down at my hands, hoping the black tendrils would suddenly materialize, I noticed how fuzzy my body looked.

The harsh light flickered and finally faded, revealing someone I wasn't expecting but missed so much.

"Herja!" I whispered eagerly.

Her smile widened. "You are very hard to find, my brilliant one!"

THIRTY

So many questions needed answers, but all I could do was stare at her. The shock of her sudden appearance quickly subsided.

"How did you find us?" I managed to ask.

Her silver eyes sparkled. Her smile grew wider at the sound of my voice.

"I—I can't believe you are here. I—I mean, we've been through a lot in this realm, and I have so many questions to ask you."

I choked back tears, not realizing how much I needed her until she suddenly appeared.

Herja immediately raised her hand, stopping me before I could proceed any further.

"My dear, we only have a short time to talk, so many of your questions will have to wait until we are face-to-face," she smiled again when she noticed I pulled back from her. "I know you are tired, my dear, so I will only take a few minutes of your dreamworld."

My excitement quickly faded. Yes, I completely forgot she was only in my dreams, not truly standing in front of me. To prove I was really within the dreamworld, I reached down and touched Elric's arm, but he did not wake up.

Sighing, I sat down again and bowed my head.

"It's just—I haven't had any contact with you or even Freyja since we entered this realm, and I, well, I miss that connection. And right now, we're not having much luck in finding the spear."

Herja sat silently beside me, waiting nearly a minute before sharing her wisdom.

"I know it has been difficult for you, Anwen."

I looked up at her and tried to smile, but its weakness made Herja lean in closer. Her hand rested beside mine, not touching, but the gesture of comfort radiated from her small act.

Her eyes flicked to Elric, where they briefly lingered before meeting mine again. Her brow furrowed more deeply.

"It has been difficult for both of you."

Herja looked around, and recognition slowly spread across her face. The small smile returned.

"I know this realm very well, my dear, and you have navigated through it with more bravery than I did so many years ago."

I felt her hand pressing down on mine. Tears threatened to fall.

Although she gained many of her powers in this realm, she also lost something of herself—free will, innocence, and trust. The gods traded Herja's life for the Shadow. They valued powers and knowledge more than a simple elf.

"I am so sorry, Herja," I whispered.

A sadness flashed across her face at my words.

"What the gods did to you . . . what Odin made you go through . . . how can you still worship them?" I wiped the tear tracking down my cheek. Anger bubbled up inside me. "What they pressured you to do was unforgivable."

She immediately noticed the increase in my energy. My hands emitted a soft glow, and the symbols on my tattoos pulsed faintly. My energy surged in my dreams. Apparently, there were no barriers or rules in the dreamworld.

"Control yourself, little one." She nodded at Elric's sleeping silhouette. "He will feel your energy, and our conversation will end. Besides, he needs his rest because his father's dark magic is trying to take over him."

My energy immediately flared up. I stood and turned away from her. I threw my hands toward whatever was trying to hurt Elric, but I forced my energy down.

"What can I do?" I whispered desperately.

Hearing the frantic and worried harshness in my voice, she stood up but kept staring at Elric's sleeping form.

"Whatever battle our dear friend is fighting must be stopped by him, but I am afraid he may not have much time left." She turned and rested her hands on my shoulders. "And do not feel sorry for me, Anwen. I did have a choice—the gods did not force me to come here. Many elves have clung to that version—that falsehood of my past—maybe it is their own way to reconcile my decision to leave them. But I offered myself to the gods, to Odin.

It was my decision with no regrets."

Her hands pressed down on me briefly, as if emphasizing her point with her declaration.

"The Shadow have given you a great gift, little one. Their trust in you reflects the trust they had in me so long ago." She paused. A slight smile lifted the corner of her mouth. "I know about the book. I have always known. It was important that you find it and learn from it."

"But why didn't you tell me? I felt guilty about hiding it from you."

I let those words fade away as Herja's smile widened.

"But not guilty enough to stop?"

I tried to pull away from her, my shame visible, but she held firm.

The excuses began to tumble from my mouth.

"I couldn't stop. Something compelled me to keep going. I really would have, truly."

My weak apology fell flat. Herja's smile grew even wider, so much that her white teeth shone brightly.

"Guilt aside, the book and I are intertwined, so if you had stopped, I would have called you back. I can be very persuasive."

Elric's earlier confession about Herja and the book felt genuine.

"So, it is true—you and the book are connected."

She arched her eyebrows in humor, then grew somber. Her eyes drifted to my bag lying on the ground. Although the book wasn't with me, its essence lingered inside the bag.

"We will always be connected, Anwen—in more ways than

you can imagine. The Shadow has ensured that."

Her eyes now searched mine. "The situation that you are unfairly facing took precedence over your so-called deceit. We knew that you held truth, skill, and courage within your heart. The Shadow believes in your intentions, even now, as the doubt in your power still controls you. They would not have chosen you if there was anything but goodness within your heart—we all have learned that lesson the hard way."

"You mean because of Brynjar?" I quickly glanced at Elric's sleeping form.

"What was he doing to Elric, Herja? What made him kill his own beloved wife when she found out about his deception?"

Herja looked shocked. "How do you know about Brynjar's crimes?"

"The Shadow told us. But more importantly, I believe Elric is in trouble—the dark magic you sensed is harming him. The Shadow said his father controls him."

Herja took my hand, and we both sat back down, our eyes refusing to leave Elric. When she didn't offer any words of wisdom, I voiced my concern again.

"Elric told me Corvus came to him in Wynfalle while he was with the recovery group. Corvus did something to him, but he couldn't remember—only that Corvus told him to bring me so he could take my Shadow."

Herja frowned. She released my hand and approached Elric again, placing one hand on his chest and the other on his head. Closing her eyes, her hands started to glow white, gradually shifting to dark purple.

I quickly sprang to my feet in shock when I saw the purplish haze flowing from her hands and surrounding Elric's body.

The haze gradually faded from her hands. Her eyes stayed closed, and her hands remained on his body. Several minutes went by before she slowly turned to me, and her expression frightened me.

"What did you find?" I asked expectantly.

When she still did not respond, I asked more firmly.

"Herja, what is wrong with him?"

Frowning, she shook her head quickly as if clearing terrible thoughts. Turning back to Elric, she closed her eyes and muttered something under her breath. Her right hand flicked sharply toward him. A small white ball of light burst from her hand and entered Elric. He flinched at the impact but did not wake up.

I hurried over to him, dropping to my knees in a panic. "What did you do?"

When she still did not respond, I looked up and found that she was gone.

The last thing I remembered was a gentle voice in my mind.

Find the spear now, Anwen. You need to hurry because all the children of the gods are in trouble.

***

Answers.

That was all I really wanted from Herja. And maybe a little guidance on how to successfully steal the spear without fighting a deadly serpent and other enemies, and on top of that, save everyone from a fate worse than death.

Apparently, all she could do in her rush out of my dreams was tell me what I already knew. Typical, I guess.

But what about saving the so-called children of the gods? Who were they? Was she referring to the powers of Freyja and Odin?

My eyes drifted back to Elric's sleeping form. He faced me with a deep furrow carved into his forehead. His sleep didn't erase the worries of his reality.

And Jack.

With all the chaos happening in this realm, I temporarily forgot about the others in our world. How were they doing? Were they still waiting for us back at the camp? Was Amastan keeping his part of the deal and protecting them from his people?

Shadow Mother said the entrance to this realm was now closed, so how would we get back to our friends? Where would we end up in our world?

Elric mumbled incoherently in his sleep, his eyelids fluttering rapidly as his eyes underneath darted back and forth. His breathing came in sputters and gasps.

I quickly moved over to him, placed my hand on his arm, and squeezed firmly.

He suddenly jolted upright, screaming my name in terror.

"Anwen!"

He took my hand from his arm, squeezing it tightly. "Anwen! Please, don't . . ."

His words trailed off.

I tried to pull my hand away from him, but his grip was too tight. Instead, I leaned in and used my other hand to pull him closer, resting his head on my shoulder.

"I am here," I whispered, calming him down as I rocked back and forth. I knew he was still asleep—he didn't try to pull away. His body relaxed, and he brought his other hand around my back, pulling me tightly to him.

We sat like that for a long time until I knew he was calm enough to lie back down. I gently pushed him back. His eyes stayed closed, but his face was now relaxed and peaceful.

Movement along the neck of his tunic caught my eye. I reached down to pull the cloth down a bit more. His markings on his chest changed from black to silver, as if he were using his magic.

But the silver was changing to another color.

Red swirled within the silver now, making it appear as if Elric was swimming in blood. I opened his tunic further. The pulsing patterns moved in such a chaotic manner that it was hard to believe he wasn't using his powers. The magic extended further down his chest, disappearing into the waistband of his trousers.

I placed my hand on his chest, focusing my energy to soothe him. The power enveloped Elric. I expected our connected energies, the calm feeling that usually flowed between us, to course through me, but something felt off. An unfamiliar, dark force held me back—this was not Elric's energy. I withdrew my hand, but I felt my Shadow urging me to keep touching him, so I placed both hands on his chest. This time, I kept my eyes open, determined to see what was resisting me.

A swirl of purple energy drifted from my hands into Elric. His markings flickered, and I saw a flash of silver, indicating I was winning the battle against whatever was stirring his dreams. The red magic faded away.

When his markings finally calmed, I lowered my hands from his body. I heard him sigh with relief and turn onto his side, now able to sleep peacefully.

I gently lifted his arm and snuggled against his chest, hoping the contact would continue to bring him comfort throughout the night.

As my eyes closed, my last thought was how familiar the cold and unsettling energy inside Elric felt—magic that I knew well.

THIRTY-ONE

Elric couldn't remember his disturbing dream, but he did recall feeling unexpectedly peaceful—something he hadn't experienced in a very long time. I told him about Herja's dream visit, the urgency of finding the spear, and the lack of guidance on how to do so. What I didn't mention was that the conversation centered around Corvus' experimentation on him, both in the past and apparently in the present.

As I finished packing my bag, Elric kicked dirt onto the remains of our fire. The wind began to pick up around us, howling along the length of the steel wall. The ground shifted beneath us. An ominous growl sounded from the other side of the barrier.

Elric grabbed his pack, focusing on the noise.

"I believe we shall not venture on the other side of the wall today, or any other day, for that matter," he murmured. "I would not like to see the maker of that frightful sound."

I nodded in agreement. "Yes, definitely. We should keep following the wall, but let's not walk too close."

Elric smiled.

"I believe we are in agreement, my love. I think---"

He paused, not finishing his sentence when he realized the slip of endearment. His gaze remained fixed on the wall, not on me.

I sensed his hesitation, but I didn't want him to think that I didn't appreciate his feelings. In fact, my heart lifted with every loving word he directed at me and the look he would give me. The only hesitation I had in responding was due to doubt about his intentions. Did he stop talking and refuse to look at me because he regretted what he said?

I cleared my throat, deciding not to acknowledge his endearment or his hesitation.

"Good, so let's make our own path right down the middle, like before. Equal distance from the forest and the wall. How does that sound?"

I offered him a hesitant smile. His smile gradually widened. "Sounds like an excellent plan."

We walked for several hours—Elric's focus on the forest side while I kept watch over the wall. Both sides produced unsettling screeches, hair-raising howls, and disturbing murmurs. The distance between Elric and me shrank to inches. The close proximity of our energies provided us comfort against the never-ending disturbances.

Our hands brushed each other now and then. Small pulses of energy shot up my arm with every touch, making my heart flutter suddenly. My emotions lifted with each contact.

I stole a few quick glances to see his reaction, noticing a slight blush on his cheeks.

Did he experience the same sensation? Why are our energies stronger today, causing such intense reactions with just a simple touch? Normal contact never triggered such a physical response. Like with Elric, did Herja use magic on me last night, too? Or was it the close contact with our Shadows and the growing power linked to this realm?

At least he wasn't doubled over in pain anymore from my touch. Or the sinister powers I sensed last night were nowhere to be found. Maybe Herja helped Elric with his pain without my knowledge.

I was just about to comment on this new revelation when the ground suddenly shifted beneath me, tossing me up in the air like a rag doll, and then I landed with a thud.

Elric didn't fare much better. He lurched to the side, but instantly sprang back up on his knees with his arrow ready to take down the offender.

A loud growl filled the air, followed by another thunderous jolt. The soil began to shift.

"What was that?" I yelled over the continuous rumbles.

The steel wall quivered and rippled as if it were made of liquid. Several trees from the forest were uprooted and fell across our path. But as quickly as the destruction began, it ended with barely a sound. Only a faint hiss pierced the air.

"Apep," Elric whispered as he scanned the area around us.

When nothing else happened, he finally stood up, but with

his weapon still drawn.

I shook my head in denial.

"Surely not. That was more like an earthquake."

Elric swung his bow around his back.

"We both know that he is capable of causing chaos, Anwen. He wants the spear." He paused and kept looking around us. "He knows that we are after the weapon now. So, we must hurry."

He held out his hand to me.

I only looked at it for a few seconds before grabbing it. The connection took my breath away. He pulled me closer. His face turned red, and he struggled to breathe. I reached up and touched his cheek. It took me a few more seconds to find my voice.

"Yes, we must," I managed to mutter in agreement.

I pulled away from him slightly but still held his hand. I didn't realize I was holding my breath until my lungs ached. "The river cannot be too far away now."

"Yes, let us not tarry," he smiled and began to walk, but the large tree blocked our path.

He easily climbed the trunk, helping me, never letting go of my hand. When we finally jumped to the other side, several more trees blocked our path. The destruction was extensive.

"Great," he muttered. "This will take longer than we have."

I scanned the wall, hoping to find a better path around the tall trees, but the tops didn't leave much room along the wall. I sighed, knowing the easiest way around the fallen timber.

"We can climb the wall and walk along the ledge. That

would save us some time."

Elric followed my gaze to the wall.

He hated to admit it, but it was easier than climbing over the fallen trees. He glanced back into the forest, knowing that going back in would only provoke more anger from the dryads.

"You're right. It will save us hours of climbing. But be extra careful. We don't know what dangers may be on the other side."

When we moved closer to the wall, our earlier concerns proved to be justified. Several large bulges blemished the surface. A few of the marks appeared side by side, at least four feet long and a foot wide.

"Are those claw marks?" I asked in disbelief.

My hand raised to trace the protrusions, but stopped short when a loud growl sounded from the other side.

"Something trying to escape their steely cage," Elric whispered timidly before he started to climb. "Let us begin."

I quickly followed him.

Every few feet we climbed, I couldn't help but look down at the ground, wishing we were climbing over the fallen trees again. The steel wall was definitely much higher than the brick wall, and as we finally hoisted ourselves onto the top ledge, it was wider than I had expected.

Elric thought the same.

"It appears to be six feet wide and quite sturdy."

I looked over the side we just climbed, noticing that the ground was barely visible. A blanket of white mist slowly moved below. My curiosity got the best of me, and I risked a glance at the other side where the monster with sharp claws was, but dense mist also hid the ground and anything farther than ten feet away.

"Maybe it is for the best that we not see what lies below." My eyes trailed to his.

"Maybe," I answered. "I don't like not knowing what could be creeping along with us, though."

He frowned at the truth of my words.

"Be aware of everything around you. Although our sight is hindered, use your other senses. Keep your Shadow ready. Together, our energy is amplified; let's use that to our advantage."

We crept along the ledge for several hours, noticing that nothing screeched, roared, or growled on either side of us. I was hypersensitive to everything around us. The silence filled the thick, misty air. My heart pounded like a hammer inside my chest from the nerve-racking silence, even more than the piercing screeches that had followed us earlier in the day.

The mist thickened around us, turning into a dense fog that slowed our progress. The sound of crunching gravel and soft growls below hinted that we were being followed.

Or even more accurately, stalked.

I followed Elric. My eyes kept scanning the wall, hoping—and a little afraid—that the ground would suddenly show through the fog. Elric's focus was on both sides, wondering if Apep would show up again.

Several hours passed without incident. Eventually, the thick fog began to part in some areas, offering us glimpses of the surroundings. A large hole suddenly appeared above us, and I gasped at what I saw. I grabbed Elric by the arm.

"Look," I exclaimed. "I don't remember being close to mountains, do you?"

He was about to respond when he tilted his head to the side.

"Do you hear that?"

Surprisingly, I heard rushing water in the distance.

"The river," I proclaimed excitedly. "We must have been closer than we thought."

Elric suddenly turned to me.

Shock spread across his face. He pulled me into his arms and pushed us down onto the ledge. I was about to yell at him, but spotted a leathery wing vanishing into the mist.

He pulled me up suddenly without any explanation and took my hand.

"Run," was the only word escaping. A large pointed object erupted from the fog, piercing Elric's shoulder before retreating back into the gray wall of mist.

I screamed, but Elric pushed me ahead, seemingly unaware of the blood spreading across his tunic or the next attack.

The flying beast landed on the ledge.

"There's a tower, run for it. NOW." The beast's beak pierced his side. His hand slipped from my back.

I turned just in time to see another monster emerge from the mist, landing on the ledge right behind its flying companion.

Elric struggled to his feet.

The beast bent over Elric's body. A victorious shriek escaped.

A sharp pain burst along my back, but all my attention was

on the monster about to attack Elric.

I raised my hands to my sides and swung them forward. Black and purple light shot out in all directions, hitting the winged beast square in the chest and knocking it over the edge of the wall.

I sensed another beast in the fog and shifted my energy to my side, hearing the monster's yelp as it felt the full force of my magic.

Not sensing any other immediate danger, I leaned over Elric. Blood poured from his chest, but he was only concerned about my wound.

"You're bleeding," he barely muttered.

Blood oozed from the corner of his mouth.

I looked down at my chest, noticing the crimson blossom on my shoulder.

"Yeah, well, so are you." I pulled him to his feet. "We need to get out of here. There are three so far, but there's probably more."

Several more shrieks pierced the air, enveloping us from all directions. The mist thickened around us, blocking any view of the next attack.

Suddenly, a familiar hiss filled the air around us.

Our eyes studied the length of the ledge, curious how Apep might have climbed the wall.

"Anwen," Elric whispered. "He's right in front of you."

My eyes narrowed in concentration, scanning the gray wall for any monstrous shape.

The hiss sounded again.

I swiftly turned.

"No, it's coming from behind you."

Gathering his strength, he pushed me forward again, not very gently. I clung to him, flinging him ahead of me.

A slender figure appeared from the foggy mist.

"You go first, and I will cover your back," I shouted. Another spike of pain burst from my side.

Doubling over, I stumbled near the ledge but managed to regain my footing.

Apep's faint outline grew darker. He swung upward to strike again.

My hands clawed at the air, sending a black tendril toward Apep's stretched body and knocking him backward.

Elric pushed me behind him and raised his hands just as the mist cleared, revealing hundreds of flying monsters rushing toward us.

We both gasped at the approaching battle with the beasts.

I couldn't believe this was how we were going to end.

Not now, and definitely not as shish kebabs for giant flying crane-like birds or swallowed whole by a vengeful ex-god.

"Anwen," Elric whispered.

Defeat was clear in that one word. His hands dropped.

He coughed, dropping to his knees. Dark red spread across his once-white tunic. He looked up at me and, surprisingly, smiled.

"I love you . . . I always have. Even in death, I shall find a way to be with you."

Hearing his words, something inside me broke.

No, this was not how we die. We have too many people relying on us. This realm was nothing—home to forgotten gods and ancient magic.

But we are something different—Elric and I. We can't give up now. We're a blend of new and old, and that will save us.

I helped him to his feet, holding him against me.

My strength caught Elric off guard. Normally, his expression would have made me laugh, but right now, flying dinosaurs and an angry snake were coming straight at us.

Deadly beaks and a mouth with multiple rows of sharp teeth opened wider at the chance of sharing a meal.

"We are not going to die," I said to him confidently.

My focus was on the terrifying monsters nearly upon us.

"Raise your hands, Elric. We can defeat them. By the power of the Shadow and with the aid of the Ancients."

Elric hesitated but remained standing. He quickly nodded, pushing his hands out with resolve.

"We won't go without a fight."

It was my turn to smile at his words, his absurd and completely ridiculous words, but yes, we weren't going down without a fight.

"*Vér eruey sem einn.*"

The phrase flowed from my lips like a lover's promise, words resonating in every bone within me. The veins in my body swelled with blood, throbbing, as magic begged to be released from the pain it caused.

We are forever as one.

Instantly, in that final declaration not to give up, something was released within me.

An old but familiar feeling swept over me, taking my breath away.

My eyes closed in pain as every part of my body throbbed from some unknown pressure. My hands reached higher, as if trying to grasp something just above me, hovering just out of reach, but if I could only try harder, something precious beyond anything I have ever known would be revealed.

I reached out, knowing that my body was on its tiptoes, just reaching for that mysterious force that had eluded me from the very beginning of my magical lessons. The powerful force that Hrafn did not want me to access, but now, I felt it again within my reach.

Calling me.

In a language I shouldn't be able to understand, but there it was, telling me that it was my destiny to become one with it. To finally grasp what it meant to harness the power within me—something ancient, yearning to be unleashed.

A purple cloud swirled around me—and within the mist, more colors appeared. Familiar shades of gold, blue, and black. Other colors spun around my fingers—green, red, and yellow linked with the purple. All my energy merged into a white blur that spiraled around us.

"Anwen?" I heard Elric call out, but the name sounded distant and unfamiliar.

I turned to him and saw that he was holding his hands in front of him. His silver-and-black energy marred my beautiful, pure white energy.

I grimaced at his audacity—that his energy wasn't evolving like mine. I had to do something about his interference, but shrieks of pain interrupted my thoughts.

My eyes followed the flying creatures as they erupted into red splashes of liquid clouds. Their suffering shook me from the unfamiliar thoughts. My hands wavered. My senses snapped back.

My energy shifted to purple. A voice echoed in my mind.

Jump. Jump into the river.

Without thinking, I grabbed Elric and pushed off the ledge, hoping the voices were right and the water would break our fall.

The impact of hitting the water stunned me. The cold water enveloped me, pushing me deeper into its colorful depths.

Stretching out desperately, my fingers brushed against Elric's tunic, but the force of the impact shoved him roughly away from me.

My hands waved and clawed, trying to grab his clothing or an arm or leg, but all my thrashing only created a wall of airy bubbles.

Red liquid clouds formed. Elric's bleeding body must be close, but then a burst of green pushed the red away. Yellow and blue followed, and suddenly purple exploded in front of my eyes.

Startled by the flood of colors hitting me and feeling the ache in my chest from lack of air, I shot upward with what little strength I had, shattering the calm surface of the water like prey fleeing from its predator.

Gasping for air, I quickly brushed the hair from my eyes and looked around for Elric.

My breath quickened, despite my efforts to quiet the tremors in my chest. I blinked repeatedly, unable to believe what I was seeing.

Bright colors wove their way through the rippling water, making it look as if a rainbow had exploded in the river.

The mist and clouds visible from the top of the wall had vanished. Bright sunshine bathed the shores, causing the rainbow sand to shimmer like sparkling gemstones.

The sharp crashing of water on rocks drew my eyes upward, where the mountain I thought I saw from the wall ledge now floated above me, not hindered by the ground but actually hovering. The gravity-defying rock not only caught me off guard, but the idea that the water's flow was actually hurtling upward instead of crashing below really shook my sense of direction.

How was this possible?

Suddenly, Elric's gasp echoed around me.

Bobbing up and down, twisting and turning, I couldn't determine his location. An arm broke the surface a short distance from me, about twenty feet away, so I pushed forward, only to go underwater again.

My deepest fears got the best of me.

I couldn't swim.

I thrashed in the water, desperately trying to save Elric.

My body felt heavier than usual, as if suddenly a weight was resting on my chest. My arms felt like lead, and my legs were useless, dragging me straight down to the bottom of the river.

Relax, do not fight, let your energy lift you.

But, when I tried to relax and follow the voice's command,

my energy didn't lift me but only made me heavier.

I fought, but without success.

My mouth opened in a desperate plea, but water quickly filled my lungs. The pull was too strong. My foot touched the bottom of the riverbed. Sharp rocks scraped against my leg. My body slipped to the side. Rough edges cut into my cheek. The final hiss of breath escaped.

But the rocks transformed into something light and gentle.

A large hole opened beneath me. I raised my hands toward Elric's floating body. A pulse of energy shot out from my palm.

Blackness finally embraced me.

THIRTY-TWO

Water burst from my mouth. An ache spread through me as blessed air pulled back into my lungs. My constricted chest struggled with my long breath. I continued to thrash, not completely realizing that my feet were already planted squarely on the bottom.

When I understood the situation, I calmed down, warily crouching just above the water where only my eyes scanned the new environment—different from what I could see from the river below. Or even as I was falling to my inevitable death.

The steel wall and forest were nowhere to be seen. Only lush greenery surrounded me, and vibrantly-colored moss covered the shoreline rocks. Strange songs escaped from brilliantly-colored birds as they sat in the trees. Their eyes watched me, bowing their heads with their energetic songs. My eyes drifted shut as the gentle ripples of the water caressed my face. The air was heavy, and the smell sweet as it wafted around me.

A wave of water crashed against my head. Strong hands pulled me up and turned me around, guiding me toward a wall of hard flesh. I looked up to see Elric holding me tightly with one hand while the other explored my head, neck, and arms.

Before I could say anything, he pulled me closer as his hurried, slightly rough handling shifted to gentle caresses along my face and down my neck. His worried expression revealed his feelings. He continued exploring, his fingers loosening my tunic and exposing my shoulder, kneading the untouched flesh as if he couldn't quite believe what he was seeing.

"How?" he sputtered disbelievingly.

How, indeed.

I suddenly understood why he was surprised. His rough handling was nothing compared to mine as I mirrored his actions, pulling his tunic down and ripping the already holey and bloody remnants of linen. I frantically ran my hands along his perfectly sculpted chest—no life-threatening injuries were to be found.

"How are you still alive?" I asked breathlessly. My hands kept skimming his side, now with gentle movements. "You should be dead."

Elric caught my hands as they moved toward the top of his trousers. His breathing was uneven, almost as frantic as mine. I hesitated to look up, my hands drifting to his chest where they rested on his pulsing tattoos. Silver called to my gold.

"The water . . . it called to me . . . I had to save you," my words were lost as his lips found mine—hungry, almost starving, for closer contact. I matched his eagerness by fumbling and grabbing his shoulders, then his head, pulling him in closer. Our teeth ground together in the urgency.

There were no words for the emotions flooding through me, through us. Our energies connected in a way that took my breath away, and from Elric's sudden intake of his, the feeling was mutual.

He pulled back slightly, our lips just barely touching, our breaths blending warm and damp.

"We—we need to—to make sure we're safe here." His erratic breathing matched mine.

My first thoughts were selfish—enemies be damned. Something was pulling us here. During our trek along the wall, our energies grew stronger, reacting with each other in ways we couldn't understand. And now, we couldn't keep our hands off each other. Whatever was pulling us here kept drawing us together even more.

He pulled away, grimacing as if it hurt him. His eyes lingered on my face. Gently, he brushed a damp strand of hair from my cheek. The touch sent a shiver down my spine, settling into parts of my body that were awakening.

"I love you."

Those three words pushed me into action.

Smiling, I turned toward the shore. My heavy, soaked clothes were a hindrance to my progress. When I reached dry land, I pulled off my boots and unbuckled my trousers, letting them fall to the ground with a wet plop. My tunic now barely covered my upper thighs. I wiggled my toes into the fine sand, relishing the feel and freedom from the tight boots. The anticipation of walking in the soft greenery was almost too much.

"Let us inspect the place and make camp." I glanced over my shoulder and smiled. It wasn't the most romantic thing I could do, but his expression suggested otherwise. He was still recovering from our quick but passionate embrace.

He shook his head slightly with a smile and followed me onto the shore. He didn't disrobe like I did, but he took off his boots and laid them next to mine.

We made our way through the lush underbrush, checking every nook to make sure no one was hiding. I especially examined each tree large enough to hold a person—dryads heavy on my mind.

After nearly an hour of scanning the woods and seeing nothing unusual or another creature about to attack us at a glance, I caught a glimpse of sky-blue peeking between the tree trunks.

How odd.

Maybe the forest suddenly ended in a desert or prairie. Why else would there be empty space so abruptly after such lush greenery?

However, as I moved closer to the blue gap, nervousness crept into my gut.

"Elric," I muttered, and when I realized my voice wasn't loud enough for him to hear, I yelled with more intensity. "Elric!"

Without hesitation, he dashed through the forest quickly

and recklessly.

"Anwen, what is . . . ahhhh---" he cried out as my arms pulled him back from plunging to his death.

Elric held onto the tree trunk while grabbing my waist.

"What the . . ."

"Yes, I know!" I mumbled now in awe of our predicament.

"How, in the name of Odin, did we end up in the sky?" he asked, turning to me with the same wonder.

Not only were we in the most beautiful forest, but it also happened to be floating in the sky. How that was possible was beyond me, whether magic or not—our oasis was not connected to the ground.

I craned my neck to see further around the floating rock and spotted what looked like falling water. Or rather, water flowing upward on the mountain.

"The floating mountain we saw from the wall, this must be it," I said.

The ground rumbled beneath our feet, softly and barely noticeable, but it was definitely a rumble.

Elric gave me a knowing look.

Was the shifting caused by normal air turbulence, or was Apep closer than we expected?

"Do you remember how we were transferred here?"

I shook my head as I watched a flock of birds fly past us, ignoring the two surprised beings hovering over a cliff. "All I remember was hearing a voice tell me to jump into the river, and then I lost you on impact. I tried to reach for you, but realized I was drowning, and then the voice told me to relax. Everything went black after that until I suddenly lurched out of the water here."

Elric furrowed his brow. "Voice? From the Shadow?"

"No—no, the voices felt different. Stronger." I shrugged indifferently, as if it was just another ordinary day, with a cacophony of commanding voices ringing through my head.

"Voices? There were several different ones?" he asked, eyeing me with uncertainty. "Have you heard these particular voices before?"

Even though I knew he didn't mean to, his tone suddenly came across as judgmental.

I pushed off the tree in a huff, fuming at his questions but also more at my own stressful insecurities about what was happening. Herja touched on it briefly, but hearing Elric voice it sparked my anger.

How was I supposed to explain each phantom voice that suddenly appeared in my head?

Elric sighed, aware he had angered me.

Why did he always seem to trigger me at the wrong time, and definitely in the wrong place?

"Anwen, listen, I didn't mean to sound so harsh. I mean, you can be so sensitive sometimes. No, I take that back—you're sensitive all the time," he pulled at my arm to stop me.

I wanted nothing more than to wrench it free from his grasp, setting aside all loving thoughts, but I knew what he said was true. I was being overly sensitive. Voices were just voices to anyone else, and most would see them as an illness. But I knew there was a difference. I wasn't sure how to explain this to Elric.

Or even if I truly knew what was inside me wanting—no, needing—to break free. Hrafn sensed it during my lessons, and even Herja noticed something was different with me. Then, something happened on the ledge—a new power pushing deep inside.

The knowledge was right in front of me, and all I needed to do was fully accept it and open my eyes to see the truth. But I wasn't sure if I was ready for what that truth meant, and I didn't know if Elric would truly understand.

My arm relaxed in his, so he pulled me closer, but I refused to face him. He studied me silently for a few seconds, making me look up into the questions forming in his eyes.

"Let us make camp and find something to eat," he said, gently squeezing my arms before letting go and walking past me.

I was stunned that he didn't push me for more information, but I knew his questions would always be there, waiting for the right moment to ask. He knew enough about me not to press. Not when I wasn't ready.

A smile flickered at the corner of my mouth before fading away. The spear was nearby; I could feel its power vibrating through everything around us. Watching Elric's stiff back as he moved into the forest, I knew he felt it too.

***

"Not bad for hunting without a bow," I proclaimed as I reached for another piece of the once colorful and beautiful bird. "Although I don't think it really knew that we were a danger to it."

I kept my attention on the tasty morsel because, if I truly wanted to feast my eyes on anything, it would be Elric's somewhat exposed state. My modest shift covered me while his braies barely covered him. Our clothes hung over several branches to dry. I, at least, had to keep forcing my eyes away from Elric. However, I caught him looking at me several times, too. I imagined the constant blush creeping up my neck and staining my cheeks.

Elric eyed his piece of meat, considering my statement, but didn't hesitate as he took the savory meat into his mouth and closed his eyes in satisfaction. "Well, he realized his fate once I grabbed his neck, didn't he? He put up a fight."

He raised his hand at the small dots of blood still trying to ooze from his wrist.

"Poor thing," I rolled my eyes and laughed. "The bird, not you, of course."

A soft chuckle escaped. He leaned over and gently caressed the pile of vibrantly colored feathers sticking out of his bag before he plucked one up and examined it by firelight.

"Well, I know one thing—a certain special elf will receive a grand gift wisely offered by our feathery friend." A slow but sensual smile appeared. He leaned slightly toward me.

"Hmm, is this special elf someone I know?" I asked softly.

Was I really flirting? Is this how it's supposed to be done?

Elric's smile faltered for a moment before he caught himself and responded with an even broader smile. But as his smile widened, my old insecurities kept up.

I noticed the hesitation. Did I make a foolish assumption?

Would Sigrún receive the feathered gift instead of me?

Suddenly, my confidence was replaced with doubts about his feelings. Over the past year, no matter what he had declared, it took a toll on our relationship. We have both changed in many ways. Our separate experiences weighed heavily between us.

The same questions that haunted me for nearly a year resurfaced, but I was too afraid to finally ask them. To confront him about why he truly broke my heart, family obligations be damned. There had to be something more. But I wasn't ready to open that elusive can of worms right now. Exhaustion, and the repeat of a heart shattering into a million pieces, made me give up.

"I'm tired. We should get some rest." I crawled to my soft bed of moss.

I felt his eyes on my back, confusion evident with my sudden declaration. His energy surged then settled, but I chose not to acknowledge it. His focus shifted to the fire, calming the flames until the remaining logs burned with a deep orange glow. At last, he turned to his bed, sighing the unspoken words that lingered between us.

It might have been only minutes, but it felt like hours as I stared into the darkness above me. Sleep avoided every attempt I made, and from the sound of Elric's irregular breathing, slumber was also slipping away from him.

The fire flickered sporadically, causing the shadows and my heart to synchronize with its rhythm. I shut my eyes, trying to calm the restless energy building inside me. Elric's sudden gasp of irritation told me that our energies were likely influencing each other.

The disturbance was overwhelming for him. Without fully opening my eyes, I watched him sit up, clutch his head in his hands, and rub it across his face in frustration. I instantly closed my eyes when he glanced my way. Several minutes went by before I heard him leave the camp.

I slowly sat up, watching his retreating figure. He was moving toward the water. I wondered if he felt the calming yet intense pull of the vibrant pond that had been overwhelming me all evening.

I followed him, but then hesitated in my steps. He left the camp to get away from me and our battling energies. Maybe I should just leave him be.

But the mighty song of the water pulled me forward. The gentle whispers hummed inside my chest, letting me know this was what they wanted.

They needed me. Elric needed me.

He stood with his back facing the shore. His arms were extended to his sides, lightly skimming the water's surface with his hands.

My eyes caught the linen heap of his braies lying next to my feet.

Elric still hadn't turned around, but I was sure he knew I was on the shore.

Without giving in to my nervousness and shyness, I pulled the shirt over my head, standing for a brief second completely nude. A change in the warm breeze caused my hair to billow around me, lifting it off my shoulders. I closed my eyes, letting the air caress my skin freely, and when I opened them, Elric was watching me.

I slowly stepped into the water, my heart pounding as he approached me. We came to a stop about a foot apart, his eyes never leaving mine.

I was the first to close the gap between us, reaching out to touch his chest. My finger traced along the outline of his tattoos across his collarbone and then slowly moved to his shoulder. The intricate swirls extended further down his back and chest, as well as his arms. My hand gently followed the pattern until his hand caught mine.

He brought it to his lips and pulled me closer. Our bodies, now touching, skin against skin. The sudden contact left me breathless. My heart felt like it would burst out of my chest, but then I felt his own beating rhythm matching mine. His other hand reached up and caressed my face, lingering along my hairline, brushing the deep red tendrils out of my eyes.

"You are so beautiful, Anwen. My heart sings when you are near and weeps when you are not." His finger traced down to my lips, where they parted at his touch. He gently brushed the fullness. "You are everything to me—my world, my life, my love."

Suddenly, the light touch of our skin wasn't enough. My free hand grabbed the back of his neck, pulling his body close to mine. His gasp of pleasure only gave me more confidence.

I turned to pure, uncontrollable fire. His mouth captured mine.

His arms wrapped around my back, pressing our bodies

together. My skin fluttered at first, tingling from his touch, then a slow warmness spread through my body. My energy sparked along with his—gold and silver blending into one. We fit as if we were always meant to be. My new-found bravery surprised me, but it didn't stop me from pressing my hips confidently into his. He responded fiercely, lifting me up with my legs around his waist. His kiss deepened with wild urgency, and I responded just as passionately.

Quickly, we reached the shore, kneeling on the lush grass that bordered the water. Our hands competed with our mouths, exploring and stroking, gasping and writhing with each sweet discovery. We devoured each other, our energies igniting within and consuming us—driving us to complete each other.

Our names were on each other's lips, our bodies pressed together. The space between us disappeared. His hands grasped mine as our rhythm quickened. His eyes flashed, whispering my name in shallow breaths. I kissed him deeply, repeating his name, until we were both breathless. Silver and gold gleamed from our hands, mingling and intensifying until they transformed into vibrant, animated colors—colors like the water surrounding us. Our energy swirled around us as we both broke apart in each other's arms, shattering our energy into a bright, white blaze that hovered over us before slowly dissolving into an enigmatic glow.

***

We laid afterward, legs and arms intertwined. My fingers seemed to have a mind of their own, gently tracing the swirls along his chest. They moved up to his mouth and face, outlining the contours of his ears. Everything about him needed to be touched. To be remembered.

He did the same with me. Our hands still exploring, rediscovering parts of our bodies that were hurriedly touched earlier, now needing gentler attention, until we couldn't stay apart any longer. Soon, our energies ignited, driving us to the brink of darkness, holding onto each other until we exploded into thousands of dazzling stars, lighting the universe and the world with our magic.

"I love you," I whispered before closing my eyes.

Sleep finally found me.

***

My eyes fluttered open as Elric's fingers softly and affectionately stroked my arm. His touch traced down my spine. Every gentle contact sent a shiver through my body. A slow smile crept across my lips. A long-ago memory of waking up with his arms around me, my head tucked into the crook of his neck, floated through my mind. I shifted slightly, only to feel his arms tighten around me.

"I don't want to let go of you this time," he said, kissing the top of my head. "I should have held onto you back in the cave."

I smiled at his reference to the shared memory—our time in the cave when he was injured. We barely knew each other—me as the hostage and Elric as the kidnapper—but I crawled into his bedding when he was shivering with fever. This time, I didn't pull away; I only moved closer to his body. My chin rested on his chest. I looked into his eyes and smiled.

"You remembered," I said. My satisfied grin grew wider.

His expression grew serious. "How could I forget the first time I held you in my arms? I remember reluctantly letting you go."

I tweaked his nose in fake irritation. "I remember how my heart leaped at the feel of you near me, but I also remember that I was a captive."

Suddenly, my humor faded. My finger gently traced the curve of his mouth. I leaned over and softly pressed a kiss on his lips. Love shadowed his features.

"I should never have let you go," I whispered, peering into his eyes with sadness.

But my statement had a different meaning—Sigrún took him away from me. I should have stood up to her.

He didn't answer, but he knew what I was thinking. Everything changed for us when we entered the kingdom of his people. We could never change the past, but we could fight for our future.

I settled deeper into his arms, silently promising never to leave his side. No matter what Kenrick, Corvus, and Loki were planning, our fates were connected. Sometimes our path was messy, but we were following the one our ancestors laid out—not just for me. I knew that now as our bodies fit perfectly together. All my life, I felt like an unfinished puzzle, pieces scattered, maybe some missing at times, but at this moment, I finally felt complete—the missing piece being Elric.

My eyes drifted up. The tree canopy moved briefly in the breeze, revealing a small patch of the night sky. Not a single cloud blocked the bright stars as they winked at us from above. Suddenly, a flash of light shot across the tiny sky window. I tensed up, then shivered. An instinctive feeling took hold of me.

Something ancient floated down from the sky. Instantly, my focus shifted—my eyes darted to the water.

Elric's arms tightened around me. "You're shivering. Let us move back to the warmth of our fire."

I concentrated on the water, ignoring Elric. Something was out there watching us. I sensed their energy, but it was unlike anything I had ever experienced.

"Anwen?" Elric whispered, concern now clear in his voice. He looked where I was pointing.

I sat up, my eyes still focused on the water, slowly gliding across the calm surface. Looking for anything that might have caused the hypersensitive force that now seemed to weigh me down.

Elric sensed something was wrong, so he quickly and stealthily grabbed his braies along with my shift. We hurriedly dressed and knelt back on the mossy bed, not moving any closer to the water.

We waited.

A sudden gust of wind pushed against us. A melodic voice floated up from the vibrant depths of the water. I tilted my head slightly, hoping to catch a few words from the air, but they weren't just words—they were a song.

"Am I dreaming?" I asked Elric, desperately hoping that someone else was seeing the same supernatural sight. But his surprised expression was all I needed to see.

“By the gods, I cannot help but be mesmerized by the enchantress singing from beyond,” he murmured softly. "But I do not believe we are in danger of falling under her spell.”

He turned to me and, surprisingly, smiled. “I feel she is singing us a love song.”

Soon, the ‘she’ was joined by several other ethereal voices—some deep and smooth, while others lilted higher than thought possible.

Now, the voices came not only from the water but all around us. We turned every which way to find the omnipresent presence, but to no avail. When we twisted back toward the water, the mysterious beings stood on the shore.

THIRTY-THREE

They pulsed with the brightness of a million stars, flickering in and out, where only within a precious second could one catch a glimpse of an actual outline of a figure. There were nine people in total, swaying slightly to their own droning hymn.

We stumbled to our feet. Elric automatically went for his weapons, but they were still back at camp. Instead, he shifted slightly in front of me, raising his hands with palms out in a defensive stance.

Although I appreciated his desire to protect me, I knew these beings weren't here to hurt us. I felt their melody drift on the breeze, softly floating toward us and weaving through the wind until it gently entered my body. The sensation might have overwhelmed me, but the lyrical invasion only brought me peace and calm, along with the reassurance of safety.

The figures made no move toward us, but continued to sing, now their voices melding into a soft hum. The beautiful love song transformed into a gentle drone, altering both the brightness and the color of their bodies.

Various shades of red, orange, green, purple, and blue circled around them, reflecting the hues of the water.

I moved closer to Elric, leaning into him and whispering. "Look at the water."

The water rippled gently before swaying back and forth, as if dancing.

He moved his hands higher, but I quickly placed mine on his arm, gently pulling it down to his side. The figures began to move inland, single file, and away from us. Their chanting continued, but it didn't fade when they walked away—it grew louder and surrounded us.

Beckoning.

"I think they want us to follow," I tilted my head up to the night sky peeking through the tree branches. Strangely, where the sky was filled with twinkling stars just a few minutes ago, only solid blackness remained.

Elric observed the dark, starless night. "It seems the gods are visiting us tonight."

I let his declaration sink in, but I didn't sense the gods were involved in this light show. I slowly shook my head in thought. "I think it is something more ancient than the gods."

Elric took my hand. We followed the light people. As we ventured farther into the forest, their humming turned into a whisper. The breeze that brushed our skin along the shore stopped in the forest, leaving oppressive heat radiating down on us. Silence, except for the soft hum, filled our surroundings. Not a single animal dared to make a sound of protest as we moved deeper into the forest.

We must have been following them for at least an hour, but in reality, it could have been less or even more. Our bodies moved automatically, not noticing that our feet were bare and sensitive to the sharp brush of branches, pine cones, and rocks.

Finally, the nine figures stopped in a small clearing. A square, flat stone altar sat in the center. Behind the altar stood a tall obelisk. The dark greenish-black stone towered over everyone as the figures formed a circle around it.

My breath hitched. I recognized the obelisk.

Elric pulled me closer. "What is it, Anwen?"

"I—I've seen that obelisk before—a smaller one. Herja and the others said it was ancient, but Herja couldn't read the symbols." I looked up at Elric. "Apparently, I knew what it said, and I spoke in a different language, but I didn't realize it at the time."

"Why didn't Herja say anything to me?" His frown grew into a scowl. His hand gripped mine tighter.

I shook my head. "She didn't know what it meant, so she made us swear not to tell anyone until she figured it out."

Elric's scowl deepened, and I guess I couldn't blame him, especially now, as we stood in front of strange beings surrounding the same type of obelisk.

But he soon relaxed, bringing my hand up to his lips. "Herja always had a problem sharing her thoughts, but she must have had a good reason for keeping it from everyone." His eyes shifted to the figures. "And now, I believe we shall discover the truth—hopefully find the connection."

The humming ceased. They raised their hands above their heads, then slowly lowered them to their sides, where they clasped each other's hands. The surrounding light diminished until only a gentle glow remained from their bodies—a radiance that emanated from within.

The figures fell to their knees as the obelisk gradually started to glow—not just any quick flash of light, but a blazing sun-like brightness. Elric and I covered our eyes, barely able to withstand the intense whiteness of the beam. Surprisingly, the light was free of heat.

As quickly as the light appeared, it suddenly faded away, revealing a lone figure standing in front of the obelisk. Her white robe was covered with black symbols—the same symbols etched on the obelisk. Long, dark hair curled around her shoulders, but when she shifted slightly to the side, silver shimmered within her strands. Yet, when she moved again, a flash of blue radiated. Every movement the figure made shimmered with brilliant colors.

Elric's hand tightened around mine, but neither of us could look away from the beautiful figure. Her brilliance hypnotized us. So much so that we didn't notice all the figures had now turned to face us. Their bodies had lost most of their glow—just enough to show their strange yet familiar features.

They stared with dark eyes, probing mine as if daring me to voice what was creeping closer into my consciousness. Each one embodied a single trait of those we left behind—family and friends. They were a mix of everyone I knew in our realm, from the pointed ears of the elves to the pebbly skin of the Rock Giants. But their features never stayed fixed. Their bodies shifted from one form to another until they became a blur of all.

I stepped forward, my eyes fixed on their beckoning hands. Elric reached for me, but his hand slipped from my arm as if it were coated in oil. The pull of the figures was too strong. My body moved instinctively. Elric fell in beside me—either drawn by the same force tempting me onward or for some noble reason to keep me safe.

I smiled at the memory of us together, just minutes ago, but it felt like a lifetime. Or maybe it was the feeling of time standing still in the presence of these otherworldly beings.

Otherworldly.

The idea of their arrival into this world, landing on the floating forest, only made sense with that one word.

Who were they and where did they come from?

And why were they here?

I suddenly stopped when the dark-haired figure moved toward me. She got within several feet, close enough to reach out and touch me.

And she did. Her hand rested on my cheek, then gripped my shoulder.

She gave me the most radiant and affectionate smile. Every worry or doubt vanished. I closed my eyes and took a deep breath as an understanding flowed through me.

Startled by the woman's sudden touch and my reaction, Elric lurched forward but was immediately stopped when she turned her attention to him. She reached out and brushed his shoulder, placing a firm yet friendly hand on it. He relaxed instantly.

"We have been waiting for you, Healer Anwen of Vardia and Volun Elric of Wynfalle. It has been a long, perilous journey in both realms, both separately and together," she spoke softly but with authority. Her words, spoken aloud but whispered within our minds, gently flowed through our bodies. Her eyes drifted over us slowly, silently letting us know that she understood the difficulties of our past. A slight smile touched her lips. "But all hardships between Vardia and Wynfalle, between the Healer and Volun, were meant to be united . . . in more ways than one."

I felt the blush creep up my neck, burning my cheeks.

How could she possibly know about tonight? Her insinuation should have bothered me more, not because I regretted what happened, but because of her attitude that she knew everything about us.

Feelings of wonder and reverence aside, I frowned.

"It seems you know everything about us, but yet, we know nothing about you," I smiled heatedly in return. "Who are you? Why are you spying on us?"

Elric tensed beside me, but I sensed the same questions burning inside him.

The woman smiled even wider, showing no signs of being offended by my accusation. Surprisingly, she seemed to thrive on my assertiveness. I noticed that the other beings started to fall back behind her, grouping together.

The woman reached for my hands, gently grasping them

and pulling them close to her chest. Her smile faded, and a look of concern crossed her delicate features.

"We are known by many names within your realm—creator, traveler, voyager, even destroyer—but one name that commands respect among your people and the Mountain Elves is Ancient."

One hand gently touched my cheek while the other rested on my chest. "Every experience, every trial, every triumph—every tear and every smile—has led you to this point in time."

Her smile deepened. She closed her eyes. "I feel their thoughts inside you, Anwen—so lonely and frightened—but I also feel their trust and faith in you."

"The Okri," I stated.

"Yes. My sons and daughters have been watching the events in your realm for a long time. When the god Loki became uncontrollable, Odin and the others should have stopped his violence—the gods needed to look out for their own."

"Yet, you did nothing when the gods couldn't control him," Elric whispered hotly.

"On the contrary, my Volun," she said calmly, eyeing Elric. "We observed from above, knowing that certain events must happen for our interference—to restore things to their original order."

"And what is that original order?" I asked. "How far back do you go to put things right again?"

The woman's hand pressed a little more against my chest, causing the Okri to start whispering.

"Your destiny, Anwen, and even yours, Elric, has always been written among us, told in the heavens, blessed upon the stars—for your histories, it is as it will always be—there is nothing to change. But, for your world and recent events, order needs to be restored."

"Tell us our purpose," I pleaded. "If our past is not to change, then tell us why we are who we are and what needs to be done to defeat Loki."

A look of admiration flickered across the woman's face. "Anwen—born of the red moon, chosen by the goddess of love, keeper of the gods' power, gifted with the magic of Hrafn, answered the call of the Shadow, and protector of the Okri. It is only fitting that your blood calls to the most ancient of magic. Your purpose is entwined with the stars—with us. Only you can answer to your own destiny. You are the key to Saerún."

The woman placed her hands on either side of my head. Her fingers of knowledge prickled within my mind—layer by layer, the answers burst free in intricate fashion. My heart stuttered and my body pitched. Elric's arm snaked around my waist, but he didn't pull me away. Somehow, he understood the importance of this moment.

For the first time, everything I knew about my surroundings fell into place, like the story of my life unraveling—the characters, the plots, and even the start of the climax became clear. All that remained was a happy ending—and I wasn't sure if that was even possible.

"Of course, your story hasn't ended, my dear—it's just beginning. Everything you have endured has led to this moment, this particular point in time, and what comes next will alter the course of your fate. Your parents recognized how special you were at your birth. The mark of the Healer set you apart, but it was the sacrifice of your mother and the influence of the gods that set your destiny in motion—Kenrick and Brynjar understood this and made a deal with another god driven by vengeance. The Ancients created the gods, and then the gods chose to create others—Lirreans, elves, humans—all their powers are connected to the future of your realm. Loki will use everything and everyone—even his trusted allies—to seek revenge. You are a powerful force, Anwen. The key to stability. The one who can open the door between order and chaos. The one who can save the realms from Loki's destructive plans. Loki knows this and will use you, along with your family and friends, to succeed in his goal. In the beginning, chaos ruled the worlds, and that is what Loki aims to recreate.

"A new chapter awaits you, Anwen. The Shadow recognized the ancient blood and power within you, and you answered their call—granting you their sacred power. I feel it stirring inside you now. They know you are their only hope for survival.

"And you, Volun," she placed her hand on his chest, briefly closing her eyes before opening them and gazing deeply into his. "Your connection to Anwen is tangible—a relationship initiated by your father, a bond that united you. Brynjar's desire to conquer death and use you as a conduit opened the pathways to your ancient blood. You are the key to holding back chaos. Your father believes he has overcome your Shadow, your powers, and your desire to protect Anwen, but it has only made them stronger. You have become her protector. You are bound by blood and magic. Without you realizing it, the gift of the brooch—the spell of protection—has linked you even more. The powers of the Shadow and the Ancients combined to guard you." The Ancient paused. A troubled expression flashed across her face, but quickly faded. "What you have been experiencing is the residual Death magic brought forth by your father—your Shadow is defending you, my dear Volun—fighting the foreign enemy inside you. The battle has been fierce, but the end is in sight."

"What can I do?" I asked. "There has to be something I can do—with all the powers within me, how can I help Elric defeat this Death magic?'

The woman's eyes never left Elric. "The Volun knows what he must do—what needs to be accomplished at the end."

I faced Elric. "Tell me, and I can help."

Elric kept staring at the woman, a grim smile curling the corner of his lips. "It is already written in the stars, Anwen. My task is to protect you at all costs."

I glanced at the woman and then back to Elric. "What does that mean?"

Fear took hold of me—the 'protect at all costs' statement triggered alarms.

"Your mother tried to protect you." The Ancients' eyes never left Elric. "Her sacrifice was felt across the stars."

"But was it enough?" Elric whispered.

The Ancient's brow furrowed, unsure how to answer his question.

"No," she said softly. "No, it was not."

A frown creased Elric's lips.

Panic gripped my heart during their exchange. But before I could voice my concerns, the group moved toward the altar.

The Ancient finally turned to me. "We have been monitoring your lives. Stories will be told of Healer Anwen and Volun Elric's bravery at the shores of Saerún—chronicled in the heavens and the stars. But, alas, you are needed elsewhere, so let us give you what you came for, and then the rest of your story, and how it shall end, is up to you."

She motioned us forward. We carefully made our way to the altar. I was expecting the spear to be easily available for us to take back to our realm, but the smooth surface remained bare.

The Ancient stood before the obelisk. My focus shifted from her to the black monolith—chaos erupted across its surface. The runic symbols swirled and rearranged until forming a circle. A small engraving of a raven appeared on each side of the circle. As Elric and I moved closer to the obelisk, soft voices emanated from within, calling to us.

"The monks are aware of your mission and have summoned the mighty spear of Odin. It will be yours to command, but be warned—Gungnir's power is immense and captivating, yet it can also be manipulative for the wielder. Only a steady hand and a clear mind can control its strength. The magic perceives only good or evil—there are no gray areas in its truth. As its master, you will be protected, but it will also destroy those it considers deceitful."

Her eyes never left mine, piercing the meaning of her words deep into my subconscious before placing our hands on the drawings of the ravens on the obelisk. She positioned her hands on each side of the circle. The group moved around us, encircling the obelisk. Elric and I barely had a chance to speak before a bright light erupted around us.

Soft words caressed my thoughts.

Vér eruey sem einn.

We are forever as one.

THIRTY-FOUR

The bright light that had previously surrounded us suddenly plunged us into a dark, stormy gray. Waves crashed, thrashing and clawing at the rocky butte we now sat on. I lifted my head slightly but quickly covered it with my arms. An enormous wave surged across the surface. I reached out and grasped Elric's hand tightly, holding on with all my might.

Where did the Ancients send us?

"Anwen?" Elric yelled over the crashing waves. "Can you see anything?"

I tried to lift my head, and this time with success as the last wave sprayed across the rocks. "I think the waves are dying down a bit."

We quickly got to our feet.

"Where are we?" Elric muttered in awe. He spun around in a circle, trying to understand how we ended up on the rock in the middle of the sea. He looked down at his body. "And what are we wearing?"

Strange tunics and trousers covered our bodies, close-fitting yet comfortable. Woven into the gray fabric were small black runic symbols—the perfect camouflage for the stormy darkness surrounding us. Another wave crashed against the black rock, sending cold spray across our faces. Water, dark and wild, hammered against the scraggly island, which was no more than fifty feet across but at least several stories high, protruding into the sea. The dark gray clouds churned, offering no sign that the sun would break through anytime soon.

"Elric, look." I walked to the center of the butte where a tall obelisk stood. "It looks like the one on the floating mountain, but the symbols are different."

Elric's hand reached for the obelisk, gently tracing the symbol that resembled a spear. Two ravens were carved on each side, their wings extended and touching the spear's staff.

"I don't understand," he shook his head. "Why are we here? Where is the spear?"

I scanned the horizon slowly and deliberately. This place felt familiar—the water, the movement, the darkness. My brow furrowed as I tried to see farther out at sea—something was there, but it was hard to make out with the chaotic clouds, twisting and swirling. The sudden movements played tricks along the horizon.

"Elric," I murmured as I pointed out to the sea.

He followed my gaze and gasped.

Several towers emerged from the water, followed by shorter spires with fortifications forming between them. Four more rocky peaks burst from the sea, rising from the bottom as if pushed up by the land's faults. Yet, no quakes or rumbles followed its disruptive and violent rise into the sky. A calm glow bathed the castle even though the sun remained hidden behind the streaking, ominous clouds—a jewel amid the turbulent darkness of the sea. The gleaming tranquility of the sea castle contrasted sharply with the violent white caps of the waves crashing against it.

My eyes refused to stray from the marvelous sight, but Elric kept watching the sea around us. Danger was always nearby.

He walked to the far side of the island. "Anwen, look. To the east."

Something in his voice made me reluctantly turn away from the grand coral castle. Majestic rock formations lined the shore, creating the illusion of more castle-like spires rising from the depths. My breath caught as a miserable scream of anguish escaped.

How could this be?

Instant denial descended deep within me. Impossible. The scene unfolding before us seemed unlikely.

But I knew for a fact we were at the end of our journey.

"We are in Saerún," Elric stated before the words formed on my lips.

Our friends. We left them in Sorayn to die at the hands of the Kaftar. But here, in Saerún, a battle was raging.

Snippets of the war swept in and out with the wind—clashing steel, roaring commands, screaming soldiers. It was hard to tell the soldiers' jumbled bodies apart from the blackness of the sand. It was a nightmare, but still, I couldn't take my eyes away from the chaotic scene. A horn sounded, bringing more cries of fury. My eyes quickly scanned the cliffs surrounding the shore—nine dark obelisks towered along the edge. My hand flew to my mouth in dread. Between the shadowy towers were the warriors of Vardia. Their white-and-gold armor contrasted with the dark monoliths. The flag bearers sat majestically atop their stallions, the blue Vardian flags held high above them. Several lines of warriors dismounted, grabbing ropes already slipping down the sides of the cliff, ready for the signal to lunge over the rock, rappelling into the fight.

My eyes drifted back to the unusual flags flapping in the gusty wind—three black, interconnected triangles with a golden hourglass at the center. My hands moved to Odin's mark along my face and then grasped the necklace hanging from my neck. Their tribute, a huge display of faith in me, only heightened my apprehension—and sense of duty.

Elric must have recognized the symbol on the flag. He grabbed my hand and gave it a gentle squeeze. "I am not sure how we ended up in Saerún, and I know you are thinking of our friends still being held by the Kaftar, but it is up to us to bring this chaos to an end. We need to focus, Anwen, and find the spear."

I nodded faintly, but I couldn't tear my eyes away from the fight. "Our people are there, Elric. My grandmother is fighting."

Elric pulled me toward him and turned my face so I was looking at him. "Then we must hurry and help them."

A tremor shook beneath our feet. We looked west again,

noticing a bridge that connected the rock formation to the castle. The blue-gray waves crashed over the jagged crossing, making the journey uninviting for anyone crossing the narrow ledge.

I walked to the cliff, cautiously eyeing the dangerous bridge. Elric put his hand on my shoulder, giving it a confident squeeze.

"We can do this, Anwen. Have a little faith." I felt his self-confidence through his touch. He squeezed my shoulder again. "Let us hold on to each other as we cross."

I nodded, hoping my self-doubt wouldn't show. "Follow me."

Elric didn't argue but stayed close behind. Waves slammed against the rock, splashing freezing spray over our already soaked bodies. I tried not to look into the water, knowing that peering into the bottomless depths would only intensify the feelings inside me—dark, cold, and unforgiving. My family and friends were fighting our enemy. Kenrick, Corvus, the Lokrum, and Loki were only a few hundred yards away. Doubt crept into my soul.

What if I couldn't save them? What if the spear wasn't here?

Screeches sounded around us. Elric tugged on my tunic and paused.

I looked down at the water, wondering where the sad cries were coming from.

Dark shapes swirled in the turbulent water, crossing over each other in a hurried whirl.

The high-pitched squeals became more frantic. A small, delicate tail fin broke from the water, giving a quick kick and spraying water over us. Another larger fin emerged right behind it, but came up further in the water, revealing the dark turquoise body of a man. Iridescent scales reflected as he dove back into the water.

"The merpeople are restless," Elric yelled above the howling wind and the rolling waves. He gave me a slight push. "Hurry, Anwen. We must cross quickly."

My heart raced with the fury of the waves as I sped up. More merpeople gathered around the bridge, not angry or violent, but as if they were encouraging us, offering support for our quest. When we finally reached the castle, a portcullis barred our way.

"Hello?" I yelled, examining the other side of the grating.

A short but dark, narrow hall led to another black double door.

I clutched the shell-encrusted grates and shook them until my hands bled from the sharp coral. Impatience riddled my words as I yelled even louder. "Hello, is anyone there?"

Elric placed his hand on mine, stopping the shaking. "They know we are here, Anwen." He paused and closed his eyes. "I feel them, don't you?"

I stared at Elric in frustration. His face showed calmness and serenity. How can he be so relaxed when all of our loved ones were dying? His lack of urgency angered me.

"I don't *feel* anything, and all I want right now is for someone to wake up and let us in so we can save our families!" I shook the portcullis again, now calling to my powers.

Purple mist escaped my hands and wrapped around the grate, encompassing every inch until the portcullis disappeared under the cloud. To my satisfaction, the heavy quaking of the portcullis raising met my ears.

"Well, that's one way to get it open," Elric muttered under his breath. I chose to ignore the disappointment in his voice, knowing what he was hoping. Because I was wishing the same thing—why was everything so difficult? The monks should have known we were coming, so why didn't they open the doors for us?

Or was this a test?

Maybe our quest for the spear wasn't over.

We quickly moved into the dark hallway, only for the purple haze to descend on the black door, but it held firm.

Without thinking, I slammed my fists against the encrusted metal.

"Please, open the door. We are wasting time," I yelled at the top of my lungs.

Nothing happened.

Elric scanned the frame, running his hand along the coral. His frustration boiled over, and he, too, suddenly slapped the door, yelling out in anger. His hand came up again, ready to hit the door with more force, but suddenly hesitated. He leaned down and gasped.

"Anwen, look," he pointed to a small niche beside the door. Dead corals marred the area around the hole, but the shape was surprisingly familiar.

I pulled the necklace from my throat and placed the hourglass within the hole. The amber stone shimmered brightly. The metal door shuddered open.

My eyes met Elric's, not yet understanding the significance

of why my necklace opened the tower of Saerún. He took hold of my hand, accepting his reassurance without a word as we walked through the door together.

Cold, dank, and eerie silence met us as we slowly traveled down another dark hallway. Coral embedded within the rocky surface left the feeling of death all around. The only noise was the soft clicks of our shoes on the crumbling path. Elric gently removed his hand from mine.

"We should be on the defense at all times," he whispered as he moved his hands to the front of his body.

I mirrored his movements but was only half paying attention. Questions swirled inside my head.

Why was my necklace the key to opening the door? A door meant only for the monks of Saerún?

I knew I had to pay closer attention to the situation and our task, but it was becoming more difficult as we walked further down the hall. My necklace felt heavy around my throat, tingling against my skin as if it knew it was nearing something important.

A light at the end of the hall spurred us into action. We moved forward more swiftly but remained highly aware of any lurking danger. The necklace continued to hum, if not more intensely, against my skin, sending tremors down my body. We stopped just outside of a large chamber.

We entered the chamber cautiously, still noticing the mixture of rock and coral embedded within the floor and walls, but now they were smooth and polished to perfection. Unlike the ghastly, tomblike feeling of the hall, the chamber offered vitality and energy—a most powerful and unyielding life force.

Marble statues lined the sides, each at least twelve feet tall. Finely chiseled hoods obscured the cloaked figures, making it impossible to see the details of their faces. But I felt as if their eyes were following us as we moved through the chamber. Elric's body tensed up, expecting a fight. His cautious behavior rubbed off on me. Maybe he also felt the stone-cold eyes of the cloaked figures watching us.

That was impossible, I thought. Statues were not alive, and they certainly couldn't hurt us.

But the feeling of something otherworldly surrounding us never left me. We continued to walk toward the bright entity.

A burst of light shattered the darkness, making it almost impossible to see. Elric shielded his eyes, but something prevented me from doing the same. The vibration from my necklace became almost intolerable. The light grew brighter. My hand wrapped around the hourglass, surprised at the power emitting from the amber. The chamber's light dulled, leaving only a pulsing object floating in the air.

Elric instantly stopped. His hand touched my arm.

"Anwen. We found it. We found the spear."

THIRTY-FIVE

The spear floated high on a circular pedestal. It shimmered, vibrant and alive. Its golden flecks sparkled on my skin. I couldn't look away from the legendary object—the mighty Gungnir. Odin's enchanted weapon.

It was larger than I imagined, but if it was used by a god, the bigger the better. Symbols decorated the staff—magical spells that granted the wielder powers in battle. Several hieroglyphs accompanied the runes, possibly enhancing the already powerful weapon with the forces of the sun god Ra. Just like the legend told by the Kaftar.

The spearhead pulsed in the light, inviting us closer. Each angle warned that anyone who touched the lethal point would face death. Three interconnected triangles—Odin's mark—were engraved into the head, leaving a strange empty space in the center. Scrollwork and runes lined each smooth edge of each triangle, but as the light played over the surface, the runes punched out, revealing a three-dimensional look.

My necklace buzzed, tingled, and jumped from my throat. I quickly grabbed the gold hourglass and held it against my skin. Elric noticed my actions, looking from the necklace to the spear. His eyebrow lifted with an unspoken question.

"Anwen," he pronounced. "Let go of your necklace."

My brow furrowed at his strange request, but I did as he asked.

The necklace remained motionless for a few seconds before vibrating again. The amber stones started to rattle inside their hourglass cage. I raised my hand to stop the strange feeling, but Elric held my hand at his side and kept it there.

"Wait," he said. "I believe your gemstones may find a new home."

As I began to speak, the amber gems slipped from my necklace, and like metal to a magnet, they shot into the empty space within the spearhead and fused into a single large gemstone. Once inside, the amber brightened, revealing a brilliance I'd never seen before; even the brightest star in the sky couldn't compare to the stone's vitality and radiance. A golden burst of light encased the spear before dimming to a gentle shimmer. But the addition of my amber unleashed a new surge of power—a power that called to me. Another space appeared at the top of the spear. Something pulled at my waist, and Elric noticed the sudden movement.

"Anwen, your bag." He reached down at my side and unclasped the cinch.

Loki's dagger flew out and twisted in midair. The large

amber stone pulsed and vibrated until it loosened, tearing away from the hilt and jumping onto the spear.

A thrumming noise echoed in the chamber. The spear shot into the air like a rocket. Light burst from the amber.

My hands itched to grasp the spear, eager to release the turbulent energy swirling beneath my skin. As I reached up to seize the weapon, a faint shuffle sounded from behind.

Bringing our hands up in self-defense, we both turned and gasped in surprise when we saw the marble statues were now surrounding us. The cloaked figures pulled their hoods down. They were no longer statues, as their flesh and bone faces stared back at us.

Their light gray cloaks contrasted with their darker skin, while their bald heads reflected the golden brightness from the spear, giving them all an ethereal glow. An equal number of men and women stared with wide, yet kind, dark eyes. They behaved not as if we were intruders but as honored visitors to their castle. A slight smile appeared on each of their faces.

One of the men stepped forward, his smile widening.

"By the god Njord, and his daughter Freyja, you have arrived," he stated breathlessly. "You bear the mark of Odin. Anwen, Healer of Vardia."

The pleased expressions evident on all of the monks' faces gave Elric and me pause. Did they not understand the battle raging on their shores? That I was only here to use the weapon to kill an evil king, his magical Mage, and even, possibly, another god?

As if the monk heard my thoughts, he bowed his head in

sorrow. "The realm is in peril, the need for action is great. Our pleasure comes only from meeting the one who was foretold by the great god Njord."

"The god of the sea?" I asked with confusion.

A female monk stepped forward, pressing her hands together as if in prayer, and bowed.

"Yes, Healer. His exalted one, Njord, keeps the spear safe—ready to be used by the keeper of Freyja's sorrow. Only when the two—the amber and the gold—are reunited can the power be truly realized and utilized."

"But, Loki, not Freyja, had the spear created for Odin," Elric stated. "How is the great god Njord involved with Loki's plan?"

"Young Volun, the god Njord, along with the other heavenly gods, contributed to creating this special gift. Each gave a part of their essence to forge a magical symbol of their divinity. It was given to the great All-Father, but he lost control of its power when he loftily handed it to a human to wield. The Ancients took the spear away and placed it within our monastery for safekeeping—away from the gods' grasp."

"Why does Anwen have a connection to the spear, besides being blessed with the All-Father's symbol? Why does her amber, from the necklace that belonged to her mother and was given by the goddess Freyja, fit within the weapon?" Elric's voice rose slightly in anger. More questions formed, and we needed answers. We were running out of time with these new revelations.

Another monk stepped forward, placing a hand on my arm.

In that single motion, that single gesture, no matter what the Ancients revealed to us on the floating mountain, I felt a sense of oneness. The runes on my body lit up, glowing brighter than ever before, but they were immediately overshadowed by the spear's radiance as the runes along its staff glowed from within. The magic of the gods whispered through my body, leaving me breathless and invigorated. Understanding dawned.

My feet were on autopilot. I walked toward the floating spear, pausing briefly before reaching out and grasping the staff. A rainbow of energy surrounded my hand and then enveloped the spear. Power surged through my body, pulsing painfully through my veins. The voices softened as they yielded to the unity.

The runes carved on the spear began to move—scrolling down the staff and onto my hand.

Elric grabbed my arm and pulled up my sleeve to my elbow. The runes were familiar to us both—the same spell etched on my brooch and written on the cover of the Book of Shadows. The runes spiraled around my arm, burning into my skin and becoming a permanent part of my forearm. But the spell didn't stop with just inking my skin. It flowed down my arm and slithered up Elric's arm, leaving the same mark.

"Tears of amber and gold," I whispered, locking eyes with Elric. "Weakness becomes strength. Grief becomes joy. Death becomes life—the power of Freyja—the power of unity. We are forever as one."

Elric's hand squeezed my arm, unsure of what to say. We were both stunned, but understanding dawned: order couldn't exist without chaos. Our connection felt whole.

"The goddess Freyja lost her one great love." The monk placed her hand upon ours, "and when she cried upon her father's shores, amber fell in grief, so she melded them together to form an amulet so that she would never forget love lost. Your mother, Anwen, helped Freyja through her grief, offering her solace and friendship during a time when the gods were fighting each other—arguing over petty grievances. Freyja's love for your mother inspired her to give her the power of the goddess—the gift of gold. Their love truly blossomed into a beautiful relationship. But Loki's power and threats proved too overwhelming for the gods. In true honor and loyalty, Eira offered Freyja and the beloved gods her most treasured gift—her precious symbol of love and devotion—you."

The female monk smiled. "Like the magical spear, you were given a piece of each god—a part of their divinity. The spear is a mighty weapon on its own, as are you, Anwen. But when the tears of Freyja complete the spear, and the magical spells within you both unite, one can only speculate on the outcome. And the power. It is the key to protecting the sacred land of Saerún."

The spear buzzed in my hands; energy pulsed through my body, connecting with me physically, mentally, and emotionally. I closed my eyes as feelings overwhelmed me—the power to take life flowed through my veins like an electric current.

Several minutes went by before Elric's worried voice broke through the static in my mind.

Anwen? Can you hear me?

I nodded, but I couldn't respond. The words were trapped

in my throat. Violent thoughts and horrifying images raced through my mind.

Could I truly use the weapon to kill? Even my most hated enemies? The power-hungry Kenrick, the evil Corvus, and the vengeful god Loki?

"Yes, you feel the pull of the powerful magic, what the spear is capable of, the ability to dominate everyone and everything around you—the power of the universe," the female monk muttered as she stepped closer. All the monks followed her, crowding around us.

A burning sensation exploded behind my eyes. I saw my reflection in the golden surface of the spear—my pupils were bright, piercing, and deadly.

"You must restrain them, Anwen," Elric whispered in my ear, wrapping his arm around my waist. "Use the Shadow within you—you are in command, not the other way around. Make the gods—the spear—see who is in control."

Worried expressions drove me to close my eyes again, gather my energy, and command the frantic thoughts into submission. When I opened my eyes, my reflection looked normal. The golden eyes vanished.

"I—I am in control," I stuttered softly, now feeling only a slight buzz of adrenaline pumping through my veins.

The male monk frowned. "That is why, when you have defeated your enemy, the spear must be destroyed. The connection must be severed."

Elric stepped forward. "And what will happen to Anwen once the weapon is destroyed? Will she be able to break the connection without harm?"

The monks stayed silent. The lack of guarantees sounded louder than any declarations.

And I knew the answer even before Elric made the connection—the weapon and I were vessels of destruction. By surrendering myself to hold the spear, I sealed our bond and our fate. We were created for two separate purposes—one for the love of the gods, and one for the life of the gods.

Elric shifted his stance, shaking his head in denial. "You must do something to protect her. How can the love of Freyja bring Anwen's destruction? It goes against everything the goddess upholds."

"Elric, we have to go," I said softly, placing my hand on his chest as he moved toward the monks. "We need to save our people."

Tearful eyes turned toward me. Elric cupped my face within his hands. "I cannot lose you. Not now."

A wistful smile escaped. "I will not go down without a fight; you must know that. Have faith in me. We just found each other—I will not lose *you*."

He answered me with a sad smile, knowing my words were merely bandages covering the bloody truth. But he didn't argue.

It was time. The cries of the battle echoed through the chamber.

My eyes lingered on each monk, letting them know I understood what needed to be done once the end was near. They nodded in response, never breaking their focus. But I sensed their tension and doubts about my ability to destroy the spear.

I grabbed Elric's hand as we ran toward the bridge. The monks' reservations were now an afterthought. More pressing matters were at play.

Water crashed against the bridge, covering it with at least a foot of water. We sprinted across, ignoring our safety until we made it back onto the platform. Unfortunately, the tumultuous sea didn't provide another bridge to the shore.

"Well, another bridge would have been nice," Elric muttered in contempt. "How are we supposed to get to the shore?"

Frustration erupted from my lips. How indeed?

A screech echoed around us. My eyes scanned the waters. A cry sounded from the sky.

Something was flying toward us at top speed. For a few seconds, I thought it was the Hraesvelgr emerging from the In-Between Realm to finish us off, but the call became clearer. A startled but happy yelp escaped me as I jumped back, just in time for the beast to land.

His majestic wings unfurled in the air with an elaborate sweep, while throwing his beak into the air with an equally boisterous screech.

"This is how we will get to shore," I exclaimed as my hand curled around the griffin's feathered neck. "Hello, Bane, my dear friend."

THIRTY-SIX

Bane dropped us near a rocky outcrop protruding from the cliff. No one had noticed us yet, but that was about to change. The weight of the spear rested within the curve of my back. A low hum resonated from the weapon—the vibration reverberated in my bones. I could feel its urge to fight.

Elric knelt beside the cliff wall. His hand brushed over the small black stones covering the beach. The porous lava rock would make fighting difficult. He quickly glanced around the corner. Packs of warriors fought nearby, seemingly unaffected by the stones beneath their feet. Metal clanged against metal, interrupted only by grunts of pain and cries of death. The spear hummed even louder as the sound of clattering increased.

"There are too many around us to slip by unnoticed," he muttered. He continued to survey the fighting. "The shoreline. If Bane could cause a diversion, we could make it towards the waterline and go from there. It will be easier to fight on the smaller volcanic sand."

Bane heard the plan and spread his powerful wings, pushing off forcefully and causing the sand to swirl around us like tiny tornadoes. Shouts of surprise alerted us, so we immediately jumped out of our hiding spot and sprinted toward the water. I glanced back to ensure Bane was unharmed. He was already flying toward us, encouraging us to speed up.

Some of the Vardian warriors called out our names, surprised but relieved. With the gratitude of our people came the anger of our enemies.

Elric blocked multiple sword swings from the loathsome Lokrum, and the fight only worsened as we moved further down the shore. Several times, we had to stop and face two or three soldiers at once. Our hands sliced through the air, unleashing our energy on the foolish men. Several traitorous Rock Giants tried to smash and grab Elric when his back was turned, so I pushed my hands out, destroying the giants into a rocky heap. Their protective amulets were useless on the shores of Saerún.

Elric looked at the remains and gave me a crooked smile, mumbling a grateful 'thanks.'

My eyes scanned our surroundings, hoping to find any sign of the evil threesome. I could feel the eagerness of the spear—the yearning to finally release its power. And I had to agree. My hands itched to hold the gold and amber again, to feel the release as the sharpened point found its mark.

The hiss of an arrow shrilled in my ear, dropping me to my knees. Elric swung his bow around, aiming at a soldier no more than fifty feet away. A sardonic grin spread across the soldier's face as he readied another arrow and quickly shot it at Elric. I raised my hands to protect him, but Elric dodged the arrow with lightning speed and fired his own, hitting the soldier in the chest.

The reprieve was short-lived. Several more of Kenrick's men stepped over their fallen comrade, waving their swords in the air with wicked grins.

Elric quickly grabbed a sword from a fallen soldier, switching it from one hand to the other. A grin cut across his face as well, but he did not delay in the attack. He swung the sword up and across one man's chest, disemboweling without hesitation. He pivoted around to the other man's head. But the Lokrum soldier was just as quick, stabbing and slicing across Elric's stomach. Luckily, he twisted away in time, but the cut found its mark on his forearm. Blood gushed and pooled within his palm, but Elric didn't seem to notice as he twisted away from the soldier, sending the hilt of the sword crashing down on his head and then pushing him away in order to land a deathly slash across his throat. The soldier never saw Elric's quickened response.

A sigh of relief escaped me as I hurried to Elric's side. I grabbed his arm and placed my hand on the cut. The wound quickly puckered and sealed.

He raised his hand to my cheek, but then quickly pushed me away. A dagger slipped from Elric's hand, followed by a sickly thud. I heard a quick intake of breath. I turned around and saw the Lokrum slumped on the sand behind me.

Elric dashed around me and pulled the dagger from the soldier's chest. It was my turn to return his smile with a grateful one.

Something drew my attention near the shoreline, no more than a hundred feet from us. A flash of white blond hair was pulled against the hands of a Lokrum soldier.

"Jack?"

How was he here in Saerún? Shouldn't he be with the Kaftar along with the others?

Elric looked further up the beach, now realizing our group of friends was here at the battle. How that happened was confusing, but as we both scanned the area, we saw Thyra and Halvard moving behind the Lokrum, nocking their bows. However, they didn't shoot. That was understandable, since Jack could be hit in the crossfire.

The Lokrum soldier yanked the helmet off his head, laughing at the elves' hesitation and mockingly shouting at them. His words were hard to understand, but from Thyra's expression and the quick draw of her bow, they were enough to make her act.

Her arrow, along with Halvard's, hit their target, each in the eye socket of the still-jeering enemy. Jack was instantly freed and fell to the bloodied soldier's feet.

Even before the first arrow found its mark, my legs responded instantly, sprinting toward Jack. I had to reach him, keep him safe.

Several warriors lunged at me with strange-looking broadswords. I didn't recognize them, but they resembled a Tolkienesque orc. Their pale, mottled skin accentuated their unnaturally large black eyes and oversized mouths filled with sharp, black teeth. Horns protruded from their heads, most of which gleamed with blood from their battles. I swung my hands at them, but felt resistance to my energy. I tried again, slashing across their throats with more force, until they finally stumbled on their stubby feet. Their heads separated from their necks.

Elric and I kept moving, even when more pale creatures approached us. We were nearly to Jack when another Vardian horn sounded from the cliffs. Elric recognized the signal, grabbing my arm to stop and raising his other hand in the air, just in time as a volley of arrows bounced off his Shadow shield.

I struggled to break free from his hold. My eyes searched for Jack. He was about to be skewered alive.

"Thyra and Halvard have shields, Anwen," he mumbled in my ear. "Jack is safe."

And he was right. I finally found Thyra and Halvard hovering over Jack with their battle shields held high above them.

Relief swept through me, but only for a brief second, as the volley ended, and more soldiers surrounded our friends. Elric and I pushed forward, now more than ever. Thyra and Halvard placed Jack in the center and engaged with the mottled group of soldiers circling around them. Their swords tore and gutted flesh in close quarters, all the while keeping Jack safe and out of reach. I was in awe of how well Thyra and Halvard synchronized their combative skills with their quickened movements, never hesitating as one slashed low while the other slashed high. Their fighting adeptness amazed me.

My breath caught when Jack suddenly lunged from the

center, stabbing his dagger into the throat of a white creature. Jack's face mirrored the surprised expression of the creature.

A proud smile stretched across my lips. Halvard leaned in and murmured something to Jack. A wide grin appeared but was quickly replaced with determination. Jack sidestepped another sword attack. His dagger swished back and forth, jabbing and countering as he completed the triangle of defense. Jack's skill with the weapon was just as impressive and remarkable.

More Lokrum approached the group, but Elric and I joined them, lunging at the unsuspecting soldiers. When the soldiers were defeated, and we reached the center to confront our friends, their eyes widened in disbelief. Jack threw his arms around me.

"How did you get here?" Thyra asked.

"How did *you* get here?" I countered. "The Kaftar let you go?"

"We waited over a month—hope and faith in the mission dwindled every day that you were gone," Thyra said, still astonished at our sudden appearance.

Halvard grasped Elric's shoulder, relieved and exuberant now. "We shouldn't have doubted you."

Elric returned Halvard's embrace and accepted Thyra's hug.

They turned to me, taking me in their arms.

"The Kaftar didn't just let us go, Anwen. They are also here, fighting alongside us. Amastan is fighting beside the queen. They have become great allies."

Her words left me stunned.

"You said we were gone for a month?" I asked. "But that's

impossible."

Jack stepped back from me. "I thought you were dead. We waited and waited, until we couldn't anymore."

Elric and I exchanged surprised and confused looks. "Within the realm, it couldn't have been more than four or five days, at most."

But they were not paying attention to his explanation—their eyes were fixed on me.

"You found the spear," Thyra stated with awe.

Her eyes focused on the glowing spear cradled against my back.

Suddenly, Jack lunged forward with his dagger. I turned just in time to see him impale a creature in the heart.

Elric spun around and deflected another wave of attacks.

"We need to find Loki," he yelled over his shoulder as he parried a blow to the head.

"Loki hasn't been seen yet, but Kenrick and Corvus are here," Halvard grunted. He countered a jab and then swung low to cut the legs off of his assailant, only to stand over him and plunge his sword into the chest. Blood spouted from the soldier's mouth. His last breath hissed from his lips. Halvard turned to us. "Near the water, about half a kilometer to the south."

"We will make a path for you," Thyra exclaimed over her shoulder as she dealt the deathly blow to her opponent.

Familiar faces crossed our path—Menhit and Shu fighting off Lokrum soldiers, Ciar leaping at several of his treacherous brothers, and Zira in human form, holding her own, waiting until darkness transformed her into a more formidable monster.

But I didn't see Anu. Where was she?

A group of soldiers rappelled down the cliff, many swinging outward to loosen their arrows on the enemy below. As soon as their feet hit the sand, more soldiers followed down the rope. This time, differently dressed soldiers jumped over the cliff—the dark trim of their armor contrasting sharply with the golden trim of the Vardian equipment. Worried for our soldiers, I started to yell a warning, but I noticed the emblem on the dark armor and shields—a mountain peak with three stars above it.

Wynfalle.

"Elric, look."

Elric followed my gaze. "I expected no less from the queen."

"I guess better late than never," I muttered, but gratitude and pride swelled inside of me—and hope.

We sprinted along the beach, staying close to the water's edge. I looked over the entire shoreline, wondering where Anu was fighting. And where was my grandmother?

I knew I shouldn't worry about them, but anxiety swelled inside me. My gaze landed on the backs of Thyra and Halvard, then shifted to Elric and Jack running beside me. The foreboding feeling intensified. Soldiers in their death throes echoed around me.

Where was Loki? He wouldn't miss this battle—his own personal display of dominance and destruction.

Ahead of us, a mesa rose from the sand, blocking our path right along the shoreline.

Waves crashed against the west end while the cliff pressed tightly against the east end, leaving only a narrow trail in between. The warriors fought near the rocky growth, blocking our path.

We stopped abruptly, unsure how to cross the platform. But for some reason, I sensed this was where I needed to be—a shiver ran down my spine, and the hairs on the back of my neck tingled. A group of obelisks lined the cliff, arranged in a half circle, marking an entrance to the stairs carefully carved into the side of the cliff, leading down to the mesa.

Something was different about this particular rock formation—a coldness curled around me. My hand reached out and grabbed Elric.

"Do you feel something different here?" I asked hesitantly, hoping he sensed the same energy flowing through the rock.

He examined the mound, narrowing his eyes at every small detail, both physically and magically. Confusion washed over his face, but then he reached out to me in panic. Everything appeared to move in slow motion. Elric's hand brushed mine, almost grasping it, but then he was thrown backward, harshly and mercilessly. Elric struggled to get up but was lifted into the air and carried over the mesa.

A brutal stabbing pain erupted in my gut, and as Elric was yanked backward, I was thrown forward, crashing against the side of the mesa. Thyra and Halvard reached for me, but I was suddenly and forcefully jerked into the air.

My body hurled onto the top of the mesa, skidding across the surface at such a high speed that I thought I would fall over the edge. Luckily, the mesa was larger than I expected, and I ended up near the center of the large rock.

Before I could react to the situation, Jack slid across the mesa and slammed into me. I quickly pulled him close, shielding him from whatever threw us onto the platform. Elric was a few feet ahead of me, already on his knees, his arms rigidly pressed to his sides.

A low, cynical laugh erupted.

My body ached, and pain shot up my arms, but I pushed myself from the ground, pushing Jack behind me.

"We meet again, Anwen."

The sound of his voice wrapped around me, pressing into my body and tearing my heart in two.

I knew he was here; I was looking for him, dreaming of killing him for all the pain he caused my family. His demise haunted my dreams.

But now, face-to-face with my tormentor—the annihilator, the killer of my parents, the kidnapper of the Okri, the man who triggered the fall of my world—left me feeling confused inside. Uncertainty about my abilities haunted me. Can I really defeat him?

Our eyes met. A fleeting spark of humanity flickered across Kenrick's face, but he was no longer a man. The sickly shell of a man I had met years ago was gone; in his place stood a gruesomely muscular beast. Standing over six and a half feet tall, his overly long arms and legs jutted from his short torso. His white, bald head glistened as larger-than-human eyes stared with a hollowness that stole my breath. A smile spread wide, carving a sharp, jagged line across his pale face.

Corvus stepped out from behind Kenrick, a sneer on his face.

"Yes, Healer. So glad you could join us," he muttered. His hands sliced through the air, sending Elric sprawling to the ground. He was slow to get up, but he managed to stand, facing me. Torment marked his features as if he were battling a silent force within his mind.

"Welcome to the end of the world," Corvus yelled. His hands swished through the air, releasing a bright red-and-black burst of energy. It spiraled around the mesa with intensity, obscuring the battle and everything around us. We shielded our eyes from the force of the whirlwind.

As quickly as the tornado started, it suddenly stopped.

I pulled my hands away from my face, uncertain of what I would see.

Instantly, I doubled over in pain as if someone had punched me in the stomach. Elric shouted my name, but his voice sounded distant. I reached out for Jack but noticed he wasn't near me anymore. I looked around from my crouched position. A strange sensation thumped beneath my feet. A fleeting wave of unease froze me, but I slowly relaxed my body.

I stood on three triangles—blood red and pulsing with powerful magic.

A breath brushed against my ear. A presence loomed over me. Without fear, my eyes locked with Loki's cold stare.

THIRTY-SEVEN

Everything around me came to a standstill—the turbulent wind, the raging sea, the chaotic crusade. Only the sound of my pounding heart echoed with each ragged breath. Something deep inside me stirred under Loki's cold stare. The way he stood before me, the way they all held themselves, confident and victorious, made me angry.

"It seems you have something that belongs to me," Loki smiled triumphantly. "It was so nice to hand deliver the gift to your god."

Words refused to form and answer his bold suppositions. Kenrick smirked, but Corvus remained impassive—his eyes darted to Elric and then landed back on me.

Jack stood a few feet away and to the right, swaying slightly on his feet. Fear appeared in his eyes, but so did courage—he knew what needed to be done to save the world.

A slight movement to the left caught my attention—Anu,

looking battle weary, stood at another corner of the triangle. Her eyes caught mine in a panic as she gestured behind me.

Herja stood calmly at the tip of a triangle. Her eyes never left the trio of evil.

Elric's body remained rigid. An inner battle showed on every tight line of his face. His hands kept clenching and unclenching by his sides. His eyes drifted upward. Floating a few feet above my head was the Okri, bundled together like a cluster of marbles. Their voices overwhelmed me.

I took a steady step forward, hoping my smile reflected Loki's confidence. But inside, fear surged.

"I see you're paying homage to your All-Father, Loki," my hands gestured toward the glowing triple triangle beneath our feet. "He, after all, is the owner of my special gift, not you." I tilted my head to the side, pondering my statement. "Ah, well, that's not exactly true, though, is it? All of the gods contributed to this special weapon."

Loki's righteous expression remained steady, but his energy increased with his anger.

"So, you know the circumstances of the spear," he countered with a mischievous gleam in his eyes. "And, of course, your connection to it?"

"I know that we were both created from the power of the gods—with devotional purpose."

Loki burst into laughter. "Oh, please . . . do you truly believe you were blessed? I see it as a curse! My brothers and sisters caused you undeniable pain and suffering. Devotional purpose? Stop spouting their rhetoric! Embrace your power, Healer. Take control of their 'gifts' and join us . . . your sacrifices don't have to be in vain. The gods don't care about you or your loved ones; they only care about their survival."

I bristled at his words. "Join you? So that you can use me to slaughter your enemies? Everything you touch turns to chaos and death. What I don't understand is what you promised Kenrick and his Mage. What can they possibly gain from the destruction of their world?"

Loki threw his head back and roared with laughter—confidence radiated from him.

"Power, immortality, godlike status . . . the list can go on, my dear Healer, but the king and his Mage truly envy *your* powers—the Shadow, the Ancients, and of course, oaf Odin and fickle Freyja and the rest of my brethren—abilities that can motivate any mortal, human and elf, to commit those unspeakable acts."

"And what do you get out of all of this?" I muttered in disgust.

Loki's smile widened—sharp and toothy with fanatic intensity.

"Vengeance."

Kenrick stepped forward and motioned to Jack. "Come here, boy."

His disfigured mouth struggled to form those few words.

Jack glanced at me; fear now consumed him, but he didn't move.

Kenrick sneered and then gave Anu a piercing look. "Bring him to me, girl."

His condescending tone made Anu scoff. She straightened her back with confidence, though a hint of annoyance remained. "Get him yourself, you insignificant human. Or are you still even that—a man or even a king?"

Before any of us could react, red lightning erupted from Kenrick's hand, wrapping around Anu's body and pulling her into his arms. The rope-like stream of red energy sank deeper into Anu's skin, causing her to scream out in pain. She writhed at Kenrick's feet. Herja stayed in her corner, though anguish and rage swirled within her.

Anu continued to cry out, but Jack stepped forward and slowly walked to stand in front of Kenrick. Although the red energy still held Anu captive, her pain appeared to lessen. She looked up at Jack and mouthed her apologies. Jack locked defiant eyes with Kenrick.

"What an obedient son," Kenrick said sarcastically.

Still reeling from discovering Kenrick's new power, I barely noticed the unexpected endearment.

"What did you say?" I asked.

"Come now, Anwen," Loki crooned. "Look around you. Why do you think they are here, these specific vessels of power?"

When I didn't reply right away, Corvus stepped forward. Hatred poured from him. "Blood. Blood is power—the first-born children created by and connected to the gods, the guardians of Saerún, are the reason for their downfall, and the reawakening of a long-forgotten world."

A flood of questions raced through my mind—what exactly was Corvus implying? The answers gradually emerged and then stopped suddenly. Disbelief overwhelmed me.

Jack shook his head in denial as Anu began to cry. I quickly turned to Elric and then Herja, hoping a rebuttal would come from them, but all I saw was a revelation.

Kenrick grabbed Jack by the shoulders and turned him toward me.

"Yes, my dear Anwen. Jack is my son—and a worthless one at that. His mother had Lirrean blood and was my captive, hidden well beneath the dungeons of the Lucian castle. My father, mother, and meddling brother never knew of her existence. Corvus began the age of renewal with Elric, using him as the vessel to connect this world to the Underworld—chaos flows in his veins. But another child was needed, and unfortunately, you were gone. Neither of my son's useless powers nor any of his Lirrean traits showed. A servant sensed something was wrong and found the dead captive with the boy. She kidnapped and hid him from me. If only he had your power—the energy flowing through you, the power so intense, even before the gods used you—power I hoped my offspring would have." Kenrick's maniacal smile grew wider. "But now our journey has come full circle—even more so with the discovery of Anu and the link to her traitorous mother. I almost feel giddy with anticipation. You see, Anwen, their deaths are unavoidable—their magic, along with yours, is a treasure trove of power, and you are the key to unleashing that force. The spear will bind you to us—enslaving you to our will."

"I will not let you hurt Jack," I hissed, glaring at all three hated beings. "I'd rather die than let you touch any of them for your crazy plan."

Loki shrugged indifferently. "Well, of course, you will."

With his last words, I pulled the spear out of its sheath on my back. Sweat ran down my arms and pooled in my palms, making it hard to grip the weapon at first. But the energy's force helped keep the spear steady in my hands. I pulled the weapon even closer to my chest, relishing the connection once more.

"I will stop you, Loki, in the name of Odin and Freyja and with the power of the Ancients," I called out.

But I couldn't figure out how to do that. Doubt crept in again. No one handed me a 'how-to-kill-Loki-with-a-powerful-spear' manual. How was the spear supposed to work? Do I just throw it at Loki and hope for the best? Or do I need to say some magic word and jab it into him? It would have been helpful to have guidance on how the weapon was supposed to work.

Seeing my hesitation, Elric took action by throwing his silver energy at Corvus and Kenrick, aiming to distract Loki so I could stab the spear into him. But Corvus and Kenrick predicted Elric's move and shielded themselves with both Anu and Jack. Elric quickly withdrew but still attacked, lifting his dagger at Kenrick, who appeared to be the easiest target.

But we all underestimated how much Kenrick had changed and what his new powers involved. He swept his free hand at Elric. Another bolt of energy, this one silver with a hint of black, shot down at Elric's dagger hand, slicing his arm deeply so that the dagger fell to the ground with a dull thud.

The lack of weaponry and his injury did not stop Elric's movement as he clenched his bloodied fist and delivered a powerful blow to Kenrick's chin, causing him to fall backward and loosen his grip on Jack.

"Jack," I yelled, but he already knew to jump away from Kenrick's grasp. He ran behind Herja, who was now moving her hands back and forth, conjuring up a mystical veil of dark mist.

Corvus threw Elric aside, his energy wrapping around Elric's chest, but Elric countered as his Shadow encased Corvus' arms and traced down his body, rendering him immobile. The anger and hatred radiating from Corvus' Shadow made Elric's Shadow hesitate.

I knew I had to help when my own Shadow shivered inside me; her brothers were in turmoil. But my eyes cautiously followed Loki as he slowly moved to the side, pleasure glinting in his eyes from the pain and blood spilling around him.

Seeing the hesitation from both Shadows, Herja moved toward the fighting trio with her arms outstretched. The sleek mist flowed from her palms, and with her eyes fixed on her enemies, the vapor encased Corvus and Kenrick. They both responded and used their own powers to try to stop her Shadow, but Herja's magic proved too strong. Corvus grabbed Anu. She screamed as he pressed a dagger to her throat.

Herja pulled back, but not before Loki, tired of the fight, appeared and grabbed her by the throat. With her feet hanging, Herja tried to pull Loki's hand away, but failed. Jack lunged at Loki and kicked him in the leg, only for Loki to quickly grab him by the throat.

"I wouldn't do that, boy," he hissed. "You have something that I want, so don't test my patience."

The spear trembled in my hands. Without hesitation, I jabbed it at Loki, grazing his side. He swung away, falling to the ground and knocking Herja and Jack down. His hand reached for the spear, but when his fingers brushed the spearhead, he yanked them back with a furious, shocked howl. Smoke appeared where his fingers touched the metal, burning his divine flesh.

I pulled the spear back, ready to attack again. We stared each other down. My mind raced to form a plan.

Herja recovered quickly from Loki's chokehold, moving her hands again and creating another cloud of purple vapor. Elric kept attacking Corvus, using both his magic and the dagger. Anu, now in her Lirrean form, twirled and lunged at Kenrick, whose power surprisingly matched that of any godly chosen.

Magic was all around us. I wasn't sure how to stop the attack before my friends and family were killed.

Loki seemed to read my mind. "How convenient that the gods bestowed a great gift, yet didn't tell you how to use it." A sneer appeared. "Typical."

Impatience overtook Loki. He spread his arms wide and used magical force to grab Herja, Anu, and Jack, sending them to different positions in front of Corvus and Kenrick. He pointed a finger at Elric, forcing him to stand beside Corvus with arms at his sides.

"Enough of this useless playing," he muttered with annoyance as he stood in front of Elric. A satisfied grin slowly grew. "Anwen, my dear, let us begin."

I held the spear tightly in my hands and felt a surge of magic flow through my veins, tensely awaiting Loki's next move.

Loki placed his hands on Elric's chest.

All hell broke loose.

THIRTY-EIGHT

Anu threw her head back, screaming as loud as she could. Her body became stiff, her arms and legs like boards. Herja tried to fight whatever Corvus and Kenrick were doing to them. Her body tensed up against an unseen force. But it was Jack's deep howl of pain that pushed me into action.

Throwing my arms in the air, I felt the Shadow escape, swirling around Corvus and Kenrick, but Loki was quick and immediately at my side, grabbing my arms and pulling me into his chest. His arms were strong, matching his large frame, but I was smaller and quicker to anticipate his move. I slipped beneath his arms, launching my body back and between his legs. I jabbed the spear into his shoulder, but he deflected it. He growled in pain as the back of his hand made contact with the spear.

A scuffling noise drew my attention. Herja broke free from the magic and hurled her purplish-black mist at Kenrick and Corvus. Anu and Jack struggled on the ground, with Jack now fully Lirrean in form. Their bodies pulsed with a copper haze. My focus shifted to Elric—the pain clear as he fought the magic Loki unleashed inside him.

Elric doubled over, briefly losing control of Loki's magic. "Kill him, Anwen . . . use the spear."

Easier said than done, I tried to wield the magic within Gungnir. I raised it again, ready to throw it at Loki, but he drew a dagger from his sheath. I gasped at the sight of the weapon.

"Where did you get that?" I exclaimed.

"Oh, I plucked this from a broken body on the shore," he eyed it with a smile.

The familiar design gave me pause.

"It—it belongs to my grandmother, but . . ." I couldn't continue. My heart raced.

I stared at the dagger, unable to believe Loki had it in his hands, arrogantly waving it in front of me and taunting me.

He pretended to pout. A brief frown crossed his lips. "Oh, well, yes, I guess I do remember the warrior who clenched it in her hands . . . hmmm, she was very angry, not at all courteous or respectful to her god." He smiled haughtily. "So, I struck her down—she did fight quite bravely, though, until her unfortunate end."

Rage consumed me.

I threw the spear at him, not caring about the consequences if the weapon hit its target—my death, regardless of the connection to the spear, was inevitable.

But surprisingly, Loki deflected the spear as if it were a stick thrown in frustration.

He started to laugh.

"The Ancients and your precious gods really didn't give you the knowledge to unlock the spear's power . . . and yours."

He kicked the spear to the side so it landed near Elric's feet. Kenrick launched himself at Elric, knocking him to the ground and landing on top of him. His hands grabbed Elric's throat. Kenrick's face twisted with madness. Elric grabbed Kenrick's hands, slowly pulling them away from his throat. The Shadow released from Elric's palms, curling around Kenrick's arms and body. Kenrick screamed in agony as the Shadow hurled him off Elric and into Corvus.

Corvus moved to the side, now ignoring his writhing master at his feet. Corvus eyed the spear, envy and madness etched on his features.

He pointed to Elric and commanded. "Grab it."

To my surprise, Elric responded and reached for the spear.

Herja yelled for him to stop, but it was too late. Elric's fingers gripped the staff. His features relaxed briefly, then a silent scream escaped from his open mouth. His eyes rolled back. He struggled onto his knees and barely managed to stand. He turned toward me, stunned by the power surging through his body. But he wasn't meant to hold the spear. Herja rushed to his side but didn't touch him.

I kept staring at Elric, confused about what was happening to him. Meanwhile, Corvus and Kenrick grabbed Anu and Jack, moving them to different points of the triangle. Loki took Herja, who looked too stunned to resist, and placed her at the point of the triangle.

Everything around me moved in slow motion.

The Okri started churning in their bundle. Their cries echoed around us. Their pain tore at my heart.

Elric's body remained rigid. The spear was controlling him.

Loki laughed, a victorious sound that grated on my nerves. Corvus and Kenrick returned to their original spots, with Corvus standing directly behind Elric.

Faltering slightly from the Okri's distress, I threw my hands outward, letting my Shadow swirl around me. The black mist now shifted to purple. I could feel my Shadow's desire to connect with the spear, but I wasn't sure how to take the spear away from Elric. In the back of my mind, I knew that if I took it from him, something horrible would happen. I was missing a piece of the puzzle.

Loki's laughter grew louder. He tossed the dagger to Corvus.

"It's all about sacrifice, my dear Anwen—sacrifice for those we love. But you always thought you would be the sacrifice . . . that you would be the only one to bear the responsibility of saving your world." Loki tilted his head, smiling like the maniacal trickster he was. "Corvus has been plotting for a very long time, my dear. His plan, although it may not be on par with yours, is to save this realm in his own way. And, fortunately, or should I say unfortunately for you, your beloved has always known that he was the link to finish his father's plans. His betrayal must devastate you." Loki's sneer widened to almost comical proportions—but this was not a joke.

Elric's lips moved, his pleas silent but desperate for me to understand. The missing piece was just a few words away.

Corvus placed his hand on Elric's shoulder and closed his eyes at the sensation of contact. A slow smile spread across his face. When Corvus opened his eyes, black orbs met mine.

"Dark shall rule over light. Blood for blood," Corvus bellowed. "Death the Destroyer released with sacrifice. Chaos shall rule the world."

Corvus tore Elric's tunic and threw it aside. Elric's tattoos shifted from swirling silver to coiling red. Corvus' cloak fluttered slightly in the breeze before he shrugged it off. Tattoos covered every inch of his skin, swirling chaotically and shifting from black to red.

Corvus grabbed Elric's shoulder with one hand, then plunged the dagger into Elric's neck and quickly impaled him in the side. Elric's head tilted back, his mouth wide open in a silent scream, but he still stayed upright, held stiffly in place by the spear clenched in his hands.

Corvus stepped back from Elric, mimicking his son's stance, head thrown back, eyes and mouth wide open. Corvus began muttering, deep and guttural. His face contorted in pain as if something deep inside him ached to escape from his chest. Suddenly, dark mist burst from his mouth, churning chaotically around him. Elric clenched the spear even tighter, his knuckles turning bright white. A low moan escaped from Elric's mouth, only to grow into a gut-wrenching cry. His body tensed further as a red mist erupted from his mouth, eyes, ears, and nose.

My feet were frozen, my mind racing, and my head was screaming. I gathered the energy now raging inside me and threw it at Corvus. He raised his hands, shielding both himself and Elric from my power. The red and black mist now churned, twirled, and melded in front of us.

Herja, Anu, and Jack ceased writhing on the ground, only to become painfully still. Their fingers bent and folded in strange, painful directions, reaching toward the sky. Black mist rose from Herja, while a silvery white mist ascended from Anu and Jack—all enclosed in the swirling tornado.

Loki cut through the air with his hand. Blood sprayed from a jagged slash on Anu and Jack's wrists.

I started to run toward them, but felt a strong hand grab my arm, pulling me back.

Freyja appeared beside me, cool and reserved as she watched the events unfold. Another strong hand brushed my shoulder as Odin appeared on the other side. He seemed unfazed by Corvus' actions.

My heart and soul called out to Elric, urging him to fight back, but his whole body was covered in red—blood from his body or from the magic, I couldn't tell. I took a few steps toward him, only to have both Freyja and Odin hold me back.

"What are you doing? He's killing Elric, I need to help him," I cried out while trying to wrench my arms free from their powerful grasp. "He's killing them all."

"Corvus is unleashing the Underworld. Your world will fall into chaos if we do not stop him," Freyja said. "Elric is now bound to the spear. He is the key to opening the portal—it must be destroyed. I am so sorry . . . it is too late for him, Anwen."

I shook my head, unable to believe what was happening and

refusing to accept Elric's fate.

"Darkness and disorder cannot be unleashed, Anwen," Odin bellowed over the increasingly turbulent wind and crashing waves. "Elric knew what he needed to do; he knew what Corvus was doing to him all those years ago—using him as the bridge to the Underworld. It only took a god to help finish their plot—the gods knew Loki was planning something against his kin, but we didn't know the extent of his vengeance until now."

"So, we were all just pawns in your game—Herja, Anu, Jack, Elric . . . me? Just so you could discover what Loki's true intentions were for our world, and for your destruction?" I seethed. I pulled my arms from their grasp. "Well, that's not good enough. It's now my time to stop them, save everyone I love from your godly squabbles."

I took a step forward, but was suddenly stopped. My feet wouldn't move. I looked up and saw Elric staring at me, his hand extended. His face twisted as another painful wave of red mist left his body.

"Kill me, do it, stop me before . . ." He couldn't finish as another agonizing scream escaped. His words tore at me. I shook my head, refusing to do what he commanded.

A thunderous clapping sound echoed from the swirling tornado. Dark tips of an object began to appear from the center, and as it rose, black leathery wings broke free from the mist.

"Anwen, you can stop this," Freyja shouted at me, grabbing my arm. "Deep inside you, the Ancestors gave you the power and knowledge to prevent the Underworld from unleashing itself—we can't stop her. Look into your mind, feel the power ready to be unleashed."

Several more winged creatures burst out of the mist. Red eyes, set deep in pointed faces, stared in my direction. Where their mouths should have been, only small webbed holes showed. A high-pitched shriek echoed. More vile beasts appeared. Blood-curdling screams reverberated through the night as the evil predators found their victims on the shore.

Loki propelled a section of mist toward Odin and Freyja. He began to laugh as the slender tendrils wrapped around the gods, small fingers of mist burrowing into their divine skin as if it were nothing more than tissue paper. Their surprised expressions only made Loki laugh harder, viciously and mockingly.

"My daughter and I will be the only ones ruling the realms now," Loki seethed as he moved closer to his struggling siblings. "But maybe I will keep you both as pets. Slaves to my newfound minions of the dark and disorder."

Odin seethed. "Do not unleash her, brother."

Loki's smile deepened as he turned to me. "Anwen? Shall we begin?"

I was caught off guard, suddenly realizing my feet were moving toward the misty tornado. I threw my hands out and called on my powers, but they didn't respond. Panic took over as I threw myself on the ground, clawing at the rock until my fingers were bloody and raw. My body kept moving toward the swirling abyss. Everything around me echoed like I was in a long tunnel—Loki's laugh, Corvus' chanting, Kenrick's snarls. The chaos overwhelmed my senses; I couldn't think straight. How could this be the end?

I glanced at Elric, hoping he would regain his senses and help stop his father, but a slow, sardonic smile played on his lips. He grasped the spear with determination. A maniacal laugh erupted. He was no longer a protector of Saerún—he was the destroyer. A pawn in Loki's game.

My eyes closed from pain and sorrow. Suddenly, a strange feeling swept over me. A small pinprick of light appeared. I opened my eyes, but the light vanished, so I quickly closed them again. As the light grew larger, a blurry silhouette emerged. I couldn't see their face, but I felt their presence.

My mother.

Let go, my love. Let Elric go.

The figure's blurry hand grew bigger until her finger reached out, clear and sharp, and touched something behind my eyes.

Look to the east.

My eyes shifted to the cliff. Nine figures stood where the obelisks used to be. The Ancients.

A vivid burst of color exploded in my mind—a flood of images downloaded into my brain. Fast and intense, the pictures imparted knowledge, power, and energy. Along with that came a sense of responsibility—given by the gods, the Shadow, the Ancestors, and even those beyond. The brightest stars surrounded me, holding me close with their fiery presence, giving me a quick sense of why this moment would define everything and everyone around me.

The key to Saerún appeared—not as a weapon, but as a thought, a promise. A vow made by the first Ancestor, the first god, the first Lirrean, the first elf, and the first human—to always keep darkness and chaos at bay, never letting the light of goodness fade. Every beast and being across all the realms pledged an oath at the birth of their firstborn—that they would always protect the balance. Many forgot that oath, but some still held order, truth, and wisdom close to their hearts and souls—that they would die to keep the light of Saerún protected from the darkness of chaos.

Saerún was the birthplace of all beings, and I was its guardian and protector. One half of a whole. That knowledge flowed through me. The power of the words, their meaning, coursed through me. I truly understood my destiny now—my role in keeping Saerún, my world, safe from Loki.

My hands reached out for my mother, but all they found was the ground. I curled my fingers into the rocky mesa, pulling my legs underneath me. My movement toward the mist paused. My lips pressed firmly with determination.

Loki was too busy hurling taunts at Odin and Freyja to notice my sudden stillness. A warmth began to surge inside me—working its way through my blood and around my muscles, veins, nerves, and bones. The sensation was familiar, first experienced in Hrafn's training room and later during the fight against the dryads. Voices whispered within me, flooding my thoughts, weaving through, and then sinking into every cell in my body—the Shadow, the Ancestors, the gods, and the Okri. I felt the power of all.

The spells shimmered on my skin with vivid colors. The power of the gods awakened within me. I enjoyed the moment as my beloved Shadow was released, purple mist rising above me. The amber's magic called out—my spear needed me. My gaze glowed gold; my sight was all-seeing. I knew everything. The power and knowledge settled inside me like a second being, warmth and understanding spreading through my body.

And I knew what I had to do.

I had to restore the balance.

I reached out my arm toward the weapon. It trembled and shimmered in Elric's stiff grip, but he couldn't deny the true owner of the spear. His lips curled back into a sneer as he struggled to keep hold of the weapon. He raised his hand, sending a bolt of energy racing toward me. I flicked it away. He immediately shot another. I barely had enough time to deflect the magic. It knocked the wind out of me. I faltered in my steps, dropping to my knees. I slowly rose again.

"I will not fight you, Elric. We are one. We are the protectors. We need each other. Fight against the magic binding you."

Elric paused, his features twisting with the pain and confusion raging inside him. I thought he was winning the battle until his hand gripped the spear and lifted it to throw.

Instinct took over. I raised my hand. Elric let out a scream of anger as the spear tore from his grip and slammed into mine with a burst of sparks.

Loki snarled at me and lunged for the spear, but I pulled back and slammed the staff into the ground. The entire mesa platform erupted into a golden bubble, surrounding everyone. Loki hesitated, but then tried to move toward me again, but his feet were planted firmly on the ground.

When I raised the spear, Loki cried out. His howl was pathetic and grave.

A sad smile tugged at the corner of my lips. A voice that wasn't mine boomed from within me. "You caused this, Loki. A god who chose to embrace chaos and unleash death upon those who could not defend themselves from your evil, wayward ways—you will accept the consequences of your actions, as those who followed will forever be entombed in the Underworld."

The spear shot out of my hand, screaming with fury as it struck each of its targets for eternal punishment—Loki, Corvus, Kenrick, Draugr, the Lokrum, and every soldier who followed Kenrick's madness.

The voices called to me, so I urged the spear to fulfill its duty to Saerún—to restore the balance. The spear's path of death was quick, and when the voices began to quiet, my hand reached out for its return. But there was one last soul to condemn. The voice of the Ancestors rose above everyone else.

The spear raced toward me, but first pierced Elric's body and claimed its final victim.

Chaos ended with a peaceful sigh of relief.

THIRTY-NINE

Gold and amber shimmered in my hands, the spear still hot from the blood of its victims. I looked down at the weapon, seeing my reflection among the crimson streaks. Gold irises gazed back at me with reverence and an unnatural fervor.

The images of Freyja and Odin appeared behind me. Their hands reached out and clasped my shoulders. Their eyes were regretful but thankful. They knew the sacrifice was great but necessary—that it tore every bit of my humanity apart before putting it back together.

Yes, the sacrifice tore my heart into pieces. My eyes stayed on Elric. The image of his broken and bloodied body will never fade from my memory.

I dropped to my knees. A piece of my soul tore away from my body.

Odin and Freyja knelt beside Loki's body, gathering him into their arms and weeping. Herja, Anu, and Jack slowly sat up, clutching their heads and sobbing as if everything they had seen and experienced would magically disappear with their tears. Blood trickled from their wounds, reminding them how close their lives and those they loved were to being lost.

My eyes trailed back to Elric.

I slowly crawled toward him, the spear still clenched in my hand. The harsh, unforgiving sound of the gold sliding across the stone clashed with the pounding of my heart and the raspy, quickened breaths.

"Anwen, the spear," Freyja's voice echoed deep within the recesses of my mind. "It needs to be destroyed."

What? Destroyed?

My eyes closed briefly before opening with renewed determination. I reached Elric. His eyes opened, gazing at the sky. I leaned over him, tears falling on his skin. I gently kissed his lips. Warm breath brushed against my skin. I pulled away suddenly. His unfocused eyes were fixed on me. Although pain rippled through his body and blurred his vision, he offered a small smile. Hope flooded through me, but was quickly taken away by his next words.

"Death is calling me, my love," Elric whispered, barely moving his lips. Blood appeared at the corner of his mouth. "I tried to fight him. I tried to fight the darkness." He briefly closed his eyes, gasping for air. "You are safe, that's all that matters. You had a duty to save our world, and I wouldn't have it any other way."

His hand slowly moved up to my face, wiping away my tears. That single gesture drained his energy. His hand dropped back to his chest.

I pressed my hands to his wound, hoping to stop the steady flow of blood.

"I love you, Anwen, always. Death is not the end."

He raised his hand and brushed my cheek. Tears streamed down my face as I pressed his hand more firmly against my cheek. I kissed his palm, trying to stifle a sob from escaping my lips. My whole body ached—shattering into a million pieces.

Elric shuddered, and I clutched him tighter to me.

"I love you," I said as a sob broke free.

His breath rattled. More blood seeped from his lips. His chest stopped moving.

I felt his energy, his magic, fade away from his body.

I cupped his face, letting my fingers glide down his cheeks, over his eyes, and across his lips, all the while shaking my head in denial. I leaned in and kissed every part of his beautiful face. My hands, trembling uncontrollably, moved to his chest, where blood pooled around the wound. Elric's once vibrant tattoos now lie still and dark.

I was supposed to be the sacrifice, not Elric. He was the one who needed saving.

A hand pressed against my back. Herja sat beside me.

"I am so sorry, Anwen. He is finally free and at peace," she whispered. Tears streamed down her face. Her pain was obvious, but I couldn't find solace in her words.

Where was the balance now? Light must exist alongside darkness. Order cannot be appreciated without the chaos that opposes it.

My eyes scanned the shoreline, needing to justify Elric's sacrifice. The violent aftermath of the battle met my gaze. Hundreds, if not thousands, of bodies littered the beach. The black sand concealed the evidence of death and brutality, only to be exposed when the tide pulled crimson streaks into the water.

Movement around the mesa caught my eye. An equal number of soldiers assembled around the large rocky platform, heads and arms raised in a salute, honoring their commander.

Thyra and Halvard stood shoulder to shoulder. Tears ran down their bloodstained, battle-worn faces. They understood the sacrifice of their commander, their friend.

Another figure approached from behind Thyra and placed her hand on her shoulder. A small smile tugged at the corner of my lips. Grandmother was alive. My smile grew wider, but it was more scornful than joyful. Not because I wasn't thankful and happy that she survived, but because of Loki's continued falsehoods.

Several familiar faces appeared, but others stayed out of reach. Most of my family and friends made it through. But not all.

Corvus' crumbled body lay a few feet from Elric. His skin almost appeared black due to his unmoving tattoos. He was covered with curling graphics. His pledge to the Underworld, to Death, took control of both his mind and his body. His obsession with power drove him mad, leading him to murder his wife and then bargain with Death to revive her. I wasn't sure what happened to his Shadow, but no presence could be felt within his mortal shell. Hopefully, for Mother Shadow's happiness, he escaped and returned to his people.

Warmth radiated beside me. The amber suddenly glowed brightly. The power of the gold and the amber tears of sorrow pulsed rhythmically. An idea took root in my mind. My fingers tightened around the spear, lifting it upright.

Herja's hand clenched my shoulder, as if she knew what I was thinking.

"Anwen, no," she whispered at my side. "There will be consequences."

She knew what I was about to do, but she was too late. Before she could cast her Shadow, I brought the spear down on the ground with a thunderous crack. The force knocked Herja away from me, leaving a protective bubble surrounding my body along with Elric's.

My actions caught Herja by surprise, but that quickly turned into shock and then fear. Anu, Jack, Odin, and Freyja all yelled for me to stop. They understood my intentions.

I called upon my Shadow, the gods, and the Ancients—the power of gold and amber, the strength of Ra and every being on this earth. The power within the In-Between Realm. And all realms under the rule and care of the gods across the universe. My plea reached out to the power of Saerún.

Energy, light, and mist radiated around us as the bubble pulsed with each prayer and command I made. Colorful clouds gathered above, then turned black. A void formed. The amber shimmered brighter than ever, knowing a light was needed to illuminate the abyss. The black space, cold and unforgiving, slowly descended upon us, leaving no doubt that what I was conjuring was the home of Death itself.

Cries from my family and friends stopped. The darkness swallowed the light.

The bubble disappeared.

Gloom and silence brushed against my skin. I tightened my grip on Elric's body. My rapid breath pierced the cold void. But I wasn't alone. I sensed a presence nearby. The warmth of the spear still vibrated beneath my hand, so I pounded the spear against the ground. The amber glow was less bright, but it provided enough light to cast a golden umbrella around us.

"Hello?" I muttered, squinting my eyes into the shadow spreading beyond the glow.

Would Death answer?

"You have denied me," a voice spoke, crisp and cold like fall leaves crunching under trampling feet.

Cold, wispy fingers traveled up my back and encircled my neck, but then disappeared.

I twisted around, hoping to glimpse the mysterious figure.

"You had no right to my world," I said softly. "Corvus promised to release you, help you destroy my world, but he is dead now, along with his god and his king. The Volun didn't deserve to die. His father used him when he was a child—forced him to follow a cruel and deadly plan. He shouldn't have been punished—killed—for his father's sins."

Silence lasted for several minutes. I believed Death had gone, but then an icy finger brushed my cheek. I fought the urge to shiver from the chilling emptiness it left behind.

"Ah, but the spear made the decision to take the life of your

Volun, not I," the voice whispered close to my ear. "You were the wielder of Death this time, my dear."

My thoughts raced. "How do I save him?"

"You are asking me—the Collector of Souls, the Bringer of Death, the Guardian of the Deceased—to part with the one soul worthy enough to join his ancestors in the great hall? To deny him that honor?" Death's mocking tone infuriated me.

"The request does not, in any way, undermine Elric's worthiness to join the halls of Valhalla or Fólkvangr. His heroism is not in question, nor is the honorable life he led; it's the fact that it wasn't his choice to be used by his father, Kenrick, or Loki. Although he was a warrior, he did not strike first, nor did he ask to be involved in the release of your chaos and wrath upon our world. He was a pawn—and his people need him. I need him."

"Ah, I see," Death's breath gently touched my hand as I held Elric. "Love—the chaotic force we inflict on ourselves that overwhelms your senses, your mind, your body. I would give anything to feel that helpless sensation ripped from my own miserable flesh—to experience the emptiness that comes with the soul's departure.

"Alas, I am merely a messenger of Death, the lone collector for souls, for the ones who hide." Death's raspy whisper faded.

"Who do I need to talk to?" I yelled into the darkness. My voice broke into sobs.

A lone figure entered the edge of the spear's glowing light.

"My father is dead, isn't he?" the figure asked.

The figure's white robe was like a beacon in the black void, yet it billowed and shimmered with a heavy shadow surrounding her. Hidden beneath a translucent veil, her guarded expression oscillated between beauty and beastliness.

"I don't understand? Your father?" I asked carefully. A familiarity with this mysterious figure gave me pause.

A cruel smile curled her lips. She lifted her hand and flicked her index finger at my chest. I felt immediate heat on my skin just above my heart—a spell glowed beneath my tunic. Recognition dawned. I pressed my hand over my heart.

"It is ironic that the gods even included me in their plans, especially placing my essence on the heart," the figure muttered, tilting her head as if in deep thought. "I can only imagine the indecision, and possibly the arguments against allowing such an action, particularly as the great All-Father marked your perfect skin with the key to their survival, my survival.

"Even though my father wished for my release, I did not want it," she mumbled softly. She took a few more steps into the glowing bubble. Her eyes lingered on the amber gemstones shimmering within the spear. "Freyja was always kind to me, probably because she pitied my circumstances, but she never denied my placement within the gods' temple."

"Your father is Loki," I said, finally understanding who the figure was talking about. "And your name is Hel."

A satisfied smile appeared. "I am not a cruel god; only my lineage and, of course, my home generate fear in others. Death is not an end but a beginning. The lives of noble warriors lost in battle do not walk my halls. Instead, the unworthy, the sick, and the depraved roam the Underworld, searching for their lost souls and purpose. Do they not deserve to find peace as well?"

"Of course, only if they truly led meaningful and kind lives before death. If they loved and were loved," I whispered, glancing down at Elric's face. "Circumstances out of your control can be cruel, and if something can be done to change those circumstances, wouldn't you try?"

Hel's eyes drifted from me to Elric, briefly examining his pale face before falling to the dark wounds along his neck, side, and chest.

"You control the spear; therefore, you condemned your Volun to his death," Hel stated, kneeling beside me. Her hand slowly grasped the staff of the spear. Surprisingly, she did not react to its power.

A sense of wariness spread through me. She placed her other hand on Elric's chest. I moved to stop whatever she was doing, but the loving expression on her face caused my guard to fall away.

She stared into my eyes, silently searching for what lay beneath.

"Sacrifice," she said. "Love."

"Yes," was all I said. My lips quivered as a tear rolled down my cheek.

Hel's gaze penetrated my soul, examining every facet of my thoughts. My life unfolded like a movie. She explored my past, then quickly fast-forwarded to my future. Her brow furrowed briefly but then relaxed into a small, satisfied smile.

"I see greatness in you, Healer," she sighed. "Your Volun's soul would have been a wondrous addition within my halls. But, his connection to you and yours to him is undeniable—and admirable. And, of course, will only enhance the power within both of you."

I dared to believe in her words. She moved away from me but never let go of the spear.

"My father loved me, I know that unquestionably, but he had a strained relationship with his siblings. That ongoing tension only heightened their nervousness and even their contempt for me. I want to change that," she said, pulling me along. We held tightly to the spear. "An equal exchange of love and respect."

I waited for her proclamation, but, strangely, I wasn't afraid or worried about what she would propose.

"Freyja, and even the great All-Father, trusted you with their power and even their darkest secrets; their lives depended on you—my life depended on you." Her spell ignited again with her words. "Everyone, other than my father and a few of his minions, revered you—trusted in your words and your actions."

"As I do with all of the gods, my family and friends," I interrupted, knowing where she was going with her request. "As I will do with you, the great Hel."

She was genuinely surprised by my straightforward statement. "But you haven't heard my conditions."

"I know what it's like to be pushed aside, silenced, and berated for actions not of my making or out of my control. I understand the longing to be accepted and loved—truly and unconditionally—regardless of those circumstances. So, I declare—I promise—to never deny you that love and acceptance. My people, and all beings within my world, will never dismiss or judge you again. Your place within our realm of gods is protected, not shunned."

Hel bowed her head, pausing to gauge my words, knowing she could sense any lies coming from my lips.

When she lifted her head, a sense of gratification radiated from her. She snapped the spear on the ground, causing tremors beneath my feet.

"Anwen, upon your return, do not destroy the spear as demanded by the Ancestors," she smiled. "The weapon answers to you, and will be useful in the future. You are the keeper—protect it as it will protect you."

She cracked the spear on the ground again. I lost my balance and fell over Elric's body. Black mist swirled around us, shimmering with vivid colors as the cloudy mass grew more chaotic.

Everything happened so quickly that I didn't realize we were sprawled on the mesa until yells and screams echoed around us. Dull gray skies replaced the pitch black of the Underworld.

A loud gasp escaped, and Herja hurried to my side.

"Anwen," she sputtered and took my face in her hands. "You're alive . . . and you're---"

I smiled at her worried words and her surprise that I was not a raving mad Mage ready to destroy the world. Yes, I was alive and myself—just me, not a monster like Corvus. Hel wasn't to blame for any of Loki's or even Corvus's actions—they were monsters of their own making.

Jack jumped into my arms, holding me tight. "I thought I

lost you."

Anu was speechless for once.

A raspy breath caught my attention.

Elric's eyes locked onto mine. A slight smile appeared. My heart raced with love.

"And I thought I lost you," I whispered just to him.

He exhaled slowly.

"You did, but you saved me. How?"

I smiled knowingly. Hel kept her promise. And I will keep mine.

I gently kissed his lips. A half-laugh, half-sob escaped.

"Because we protect each other. We are forever as one, my love. Always."

EPILOGUE

Lights flickered and danced along Jilneim's branches—new life flooded the Great Tree of Vardia. Soft, mesmerizing songs drifted through the branches as the fairies soared and tumbled among the green leaves. Joy burst from their tiny lungs at the ongoing new growth of their beloved and sacred home.

My smile widened as I looked around the dell in the soft glow of the lanterns. The star patterns of their light shimmered through the darkness of the forest. Twilight was here, but even in that dusky transition between the setting sun and the coming night, life burst from every corner of the clearing. This time tomorrow, we will be in a new era—a fresh beginning for Vardia and Wynfalle. Maybe even a new age for all the realms.

Rows of golden benches lined the area, all facing the Great Tree and waiting for the hundreds of people traveling to Vardia for the wedding between their beloved Healer and equally cherished Volun.

My wedding.

I closed my eyes, inhaling the sweet, fragrant air. Every corner, crevice, and gap burst with vibrant, colorful garlands of flowers. It was truly a beautiful fairy-tale setting—a perfect end to an amazing, yet dangerous, journey.

His energy was the first thing I felt as gentle hands wrapped around my waist. Elric leaned down and kissed the top of my head. A soft hum vibrated in my throat.

"I see we are making sure everything is in order for the big day tomorrow," he whispered lovingly into my ear.

I slowly turned into his arms and wrapped my arms around his neck. My lips softly pressed against his, sighing with contentment but also carrying a hint of sorrow.

"They would have loved to see their kingdom in such a state—full of new life and a hopeful future."

Elric's arms wrapped tightly around me.

"King Ansgar sits with full honor at the helm of the Underworld. Hel and the other gods look at him with respect and love—and General Vidar and Healer Hrafn are in the halls of Fólkvangr and Valhalla. True warriors who fought for our kingdom," Elric murmured as he gently lifted my chin, knowing tomorrow would be a bittersweet beginning to our life together.

Sorrow darkened Elric's features. Grief wrapped around all of our hearts. Even though the mysterious sickness claimed my grandfather nearly a year ago, all of Vardia still mourned his death. But it was my grandmother who insisted we go ahead with our wedding on the day of the king's passing.

Elric pulled away but kept a hold of my hand as he turned

to face the Great Tree. His eyes scanned the branches for the melodious voices, bringing a wistful smile to his lips. He continued to trail his eyes down the tree until they landed on the water, probing the depths until he found what he was seeking.

"The Okri seem to like their new companion."

I moved closer to the well and sat on the ledge. I reached down to twirl my hand on the water's surface, feeling the power of the spear. Its golden body shimmered beneath the water. The amber glowed brighter as the Okri surrounded the spear and then suddenly floated up to meet my hand, letting my fingers glide over their gelatinous orbs. A smile played on my lips.

Elric looked toward the clearing and frowned. "Tomorrow will be . . . interesting, to say the least. All kingdoms will be sending representatives, and even Lucia will attend."

My smile grew even wider at the mention of my homeland. "Yes, but Lord Magnus will be here for a double purpose."

A smile crept across Elric's lips as he chuckled softly. "Jack can't decide whether he wants to stay in Vardia and continue his training or travel back to Lucia and become their new king. It's quite a decision for a young boy."

"Well, there's no reason he can't be both. He can become a great Vardian warrior and rule the Kingdom of Lucia. There's no rule saying he has to choose. Besides, Lucia will need someone like Jack to restore hope again. Thyra, Anu, and Halvard have agreed to go with him to Lucia—to continue his Lirrean teachings with Anu and learn the Vardian way with Halvard and Thyra." A teasing smile grew. "And I know for a fact that another wedding will be coming soon."

Elric smiled, showing his dimple. My breath caught at the sight of the handsome elf in front of me—my future husband. I could gaze at him for eternity.

"Well, I do say if Halvard does not propose to Anu soon, we might face another war." Elric pulled me into his arms with amusement. "But, alas, with your matchmaking skills, nothing is impossible when you're around."

"I am glad you said that, my dearest," I whispered just before giving him a quick kiss on the lips. "It's good practice to agree with your soon-to-be wife, for future reference, of course."

A quick but hearty laugh burst out. "Yes, of course."

His lips met mine, but it wasn't a quick peck this time. Slow and sensual, his mouth teased and explored with careful intention. Our arms wrapped around each other more tightly.

A soft cough sounded behind him.

Reluctantly, we pulled away from each other. We both felt the different, yet powerful, energies immediately.

Hel smiled at Freyja and Odin as they appeared beside her.

"You do know that the wedding is tomorrow evening," I smiled affectionately. "Unless there is some other pressing matter that needs to be attended to?"

Freyja's smile grew even wider. "Of course not, my dear. We wouldn't miss this wondrous event. You should know that."

"Yes, of course," I said, nodding toward the tree and the chairs beside it. "We didn't know how many of the gods would show up, but we have three chairs ready for the most honored."

Hel placed her hand over Freyja's. A mischievous smile spread as she looked at Odin.

"I wouldn't miss a chance to see my kin squirm and wiggle with anxiety, my dear." Hel noticed Odin rolled his eyes. "However, most have welcomed me with warmth and open hearts."

"Nonsense," Odin exclaimed. "We have all welcomed you with open arms, my dearest Hel. I demanded that each of my brothers and sisters do the same."

Hel arched her brow in reproach. "Well, you may have commanded your family, but some still do not greet me with civility."

Elric interrupted. "They will in due time, my goddess, just give them the space they need to fully understand that you are here to stay . . . and very much loved by all."

"Yes, what our noble Volun says is true, my beautiful Hel," Freyja said while gently grasping Hel's shoulder and giving it a squeeze. "As you know, the gods can be an unpredictable bunch, but they will come around. Especially, when the great All-Father shows them that they have nothing to fear from you."

Hel looked lovingly at both Freyja and Odin, setting aside her fears about her kin.

She cleared her throat. "Well, we know you have plenty of preparations to be had on the morrow, but Freyja and I wanted to give you a gift before the festivities."

Hel pulled something from her robe and faced Elric, while Freyja did the same and faced me. Each god placed a necklace around our necks—Elric's was a black stone set within a silver ring, and mine was an amber stone set within a golden ring. I traced the runes along the circle.

"*Vér eruey sem einn*—We are forever as one."

Tears threatened to spill as I looked at Elric. He grasped my hand and gave it a gentle squeeze. Energy radiated from the necklaces, connecting to our powers. Both of our hearts briefly raced at the new magical protection.

"The power of gold and the magic of amber cannot endure without the undeniable life force of the Shadow. May peace and harmony guide you and protect your realm with strength, devotion, and love."

Our stones glowed at Freyja's words, showing the shared bond.

Odin clapped his hands happily.

"And may you be blessed with many sons and daughters."

Elric pulled me into his arms and smiled warmly. Mischief sparkled in his eyes.

"Thank you, All-Father. You honor us with your blessings."

We laughed, hugged, and kissed.

Vardia and all the kingdoms were at peace, and most importantly, Elric and I found our true home—with each other.

THE END

PRONUNCIATION GUIDE

Character Names

Alvis – ALL-vis

Ansgar – ANHS-gahr

Anu – AH-noo

Anwen – ANN-wen

Apep – A-PEH-P

Arnbjorg – ARN-yorg

Áslaug – AHS-lowg

Asmund – AHS-moont

Barik – BAR-ick

Brynjar – BRIN-yar

Ciar – KEY-ih-r

Corvus – CORE-vus

Draugr – DROW-ger

Einar – IE-nahr

Eir - Air

Eira – AY-rah

Elley – EH-lay

Elric – EL-ric

Embla – Em-bler

Eydis – EY-dees

Fanndís – Fan-dis

Flóki – Flo-kee

Freyja – FRAY-ah

Gamila – GAME-ill-ah

Glaesir – Glay-seer

Grannir – Gran-near

Hagen – HAH-gen
Halvard – HAHL-vart
Hel - HEL
Herja – Her-YA
Hjalmar – HYAL-mahr
Hrafn – RAH-ven
Inka – EENG-kah
Ivar – EE-vahr
Jerrick – YEH-rik
Kenrick – KEN-ric
Laga – La-GA
Leofric – LEO-fric
Loki – LOW-kee
Lyfir – Lie-fur
Mangus – Man-GUS
Menglad – Men-glod
Myrk – ME-ark
Odin – OH-din
Ragnhild – Ragn-hild
Sigrún – SIG-run
Sigurd – SIG-urd
Sindri – Sihn-dree
Sulwen – SIL-wen
Thrym - Thrimm
Thyra – TEE-rah
Torvald – TAWR-vald
Tyr - Tire
Tule - TOOL

Vidar – VEE-dar

Important Names

Fólkvangr – FOKE-VAHN-gerr

Hraesvelgr – HUR-race-vel-ger

Jilneim – YIL-neim

Jordanna – Jor-DAN-nah

Kaftar – Kuff-tar

Lirrean – LEAR-e-ann

Lohrhan – LOR-han

Lokrum – Low-crumb

Lucia – LOO-sha

Máni – MAH-nee

Myrar – MY-rare

Navalen – Nav-ALL-in

Okri – OH-cry

Rydlyn – RID-lyn

Saerún – Sah-RUN

Scykra – Sky-craw

Sessrúmnir – Sess-room-near

Skovmal – Skow-maul

Sól - Soul

Sorayn – SORE-ann

Urora – YOU-oar-ah

Valhalla – Val-hah-lah

Valkryie – Val-KEE-ree

Vardia – VAR-dia

Wynfalle – WIN-fall

ACKNOWLEDGEMENTS

The Power of Gold trilogy was my first writing adventure and will always have a special place in my heart. So many happy moments, and a few distressing ones, came with this endeavor.

To Gabriella Regina of GR Book Covers for completing the best trilogy designs ever. You are an inspiration and a truly talented artist. Fragmented ideas churned inside my mind, waiting for just the right person, a visionary, to coax them out and create exactly what I was hoping. The design for the final book is perfect.

To Jennifer Noffze, for being my editor, friend, and sounding board. As with everything related to 2020, I know it was particularly hard. But you are a survivor. Your positive attitude has inspired me in more ways than you can imagine. You are the best, and I love you. Thank you!

Thank you to my family—for your support, your encouragement, your marketing skills...I truly have the best family in the world.

To my brilliant friend for their encouragement and support.

I left a successful museum career and many wonderful co-workers and colleagues to follow my dream! I appreciate everything you do and more!

Shout out to my library ladies—your continuous support and encouragement always lift me up. The self-proclaimed GDPL reading club, a.k.a. the GGYALCWOWOS (yes, I do believe we need to have a title...guess the acronym!)

Most of all, thank you to my husband, my love and my best friend, Joey, and my two brilliant sons, Connor and Reece. Thank you for putting up with my constant late nights, the endless hours of rereading my drafts, and the 'moans and groans' of editing. I could not have accomplished this journey without your support and encouragement, and I love you all to the end of the universe and beyond.

And finally, thank you to my beloved readers—thank you for your continuous support...and patience...to finally see the wondrous end to Anwen and Elric's journey...or is it? Maybe Jack needs an adventure....

Thank you, thank you! Until next time.... cheers!

www.ingramcontent.com/pod-product-compliance
Lightning Source LLC
Chambersburg PA
CBHW030516310726
48979CB00010B/1698/J

* 9 7 8 1 7 3 6 0 1 4 4 6 2 *